RUSSIAN TREASURES

BOOK ONE

ELVIRA BARYAKINA

Translated from Russian by Elvira Baryakina, Rose France and Simon Geoghegan

This book is a work of fiction. Any references to historical events, real people, or real places are used fictitiously. Other names, characters, places, and events are products of the author's imagination, and any resemblance to actual events or places or persons, living or dead, is entirely coincidental.

ISBN: 978-1-7325840-0-6

For Pavel Mamaev

1. THE PRODIGAL SON

1

When Klim Rogov ran away from home, he took what his father cherished most—his dreams of Klim's bright future. At the time, it felt gratifying. *Did you seriously think I would want to follow in your footsteps and become a Public Prosecutor, a man who preys and profits on others people's misfortunes?* Klim had thought. *No way, Father. No way.*

Ten years had passed, and Klim found himself once again standing indecisively on the threshold of his family house on a balmy summer's night. It was shabby and overgrown with lilac and ivy but still luxurious with two marble bears guarding the entrance and a white balcony protruding like the open drawer of a dresser.

There had been a time when Klim had dreamed of his triumphant return to his hometown as a successful foreign journalist whose writing had made him famous all over Argentina. But in the summer of 1917, this would not have been the safest guise to assume in Russia. Klim's home country had been at war with Germany for three years now, its economy had collapsed, and the railroads were packed with armed deserters. Foreigners with their fancy suitcases were easy pickings for them, and Klim decided it would be wiser to melt in with the local population. He grew a layer of dark stubble, acquired a soldier's uniform and a shabby trunk for his belongings, and arrived in Nizhny Novgorod looking more like an opera villain than an heir to a fortune.

He felt uneasy in the knowledge that the moment he knocked on the door and reentered the once forbidden family home, the life that he had cultivated for himself would become irrelevant and meaningless. Cousin Lubochka, who was renting the second floor in his father's house, would come running to greet him, and the sleepy servants would gather at the doorway, oohing and aahing at him. The renowned traveler and journalist would once again be regarded as no more than his father's son, and he had no idea where that was going to lead him.

Klim took a key out of his pocket, the only thing from home that had survived his extensive travels around the world.

I wonder if Father ordered the lock to be changed?

But the key turned, and the door opened noiselessly. With his heart pounding, Klim found the switch on the wall—a familiar gesture that had never faded from his memory.

Nothing had changed in the hallway. There was the same big mirror in the silver frame in patina and shoe horns and brushes on the carved shoe rack. A set of knight's armor complete with a lance and shield was still standing in the corner. Klim lifted the visor on the helmet and peered inside. When he was a child, he had convinced himself that there would be the body of a tiny knight inside that had become shrunken and mummified over time.

There was a patter of footsteps, and a young maid with loose dark curly hair ran into the hallway.

"How did you get in here?" she asked in a frightened voice.

"I just walked through the door," he replied with a smile. "I'm Klim Rogov, the heir."

The girl was lovely, slim, big-eyed, and graceful, and even her dull black outfit looked good on her.

"How long have you been working here?" Klim asked.

"Oh…" She looked confused as if she didn't know what to say. "Not that long."

Klim walked around the hallway and examined the familiar things that had not changed at all: the hall stand with legs chewed by one of his puppies, and the carpet still bearing the traces of a "chemistry experiment" that had gone wrong.

He patted the maid on the shoulder. "Would you take care of my trunk, please?"

That's the type of a girl that should be cuddled and tempted with sweets, he thought.

His gaze went from the open door to the library, and Klim forgot about everything else around him. He entered the room and froze, touched and overwhelmed by his memories. The light from the electric lamp was reflected in the glass doors of the bookcases and gilt spines of the books. Once, this room had been both a treasure trove and torture chamber for Klim. He remembered himself sitting in a red armchair and taking delight in the humor of Mark Twain, but it was also here, at the desk covered with ink-stained leather, that he had repeatedly copied out Latin phrases under the strict supervision of his father. *Dura lex sed lex*—"The law is harsh, but it is the law."

There was still an inkwell in the form of a compass on the desk, and the map of the world still hung on the wall. The colored pins dotted all over it indicated the cities Klim had visited. Before he had escaped from home, it had been just Moscow, Saint Petersburg, and Berlin where his mother had taken him shortly before her death, but now, pins were scattered all over Persia, China, and Argentina.

It seemed Lubochka had shown Klim's father all the letters she had received from his "prodigal son" after all.

Klim noticed his own framed photograph on the desk—*goodness me!* He had sent it two years ago when he had been invited to Casa Rosada, the pink presidential palace, for the first time. What emotions had been going through Father's head when he looked at this picture? Had he remembered yelling at Klim, "You'll end up serving hard labor! Stand up straight when I'm talking to you, you dunce."

Klim heard the lock click softly, and he raised his head. Had he been locked in?

"Hey! Stop fooling around!" he raised his voice, but the maid didn't answer.

Klim pulled the heavy oak door. "What if I'm the type of man to bear a grudge?" he asked even louder. "Are you not afraid that you might lose your job?"

He heard women's voices behind the door.

"I have no idea how he got into the house!" the maid said. "Someone probably told him that you're waiting for Mr. Rogov and that Dr. Sablin is on the night shift."

"We must call someone," the other woman replied.

"Do you have any weapons?"

"Well…only the knight's lance, I think."

Klim pounded the door with his fist. "Lubochka, open up! It is really me."

The women behind the door gasped, the lock was opened, and a delicate lady with a porcelain complexion and a mass of wild and frizzy hair threw herself on Klim's neck.

"I've missed you so much!" Lubochka said, laughing and crying and kissing him on the cheeks.

They stared at each other, hardly able to believe their eyes.

"Look at you!" Lubochka exclaimed. "A beard, a soldier's tunic…you look like a deserter!"

Klim also couldn't believe that the little girl he had teased as a child, calling her a "dandelion clock," was now an elegant young lady with a wedding ring on her finger.

The vigilant maid looked at them, confused. "I'd better be going," she said, taking a step backward.

2

It was well after midnight, but Klim and Lubochka were still sitting in the library and talking in much the same way they had in their childhood.

"Do you remember our parents had put us to bed," said Klim, "and we tiptoed to the drawing-room door to eavesdrop on the adults playing the piano?"

Lubochka nodded. "Do you remember my father taking us to dance classes? You wore white knitted gloves, and you were always the very best student. And the instructor told me, 'Mam'selle, you have perspired so much that your clothes are wringing wet. Go and change.' I could have died of shame."

There was so much to share! And it was so nice to see each other again and talk as if they had never been separated for the past decade.

"I wish you'd never run away," Lubochka said. "We all loved you so much…especially your father."

"I find that difficult to imagine," Klim said, smiling wryly.

Father had felt he had the right to lash out at Klim whenever he pleased, either with sharp words or with his fists. At work, his father had been strict but fair, and at home, he had been polite—albeit aloof—in dealing with the servants. But with his son, it had been different.

"He regarded me as his own property—" Klim began, but Lubochka interrupted him.

"That's not true! Why do you think he left you the fortune?"

"Out of revenge to force me to come back all the way across the Pacific Ocean and Siberia. While I was on the train, deserters tried to rob me five times."

"But they didn't, did they?"

"I'm good at boxing," Klim said, rising. "Remember, you asked me to bring you phonograph needles? I've got you some. Has your maid already taken care of my luggage?"

Lubochka frowned. "What maid?"

"The one who locked me in the library."

"That's my friend, Countess Nina Odintzova. My husband is working tonight at the hospital, and I asked her to stay with me. I'm afraid of being on my own in such a big house. And there are no servants besides the cook."

Klim was at a loss for words.

"And why does this countess of yours wear a maid's uniform?"

"It's not a uniform; it's her mourning dress. Her husband was killed in action."

Klim was mortified. As far as he remembered, he had addressed the countess in the most familiar terms and threatened to fire her.

"I'll bring her round, and you'll make it up," Lubochka said and went after her friend.

But it turned out that Nina had already gone home. Alone in the middle of the night.

3

Two years earlier, Lubochka had been flattered to be the wife of a brilliant surgeon, but her marriage had resulted in bitter disappointment.

Dr. Sablin was mild mannered and polite, but just as the color-blind are incapable of perceiving certain shades, so he was incapable of feeling delight in a woman. He had no idea how to pay a compliment, never made any physical show of affection, and had only confessed his love for Lubochka once—on the day he had proposed marriage. His passion for his wife consisted of occasional inquiries after her health and regular contributions to the housekeeping money.

For a long time, Lubochka refused to admit that she was bored to death with Sablin and his eternal conversations about the war and medicine. In order to prove to herself that her life still had some meaning and that at least some people needed her, she started throwing parties. The guests danced, talked, and proposed toasts "to our beautiful hostess," and Lubochka felt pleasantly flattered by these gatherings. They warmed her soul and provided temporary relief like a mustard plaster to the chest.

Then Klim came and destroyed her fragile equilibrium. Lubochka had never told him that she had been madly in love with him as a child. As God was her witness, she had desperately hoped that he had changed and become unworthy of her feelings, but she realized immediately that this was not the case.

She couldn't stop marveling at his tanned face and smiling brown eyes while he was reading his thick book in Spanish or drinking his Argentinean mate tea through a silver straw called a *bombilla*, not from a cup but from a calabash gourd with a silver rim and stand.

Klim took little interest in the news about the war and the impotent Provisional Government that was attempting to rule the country after the Tsar's abdication. He didn't want to hear about ration cards and asked the cook to buy the best products even if they were the most expensive. To Lubochka this seemed both shocking and delightful—it was as though the affairs of the world simply didn't apply to Klim.

She tactfully asked him what he was going to do now that he was so rich. He told her jokingly that he was thinking about taking up a career as Tsar

Koschei, the famous Russian folk villain who spent his whole time counting his hoard of gold and entertaining himself by kidnapping fair maidens.

Many of Lubochka's girlfriends would have been over the moon if he were to kidnap them and take them away to the wonderful country that he would describe to them at her soirees. According to Klim, there were sea lions in Argentina, meat was cheaper than bread, and palm trees and cypresses grew right in the streets.

However, Lubochka was not destined to see these miracles. It did not occur to Klim to even think of treating her as a woman. She constantly noticed the unflattering difference between her casual, elegant cousin and her shy husband who looked out at everyone from under lowered brows and tried to walk as little as possible to hide his lameness. He had been shot in the leg during the Russo-Japanese War and had had a limp ever since, which kept him away from the front now.

Lubochka always accompanied Klim around the city and did her best to shield him from seeing the "wrong people." She felt jealous even of his childhood friends whenever he expressed a desire to visit them. But there was no one to visit anyway. All Klim's former classmates were in the army.

"When I knock on their doors," he told Lubochka with a sigh, "I try to guess whether they have been killed, maimed, or taken prisoner. It's hard to imagine, but half of our class is dead."

But Lubochka did not want to think about such ugly things. Klim provided her with what she valued most, the beauty of life, and she was determined that nothing would stop her enjoying his company. She took her cousin to theaters and restaurants, and he taught her how to dance the Argentine tango and showed her his old "hunting grounds." He liked to take her to the islands where he used to go fishing as a child or the ruins of the ancient Nizhny Novgorod Kremlin full of memories of playing and fighting with the other boys.

Lubochka would have given anything for her cousin to remain with her forever, and sometimes it seemed to her that this was a distinct possibility. She could tell right away that he hadn't just returned to Russia to claim his inheritance but also to reconcile himself with his past and his notion of himself. She diligently tended the seed in his mind that he should stay in Nizhny Novgorod and occupy his appropriate place among the good and the great of the city.

4

The cab took Lubochka and Klim along the promenade. Breathless, Klim gazed at the green slopes of the shoreline cut through with deep red clay ravines. The Oka River was bustling with fishing boats, wooden barges, and small, quick paddle steamers with black funnels. On the right side, there were storage sheds and the wharfs used for the Nizhny Novgorod Fair, and on the left, the high river bank was dotted with the colorful domes of churches and fancy office buildings. There were palaces, chapels, taverns, and the fearsome Millionka—a neighborhood in which every house hid a den of thieves and every day brought either a fistfight or a fire.

The cab stopped at the entrance to the hilltop restaurant, the Oriental Bazaar. There was a red carpet on the porch, and the liveried doorman greeted patrons with a bow. The guards were dressed in the traditional *chokha* coats with bandoliers on both sides of their chests and black leather belts inlaid with silver.

Klim and Lubochka followed the head waiter across the dimly lit restaurant hall onto a terrace wreathed in ivy. The orchestra played behind a screen of tropical plants, and the view was breathtaking.

"Not bad, huh?" Lubochka asked as they sat at the table covered with a white starched tablecloth.

While waiting for their order, Klim told Lubochka about the San Telmo district of Buenos Aires where he lived. It used to be a prestigious neighborhood, but after the yellow fever epidemic, all the rich people had moved away and rented their houses to émigrés.

"It's also beautiful there," said Klim. "High windows with shutters, and every door is a work of art. But there's nothing fancy about the locals."

"Will you move out of your apartment there now?" Lubochka asked.

"I don't think so. My building has a restaurant on the ground floor, and above that, there's an Italian family with six marriageable daughters. I'm on the floor above, and I have a beautiful balcony with an ornamental railing and some ancient aristocratic family's coat of arms. By default, I have come to think of it as my own. How could I give up such delights?"

"I'm sure you can," said Lubochka.

The waiters brought them some thinly sliced cured fish, golden roast quail, *foie gras* with prunes in tiny porcelain cups, and champagne in ice buckets. Here, in the Oriental Bazaar, it seemed that no one had heard of the alcohol ban that had been imposed since the beginning of the war and the empty food stores that were being besieged like fortresses.

"What do have to go back to in Argentina?" asked Lubochka, taking a sip of her champagne. "No matter how hard you try, you'll never be fully accepted there. And neither will your children. Here you have a name, you are the scion of a noble family, but there you'll always be looked upon as a stranger. You can't come from nowhere and become someone important."

Klim smiled and nodded toward the patrons at the neighboring tables: the young ladies in silks and gentlemen in evening dress or military uniforms.

Lubochka lowered her head, embarrassed. She had repeatedly told Klim that the world had been turned upside down by the war and that now everything was run by nameless upstarts. Alas, she had got so used to these new surroundings that she had often fallen victim to her own wishful thinking and failed to notice the alarm signals all around her.

The old ways didn't work anymore, and Nizhny Novgorod was not what it used to be. Its fair, which had once hosted up to two million visitors per season, was now half boarded up. There were no goods to sell and no customers to buy them. Prices were rising every day, factories were closing, and thousands of soldiers were dying at the front—every single day. Sure, Klim's inheritance might be able to buy him a semblance of civilized life, but he wouldn't be able to enjoy it knowing that there were hungry women looting the food store next door.

The more Klim thought about it, the more he wanted to leave Nizhny Novgorod as soon as possible, but he did not dare mention this to Lubochka and her guests. If something bad were to happen, he would be able to escape to safety, but they had nowhere to go.

Suddenly, Lubochka's expression changed as if she had spotted something strange behind him. He turned and noticed Countess Odintzova standing next to the terrace railing.

This time, she wasn't dressed in mourning. The evening sun was reflected in the exquisite blue beading of her dress. Her dark hair fell loosely from her parting in waves and was swept into an extravagant chignon on the back of her head. She fanned herself with a large black fan, the delicate ostrich feather fronds waving to and fro like seaweed.

And I took her for a maid, Klim thought. *What a fool!*

Should he apologize for his stupid mistake? Invite her to his table and then summon the waiters and order whatever dish might take her fancy?

The orchestra struck up a tango, and a singer in a beautiful dress embroidered with red roses started to sing.

Every evening he watches her dance,
Her beauty ablaze
As the other men gaze.
He is tight as a spring, cursing Chance
As he sips at his glass full of sadness,
His *señora*, his passion, his madness
Dances a tango—revenge turned to art.
Every blow of her heels is a stab at his heart.

Klim rose.

"I'll be right back," he told Lubochka and headed across the terrace to the countess.

What is she doing here? he wondered. *Is she waiting for someone? Or maybe she came with someone else?*

Nina turned her head, and her black fan fell out of her hand and hung limply from her wrist on its thin velvet ribbon.

"Good evening," Klim said and bowed.

His pulse beat faster. *Will she slap me across the face? Or will she laugh at me, recalling my threats to fire her?*

"Good evening," said the countess.

Her gray-green eyes looked calm and impenetrable. If she were angry or annoyed at him, Klim was confident that he would know what to say. He would come up with some joke or droll phrase. But Nina was looking at him as if she had never seen him before. Maybe she did not recognize him?

"Are you dancing tonight?" asked Klim.

To his joy and amazement, she silently gave him her hand, and he led her to the dance floor.

"It's an Argentine tango," said Klim. "You should stand closer to me."

"Like this?" Nina looked into his eyes for a moment, moved closer, and Klim felt her light breath on his neck.

"Yes, that's right." He placed her hand on his shoulder and took her gently by the waist.

"So, what do I have to do?" she asked.

"Just follow me."

They danced, and he felt the hard touch of the rings on her slender hand, the warmth of her thigh through the silk of her skirts, the tense muscles of her back, and something else: the intimate seam of a shift beneath her dress under his shameless, tingling fingers.

The singer sang about impossible happiness. Klim looked at the woman in his arms, and his heart froze with the inspiration and foreboding of something huge and inevitable.

When the tango was over, Klim stepped back and bowed. *"¡Gracias, señora!"*

What now? Should he invite Nina to his table?

But she did not answer. Next to them, there was a tall, sturdy man with a shaved head, about forty-five years old.

"Nina Vasilievna," he called to her respectfully, using her patronymic. "We need to talk."

"Sure." She turned to Klim. "Excuse me."

They left, and Klim returned to Lubochka.

"Do you know who that gentleman was?" he asked.

"Everyone knows him," she snapped. "It's Mr. Fomin, the chairman of the city's Provisions Committee."

The plate in front of Lubochka was full of grapes, torn off from the bunch but not eaten. She took one of them and squeezed it with her manicured fingers. Slipping from her grasp, the grape rolled under the table next to them.

Lubochka waved to the waiter. "The check, please."

Klim looked around the terrace for Nina, but she was nowhere to be seen.

"We're going home," Lubochka said. "I have a headache."

5

All the way home, Lubochka lectured Klim.

"You do realize that Nina is trying to hook you, don't you? She's been wearing nothing but mourning dress for three years, and now, suddenly, she's out at a restaurant, dressed from top to toe in her finest finery. I told her yesterday that we were planning to go to the Oriental Bazaar, and there she was."

"Why are you so angry with her?" Klim asked in surprise. "It was me who invited her. I just wanted to make amends, and your friend was happy to accept it."

The melody of the tango was still spinning in Klim's head. His whole arm from his elbow to his fingertips still retained the vivid and treasured memory of what it had been like to hold Nina.

Lubochka narrowed her eyes, and her lower lip trembled as it used to do in her childhood when she was about to cry.

"Don't be fooled by Nina. She owes you money."

The cab turned to Ilinskaya Street and stopped by the mansion with its marble bears. Klim jumped into the dust warmed by the heat of the day.

"Why are you back so early?" Marisha, the cook, asked as she opened the front door.

Ignoring her, Klim walked past into his father's office. Up to now, he hadn't bothered looking too closely at the papers he had inherited. Everything related to finance was a bore as far as he was concerned.

He deftly twisted the dials of the vintage American safe and took out a black binder filled with bonds, promissory notes, and contracts. A familiar name caught his eye—Vladimir Alekseevich Odintzov.

Five years earlier, Nina's husband had borrowed twenty thousand rubles from Klim's father at seven percent interest. Count Odintzov had mortgaged his flax-spinning mill, and there were all the necessary proofs of the validity of the transaction—a notary's signature, a seal, and the stamp duty. The payment was due on October 1, 1917.

So, it was true: Nina was interested in Klim not for his personal qualities but for his inheritance. He had let his imagination run wild and had now been brought back to earth with a bump.

2. THE GENTLEWOMAN

1

Klim stopped going to theaters and restaurants and now spent all his time at his bank and lawyer's office. His father had left him a little under three hundred thousand rubles, and to tie up his affairs in Nizhny Novgorod, Klim needed to sell his securities, exchange his rubles for foreign currency, renew his leasing contracts, and arrange for payments to be wired straight to Buenos Aires.

When Klim got home at night, he would go to the servants' quarters to ask who had visited Lubochka during the day. He hoped against hope that Nina might have tried to make contact with him—after all, she needed to sort out the money she owed him. But Nina never came.

Occasionally, Klim took out the promissory note written by her husband and examined it. Maybe he should go and ask her how she was planning to pay? It was a large sum, and the due date was close.

He found out where she lived, and several times he passed by Nina's house at Crest Hill and peered through the stucco-framed windows. He returned none the wiser, fretful and full of self-doubt—a sensation that was quite unusual for him.

How had this young woman managed to get under his skin in this way? Klim knew nothing about her. One emotion would follow another: first rapture, then morose bewilderment, and then outpourings of wounded self-esteem. *Can it really be that she doesn't care about me at all?*

At night, vivid fantasies kept him awake. He imagined Nina in the same glittering dark blue dress with the low neckline that attracted his lascivious gaze. The more Klim put things off, the less confident he became of having any success. And in any case, he asked himself, what possible success could he be thinking of? He would be leaving soon, and Nina would remain in Nizhny Novgorod. He should stop tormenting himself and leave it to the lawyers to deal with Nina's promissory note.

2

Klim was in his father's office, flipping through the documents filed in the binder. A fly buzzed against the window. The church bells called the local parishioners to mass.

"You have a visitor," said Marisha, knocking at the door. She gave Klim a business card that read "Countess Odintzova."

All thoughts about bonds and promissory notes flew out of Klim's head.

"Please, let her in," he said, dropping the binder into the drawer.

However, it was not Nina who entered the office but a burly elderly lady in a black lace dress.

"Please call me Sofia Karlovna," she said, offering Klim her hand.

He shook it, trying not to reveal his disappointment, and then collected himself. *This isn't all bad,* he thought. *This lady must be a relative of Nina's, and she might provide me with some very valuable information.*

Sofia Karlovna sank into the armchair and fixed her blue eyes on Klim for what seemed a long time.

"You inherited a promissory note signed by my son," she said finally, "but my daughter-in-law, who is responsible for the payment now, has got herself into a very bad situation."

"What's happened?" asked Klim, alarmed.

Sofia Karlovna took a deep breath. "Since the start of the war, we have been impoverished. Our workers and horses were commandeered by the army, and there is nobody to work our fields. My daughter-in-law met the chairman of the city's Provisions Committee, and he convinced her that she should restore our old flax spinning mill in Osinki."

Klim remembered the man who had accompanied Nina out of the restaurant and the deep fold in the nape of his neck like the slot in a piggy bank.

"So, what can I do for you?" Klim asked.

"Nina does not have the cash," said Sofia Karlovna, "and she wants to ask you to delay the repayment of her loan. Mr. Fomin went to the capital to get her a state contract for tarpaulin goods for the army, and Nina hopes that she'll soon be able to sort things out."

"What kind of deferment is she looking for?" Klim asked gloomily.

"Oh no!" Sofia Karlovna exclaimed. "You've misunderstood me. I want you to take Nina's mill."

Klim looked at her in bewilderment. "I need liquidity and cash, not a mill around my neck."

"If you defer her loan payment and leave for Argentina, you can forget about ever getting your money back. I know exactly what Fomin is after. He is hoping to persuade Nina to marry him in order to get his hands on the mill and the lucrative contracts it is set to sign. What are you going to do if he refuses to pay you? Send him a threatening letter?"

"What will happen to your daughter-in-law if I take over her mill?"

"You will be saving her from making a terrible mistake. Mr. Fomin is a most unsuitable match! He has Nina completely hoodwinked, and she doesn't have the sense to figure out what he's really like. As soon as Mr. Fomin finds out that she is penniless, he will drop her immediately. The heartless barbarian clearly doesn't care a fig about our house, library, or Nina. For him, they are all just unnecessary expenses."

Sofia Karlovna was silent for a while.

"I am terrified that I will end up on the street. If Nina marries Mr. Fomin, there's no way we'd ever be able to live together. Mr. Rogov, please, go to Osinki and talk to Nina. Mr. Fomin is currently in Petrograd, so there'll be no one to oppose you."

3

The deck of the little steamboat was crowded with monks in their dark robes, peasant women with sacks, and carpenters with saws wrapped in old rags. Some were dozing while others were talking to their fellow travelers.

You and your wild schemes! Klim thought to himself. Here he was sailing upriver on a rust-bucket steamer, guarding his trunk against thieves—fretting, wondering, and cursing himself for his presumption and ridiculous daydreams.

What if Nina was perfectly happy with Fomin? What if Sofia Karlovna had been overexaggerating the whole situation? She was clearly much more worried about her own future than Nina's.

But here Klim was, breathing in the steamer's acrid smoke and cinders, sweating in the roasting heat, and pulling his hat down low over his forehead so that nobody would see the anxiety in his eyes.

They sailed under the clear vault of the sky between thickly forested river banks. Stray, blackened, semi-submerged logs that had been left behind after the timber harvest had been floated downstream peered out of the water like prehistoric animals. A heron stood hunched on the sandbank, its reflection zigzagging across the water.

"The next stop is Osinki, sir," said a sailor pointing toward an old manor house on the top of a nearby hill.

The deckhands moored the steamboat to a half-rotten pontoon, and the wave from under its paddle wheel almost capsized a rowboat carrying two girls wearing wide-brimmed hats.

The only passengers to get off at Osinki were Klim and a blond boy of about sixteen called Zhora Kupin. All the way from Nizhny Novgorod, he had entertained his fellow travelers with his poems and stories about his father who was a tailor, famous throughout the entire Nizhny Novgorod Fair.

The deckhands pulled the gangway back on board, and the steamer continued its way upriver.

It was hot and quiet; the breeze stirred the leaves of the hundred-year-old trees, and the dragonflies hovered over the water lilies.

Shielding his eyes from the sun, Klim looked up at the manor house. It seemed very respectable from a distance, but on closer inspection, its peeling light blue paint and cracked stucco betrayed its owners' straitened circumstances.

Klim picked up his trunk and walked up the wooden stairs.

"Elena, I'm back!" he heard Zhora's voice and stopped.

Should I ask him how to find Countess Odintzova? Klim thought. Zhora had mentioned that he knew everybody in Osinki.

Klim turned back to the shore and froze. Nina, barefoot, her dress soaked to the knee, was wading out from the boat to the moss-covered pontoon. While she held the stern steady, Zhora and Elena carried a large votive candle stand out of the boat. The three of them hauled it up to the sandy beach.

"Arkhip sneaked into our chapel last night," Nina said, breathing heavily, "and took everything he could carry. I went straight over to his hut to sort him out, and Elena went with me."

"I wouldn't let you go on your own," said her friend, a tall girl with two thick braids of fair hair that fell down to her waist.

Nina bent down to grasp the candle stand again, and a small revolver fell out from the pocket of her skirt.

"Where did you get that?" Zhora asked in amazement.

"It's my husband's. Do you think Arkhip would have just let me take the family candle stand back if I had turned up empty-handed?" She put the revolver back in her pocket. "Let's go. This thing must weigh at least one hundred pounds...I don't know how we'll manage to get it up the hill."

Nina looked up and met Klim's gaze.

"Have you come to see me?" she asked, her face turning pale.

"I know Klim," Zhora exclaimed. "We met on the steamer. Mr. Rogov, let me introduce my sister Nina and my bride Elena."

Klim put his trunk on the ground and raised his hat. "Nice to meet you."

He couldn't keep his eyes off Nina's crestfallen face. If she was Zhora's sister, then her father was a tailor. Hardly the lineage of a bona fide countess! Klim could now clearly see why there was little love lost between Sofia Karlovna and her daughter-in-law.

An explosion roared out from the opposite side of the river, and a column of water shot up into the air. Elena and Zhora jumped back in fright.

"Honestly, you're like a couple of babies, the pair of you," Nina grumbled. "It's only deserters stunning fish with grenades they've brought back from the front."

"Nothing to write home about," Klim said in wry amusement.

"There's always something exploding around here," Nina shrugged.

Like Lubochka, Nina had become so used to anarchy and war that the sound of a grenade exploding was nothing out of the ordinary.

Klim picked up the candle stand. "Let me carry it up for you," he said. "Zhora, would you mind taking my trunk?"

4

Nina asked Klim to put the candle stand in the empty stillroom that was lit by the lengthening sun. Zhora and Elena went to the kitchen to give orders regarding dinner and left Klim and Nina alone.

"I think you'd be better off returning to the city," Klim told her. "It'll be safer there."

"Country or city—it makes little difference these days," she said, shrugging her shoulders.

The evening sunlight slanted through the window, leaving Nina's face in shadow but illuminating her low-necked dress.

She was an impossible and unthinkable mélange of opposites: her girlish charm and hard-nosed feistiness, her noble title and her lowly tailor's origins, not to mention her less than salubrious admirer from the Provisions Committee.

Nina was also observing Klim, distractedly twirling her engagement ring, which was too big for her finger. It was obviously very expensive, most likely an heirloom, and it didn't fit her very well.

"How did you know that I was here?" she asked.

"Sofia Karlovna wanted me to take control of your mill—" Klim began, but Nina interrupted him.

"Sofia Karlovna has no idea where our money comes from. How are we going to live if you take over the mill?"

"She said that Mr. Fomin—"

"He's the only one here who can help me. He knows all about accounting and engineering, the machines, the procurement.... If it weren't for him, we would have been out of business long ago."

She dropped her ring and bent down to pick it up, and her revolver fell out of her pocket again. She squatted down and looked up at Klim.

"Can we write you a new promissory note? I understand you need the money, but I have no way of paying you back until spring. If you want, I can give you my furniture and silverware as an additional deposit. In March—no, let's say May—I'll be able to send you the money."

Frightened and determined, Nina was ready to fight the creditor who threatened her business plans as fiercely as she had fought with the thieves who threatened her property. Klim already knew that he would never have the heart to take her mill away from her.

"We can sign the new papers as soon as you get back to Nizhny Novgorod," he relented.

"That's wonderful!" Nina exclaimed and then fell silent, embarrassed. "But I can't go just now."

"Why?"

"I have business here."

Still with the revolver in her hand, Nina drew herself up to her full height and began to explain hastily that the tarpaulin production process was extremely complex and she needed to keep an eye on it.

"Perhaps you'd like to stay with us?" she asked. "And then we can go to the city together to sign the papers. I'm afraid that if you go back to your lawyers on your own, you'll have a change of heart."

Klim sighed but, unable to resist her, laughed. "You end up doing a lot of crazy things when someone is pointing a gun at you, you know."

"It's not loaded anyway," Nina said and put the revolver back in her pocket.

5

Klim continued to do nothing to settle his affairs and lived like a lazy schoolboy skipping classes. Initially, it was just a week, but that soon changed into two and then three. Nina always seemed to have something important to attend to at her mill, but Klim didn't mind a jot. He informed Lubochka and his lawyers that he was in Osinki for his holidays and convinced himself that there was no way he could leave a damsel in distress all alone in the middle of nowhere surrounded by deserters and votive candle stand thieves.

Nina's multifaceted nature fascinated him. For Zhora and Elena, she was the wise elder sister. When she talked to her foreman and vendors, she played the role of the defenseless and unlucky young lady, convincing them that it would be a sin to do anything that might harm her. However, if someone dared to encroach on her possessions or show a lack of respect, she would be transformed into a fury. On one occasion, before Klim and Zhora could raise a finger, she personally threw a drunken deserter down the porch and out of the house, telling him in no uncertain terms that she would "bust his head open" if he ever showed his face again.

She was always polite and hospitable to Klim and graciously accepted his well-meaning offerings—a hedgehog that he had brought home in his hat, some dark purple plums, or a string of perch from the river. But she always seemed to keep herself at a distance when she felt that he was trying to get too close. He couldn't work out if this was because she was afraid of upsetting Mr. Fomin or whether a lingering affection for her dead husband still existed. Count Odintzov's portraits littered the house, and she was constantly glancing at them in a sad reverie.

The villagers regarded Nina as a feisty businesswoman. Zhora told Klim that after her husband had died, she had sold off an oak wood on the estate to a timber merchant. The merchant had offered her five thousand rubles, and she had signed the contract on the spot. Much later, she had found out that it had been worth six times the price she had gotten for it. Now, she haggled over everything and made no concessions, not even to the nuns who came to buy currant leaves for their pickled cucumbers.

"We're fast learners," Zhora told Klim with pride. "By birthright, we shouldn't have any of these privileges or a high level of education, but Nina has now earned herself a mill of her own, and I'm going to finish university, become a diplomat, and marry Elena Bagrova. She's the daughter of a prominent merchant and the owner of a steamboat line. He said he wouldn't have any objections."

Every morning, they would all wander out to the village: Nina to the factory, Elena to the market, and Klim and Zhora as their bodyguards. Klim fashioned a *bolas*, an Argentinean hunting weapon, out of a couple stones and some rope and taught Zhora how to throw it like the gaucho cowboys of Argentina. Zhora soon learned how to knock a pair of old boots from the top of a log and promised Nina that if any deserter were to attack her, he would knock their boots off too.

Klim was surprised at the energy and passion that Nina invested in her small mill. It clearly wasn't worth twenty-seven thousand rubles. The squat stone building contained two flax combing machines and eight spinners. In the dusty, noisy shop next door, soldiers' wives wove tarpaulin while in the outbuildings, women cut and sewed mittens and rifle straps, their babies crawling around half-naked under their mothers' feet.

Nina frowned at the sight of the dirty-faced, sickly children and promised to set up a kindergarten for her workers. But where was she going to find the money?

"My first priority is to replace the tension gear," she told Klim as if justifying herself to his silent reproaches. "It keeps breaking the fiber."

It seemed so strange to Klim to hear Nina talking knowledgeably with the foremen at the mill or bargaining with vendors over the vats for the retting solution. How could she combine such delicate femininity with such fierce strength and willpower?

Klim called her "my filigree girl"; to him, she was as strong as metal yet as delicate and fine as lace. She was mysterious, incomprehensible, and utterly adorable.

6

Sometimes, they would go out foraging for mushrooms in the forest, following unknown paths that were as dark as tunnels. The moss-covered earth was light and springy after the previous day's rain, and the scent of the autumn leaves, mushrooms, and the nearby river permeated the air that blew in on the breeze.

Zhora and Elena forged on ahead, and Nina followed them in her felt hat and hunting jacket, an alder cone tangled in the braid of her hair. Wandering in a daze behind her, Klim dreamed of catching up with her, pulling her toward him, and kissing her full on the lips.

Nina glanced back at him mischievously. "I deliberately left you a very good mushroom on the side of the path back there. Didn't you notice it?"

"I didn't see a thing."

"Great mushroom hunter you are," she said, laughing.

They came back to the manor house—exhausted not so much by the walk as by all the intoxicating smells and sights of autumn. They sat together companionably on the sunlit terrace, Nina and Elena cleaning the mushrooms that stained their hands dark while Zhora and Klim threaded the caps and stalks onto thin switches to dry in the sun.

Sometimes Zhora would invent an excuse, and he and Elena would go off "on a very important errand." Although it was clear that the true mission of their "errand" was to kiss in the gazebo at the far end of the garden.

Klim would stay behind with Nina, and these were the moments he enjoyed the most.

He minutely observed the light brown birthmark on her scalp right at the parting, the pattern of the veins on the back of her hand, and the topography of her dress with all its pleats, valleys, plains, and hills.

Nina asked Klim about his adventures, but not in the way that Lubochka and her friends did. They all wanted to hear about his romantic and heroic exploits, but Nina asked different sorts of questions: "What did you live on? How did you learn the languages? What was the most difficult thing you had to do?"

"The most difficult thing was to run across the roofs of Tehran after a thief who had stolen my only shirt," Klim answered, jokingly. "If I hadn't caught him, I'd have had to go to work wrapped in a prayer mat."

"I'm being serious!" Nina protested.

So, Klim confided to her what had been the most difficult part of living abroad. "When you live in your own country, you are valued by your friends and relatives, your entire clan. But in a foreign land, you very soon realize that no one needs you. If you are an immigrant, you have to be a hundred times smarter and more ingenious to get people to notice you."

"I feel like I've been an immigrant from birth," Nina said, smiling. "But I've only ever been abroad once. My husband took me to Paris for our honeymoon."

I don't care if your husband is constantly on your mind, Klim thought. *I don't even mind about that Chairman of the*

31

Provisions Committee or whoever he is. Just as long as you're by my side.

Klim was gripped by a sharp and unbearable feeling of impermanence. He might be allowed to spend the next day with Nina and perhaps the day after that, and then everything would be over.

7

Klim woke up early, but the house was already empty. He paced the dusty rooms and met Zhora dressed in a city-style suit in the entryway.

"Are you leaving?" Klim asked.

"Mr. Fomin sent a telegram," Zhora said, excitedly. "He's managed to get a state loan for us."

Nina entered the house, a happy smile lighting up her face. "Thank goodness! Now, we'll have the money, and I'll be able to pay you back."

She tried to walk past Klim, but he grabbed her hand—an unpardonable gesture. "We need to talk."

She glanced at him in surprise but followed him to the billiard room with its huge semi-circular window and billiard table spread with yellowing newspapers.

Looking at her against the light in her mourning dress, Klim suppressed a painful shudder.

"Nina, come with me to Buenos Aires!" he burst out suddenly. "This place is only full of sad memories for you. There is nothing to keep you here in Russia."

She frowned. "How could I go? I have my family and the mill."

"Nina, listen to me—let Sofia Karlovna live in your house. I'll give Zhora money—let him finish school and go to university. Don't sell yourself to Fomin!"

Nina blushed.

"What do you mean by 'selling myself?' First, you see me as a housemaid and then as a woman for sale?"

"You've got me wrong—"

"I've got you quite right!"

Klim felt as if the blood had drained from his heart. "What will happen to you if you go back to your Mr. Fomin?" he asked, his voice broken.

"And what will happen to me in that Buenos Aires of yours? You yourself said how terrible it is to be a stranger in a strange land."

"I'll take care of everything. I have money and proper connections—"

"And what if we have a fight? What would I do then? Walk the streets?"

Nina left the room, brushing against one of the newspapers as she went out. It slipped from the table to the floor with a quiet rustle. Its headline read, "Offensive becomes bogged down, resulting in heavy losses."

"Zhora, did you take the butter?" Klim heard Nina's voice in the hall. "I left it on the kitchen windowsill."

She spoke in a perfectly even and ordinary voice as if nothing had happened at all.

3. THE COUP

1

Lubochka was wracked with unrequited love. Klim had passed her over for a shameless imposter, a woman Lubochka had foolishly believed to be her friend.

Sablin could sense that something was wrong and had come to the conclusion that his wife was having a bout of "nerves." In an attempt to help her, he brought Lubochka a thick medical book describing the symptoms of and remedies for melancholia. She threw it across the drawing room in a fit of temper.

"You should never have married a real live woman with feelings and warm blood in her veins!" Lubochka cried. "The best match for you would have been a skeleton from a dissection room. Then you could have counted her ribs whenever you liked and stood her in the corner if you felt she was getting in your way."

"Darling, do be reasonable—" Sablin began, but Lubochka didn't care about being reasonable anymore. Her heart was broken, and nobody could care less.

When Klim came back from the country, Lubochka could tell immediately that something was wrong. Pale and tight-lipped, he entered the house, and without stopping to greet her, he headed straight to his room.

Within an hour, Marisha rushed in to see Lubochka, looking bewildered.

"He's ordered me to sell all the possessions his father left him to the neighbors," Marisha said. "He told me not to worry about getting a good price and to get rid of it all as soon as possible. He said he'd had enough and was leaving at the earliest opportunity."

Lubochka gasped. It was obvious that Nina had rejected her Argentinean admirer. What a fool! What a complete and utter fool!

The whole day Lubochka wandered around the house, trying to come up with a way to stop Klim from leaving. But what could she do? She had no power over him.

At dinner, he offered Lubochka's husband a choice: a long-term lease of the house or redemption.

"He doesn't want me to pay interest," Sablin marveled when he and Lubochka were about to go to sleep. "Can you believe we'll finally have a house of our own? But I hate to profit off your cousin in this way."

He glanced at Lubochka lying beside him.

"I think Klim isn't looking too healthy," Sablin said. "I hinted that I'd be happy to refer him to an expert, but he's scared of doctors just like you."

Lubochka could only feel astonishment at her husband's ability to misjudge and misinterpret the whole situation so spectacularly.

2

Lubochka's father, Anton Emilievich Schuster, was the executive editor of the local paper, the *Nizhny Novgorod Bulletin*. Slim with a solemn narrow face and a gray beard, he was a man of culture and huge erudition who lived in a 17th-century stone tower surrounded by his large and motley collection of antiques, books, and rare objects.

Lubochka liked to visit her father. It was a tradition of theirs to have dinner together once a week. But this Saturday, the dinner table was set for three.

"Are you expecting someone?" Lubochka asked her father, unfolding the napkin on her lap.

Anton Emilievich glanced at his watch with a meaningful look. "Just wait a little, and you'll see!"

She noticed that many of the Rogovs' possessions—including the iron safe—had made their way into her father's collection. Anton Emilievich had taken everything that Klim's dubious neighbors hadn't had time to get their hands on.

Klim had bought a ticket to Moscow, and Lubochka tried to prepare herself for what was to come. What was she going to do when he left? Her life would be changed irrevocably.

The brass doorbell jingled in the hall.

"That's him!" Anton Emilievich exclaimed, jumping to his feet. A minute later, he ushered the newly arrived guest into the dining room. He was a common soldier—not an officer but one of the ordinary rank and file.

"Here he is, my one of a kind," Anton Emilievich exclaimed. "Osip Drugov. What's your patronymic?"

"Petrovich," boomed the soldier in a bass voice.

Lubochka cautiously offered him her hand, and he clasped it firmly in his great rough paw. "Pleased to meet you."

Osip was tall and broad-shouldered. His face was ruddy, and the whites of his blue eyes were yellowish and threaded with tiny red veins. When he reached for a piece of bread, the folds on the back of his neck—brown from the sun—stretched out to reveal the pale skin beneath.

"Comrade Drugov is something of a hero," Anton Emilievich said to Lubochka. "He was one of the leaders of the 62nd Regiment rebellion. Soldiers who had recovered from their injuries were being forced to board trains heading back to the front, and Osip Petrovich and his colleagues managed to get them away from their escorts."

Anton Emilievich was trying to sound ironic, but Lubochka detected an unfamiliar, ingratiating note in his voice. He fawned on Osip. "Do please help yourself. This trout is excellent—it just came today from the farm."

But Osip paid no attention to his host's efforts to impress him. "It's unfair to send men back to be slaughtered while any man whose mother or father can afford to pay sits in safety away from the front," he said, fixing Lubochka with a stare. "I went straight to the newspaper office, and I met your father there."

Lubochka huddled back in her chair, her whole body sensing the contrast between the nervous agitation of her father and the confident power exuded by his guest, who was neither offhand nor insolent but felt at liberty to do and say whatever he pleased.

"Did Father interview you?" she asked with a forced smile.

"We talked about things," Osip said. "I told him, 'I've shed blood for you,' and all that. 'I've been wounded twice and suffered from shellshock, so you have to help us. And if you won't write about the demands of the people, we'll confiscate your newspaper.'"

Anton Emilievich roared with laughter. "I was flabbergasted! So I said, 'Who the hell are you?' And he said, 'I'm a Russian Bolshevik.'"

Now, Lubochka understood. The Bolsheviks were a small left-wing political party gathering momentum with young radicals and deserters from the front joining them, and now, they were calling openly for a coup d'état.

Lubochka's father in his wisdom could tell that important events were afoot. Recently, he had taken to saying that they were living like goldfish in a glass bowl. They saw everything in a distorted light without actually caring about what was going on in the world outside. Meanwhile, however, the glass in the bowl had cracked.

Anton Emilievich wanted to find out what was going on in the barracks and factories—that was why he had invited a Bolshevik to dinner.

Osip Drugov said things that made Lubochka's hair stand on end.

"We don't want Russia to win this war—this is the kind of war that should be lost. It wouldn't be a defeat for us. It would be a defeat for the Provisional Government. The bourgeoisie has forced us to kill our own brothers, workers from Germany and Austria-Hungary. Just think of it—how many people have died! And for what? Now that we have weapons in our hands, we'll put them to use against our real enemies—the landlords, the factory owners, and the other oppressors of the working people."

"And how will you tell who are the working people and who are the freeloaders?" asked Anton Emilievich politely.

"It'll be easy. Those people who are of some use to society may live. And as for the freeloaders, we'll string 'em up from the lampposts. Now, you, Anton Emilievich, have a very useful profession—"

"Wait a minute," Lubochka interrupted. "So, you think I should be strung up from a lamppost? I don't work for a living, after all."

Osip wasn't in the least embarrassed. "That's only because bourgeois society sets restrictions on what you can do. A woman Bolshevik came to our hospital and talked to us about women's rights. Think how useful women could be if they had the chance to work like men! What would you like to do, for instance?"

Lubochka looked around the room and the dining table. "I suppose I'd like to open a restaurant."

"I'm afraid that's out of the question. We intend to ban all private property. But we're going to need people in public catering who know what they're doing."

"Visit us again," Anton Emilievich told Osip as they said goodbye. "Lubochka is having a birthday party soon."

Osip turned toward her and looked at her with a piercing gaze, showing such frank and obvious sexual interest that she felt slightly weak at the knees.

"What would you like me to get you as a birthday present?" he asked.

"What kind of thing can a Bolshevik get?"

"Everything. The whole world."

"Then I'll have that."

"Right. It's yours."

3

Mr. Fomin, the chairman of the city's Provisions Committee, sat at his table in the Oriental Bazaar sweating, his broad shoulders bowed by worldly cares, his throat tightened with anger and jealousy as he stared at the dancing couples.

He had asked Nina to come to the restaurant on purpose. There would be people around him, and they wouldn't allow him to do what he wanted to do most of all.

Nina ran into the half-empty room, blushing with anticipation. She put her wet umbrella on a chair and sat across the table from Fomin. "Tell me all the details! Whom did you meet in Petrograd?"

Nina was uncommonly smart, quick, and self-assured and looked nothing like Fomin's own sturdy girls who had been living in Geneva with their mother, safely in neutral Switzerland since the beginning of the war.

Fomin tried to be calm and sober while telling Nina the news, and she was so excited that she didn't notice his mood at all. She gasped, wrinkled her nose, and, like a little girl, bit her lower lip, trying to stop herself from laughing in sheer delight. "Oh, I knew you'd make it happen!"

Fomin could barely hold his emotions in check. *Why has all this happened to me?* he thought. However, he had no one to blame but himself. It had been he who had invaded Nina's life, a big balding man whose belly hung over his belt. But how could he stop himself when he had seen her perishing, crushed by her grief and tormented by her mother-in-law? Apart from him, Nina had no one else to rely on except her younger brother.

Fomin had no illusions—he was well aware that she thought of him as no more than her patron. She listened attentively when he gave her advice and was grateful for all the help he gave her. Fomin's office was full of little gifts that she had given him—tiny jars of jam, knitted mittens, and the like. Nina was under no obligation to pay him back for what he had done, but she had decided in her own naïve way to show her gratitude: *You gave me something, so I'll give you something in return. If you don't want my jam, well, there's nothing I can offer you besides myself.*

Fomin knew that they had no future and that their little adventure could only end tragically.

Nina took a notebook from her bag and began to calculate something.

"Do you think the current ruble exchange rate will last until winter?" she asked him, meeting his stare.

And only then did she realize that Fomin was about to explode.

"What's wrong?" she asked, worried.

The walls were shaking around him; his whole world was crumbling to dust. Should he kill himself in front of her? Or smother her and then shoot himself?

"Sofia Karlovna told me everything," he said colorlessly. "While I was away, solving your problem, you had an affair with the prosecutor's heir."

Nina put her pencil down. It rolled across the table and fell on her lap.

"Don't you understand that Sofia Karlovna wants us to fall out?" Nina asked quietly. "She was the one who sent Mr. Rogov to Osinki."

"He stayed there for three weeks!"

"So what? I owe him twenty-seven thousand. I had to work something out."

People started looking at them, but Fomin didn't care. What could Nina possibly "work out" with Rogov? The same arrangement that she had worked out with him?

"Will you at least let me explain to you how we spent those three weeks in Osinki?" Nina asked and began to describe how they had visited her mill and gone mushrooming and how she had refused to go to Argentina with Klim.

"If you don't believe me, ask Zhora and Elena," Nina added. "They'll confirm everything I've told you."

Suddenly, Fomin felt exhausted. His jaw was trembling, and a cold drop of sweat trickled down his temple.

"Why did you refuse to go with Mr. Rogov?" he asked.

Nina opened her notebook in the middle and moved it toward Fomin. "Here's my balance sheet. As you can see, we've had very good results even before we won that state contract."

She leaned back and crossed her arms. "I had my workers sewing canvas sacks. That is exactly what is in high demand among people who carry flour from the grain-producing regions."

Fomin looked at her with a wry respectful smile. "You are a crazy woman. Mr. Rogov has offered you beaches and palm trees, and you have turned them down for a pile of canvas sacks."

"I don't need someone else's achievements," Nina said. "I want mine. Something that I have earned and that no one will take away from me."

4

The church was full of people. The flickering reflections of the candles shone in the gilded robes of the priests and the silver frames of the icons. The voices of the choir singing "I Call to You, Lord" flew high up into the dark vault above.

Nina was crossing herself without grasping the meaning of the service. She looked around at the anxious faces—at a young woman kneeling with a black lace veil over her head and an old man trying to light a candle with a shaking hand. Next to him, a portly merchant's wife dipped her finger into the oil of a sanctuary lamp and anointed her eyelids and the eyelids of her little son.

Nina had got exactly what she wanted: she and Klim had signed all the requisite papers, and her bank account had just received funds from her state loan. And yet she somehow felt deflated and unhappy.

In the past, Nina had always known exactly what she needed to do and diligently pursued her goals in order to never again experience the shameful poverty that had been a permanent feature of her childhood.

Her father had been a skillful tailor and charged up to thirty rubles for a fine dress, but he had also been a gambler, capable of blowing the family's entire savings in a single night and forcing Nina's mother to borrow money to feed her children.

If it hadn't been for a casual acquaintance with Count Vladimir Odintzov, who for some inexplicable reason had fallen in love with her, Nina would have been condemned to the same grinding poverty that had marked her mother's life. Nina owed Vladimir everything and felt guilty at even thinking about another man. Fomin didn't count, really—at least that was what she told herself—but after Nina had met Klim, the revered remembrance of her dead husband seemed to have lost all its meaning like an old theater ticket. Nina believed that one day she would answer for this at the seat of judgment, and it struck superstitious fear into her. After all, she had already received much more than a girl of her background could ever dare hope for.

I wish Klim had never come back, Nina thought. He had mistaken her for a housemaid, immediately recognizing her lower social status, and she had immediately recognized him as a "robber." But in this instance, he was not so much a robber of personal possessions but her personal affections.

The fact that he asked her to go to Argentina with him meant nothing to her. How could she possibly leave her mill and her brother behind? It would be impossible to take Zhora with them—he would never go without Elena. And her parents would never let her go to a foreign country with god knows who.

If only Klim could be persuaded to stay in Nizhny Novgorod! *But what could he do here?* Nina thought in despair. Work as a reporter for his uncle's newspaper? Or just be a rich playboy idler?

It didn't make sense to even dream about it. There was no way Nina could sunder her ties with Fomin. He had told her straight that he would kill Klim if he "allowed himself to take any liberties."

5

Nina left the church before the end of the service. The weather was nasty with drizzling rain and a biting wind.

A boy stood in the street with a pile of newspapers. "Read the latest!" he shouted. "Provisional Government deposed!"

Oh, no, Nina thought. *That's all we need.*

People gathered around the newsboy. "What are they saying? Is it another war? Who are we fighting with now?"

"There's been another revolution in Petrograd," the newsboy said. "The Bolsheviks have taken power."

Nina didn't manage to get a newspaper. She looked around anxiously for another news vendor. People were crowding out of the church—rumors about the collapse of the government had spread like wildfire.

Nina noticed a soldier holding a paper. "Damn, I can't understand a thing," he grumbled. "Hey, lady!" he called Nina. "Do you know your letters? Could you read this for me, please? What are they saying?"

Nina took the dirty sheet, which smudged her hands black with printing ink.

"To the citizens of Russia," she started to read loudly. People moved closer to her, listening intently and trying not to miss a single word. "The Provisional Government has been deposed. State power has passed into the hands of the Revolutionary Military Committee, which heads the Petrograd proletariat and the garrison. The cause for which the people have fought—namely, the immediate offer of democratic peace, the abolition of landed ownership, workers' control over production, and the establishment of Soviet power—this cause has been secured. Long live the revolution of workers, soldiers, and peasants!"

Beneath this Bolshevik manifesto were a number of reports that made it clear there were disturbances in Petrograd and shootings in Moscow.

"The Bolsheviks have made no secret of their intentions," said a gentleman in a felt bowler hat. "They wanted to seize power, and they have done so. Now, we'll see a bloodbath."

The crowd began to disperse.

Nina wondered what the phrases "the abolition of landed ownership" and "workers' control over production" actually meant. What if the new authorities were about to take her mill away?

I need to see Fomin, she decided. *He's bound to know what's going on.*

She hurried down Pokrovskaya Street. The reflections of the streetlights flickered in the slush on the pavement, their bleary outlines glimmering in the dusty shop windows.

"Nina, wait!"

She turned her head and saw Klim dressed in an elegant gray overcoat, hat, and suede gloves.

"Have you heard about the coup?" she asked and told him what she'd read in the Bolsheviks' manifesto. "Do you think it's serious?"

Klim shrugged. "No idea. Are you in a hurry? I'd like to say goodbye before I catch the train tonight. My luggage is already at the station. Can you imagine, I've got a whole compartment to myself and will be traveling to Moscow like a state minister, no less."

He fell silent, smiling sadly at his own thoughts. "Zhora told me you were in the Pokrovskaya Church. I wanted to see you before I leave—in order to perform an important act of *gauchada*."

"What does *'gauchada'* mean?" Nina asked.

"It's the word that the Argentineans use to describe a deed worthy of a true gaucho. The gauchos are just regular cowboys, but the people believe they have noble souls and a special talent for selfless deeds. Well—here is mine."

Klim took a white envelope out of his breast pocket and handed it to Nina.

She looked at him, puzzled. "What is it?"

"Your promissory note. I wanted to give you something in memory of our friendship."

Nina was taken aback. "Are you giving me back my mill? Don't you need the money anymore?"

"I have more than enough money to travel the world for the next ten years, and then I'll come back for you. Hopefully, you might have changed your mind about me by that time."

He looked at her, smiling. "No thanks needed. A true gaucho never asks for any reward for his noble deeds. You could just hang a commemorative plaque with my face on it at the entrance to your mill. But I'm afraid Mr. Fomin might object."

Nina put the envelope into her muff. "Thank you."

They reached Blagoveschenskaya Square in silence. Nina didn't know what to say. In her experience, men usually tried to settle their scores with the women who rejected them. She never thought Klim would display such magnanimity.

Military trucks drove past and columns of soldiers marched by.

"Tripe for sale—fried, steamed, or buttered!" a street seller shouted at the top of her voice. The corners of her checkered headscarf billowed over her head in the wind.

It was dark and quiet in the Kremlin fortress. Only the windows of the Governor's Palace shone with a bright electric light. Nina noticed a long red cloth hanging from the railings in front of the arsenal—"All power to the Congress of Soviets of Workers, Soldiers, and Peasants!"

Nina walked up the porch steps. "Well— goodbye," she whispered, her voice faltering.

She felt keenly that her words didn't do justice to either the gift she had just been given or the fact that she and Klim were about to say goodbye to each other forever.

Droplets of rain shimmered on the fibers of his overcoat. He was clean-shaven and smelled of cologne. He didn't fit into this benighted country; he belonged on the other side of the world where it was spring now with the purple jacarandas in bloom.

Klim took off his hat and kissed Nina's hand. "Farewell."

6

There were no guards or visitors in the corridors of the Governor's Palace, and Nina made her way slowly across the entry hall and opened the door that was smudged with muddy footprints. The smell of burning paper hung heavy in the air.

I don't suppose I'll ever see Klim again, she thought, and the very idea seemed outrageous to her.

How could she just let him disappear like that? It would be a mockery of everything that had been between them and even common sense itself.

Nina turned to run back after Klim and almost collided with Fomin.

"Follow me!" he ordered, his voice like a prison guard's.

Grabbing her by the hand, he dragged her into his office. The floor inside was covered with ashes. The inkwell on his desk was overturned, and there were pens and pencils scattered everywhere.

"Listen to me carefully," Fomin said, standing close to Nina and looking at her with troubled eyes. "Tens of thousands of soldiers have gathered in Petrograd. They've been doing nothing but robbing, drinking, and gambling. The Provisional Government tried to send them to the front, but now, they've mutinied." He grasped Nina's shoulders. "We have to leave immediately! These gangs of armed, hungry deserters will soon be in charge of the country."

Nina gasped. "What about the Bolsheviks? After all, they're the ones who have seized power."

Fomin roared with coarse laughter. "And do you have any idea who these Bolsheviks are? They're a small group of emigrants and political convicts who have accidentally found themselves at the head of a spontaneous rebellion. It's the deserters who are propping up the Bolsheviks because they are promising them immediate peace with Germany.

"Now, who do you think is going to feed and clothe our hungry, threadbare, gray-coated heroes? We have three infantry regiments of them in Nizhny Novgorod alone, and these guys have spent up to three years at the front. They have gotten out of the habit of working and become rather accustomed to making a living by slitting throats. Mark my words— they won't hesitate to loot your house just as they did the Tsar's Winter Palace."

"Lord, help us!" Nina whispered.

"They burst into the Palace, broke everything they could lay their hands on, opened up the wine cellars, and now, the whole of Petrograd has been carousing for the third day running."

"Maybe the rebellion won't get as far as Nizhny Novgorod—"

"Don't be a fool! I have it on reliable intelligence that the Bolsheviks will try to seize the Nizhny Novgorod Kremlin tonight."

Nina stepped back from him in alarm. "I won't go with you—"

"Then who will you go with? Your gentleman from Argentina whom I just met outside on the street?"

The telephone rang, and Fomin snatched the receiver. "Yes…yes…arrested? All right, I'll be there." He closed his eyes for a moment and then turned to Nina. "Wait for me here."

"I told you. I'm not going with you!"

She made a dash for the door, but he yanked her hand so hard that she almost fell over. "Stay here, I said!"

Fomin left the office, and the next moment there was a sudden clatter of footsteps thudding down the corridor and the sound of male voices cursing crudely. Then there came the unmistakable crack of gunfire.

Terrified, Nina shrank back against the wall. "Lord, have mercy on us," she kept repeating.

She parted the curtains, opened the window, and threw her legs over the side of the windowsill.

"Be careful. There's broken glass on the ground here," Nina heard Klim's voice say.

Without asking her any questions, he helped her out of the window.

"Now, run!" he whispered.

They ran, holding hands, splashing through the icy puddles in the darkness. Next to the Kremlin gates, they almost collided with a group of soldiers and hid in the shadow of the wall, waiting for them to pass. One of the soldiers struck a match to light his cigarette, and its flame illuminated his bearded face and gleamed in the polished blade of his bayonet. Barely daring to breathe, Klim and Nina listened to the sound of footsteps and the creaking of machine-gun wheels bumping along the paving stones.

As they got to Blagoveschenskaya Square, they saw people hunched into the upturned collars of their coats, darting in and out between the two main city cathedrals.

Nina glanced at Klim. "Where now?"

"To my house—just in case Fomin comes looking for you at Crest Hill."

"But what about your train?"

Klim gave a dismissive wave of his hand. "Who cares?"

7

They were stopped three times on their way home by the patrols. Men in padded jackets and cartridge belts slung over their shoulders demanded to see Klim and Nina's documents. However, on each occasion, a five-ruble banknote had sufficed to keep them happy.

All the way home, Klim kept a fast hold on Nina's hand, his heart pounding and his thoughts scattered to the four winds. *I suppose my train must have left already,* he thought. But it didn't matter. Something huge and awe-inspiring was manifesting itself; something that he felt he had been waiting for all his life.

"Why did you come back for me?" Nina asked.

"I heard the gunshots," Klim answered and smiled at his own thoughts. The truth was he hadn't been planning on going to Moscow anyway. The moment he had seen Nina that night, the matter had been settled in his heart forever.

The electricity was down on Ilinskaya Street, and all the houses looked abandoned. Klim walked up to the porch of his house, unlocked the front door, and conducted Nina to his room.

It was empty except for a bed, a sanctuary lamp that flickered under the icon in the corner, and a portrait of Nicholas II that no one had wanted to buy.

Klim and Nina shed their coats on the bed and sat on the floor, leaning their backs against the hot tiles of a stove.

"The stove is perhaps mankind's most important invention," said Nina as she pulled off her wet stockings.

Klim nodded. He felt the tension growing in every fiber of his body.

Nina reached for her muff and took out the envelope with the promissory note. "I won't take it," she said.

"Why?"

"I don't want you thinking that I'm only here to take advantage of you."

"What else should you do? Of course, you should take advantage of me." Klim flung the promissory note into the stove.

Nina moved closer and leaned her head against his chest. "Your heart is pounding."

"I'm not surprised."

He put his arms around her and kissed the nape of her neck, the side of her face, and the corners of her mouth. Once again, he fell into a world of dreams, luxuriating in it joyfully and losing all sense of place and time. "Nina...darling—"

She sprang to her feet, put her hands on the back of her head, and took out her hairpins one by one. Then she undid the fastenings of her black mourning dress and let it drop to the floor.

"Come here," she said to Klim. She looked different now, sitting on the bed in her white undershirt and drawers.

He went up to her, untied his necktie, and unbuttoned his shirt.

The creaking of the floorboards in the corridor made them jump. A candlelight flickered in the crack under the door.

"He must have forgotten to turn off the electric light," Marisha grumbled to herself. "He'll run up such a bill that he'll never be able to pay it off." She tried the bolted door. "Hey, I thought you'd already left!"

"I'm sleeping," Klim said, his voice hoarse with emotion.

"How come? Did they cancel your train?"

"Marisha, I'm sleeping!"

"All right, all right—tell me all about it in the morning." Marisha sighed and shuffled off.

Inflamed by the possibility that she and Klim might have been discovered, Nina pulled her undershirt over her head. She looked at Klim triumphantly, brushing the curls away from her heaving breast.

My love, I'll never leave you, he thought, pressing her to his chest.

The light in the bathroom suddenly turned back on as the electricity was restored. Marisha was right: Klim had forgotten to switch it off.

Nina lay quite still on her back, her eyes closed and her fingers grasping the sheet. Klim pressed his forehead against her shoulder.

"Do you want anything to drink?" he asked.

She gave a barely perceptible shake of her head.

Swaying on his feet, Klim headed to the bathroom. He turned on the tap, drank the icy water from his cupped hands, and then looked at his reflection in the mirror. He could hardly believe what was happening.

4. THE DELUGE

1

EL CUADERNO NEGRO

Klim Rogov's little black notebook

We have no ink left—our representative from the Neighborhood Committee has confiscated the last of it. He's been going from house to house begging for ink because the Committee has masses of paperwork and no writing materials. I didn't dare refuse. He threatened a particularly harsh punishment to any would-be "saboteurs"—they wouldn't have their cesspits cleaned out.

From now on, I'll be writing in pencil.

There is a general strike across the whole of Russia, demanding that the Constituent Assembly assumes leadership of the country. The Bolsheviks continue to delay its convocation because they only got twenty-four percent of the vote in the election.

All the banks in the city have been closed since the end of October. Nobody can withdraw any money, and since salaries are not being paid, I have no idea what people are living on. Everyone is eating up whatever crumbs happen to be left over, and that includes the representatives of the new powers that be.

The Bolsheviks are biding their time, hoping that the revolutionary movement will assume worldwide proportions and capitalism will go up in flames so that the whole question of capital will become irrelevant. Here in Nizhny Novgorod, the only thing that has gone up in flames is a storehouse where the surgical spirit was stored, which was besieged by the "loyal sons of the working people." A sight for sore eyes, these "loyal sons" in their unbuttoned greatcoats with Mausers in one hand and teapots full of alcoholic swill in the other.

When all of the alcohol had been drunk and all of the flour from the plundered provision storehouses had been eaten, the Bolsheviks headed to the banks and opened the safes. Their official objective was to check who had earned income and who had not. But in reality, they were just engaging in daylight robbery in the true spirit of the Wild West. So, I'm afraid that if my money hasn't already been transferred to Argentina yet, there will be nothing left of it—it has all been confiscated for revolutionary requirements.

All of my friends were shocked when I decided to stay in Nizhny Novgorod with Nina.

Lubochka thinks I'm crazy too. "You could have caught the very last train out and escaped the revolution," she said to me.

But actually, that wouldn't have changed anything. Instead of getting stuck in Nizhny Novgorod, I would have gotten stuck in Moscow where the Bolsheviks have been shelling entire streets to crush the opposition.

Anyway, I couldn't leave Nina behind. Strangely enough, I'm happy here. My feverish heart is untouched by all of the events I've just written about. It's not only my Argentinean passport that makes me a foreigner here but also the fact that I have no interest in the fight over our bright future.

For me, the present is already bright enough. Nina and I stroll the snow-covered streets, the snowdrifts tower over our heads, and the birch trees, shimmering with the frost, form a guard of honor specially for us. Nina recites the poems of Alexander Blok, a popular Russian poet, and I sing Spanish tavern songs to her, shamelessly muddling all of the words and tunes.

We watch the revolution as if we are watching a movie, and we are happy that Mr. Fomin has disappeared from our lives without a trace.

Sofia Karlovna holds more terrors for us than the Military Revolutionary Staff. After all, she could admonish us about our behavior. Once she caught us sitting by the stove in an embrace, and that put her in complete disarray. Suddenly, she realized that I'm an even bigger threat to her than Mr. Fomin.

After all, if I take Nina away with me to Buenos Aires, who is going to pay the old countess's bills?

Nina finds it difficult even to think about leaving the country. She believes that if she stays in Russia, she will be able to prevent the confiscation of her mill.

"They can't take away everything from everybody," she told me.

I think they can, and that's why I'm firm that we need to leave Russia as soon as possible and spend at least a couple of years abroad. Then we'll have a better idea of what to do.

Nina and I have decided to wait until the railroad strike is over and then go to Petrograd for Argentinean visas. We'll take Zhora with us and telegraph money to the old countess. (I dearly hope that I will be able to provide for us all.)

We haven't discussed it with Zhora though. We don't want to upset him with the thought of having to leave Elena.

A later entry

Of course, all that I have written here is sheer bravado, an attempt to conceal my entirely justified fear of the coming deluge. Alas, I don't have an ark and am not on terribly good terms with God.

2

Poverty means not having enough money, Nina thought. *Destitution means having no money whatsoever and no food.*

Initially, she looked for coins in her coat pockets, muffs, and purses. Then she searched through the library, remembering that in better times she had used banknotes as bookmarks.

The school was closed, and Zhora helped Nina rummage through the books. He climbed the ladder up to the ceiling, flipped through the pages of dusty volumes, sneezing and humming a Polish revolutionary anthem, "The Song of Warsaw":

Treacherous whirlwinds are raging around us,
The forces of darkness our brothers oppress.
Now, we do battle with the foe that surrounds us—

"Oh, damn this ridiculous song!" Zhora complained. "I can't for the life of me get it out of my head." But the next minute, he started whistling it again.

Nina had sold Vladimir's gold watch to buy food, but she knew that it would only be enough for a couple of weeks.

"We need to tell our Osinki manager what it's like here," Zhora said as he looked through the *Gingerbread Man, the Magic Goose, and other Fairy Tales*. "He might be able to send us food from the village."

But it was impossible to send messages when neither telegraph stations nor postal offices were working. The horizons of their world had dwindled drastically. Nobody visited their friends anymore— there was no food to share, and spare rooms were locked because there wasn't enough firewood to heat them. People had begun to live like nomads camping in an icy desert: it was as though a vast tundra separated one house from other.

Sofia Karlovna appeared in the doorway, a gray paper leaflet in her shaking hand. "The Bolsheviks have issued a new degree," she said.

Nina read through it:

The owners of wine cellars must turn over all wine and spirits to the appropriate Soviet institutions.

The Bolsheviks informed the townsfolk that they were seeking to prevent the bourgeoisie from engaging in illegal trading in wine and wouldn't let them make drunkards out of the people. An announcement that those who disobeyed the order would be arrested was printed in bold lettering.

"Why should we care?" Nina asked, but the old countess cut her short.

"We have a full wine cellar. In 1914, when the government had issued a prohibition law, I ordered the wine cellar to be bricked up."

Nina looked at her brother. "Go find Klim and bring him over. It looks like we're going to survive the winter in style."

Sofia Karlovna gasped. "What are you up to?"

"Alcohol is the only reliable currency in this country," said Nina. "We'll get plenty of food in exchange for a bottle of champagne."

"But they'll put you in jail!"

"Let them catch me first."

Seeing her brother off, Nina made a sign of the cross over him. Every time one of them went out onto the street, it felt as if they were being sent down a rickety mine where there could be a landslide or a gas explosion at any moment. The city was full of Red Guards who believed that harassing passers-by was just another way of advancing their struggle for the rights of the working class. It was useless to complain about them to authorities because they always sided with the hooligans.

When Nina returned to the library, Sofia Karlovna was still standing at the window that was blocked out by the drifts of snow.

"Your previous admirer, Mr. Fomin, turned you into a market trader," she said without turning her head. "I thought it was the most horrible thing that could ever happen to you, but I was wrong. Now, you have made friends with Mr. Rogov, and you are ready to become a criminal. There are certain things you should know about Mr. Rogov's past. Do you know what caused his mother's death? An abortion! She had an affair with an Imperial Guard's lieutenant, became pregnant, and tried to conceal it from her husband. I hope you realize that all this has affected her son's morality."

Nina wrung her hands and bit her tongue. *Sofia Karlovna is Vladimir's mother,* she reminded herself. *And I owe him everything I have.*

"What do you see in that man?" the old countess asked sadly.

"He loves me for who I am," said Nina. "But you don't."

3

Nina heard a rustling sound from outside, and the rime on the outer pane suddenly blazed into light.

Klim had made it a habit of always "digging out the sun" before he came indoors.

She dashed to the hall, trembling with joy. Klim and Zhora came in, their cheeks flushed with the cold, and Nina hurried them down into the basement.

Klim scrutinized the brick wall covered in frost. "I used to work for archeologists in the desert," he said. "We were looking for broken pots and ancient skeletons, but I think it's much more interesting to look for wine."

Nina found a couple of hammers, and Klim and Zhora began breaking down the brick wall. Their blows were so loud that it felt as though they would destroy the building. Finally, the wall gave in, and the bricks spilled onto the concrete floor.

The dusty bottles were lined up on the shelves, and the glow of Nina's lamp reflected and multiplied in their dully gleaming sides.

Zhora whistled appreciatively. "Wow!"

Shivering with cold and impatience, Nina read the labels: Moët & Chandon, G.H. Mumm, Louis Roederer.

Klim put his arms around Nina. "We've hit the big time."

"Sofia Karlovna is convinced that we are criminals," Nina said.

"That's nothing compared with what Lubochka says about us," Klim replied. "She called us fools who had frittered away my father's inheritance."

"Don't you regret anything?"

"Only one thing. I should have come home for you much earlier."

4

Later that day, Klim and Zhora brought back two baskets—the day's takings. Nina couldn't believe her eyes. There were smoked sausages, oranges, and chocolates.

Sofia Karlovna grumbled for a while that it was outrageous to feast when so many people were starving, but Klim tempted her with a small glass of liqueur.

"I remember this bottle," the old countess said. "It's a real Bénédictine from the Abbey of Fécamp—I brought it back from Normandy. See the label: D.O.M.? It means 'Deo Optimo Maximo'—'To God, most good, most great.' You should kneel to drink such a wine, and here you are lapping it up by the glass. Shame on you!"

Soon, her cheeks were flushed pink and her mood softened.

"Here, my dear," she said, pouring red wine into Nina's glass. "Bourgogne ought to be drunk with époisses cheese, but what can we do if we don't have any? Drink up. It'll be a long time before you'll ever get another chance to try the favorite wine of d'Artagnan and Aramis."

5. INTRUSION

1

Dr. Sablin had not joined the strike. Every day, he continued to go to the Martynov Hospital, put on his white overalls, and perform operations.

The October coup had unsettled him completely. Everything that had formerly been considered good was now seen as counter-revolutionary. It was shameful to be rich and foolish to fight for your country, whereas looting and robbing were now regarded as a struggle for the interests of the people. Nowadays, public enemies were identified by those in authority in terms of their felt hats and clean fingernails.

"The Soviets have used up all the money," Anton Emilievich said to Sablin one day. "The treasury is empty, and the Petrograd authorities are rejecting all requests for funds. They've given the order to find money locally. I presume that means there will be confiscations soon."

"How do you know?" Sablin asked suspiciously.

Anton Emilievich showed him a typed copy of a decree on the confiscation of private property from bourgeois ownership. "We got this today at our editorial office. They have ordered us to publish it tomorrow."

What am I going to do? Sablin wondered. *What am I to make of all this?* Every ounce of his sense of justice screamed out in protest. And yet, he thought, the people of Russia accepted the Bolsheviks. Or was that merely an illusion?

Revolutionary sailors had suppressed the Constituent Assembly, and the Bolsheviks had banned all strikes and mass meetings by the opposition. At their own meetings, they declared that they stood for the total equality of the people. "All means of production should become public property," read the front pages of their newspapers. "From each according to their ability, to each according to their needs." But these were the laws of primitive savages.

Most amazing of all was the fact that nobody was protesting. Instead, the people of the city prayed. At Candlemas, the religious procession stretched from the cathedral to Novo-Bazarnaya Square. Bareheaded, Sablin watched the huge crowd breathing out clouds of steam as it shuffled along.

Church banners fluttered, and the snow squeaked under thousands of feet. Austrian prisoners of war, looking even more miserable than usual, approached the procession to beg for bread. "For the luff of Christ—"

The Bolsheviks had declared that religion was the opium of the people, and the priests in the churches prayed for peace in the country while at the same time pronouncing an anathema against "those who act unlawfully and oppress the Christian faith and the Orthodox church."

Sablin learned about international events from Lubochka—she told him that the Germans were demanding significant territorial concessions and reparations. If these demands weren't met, they were threatening to continue their advance into Russian territory. Leon Trotsky, the People's Commissar for Foreign Affairs, had ordered the army to be disbanded and the Bolsheviks to refuse to sign a peace treaty in the hope and anticipation that the German proletariat would overthrow the Kaiser and reverse all of his greedy demands.

"But then the Germans will invade and occupy us," Sablin kept saying to himself and tried to figure out what an honest man should do if that became the case.

2

Sablin stepped onto the porch and brushed the snow from his felt boots. Klim opened the door to him. He had only come indoors a minute earlier and hadn't had time to take his overcoat off.

"How are things at the hospital?" Klim asked cheerfully.

Sablin didn't answer. He was looking for Lubochka, who had failed to come out to greet him. *Where is she?* he wondered. *Has she gone to another party?*

Klim took a bottle of champagne from the inside pocket of his overcoat and put it on the table beneath the hall mirror. "A present for you, doctor."

"Where did you get it?" Sablin exclaimed in amazement.

"I discovered a horde of treasure." It seemed that Klim was slightly the worse for drink.

He was the only person Sablin knew who wasn't taking the political situation seriously, and his nonchalance irritated the doctor. What sort of time was this to have a love affair with an officer's widow? What were the two of them hoping to gain? What were they planning to live on?

There was a knock at the door, and Klim and the doctor exchanged glances.

"I think it must be Lubochka," said Sablin as he pulled the bolt.

But instead of his wife, a group of armed men stood on the porch.

"We're the Committee for the Hungry," announced a tall, round-shouldered man in a pince-nez. "All houses belonging to the bourgeoisie are subject to official searches. We are looking for weapons, spirits, and other surplus goods."

A faceless, bustling crowd streamed into the hall. Cabinet doors slammed, chest of drawers creaked, and shoe brushes and shoehorns clattered to the floor.

"Who has given you the authority?" Sablin shrieked and stopped short when the head of the gang pointed a revolver at his face.

"Are you a doctor?" he asked. "Do you have alcohol, morphine, or cocaine?"

The blood had drained from the man's pale face, and his nose was shapeless and desiccated. He moved jerkily, his pupils were dilated, and large beads of sweat stood out on his forehead.

A drug addict, thought Sablin. The type who can kill without a second thought.

"We have nothing of that sort here," Sablin said in a shaky voice and suddenly remembered the unfortunate bottle of champagne.

Klim, still in his unbuttoned overcoat, was watching the intruders with his arms folded over his chest. The bottle was gone; evidently, he had hidden it.

"You two and the cook shall go and sit in the dining room," the man in the pince-nez ordered them. "If we hear so much as a squeak from you, you'll be wearing my rifle butt instead of your teeth as dentures."

Then he turned his face toward Sablin. "If you've been lying about the alcohol, I'll shoot you on the spot."

The members of the Committee for the Hungry darted past, carrying piles of towels, hunting boots, and crystal vases. Sablin felt a cold draught at his feet from the doors that had been opened. Feathers from ripped pillows floated in the air, and all of the family's papers were scattered around the dining table: birth certificates, diplomas, and bills. Marisha sobbed quietly.

Just so long as they don't find the champagne, Sablin prayed.

The man in the pince-nez told a young lad with a rifle slung over his shoulder to watch the arrested.

"How old are you?" Klim asked the lad.

The guard didn't even look at him but carried on picking his teeth with a matchstick.

"You look about nineteen," said Klim. "Are you a worker? You certainly don't appear to be a bishop. But you do go to church, I assume. Have you heard the commandment 'Thou shalt not covet'? 'Thou shalt not covet thy neighbor's house. Thou shalt not covet thy neighbor's wife, nor his manservant or maidservant, nor his ox nor his ass, nor anything else that is his.'"

He'll get what he's asking for now, thought Sablin. *What a time to start preaching!*

The lad threw the matchstick on the floor and wiped his chapped lips with the back of his hand. "Comrade Scherbatov says the priests are liars. We have to confiscate everything and then share and share alike."

"That's a great idea," Klim agreed. "Let's share. You've had your rifle for a while; now it's my turn."

The lad smirked. "Think you're smart, don't you?"

"So, you don't want to share after all, do you? Then how did you end up with this lot?"

"The factory closed, and there was nothing to eat. And here they pay us."

They heard footsteps on the mezzanine floor and a voice shouting, "Hey, look what I've found!"

Sablin's heart sank. The man in the pince-nez slowly entered the dining room holding a portrait of Nicholas II in his hands.

"Who is the owner of this?" he barked, shifting his gaze from one face to another. "Well, well, well—it seems we've found ourselves a nest of monarchists."

"It's mine," said Klim abruptly. "Put it back and leave it alone. I'm a foreign correspondent and have a right to take historical souvenirs abroad with me."

The man was caught by surprise. "A foreigner? Why is your Russian so good?"

"I went to a special Russian school."

"Show me your documents!"

The Argentinean passport perplexed the raiders. Klim started talking through his hat about some Foreign Press Committee and how he knew Lenin personally and would instigate criminal proceedings against the wrongdoers.

"What are your names?" he asked in a stern voice.

The man in the pince-nez pulled out his pocket watch and looked at it. "We've got other fish to fry. Let's go, boys!"

The gang poured out into the street. The doctor bolted the door and leaned his back against it. He was drenched in sweat.

"I don't get it," he moaned. "Shoot me on the spot, but it's beyond my comprehension."

"It's all as clear as day," muttered Klim. "That scoundrel holds some petty government position. He hasn't received his paycheck, so he's decided to try to squeeze something out of the bourgeoisie. The rat knows he won't be punished. Nobody will stand up for the bourgeois. As for being a foreigner—who knows? For all he knows, perhaps I have shaken hands with Lenin."

Klim took the illicit bottle from his inside coat pocket. "Have some wine, doc. You're looking a bit peaky."

He put on his scarf and buttoned his overcoat. "I'll go to Crest Hill and spend the night there. Don't open the door to anyone and burn that portrait of the Tsar. Tell Lubochka not to leave the house alone, especially at night."

3

But when Lubochka came back, she wasn't alone. Osip Drugov had walked her to her porch, saluted, and disappeared into the blizzard.

She stood in the ransacked hall, looking around in shock. "What happened here?"

Sablin, exhausted and drunk, appeared in the doorway with a bottle in his hand. "Good evening, sweetheart. Would you like a drink? Klim brought us champagne and managed to hide it under his overcoat while they were searching the house."

Slowly, Lubochka undid her headscarf and let it drop to her shoulders.

"I'll ask Osip to get us a certificate of immunity or something," she said in a trembling voice.

4

"We've had visitors today," said Nina as soon as Klim entered her house.

"Who?" he asked.

"Our friends the comrades. Who else?"

Nina's house had been trashed as well. Klim had been wrong: it hadn't been a private raid but a premeditated campaign.

"Did they find our wine?" he asked.

Nina shook her head. "If they had, we wouldn't be here. But they've taken all our valuables and almost all our clothes, and they've stamped our documents.

Now, none of us can leave Nizhny Novgorod without their permission."

"But why?"

"The rail strike is over, and the Bolsheviks can't let the bourgeoisie run away just like that. They can't do without their class enemies to blame for their own blunders."

Zhora came into the hall too.

"That's for the best," he said. "We can't just sit around anymore. We have to fight."

"They'll kill you, you little fool!" Nina moaned. "If you're not afraid for yourself, at least think of Elena and me."

She turned to Klim looking for his support.

"I'll go to Petrograd," he said, "and ask the Argentine ambassador to help me get you all out of Russia. He won't turn me down since I'm well-known in Buenos Aires and have important connections."

"Only rats desert a sinking ship!" cried Zhora. "I won't go without Elena. What am I going to do in Buenos Aires? Do you want me to become a street sweeper instead of a student? I don't know a word of Spanish."

"Sometimes people have to make difficult decisions," said Nina in a whisper.

5

Nina, Klim, and Zhora sat side by side in front of the fireplace until midnight. Klim tried to coax some heat out of the meager embers with the poker. The lurid reflection of the glowing coals flickered across his gloomy face.

How can I go with them? Zhora thought. *What am I going to tell Elena?*

What if Klim didn't keep his word and didn't take them away to Argentina? Maybe he had had enough of the Bolsheviks, and his trip to Petrograd was just an excuse for him to escape?

Zhora understood him perfectly well though. At first, Klim had seen the Bolshevik coup as an amusing adventure worthy of a couple of wry articles in his newspaper, but now, he had realized that it was no joke anymore. Klim was not foolish enough to take responsibility for so many hungry mouths, especially now when he had neither a job nor his father's money.

The more Zhora pondered about their situation, the more he prayed that Klim would never return from Petrograd. *We will be fine,* he thought. *Nina is smart, and she will find a way to manage our situation.*

He was sure that there would be an anti-Bolshevik rebellion soon, and the usurpers would be overthrown. Everything would be just fine. University, marriage to Elena, and a brilliant diplomatic career—that was the future that awaited him.

But it was painful to look at his sister. She was sitting pressed close to Klim, and it seemed she was too afraid to move.

"I don't know how long I'll be in Petrograd," Klim said. "And I have no idea if I'll be able to write to you. But I promise I'll come back for you. Whatever it takes."

Nina nodded and looked at him, her eyes full of tears.

"You won't leave me alone tonight, will you?"

As they left, Zhora remained by the fireplace, feeling shocked and ashamed. Nina was about to spend the night with a man whom she wasn't even married to. Klim may have been a good man, and she may have been deeply in love with him, but this was scandalous.

Sofia Karlovna appeared in the doorway with a flickering church candle in her hand.

"I knew that something like this would happen," she said. "First, your sister had a relationship with Mr. Fomin and ruined her reputation, and now, men see her as nothing more than a strumpet. They will lie to her saying that they'll marry her, but they are only really after one thing."

"Times have changed," Zhora replied in an unsteady voice.

But Sofia Karlovna just shook her head sadly. She picked up the portrait of her son that had been thrown on the floor by the raiders and dusted off the cracked glass over the photograph.

"See, Vladimir," she said, "what kind of a woman you have brought into our house."

6

Klim insisted that Nina did not come to see him off at the station.

"You'll only be asking for trouble with the Red Guards," he said. "What if they ask you for your documents?"

She stood on the porch and watched him tying his suitcase onto the sleigh.

Anton Emilievich, in his enormous fur coat, was already waiting for Klim in the driver's seat. On finding that his nephew was about to leave for Petrograd, he had decided to join him. He intended to travel on to Finland, which had declared independence from Russia and the Bolsheviks in the nick of time.

"You'll have to forgive me, old man, but I can't live in this chaos," he had told Klim. "I'll sit out the revolution in Helsingfors. I have friends there."

Klim went up to Nina. Her eyes were swollen with tears, and her lips were trembling.

"Promise you'll come back," she whispered.

He embraced her and put the key to his house in her hand. It was next to useless because after the raid at their house, Lubochka had ordered that a new steel-enforced front door be installed.

"What is it?" Nina asked.

"It's the key to my heart," Klim said, smiling. "At the moment, I have nothing else to give you."

"Hurry up, or we'll be late!" Anton Emilievich cried.

Nina made the sign of the cross over Klim.

"Go inside, or you'll catch your death of cold," he said, trying to lead her to the door.

But she stood trembling in the wind until his sleigh was out of sight.

7

It had been impossible to get tickets for a sleeping car. The Bolsheviks had issued another decree abolishing all classes on the railway thus making all passengers equal.

"Let the bourgeoisie enjoy the comforts of the third-class car," their propagandists said.

But there weren't even any third-class cars. The train consisted of red boxcars with notices on their sides proclaiming, "Capacity: eight horses or forty people."

The passengers took the boxcars by storm. The train stood high above the platform with no steps, but Klim was one of the first to manage to get inside. Someone gave him a leg up, and then he helped others load their luggage and pulled in the other passengers, most of them were so-called *bagmen*, small traders who carried their goods in burlap bags.

In the center of the boxcar was a small stove surrounded by plank beds. The passengers sat on them packed as tightly as herrings in a barrel.

"Close the door!" the bagmen yelled. "There's no room for any more!"

The door banged, they heard the rasp of the lock, and then everybody began to examine the cuts, bruises, and torn clothes they had received in their rush to board the train.

It was only now that Klim noticed there were no women among them. That made sense. No lady worthy of the name would ever have been able to brave the crush to get onboard, let alone countenanced traveling in a boxcar without a lavatory.

I can't imagine Nina here, Klim thought. *How on earth will I get her to Petrograd when I get her visa?*

Anton Emilievich was still panting for breath. In the struggle, somebody had elbowed him in the ribs and winded him.

"At least I'm in one piece," he said as he examined the torn handle of his suitcase. "I never thought I was capable of such behavior. Isn't it incredible how suddenly everyone forgets their upbringing and thinks only of themselves? When I used to meet my neighbor on the stairs, we would bow to each other and let each other pass, 'Please, after you!' And now just look at us all like pigs fighting to get at the trough."

The train set off, and the passengers began to unwrap their food and take out their tobacco pouches. Soon, the boxcar was filled with pungent smoke. Klim was lucky to have gotten a place next to a wall perforated by a string of bullet holes. An icy breeze came through them, but at least it was refreshing.

Now, everything in the boxcar—clothes, luggage, and faces—were covered with a white film of dust.

"That's flour," Anton Emilievich whispered in Klim's ear. "These bagmen are carrying food to Moscow and Petrograd—the food shortage there is much worse than in Nizhny Novgorod. The boxcar is shaking so much that some of the dust is escaping out of their bags."

Klim looked around him at the stern, bearded faces. The Soviet press liked to paint these bagmen as weak, cunning idlers, but nothing could be further from the truth. Those political pen pushers sitting in their offices would never understand what it took to travel across the country in a crowded boxcar carrying heavy bags and risking one's life on a daily basis. Bagmen were the only people now providing the hungry cities with the provisions that the Bolshevik government was so spectacularly failing to supply.

When the train stopped, the passengers refused to open the door of their boxcar. They could hear the soldiers outside striking the sides of the train with their rifle butts and threatening to throw a grenade under the boxcar.

"There's no room!" cried the passengers.

They passed out a kettle through the little window under the ceiling to the local boys, asking them to bring boiling water, and paid them with a dried crust of bread.

The passengers amused themselves on the long journey with gambling, scurrilous jokes, and stories about the stationmasters at the different railroad stops—which of them were kind and which of them were corrupt, tight-fisted brutes.

Gradually, the voices subsided. Surrounded by the snores of his fellow passengers, Klim buried his head in his folded arms and dozed, daydreaming sleepily about the previous night.

Nina's room had been warm. The green glow of the lamp had been reflected in the porcelain horses on her chest of drawers and the mirror tiles on the glass door of her closet.

For Klim, a sense of desperation—as though before a fatal step—had been mingled with the warm, aching joy of holding Nina in his arms. He had felt the gentle touch of her finger on his unshaven cheek and heard her voice.

"I'm drawing your portrait with my fingertips," she had said. "Here's your cheekbone, and your eyebrow…and now, your murderer's earlobe—"

"Why murderer's?" Klim had asked.

"They say that people with adherent earlobes like yours are capable of the most terrible things."

Nina had known that Klim had no choice but to carry out the plan they had concocted, but despite herself, she had reproached him for being able to leave her even for a short while.

Klim had blamed himself too, but for other reasons. He should have gotten Nina out of Russia that autumn and away from all of that danger and uncertainty.

"You'd be better off drawing me big muscles," he had said, trying to distract her. "I'm afraid that soon I'll be as skinny as a rake, living on these Soviet food rations."

"I won't," Nina had refused. "A man should be athletic but lean. Good breeding implies elegance."

I was insane to have removed myself willingly from that paradise, Klim thought. *I should have stayed with Nina even if it meant death—at least we'd have passed away together.*

He dozed fitfully as the wheels of the boxcar intoned, "You have to, you have to, you have to."

6. REVOLUTIONARY PETROGRAD

1

It took Klim and Anton Emilievich a week to get to the capital.

Every now and then, their train would stop for no apparent reason, and nobody knew what was going on. Later they learned that they were making way for the trains going in the opposite direction, carrying refugees.

The Bolsheviks had promised the deserters that they would demobilize the Tsar's Army and offer Germany a peace treaty without annexations and reparations, but the Berlin government just laughed in their faces. And now, German troops were advancing on the defenseless Russian capital.

In Petrograd, a crowd was besieging the ticket offices of the Nikolaevsky railroad station.

"The Germans are coming! The Germans!" Klim heard people shouting.

When he and Anton Emilievich turned down Ligovsky Avenue, they saw a line of loaded carts stretching as far as the eye could see. Writing desks and folded banners stuck out from under the tarpaulin covers. Women and children sat on top of the carts wrapped in fur coats and shawls. Cart drivers yelled at one another, whips cracked, and horses whinnied.

Anton Emilievich glanced at Klim. "What kind of exodus is this?"

"The Bolshevik government is moving to Moscow," a gentleman in an astrakhan hat remarked. "Along with their families, servants, and concubines."

Mounted soldiers rode toward the excited, anxious crowd.

"Move on, move on!" they shouted in thick foreign accents.

"Latvian riflemen," said the gentleman in the astrakhan hat with a disparaging shrug.

"What are they doing here?" Klim asked.

"Guarding our new rulers. They are deserters like all the other soldiers. But the Russian deserters have gone back to their villages, and the Latvians can't go home since it's become occupied by the Germans now. That's why they're willing to work for the Bolsheviks in exchange for their food ration. People say they make ideal mercenaries because they barely speak a word of Russian, so you can't even bribe them."

Anton Emilievich knew Petrograd well and told Klim how to find the Argentine Embassy.

"I'm going to visit the Bolsheviks headquarters now and get my pass to go abroad," he said. "See you tonight at Khitruk's. Do you remember his address?"

Klim nodded. Khitruk was an old friend of Anton Emilievich, and they were hoping he would let them spend the night at his apartment.

2

Klim hurried along the street, looking at the beautiful buildings that adorned central Petrograd. Handwritten advertisements had sprung up all over them like mold growing on plaster. The Bolsheviks had issued a decree forbidding advertising in any opposition newspapers to deprive them of their profits, so now all the announcements of items "For Sale" or "Wanted" had spread over the walls and lampposts of the city instead.

Hunched, shivering figures hurried past Klim. Half the shop windows had been broken, and the vacant dark shops looked like caves. Klim saw a sign in place of a storefront that announced in huge letters, "Citizens! Save Anarchy!"

So, now we even have to save anarchy, Klim thought, grimly.

It didn't take long for him to find the six-story columned building that housed the Argentine Embassy. Polish soldiers in square peaked caps and long cloaks were guarding it. Klim showed them his passport, and one of the guards shouted up for the secretary, a tiny woman with black hair.

Klim told her that he had come to Russia on family business and now wanted to get back to Buenos Aires.

"Follow me," she said, inviting him in.

The windowsills and cabinets in the lobby were covered with half-burned candles.

"The electricity is only intermittent," the secretary said. "To tell the truth, it can be frightening at night. A few days ago, some crooks broke into the Italian Embassy and took the ambassador's wallet and fur coat right off his back. We are lucky to have the Poles here, but if something terrible happens, there's not much chance they'll be able to protect us. None of the foreign powers recognize the Bolsheviks and their Soviet government, and in return, they don't recognize our diplomatic immunity."

Klim had not expected to find foreign diplomats to be quite so powerless.

"Can I talk to Señor Ambassador?" he asked.

"I'll announce your arrival," said the secretary. "Please take a seat and wait a moment."

The embassy was silent. Even the pendulum of the wall clock hung motionless.

Klim walked around the room and picked up a copy of *Pravda* newspaper dated February 23, 1918. A banner headline splashed across its front page read:

SOCIALIST HOMELAND IS IN DANGER!

The German generals have created shock troops and, without prior warning, attacked our army, which is in the process of peaceful demobilization. However, resistance is growing and will continue to grow with each day. We must devote all our energies to repulsing the German White Guard!

Who are the White Guards? Klim wondered. *Anyone who opposed the Bolsheviks?*

"Señor Martínez Campos is expecting you," the secretary called Klim and ushered him into a fancy office.

3

The ambassador was about fifty. He was sitting at his desk dressed in an elegant suit with his neat black mustache tips twirled upward and his gold pince-nez glinting in the lamplight.

"Pleased to meet you," he said, thrusting out his small hand. "How long have you been in Russia? Half a year? It would appear we are witnessing the total collapse of a great country. How could this have been allowed to happen?"

"A series of extremely unfortunate coincidences—" Klim said, but the ambassador had already changed the subject.

"I've met Lenin several times," Martínez Campos said, smiling wryly. "A man of culture but a perfect fanatic. The only decree he has made that is actually in the interests of his country is the decision to switch to the Gregorian calendar."

Klim didn't feel inclined to discuss the change in the calendar, so he got straight to the point and told the ambassador about his problem.

"I advise you to leave Russia as soon as possible," Martínez Campos said. "If you have no money, our government can supply you with a loan. At present, the only route out of the country is through Arkhangelsk in the north or Vladivostok in the far east. All the other borders are shut. You could perhaps try Finland if the Soviets provide you with the necessary pass. If you choose to go there, I'll give you a paper for the People's Commissariat for Foreign Affairs."

Martínez Campos took a pen and a blank sheet of paper from his drawer.

"I need to take my family with me," Klim said. "The Bolsheviks have prohibited my fiancée from leaving Nizhny Novgorod. Have we any leverage to get them to let her go?"

"Is she a citizen of Argentina?"

"No, but—"

Martínez Campos put his pen away and assumed a weary expression, as though he already knew in advance everything Klim was about to say.

"I'm sorry, but I can't help you. I have instructions not to grant visas to any Russian citizens."

Klim's heart sank like a stone. "But why?"

"The government in Buenos Aires is wary that the Bolshevik disease could spread to our country."

"But what if she were the spouse of an Argentinean citizen? I'm planning to marry her. We just haven't had time to draw up the papers."

"There can be no exceptions," Martínez Campos sighed. "I strongly recommend that you make a run for it, Señor Rogov, or you may well end up dying here."

4

Klim headed back to the railroad station.

The country is becoming the land of red tape, Klim thought as he hurried down the street. People needed official permission for everything. To buy food, Klim needed a ration card; to take a train, he needed a pass; and his personal happiness now depended on a visa.

He attempted to calm himself. *It doesn't matter. The main thing now is to get back to Nizhny Novgorod as soon as possible.*

The railroad station was full of passengers who had been waiting for days for their trains. A soldier with a red armband constantly warned them, "Don't fall asleep! Keep an eye on your possessions, comrades, or they'll be stolen."

There was a long queue at the ticket office, and the girl on duty was yelling at everybody who was waiting, "There are no tickets for sale! There's been a directive from the Chairman of the Central Board for Evacuation. Nobody is to leave the city except women, children, and government officials."

She was about to close the window when Klim stopped her.

"I'm a foreign journalist, and I need to get to Nizhny Novgorod as soon as possible."

"Foreigners are not allowed to buy tickets," she snapped.

Klim dashed to the departure platform. To hell with tickets! If he had to, he would break into the car by force. But the platform had already been cordoned off by soldiers. Nobody was being allowed onto the trains with or without tickets.

5

A blackout had been imposed on the city. The hazy beams of the searchlights swept the night sky, and factory sirens wailed in the distance. Petrograd was expecting a German airship attack.

Klim found Khitruk's apartment building on Mokhovaya Street and climbed the dark staircase to the fifth floor. He knocked on the padded door, and it was opened by a round-faced housemaid with a candle in her hand.

"We've been expecting you," she said when Klim introduced himself. "Anton Emilievich told us you were coming. Please don't take your overcoat off—it's cold in here."

Khitruk's apartment was full of noise and cigarette smoke. Klim headed to the dining room lit by a paraffin lamp. A group of lively and energetic men were sitting at the table in their fur coats.

"Ah! Here's my nephew!" cried Anton Emilievich.

Klim greeted people and shook hands with them without registering all of their names and faces. He found himself a place in an armchair by the wall and sat down, feeling suddenly exhausted.

"How are things?" Anton Emilievich whispered, trying not to interrupt the speech of a tall, gray-haired man who was passionately berating the Soviets.

"Things are looking bad," Klim told him. "I couldn't get any visas, and now, it's impossible to buy tickets to get back to Nizhny Novgorod."

"Did the ambassador turn you down?" Anton Emilievich whistled. "That's too bad. Are you hungry?"

He ran to fetch Klim some rye bread.

"Khitruk is a rich man these days," Anton Emilievich said when he returned, gesturing toward the gray-haired man. "His wife and children are in Kiev, and he uses their ration cards and lives like a king. Seven pounds of bread for one person! Not bad, eh?"

"How did your affairs go?" Klim asked.

Anton Emilievich fished a paper out of his pocket. "I went straight to the chairman and told him I needed a warrant," he said. "And here it is."

For a while, Klim looked at the paper with a huge purple stamp.

This document is to certify that the bearer, Anton Emilievich Schuster, is indeed a revolutionary journalist. He is granted permission to go to Finland on assignment. I order all Soviet institutions to render him assistance and support.

"How much did you pay?" Klim asked disconsolately.

"Five hundred rubles in golden tens," Anton Emilievich said.

That was the price for one paper, and Klim needed three: for Nina, Zhora, and Sofia Karlovna. Nina had promised her mother-in-law to take her with them. She couldn't just let the poor old woman starve to death.

"My advice to you," Anton Emilievich said, "is to go to the Bolshevik headquarters while you still can. The Bolsheviks know that they won't be in power for long, and they are grabbing any bribes that come their way."

"I only have two hundred rubles," Klim said.

6

"The Bolsheviks have robbed us of our revolution!" exclaimed Khitruk. "They have completely disgraced themselves. Censorship has got so bad that they don't even bother rewriting articles anymore but just leave blank spaces where the articles should have been. So, what are we going to do about it? We can't just sit around doing nothing."

Anton Emilievich had informed Klim that Khitruk was an experienced revolutionary publisher. His newspapers had been closed down by the Tsar's government, and he had been fined and sent to the notorious Kresty jail for political prisoners. But on his release, he soon went back to his old ways. He had an air of martyrdom about him and a crowd of enthusiastic young followers who were ready to go to any lengths on his behalf.

His opposition to the Tsar's Gendarmes was as dogged as his current criticism of the Bolsheviks' thugs.

"I have the funds to start a newspaper," Khitruk announced. "A merchant who has recently been released from prison will provide us with the money. We have paper, we have an agreement with a print shop, and a front man has gotten us a license."

This news was welcomed joyfully.

"When will the newspaper come out?" someone asked.

"The day after tomorrow," Khitruk said, "and it will be a daily paper. It's safe to say that we won't have any competition since the quality of the Bolshevik press is very poor. No decent reporter will work for them, so they end up hiring hacks who are so badly educated that they think imperialism is a country somewhere in Western Europe."

They argued excitedly about the policy their newspaper should adopt and agreed that it should be politically daring. Khitruk set about busily dividing and ruling his minions, allocating them tasks, and giving them advances.

"Would you like to write something for our newspaper?" he asked Klim when the guests had left. "Your uncle told me you have followed in his footsteps and become a journalist."

Klim told him briefly about his situation.

"That's not good," Khitruk muttered. "But we'll figure something out."

He led Klim and Anton Emilievich to a freezing-cold guest room and gave them two logs for the stove.

"I'm sorry, but we can't heat this room properly," Khitruk said. "I just can't afford enough firewood at current prices."

Khitruk turned to Anton Emilievich. "Are you sure you won't change your mind about leaving? We are badly in need of educated people, and your encyclopedic knowledge would be invaluable."

Anton Emilievich sighed. "You have so much energy that you don't notice how cold it is in Petrograd. But I couldn't live without hot water. My back aches in the cold."

Khitruk sat down next to Klim on the sofa. "What are you going to do now?"

"I don't know." Klim shook his head. "I was at the railroad station and heard someone saying that people are managing to get out of the city on foot or by sleigh."

"Don't be ridiculous,." Khitruk said angrily. "It's freezing out there, and you have neither felt boots nor a sheepskin coat. You'd freeze to death in three hours. But with your bourgeois appearance, you wouldn't even last that long before the Red Guards got you."

Klim said nothing.

"Listen, you need to find a place to stay while you try to get a return ticket," Khitruk said. "Why don't you live here for a while? Otherwise, I'm afraid that the Bolsheviks will force me to give over all my rooms to the proletariat. Workers with nowhere to go are being given so-called 'class mandates' so that they can confiscate spare rooms in a rich person's apartment. They've already been to see me three times and told me that I can't live here all by myself. It makes me sick to think of some bumpkin cooking on my stove or using my bathroom. Plus, as you can see, I often have company. We won't be able to talk about serious things with ignorant strangers around."

"Why don't you ask your friends to live with you?" Klim asked.

"All my friends are looking for tenants too. And most decent people have already left the city. Please stay with me! It's true that ration cards are a problem. The 'bourgeoisie' are in the lowest category and only get an eighth of a pound of bread a day. I have no idea if you have any right to a ration as a foreigner, but we can find out. So, what do you say?"

"All right," Klim nodded.

"Excellent! Tomorrow, you can go to the house manager's office and register yourself as a tenant. The lady who works there is a little strange though. You'll see what I mean when you meet her."

7

The house manager's office was in the former porter's lodge. Klim noticed a sign attached to the door. It said that Petrograd was now in a state of martial law, and all visitors to the city must be registered without delay.

Klim knocked on the door and entered a dimly lit office adorned by two portraits—one of Lenin and the other of the many-armed Hindu god Shiva. A woman in a crimson knitted cap was sitting beneath them.

"Peace be with you," she said in a disinterested voice and lit a copper incense burner that hung above her desk. A trickle of bluish smoke drifted up toward the grimy ceiling.

"I'd like to register myself," Klim said.

She stared at him with her round, crystal clear gray eyes. "Thank the gods you're not proposing to marry me," she muttered. "I recently had a visitor from Apartment Thirteen who was determined to win my hand in marriage. I'm in charge of the ration cards and accommodations, and that alone is dowry enough to tempt a great many men. Durga!" she said suddenly and thrust out a hand to Klim.

He shook her thin fingers. As far as he could remember, Durga was the Hindu warrior goddess who ensured order in the world.

"Have you heard the news?" the woman said. "The Bolsheviks have paid off the Germans. They've signed a peace treaty agreeing to the Kaiser's terms. The war is over, but the Germans have taken all our western provinces. But he," Durga pointed at the Lenin's portrait, "couldn't care less. If he's still in power, that means the gods must be on his side."

The woman made Klim sit on a small oriental drum and focused all her attention on Klim's Argentinean passport and Khitruk's petition for a temporary registration.

"So, Mr. Rogóv, Kliment Alexandrovich, born 1889," she said slowly, "you've stated that your occupation is 'writer.' What exactly do you write?"

"Recently, the only writing I've been doing is filling in forms."

"You too!" Durga cried and gazed sadly at Shiva. "Khitruk writes proclamations that nobody cares about, the man from Number Five writes poetry, and a tenant from Number Ten writes pieces for the violin and divine revelations when he has the money for his cocaine habit. Why doesn't anyone write anything useful, like how to survive all this madness?"

She stared at Klim disapprovingly.

"My friend sold me a pound of American corn flour and a jar of French margarine," Durga said. "My pantry is empty. I have nothing but salt and baking soda. So, I have a question for you, sir: What can I do with this latest acquisition of mine? I looked in the cookbook, and all the recipes sound as though they have been made up to taunt me. 'Take three pounds of veal,' they begin, but they don't say *where* this veal is to be found. I need to know about corn flour, not about veal that can't be obtained for love nor money."

"You could make a tortilla," Klim suggested. "It's a type of soft flatbread. At one time, it was all I ate."

"Then why don't you write about something useful like that?" exclaimed Durga. "Perhaps you have a recipe for potato peelings or fish heads as well? You could write a pamphlet entitled 'Dinner on a Shoestring.' That is what people need now! Tell Mr. Khitruk to stop churning out inflammatory nonsense and write something worthwhile."

Klim shrugged. "He's just unable to stand by and watch dispassionately—"

"Dispassionately means not being misled by passion," Durga barked. "If you keep a cool head and act the same way toward everything and everyone, you have no expectations and, therefore, won't suffer disappointment or disillusionment. Tell Mr. Khitruk to put that in his pipe and smoke it."

She wrote down Klim's recipe and added his name to her register. "Come over this evening," she said. "I'll treat you to some of your tortillas."

7. THE CONSPIRATORS

1

Three weeks passed, and there was still no letter from Klim. The post office had started working again. Nina went there every day, but the assistant behind the wooden counter always met her inquiries with an indifferent shake of the head.

There was no news from Osinki either, and Nina suspected that the mill was no longer in her possession. Most likely, the workers who hadn't received their wages had stolen and sold the equipment and looted Nina's house.

If she had listened to Klim back in September, they would have safely been in Buenos Aires by now. She had chosen the wrong path by refusing him and trying to save her business, and the hopeless position she found herself in now was what she had got in return.

The only memento Nina had of Klim was the "key from his heart," and she carried it on a chain around her neck like a talisman.

In the evenings, she loosened her braid and ran her fingers through her hair just as Klim had done. She buried her face in the pillow on which his head had rested. Walking the streets, she stopped at the places that still bore the invisible traces of his presence: the spot where he had dropped his glove in the snow, and the ice run where he had held her hand and had slid together.

She remembered the mixed colors of his stubble— black, fair, and red, his eyes the color of strong black tea, and the imperceptible little scar on the lobe of his left ear, the mark of an earring he had worn at nineteen on his travels in Shanghai.

Zhora told Nina that he was not going to pin all his hopes on Klim. He had only one thing on his mind: "We can't abandon Russia in her hour of need. It is the duty of every able man to go south and join the White Army volunteers to fight the Bolsheviks."

Listening to him nearly broke Nina's heart. Zhora was no more than a boy, skinny and awkward, with a great cowlick of hair covering his forehead. What kind of a soldier would he make?

Sofia Karlovna spent her days praying, visiting her friends, remembering the good old times, and cursing the Bolsheviks. Occasionally, she would come to Nina and demand money, favors, and explanations of what was going on in a world that had gone crazy.

"The Bolsheviks have ordered Princess Anna Evgenievna to bring three members of her household to clean a latrine," the old countess said. "They're doing it on purpose just to humiliate her. What if they order us to do the same?"

"I won't go," Nina said firmly. "They may shoot me—let them do whatever they please."

To cap everything else, the Bolsheviks had arrested Elena's parents. The Regional Executive Committee had come up with a new idea for inveigling more money out of the rich by demanding an "indemnity" from the city's wealthiest citizens—fifty million rubles in total.

"They're no better than kidnapping criminals," Elena wept on Nina's shoulder. "They take control of the cities, bleeding the people dry and blackmailing the wealthy merchants."

The Bolsheviks could see little difference between five thousand and fifty million rubles. For them, it was just a pile of cash, and they didn't care where the merchants got these extortionate sums just so long as they paid.

Nina told Elena to move into her house.

Now, there's nowhere for us to escape even if we wanted to, she thought. Nina and Zhora would never have left Elena on her own, and there was no way Elena was going to leave her parents.

One day, Nina went to visit Lubochka to see how she was doing, but her friend wasn't at home.

"You'll never catch her here these days," Marisha grumbled. "The mistress is playing around behind her husband's back. She and her Bolshevik friend brazenly walk the streets, and he gives her presents. Yesterday, she brought home a gilt-backed hairbrush—with someone else's hair in it."

Shocked and dispirited, Nina went home.

How could her friend—so smart and so high-minded—keep company with a man who was little more than a bandit? It was an act of utter treachery.

Zhora confirmed what Marisha had told Nina: he had seen the incongruous couple out and about a number of times—elegant Lubochka arm in arm with a soldier in a burned and tattered greatcoat. They had been so engrossed in each other that they hadn't noticed anyone else.

2

The frost held until mid-March, and then a rapid thaw set in. During the day, avalanches of snow slid heavily from the sun-warmed roofs, but every night a new palisade of icicles as thick as a man's arm bristled from the eaves again. The city stewed and began to smell as all the rubbish dumps that had been buried under the snow began to thaw out.

Usually, Nina went to the market with Zhora, afraid that she might be attacked and her basket of food stolen. But today, she had to leave her brother at home. The day before, he had declared that now that it was spring, he had no intention of wearing his scarf. He had caught a cold almost as soon as he had stepped outside the door and lost his voice.

Officially, the market was shut, but in fact, a huge crowd gathered on the central square every day. Private trade had initially been prohibited and then briefly permitted only to be banned again. Things had gone on in this way for several months, and the policemen were never quite sure whether they were meant to drive the "criminal capitalist profiteers" away from the market or not. Consequently, they implemented a "dictatorship of the proletariat" as and when the fancy took them, robbing the villagers of whatever goods they wanted for themselves or their friends and family.

The market boiled with life like a giant cauldron. Every imaginable product was on sale there: foot wrappings, Christmas ornaments, poppy cakes, and cocaine.

An old general in cracked glasses was trying to sell a gramophone horn. He stood timidly among the crowds, eyes averted, chewing on the ends of his gray mustache. An old woman with her head wrapped in a shawl was peddling two dirty frying pans. Boys hawked Swedish matches and local "Java" cigarettes and thrust a shivering puppy out toward passers-by. "Do you want a barker to guard your house?"

Nina approached one of the traders she knew, Mitya, a thin man with eyelids that twitched with a nervous tic. He was standing by the fence with his goods laid out on a torn cloth: old doorknobs, soldiers' belts, and a vintage Bible in a velvet binding.

She nodded to him, and Mitya beckoned to a man idling nearby. "Keep an eye on all this, will you?" Then he set off through the crowd with Nina at his heels.

Mitya went into an empty cobbler's shop smelling of glue and old leather. The dim light from the small dusty window lit up piles of broken wooden boxes and old cloths on the floor.

"Can you pay me in money today?" asked Mitya.

Nina pulled out some bank notes from the inside pocket of her coat.

"Give me two pounds of barley and half a pound of honey and fill up this matchbox with salt," she said. "I need tea as usual and bread. Last time I asked you for bread made with unadulterated flour, and you ended up giving me God knows what."

"That's the baker's fault, not mine," Mitya said, blinking fitfully.

She gave him her food basket, and he disappeared behind the door.

Nina stood and waited, beating a tattoo on the doorframe with the rings on her fingers.

She could hear the noise of the market grow louder and looked out the window nervously. The black crowd was churning like a shoal of fish in a trap, but there seemed to be nothing amiss.

Mitya came back at last, and Nina checked her goods. The heavenly smell of freshly baked bread rose from the basket.

"Do you know anyone who buys expensive liquors?" she asked.

"What sort of liquors?" Mitya inquired, his face twitching.

Nina pulled a strangely curved bottle from her pocket. It was filled with an amber colored liquid.

"It's a real Scotch whiskey," Nina said. "It was served in private clubs as a joke. See, the bottle looks as if it's drunk. This kind of whiskey used to cost more than three hundred rubles before the war."

Mitya hesitated. "Well…I don't know…I'll have to ask. Follow me."

They walked into a small backyard. A black guard dog with matted hair dashed toward them but began to wag its tail as soon as it recognized Mitya.

Nina glanced around uneasily. *He could take me off anywhere and just kill me*, she thought.

"Come over here," said Mitya, pointing to a lopsided gatehouse.

Nina went inside a dim room that smelled strongly of fried fish. A bearded man was sitting next to the window, having his lunch.

Nina gasped. "Mr. Fomin? You of all people!"

He sprang to his feet and opened his arms to embrace her. "Nina, darling! Sorry, my hands are covered in fish oil. I haven't seen you for so long! How is life treating you?"

3

After Mitya returned to the market, Fomin pushed his plate of cold fried fish toward Nina.

"Help yourself. I'm glad you've found me—I need to talk to you." He gestured at a box in the corner of the room. "You see, I haven't forgotten you, and I've already procured some supplies."

"Where have you been all this time?" Nina asked.

Fomin wiped his hands on an old newspaper. "I was in hiding in Osinki."

"How's the mill?" Nina asked, her heart ready to sink.

Fomin grinned. "A local Bolshevik called Utkin arranged a meeting at the village elder's house and told the men to establish a Soviet rural council and confiscate your mill together with the mansion. I had a word with them too. 'If you do that,' I said, 'who will provide you with supplies? Who will fix the machinery? Utkin? Appoint him as a manager and just see how he fares.'"

"Did you manage to save the mill?" asked Nina hopefully.

"They haven't touched the mill shops, but they burned down the house."

"Good Lord!"

"The women told me Utkin was responsible. They chased him away from the village after that. They were worried that he might decide to burn down their houses too."

To be on the safe side, Fomin had established a workers' Soviet administration in Osinki and hung a red banner from the mill gates. But when some of the youngsters began talking about the workers taking control of the mill, Fomin had made his terms clear.

"It's them or me," he had said. "If they take charge, I go." So far, nobody had challenged his authority.

Fomin put the most capable foreman in charge of production and appointed himself in charge of sales. Inflation was rising daily, so he was always on the lookout for goods that could be used for barter. He brought leather shoe soles from Bogorodsk, fishhooks from Gorbatov, and wooden spoons from Semenov. Initially, he had carried all these goods on his own back, but later, he had begun to hire teams of unemployed workers to do the job for him.

"The Bolsheviks put troops at every crossroad," Fomin told Nina, "but we always manage to get through one way or another."

"Do you think the Bolsheviks will nationalize my mill?" she asked.

Fomin frowned. "If the Bolsheviks stay in power, they'll take away the mill sooner or later. According to the peace treaty, the Germans have the right to hang onto their property in Russia. That means the owners of private enterprises will try to sell their shares to German agents to turn at least some of their assets into cash. Naturally, the Bolsheviks won't want all that property to slip through their fingers, so they'll try to nationalize the factories and mills before the Germans can get their hands on everything."

"Get out!" someone shouted from the direction of the market. "There's a raid!"

The sound of frenzied barking came from the yard. Fomin jumped to his feet and snatched the box he had been planning to give to Nina. "Run!"

They darted behind the sheds and clambered up the log pile and over the fence. As they ran down Pryadilnaya Street, peasants drove by in sled with runners scraping the bare cobblestones. Women ran by at full tilt, clasping their unsold goods to their chests.

Nina was panting, and very soon her skirt was soaked and her feet freezing after running through the puddles that littered the road.

Gunshots could be heard. Nina flinched.

"Don't cower like that!" Fomin said angrily. "If they catch us, we'll slip them some money. The only reason they're raiding the markets is because the Red Guards have nothing to eat, so their commanders have sent them to 'fight the profiteers.' They confiscate food from the peasant women, and that's what they live on. The market will be back to normal in no time. Don't you worry. The only thing that will change is that the prices will go up again."

4

Nina sensed that she had brought a dangerous man back home with her. Fomin had turned into a big criminal and was just the sort of men the new political police, the Cheka, were after. It was rumored that terrible things were going on in the basement of their headquarters.

Nina quietly thanked her lucky stars that there was no one in the house when they came in. Sofia Karlovna was in church, and Zhora and Elena had gone off somewhere, but the slightest noise made Nina flinch. Nevertheless, she tried her best to be a good host, inviting Fomin to the dinner table and offering him all of the good things they had brought home that day.

Fomin scrutinized Nina's ransacked dining room with its broken cabinets and dark spots on the wallpaper where a painting had previously hung.

"I see they've robbed you but let you keep the house," he said thoughtfully.

"My house is located far away from the main road," Nina said. "There are few locals among the Bolsheviks, and they don't know the city well. I guess they just forgot about us."

"So, how are you managing to live?"

Nina told him about the wine cellar. He nodded, smiling, and Nina couldn't tell if he was approving or, on the contrary, laughing up his sleeve at her pitiful attempts at commerce.

"Let me make a proposal," Fomin said finally. "You have an opportunity to earn a lot of money very quickly. When summer comes, the sacks we make at the mill will be worth their weight in gold at the depots and quays.

"You have a basement that would be perfect for storage, and you can keep a lookout for anyone coming up toward the house from the side of the hill.

"All you need is to set up one of these so-called 'cooperative societies' and pretend that a group of you are clubbing together to buy groceries and soft goods. Then you'll get all the necessary licenses from the Soviets, and we'll be able to bring in goods of our own."

"You won't be allowed to bring sacks into the city," Nina protested. "Do you think the Bolsheviks are too stupid to realize that you're supplying packaging material to profiteers?"

"But we won't be bringing in sacks. We'll be bringing in—let's say—birch switches for the steam baths. How will people massage their backs in the steam room without good switches of birch twigs? Or if that doesn't suit you, we could bring in straw or fallen leaves. Our sacks will just be the packaging material like you said."

Nina noticed that Fomin said "we" as though there were others involved in his scheme.

"Do you have other partners?" Nina asked. "Who are they?"

Fomin frowned. "I can't say."

"But I have to know who I'm dealing with. You have to tell me about all the risks, who knows about this business, and how are we going to share the profits."

He glowered at her. "Well—as for risks are concerned, you'll be risking your life. And you won't see a good deal of the profits."

"What do you mean?"

"Believe me, you don't need to know more. This is no business for a woman. Your job is to help us with the cooperative. We'll do the rest."

Finally, Nina realized what he was talking about. "Are you preparing a rebellion?"

"I never said as much, and it would be better for you if you didn't know. Whatever we plan to do, the first thing we need is money. Everyone is contributing what they can or helping to raise funds, but naturally, nobody will blame you if you choose to refuse. You are perfectly within your rights to forbid me to sell the sacks from your mill—after all, it is your private property. But remember, if we don't take action ourselves, we can't expect anyone else to do it for us."

Fomin gave her detailed instructions about what she needed to do to open a cooperative. Nina tried to listen to him carefully, but her thoughts kept wandering off.

What if the Bolsheviks arrested her? Would she betray Fomin right away? Would she tell them everything she knew in the hope that the Bolsheviks would have mercy on her and not rape her or beat her to death?

True, she could refuse to do her bit and sit around waiting for a miracle to happen. For some gallant knight like Klim to save her? Or some "force for good" such as the White Army that was rumored to be mobilizing somewhere in the south? But if that was what she chose to do, then she would have no right to complain. After all, if she did nothing, what else did she deserve?

Nina excused herself from the table and brought in the "drunken bottle."

"I will help you with your cooperative," she told Fomin. "And here's our family's contribution—the most expensive whiskey from my cellar. You might be able to use it as a bribe for some important Bolshevik official."

5

Zhora and Elena had spent the whole day standing in line in front of the jail, hoping to pass their parcel to Elena's parents. Visits were prohibited. The only food for both inmates and guards was provided by the prisoners' relatives.

Standing in queues in front of the jail was a torment for Zhora and drained him of all his energy, but he couldn't leave Elena on her own.

When they got home, Nina scolded Zhora for going out with a temperature and then told him that Mr. Fomin was here to see them. Zhora was thrilled with the news. Finally, a serious man had arrived who would be able to give him some sound advice on what he should do next with his life.

He had lost his voice completely, and Nina told him to go to bed. As soon as she and Elena went to the kitchen to make him some lime tea, Fomin quietly went up to see Zhora in his bedroom. With his huge peasant beard, shirt, vest, and pants tucked into his worn-out boots, he was barely recognizable.

"How's life?" he asked, sitting himself down on Zhora's bed.

Zhora shook his hand and showed him the books on his bedside table.

"I'm studying for my university entrance exams," he croaked in a barely audible whisper.

"The Bolsheviks are about to bring in forced conscription for the Red Army," Fomin said, "and most likely, you'll end up a soldier."

Zhora said nothing.

"Diplomats might be in demand in countries where there is the rule of law," Fomin continued. "But to be frank, you'd be better off signing up for medical classes at the Martynov Hospital. I hope you don't mind me speaking to you like this, but you're a grown man now. As soon as the roads become passable, there will be a war. Our people are not going to sit around and do nothing while Russia is being destroyed. The Bolsheviks have realized they can't survive without a standing army, so they've mobilized thousands of former Tsarist officers. They're keeping them on a very tight leash, giving them extra food on the one hand while threatening to put them in prison on the other."

"But how could they possibly agree?" Zhora whispered in indignation.

"Everybody has a family to provide for. The military is used to following orders, no matter who is giving them. I've talked to a lot of them. They would be happy to see the back of the Bolsheviks, but they don't see anyone capable of getting rid of them at the moment. Once the Bolsheviks have real armed forces, not just these Red Guard riffraff, it'll be much more difficult to fight them. We need to take action now."

Zhora's heart was pounding. "I wish I could go south—"

"The pivotal battles will take place here and in the other big cities." Fomin rose to his feet. "So, you see what I mean about medical classes?" he asked. "We'll be needing medics, and we'll be needing them soon."

8. THE OPPOSITION

1

EL CUADERNO NEGRO

Klim Rogov's little black notebook

I have sent eight letters to Nina but still had no reply. Mere mortals are not allowed to send telegrams; the telegraph lines are far too busy carrying the wise decrees of our esteemed government around the country. I feel as though I'm standing on the brink of some postal abyss, staring into its mouth like Dante looking into the maw of hell. Could it be possible that Nina and I have lost each other for good?

My friend Durga, the goddess of official forms and stationery, takes a keen interest in examining my soul. She is curious to know what am I doing here and what lurks behind this quasi-foreigner's gloomy mask, and she tries in various ways to find the key that will open me up like a burglar trying to break into a safe.

"Imagine your life was a painting," she said. "What genre would it be, and what would it depict?"

I told her about a type of seventieth-century Dutch still life painting known as a *Vanitas*. These pictures often included skulls as a token of the inevitability of death, playing cards to represent excitement and chance, money bags for wealth (of which I'm badly in need of right now), a rose as a symbol of love, and an hourglass to remind us of the transience and brevity of our lives. All of these objects are set against a backdrop of ruins with the encouraging motto, "All is vanity and chasing after the wind." And that just about sums up my life right now.

Khitruk, who is a smart man, has advised me to get Nina and her family passes to get to Ukraine so that we can travel into German-occupied territory. Anyone who is able to bribe officials and prove their "Ukrainian origins" is going there.

If you want to get into the occupied zone, you have to be quarantined with all the poor souls who are sick with typhoid and dysentery. Once they have died, the survivors are then permitted to travel on. But before you can even get into this hellish place, you have to get ahold of a passport with a visa— something that costs twelve hundred rubles. The permissions from the Cheka cost another thousand.

Uncle Anton was lucky—he got out when the Bolshevik officials were in a blind panic and ready to grab anything that dropped into their lap, including a paltry five-hundred-ruble bribe.

Like a dogged scarab, I try to gather an unfeasibly large dung ball of money and possibilities.

The ball started rolling when Khitruk let me into his little bookkeeping secret. His newspaper wasn't bringing any money in, and his benefactors were still waiting to see any tangible returns on their investment. Now, when Khitruk goes to them for finance, they are beginning to shrug their shoulders and tell him that times are hard.

I had a word with the newspaper vendors, and they told me that there's much more money to be had selling collections of jokes or pornographic postcards than opposition newspapers.

The all-seeing Durga was right: criticism of the Soviets is not what Russia needs at the moment.

The Russian press on both sides of the ideological divide have become completely discredited, and people buy newspapers not so much for their content but for their practical use as fire starters or cigarette papers (the thin paper is ideal for rolling tobacco to make handmade cigarettes).

There's no truth in the Bolshevik press, and the opposition can't publish the truth either. Since we have no reliable sources of information, our entire network of correspondents has long since been scattered and destroyed. And even if we did manage to dig something up and publish it, we'd be summoned to 2 Gorokhovaya Street, an infamous address from which few return. Ironically, the Petrograd Cheka is housed in the same building that used to house the Tsarist secret police.

I wrote a front-page article for Khitruk with the banner headline, "Excellent Substitutes for Imported Colonial Goods such as Tea and Coffee."

At first, Khitruk was indignant. "I'm not going to turn a serious political broadsheet into a recipe book." But I persuaded him that it would be difficult to find a more striking illustration of the times we live in, and he agreed to give it a try. Sales shot up, and now, we publish comment pieces on Soviet decrees on the left side of the front page while the right-hand side is reserved for articles with titles such as, "How to Cook Raw Rye and Wheat and Save Firewood."

In addition to the paper, Khitruk is also publishing my memoirs featuring the lifesaving recipes that I picked up on my travels from Tehran ragamuffins, Shanghai coolies, and the immigrants of Buenos Aires.

I spend days at Durga's using up government ink on my immortal manuscript, *Recipes for the Resourceful Intellectual.*

While I dictate, Durga bashes away at the typewriter. "Flour gruel. Take half a cup of rye flour and mix with boiling water until smooth."

As the rickety Underwood typewriter thunders away, paper clips jump on the desk and the lid of the incense burner rattles.

"Now what?" asks Durga.

"That's it," I reply. "That's your gruel."

"Maybe you could add some saccharin?"

"What a bourgeois notion! The rye flour is sweet enough as it is, but perhaps we can stretch to a little salt."

I visit the Public Library and trawl through the dusty volumes of *Edible Plants and Mushrooms of Our Region* for precious information. For poorer readers, we publish *Bread Surrogates: Acceptable Additives,* while better off members of the public tend to buy our more upmarket publication: *Candy Recipes with Sugar Substitutes.*

My pride and joy is *The Home Distillers Handbook*—this is the demure title of my leaflet on how to make a still for hooch. Next, I'm planning to publish two twelve-page brochures: *Maintaining Satisfaction in the Marital Bedroom* and *Contraception on a Shoestring.*

I keep the wages I've received from Khitruk in a small, old chocolate box and carry it in my breast pocket. This is my private security fund.

I don't know where Nina is, what she is doing, or even whether she is alive or not. I don't know if I'm doing the right thing staying in Petrograd and trying to get ahold of these papers.

Should I send a messenger to Nizhny Novgorod to try to find out what is going on? That would mean spending all of my precious chocolate-scented savings, but I need to hurry and get the Ukrainian papers before even that loophole is closed off by the Bolsheviks.

Every night as I get ready for bed in Khitruk's guest room, I push away all thoughts of my everyday life—or rather nonlife—and fill the room with visions of last winter, that wonderful, terrible, unbelievably happy time.

But now it's too late—a huge crack has opened up in the earth, and my love has hurtled down into the abyss.

Khitruk says, "I wish I could give you everything you need immediately, but you can see for yourself how many people I have to pay and support. Never mind, old chap. Don't despair. Everything will be all right."

But I have to admit that despair descends upon me from time to time in my lonely room. Sometimes I feel that it's too late and that I will never win back what I once had.

2

Klim threw the door open and ventured into the printing works, a cramped, damp place that stank of cigarette smoke. The room was lit by a single electric bulb under a curved round shade.

"Where's the boss?" Klim asked a bald old man stooped over the typeset.

The old man pointed to the door of the printing shop and the deafening noise of the printing press coming from behind it.

Klim entered the printing shop. Despite the pleas of his staff, Khitruk had decided to publish a report on the local elections. He was operating a press that looked as if it had been stolen from a museum, and the floor was already covered with stacks of that day's freshly printed issue.

"The Bolsheviks have lost ground throughout the country," Khitruk assured his young assistant,

Arkasha. "People have voted for other socialist parties. No other newspaper will dare to reveal this secret, but we will."

"This is suicide!" Klim exclaimed. "You have twenty-nine employees. What will happen to them if the Bolsheviks shut down your paper?"

Khitruk let the wheel go and pulled the lever that turned the sheet of paper. "You're planning to leave the country, but as long as we're staying here, we've got to keep telling the truth, or the Bolsheviks and their lies will prevail."

"Thanks to you, Mr. Rogov," Arkasha said, "our newspaper already looks more like a cookbook than a serious paper."

"You wouldn't survive another month if all you printed were political articles..." Klim fell silent when he heard heavy boots tramping through the next room.

The door crashed open, and a group of soldiers burst into the print shop.

"Against the wall, all of you!" they yelled. "Put your hands up!"

3

Those arrested were taken to Gorokhovaya Street.

"There's a shortage of paper in the country," the young investigator told Khitruk. "It's only fair to distribute newsprint according to the relative size of the target readership. Your newspaper represents the former upper classes, and since the bourgeoisie are less numerous than the workers, we are going to confiscate your newsprint and give it to the *Red Newspaper*."

The investigator told the employees at the printing shop to come back to work the next morning. As for Klim, he was told that he had twenty-four hours to leave the country.

"Your men confiscated my box in which I kept all my savings," Klim said. "I would like it back."

The investigator raised an eyebrow. "What are you talking about? I know nothing about your box." He returned Klim's passport with its visa now canceled. "Good luck. You may leave now."

Klim and Khitruk went out into the empty street. It was the time of the "white nights" in Petrograd, and the city slumbered in a bluish twilight.

"A penny for your thoughts," Khitruk asked as he lit a cigarette.

"It's hard to believe that this is actually my life and not some bad dream," said Klim gloomily.

Khitruk patted him amicably on the shoulder. "I thought you were going to say that this was all my fault, you tried to warn me, and I didn't listen to you."

"Each of us has his own responsibilities."

"Tell you what," Khitruk said, "let's go to the theater. Right now, we need the healing power of art."

4

The small concert hall was packed. People were sitting in the aisles and on the floor in front of the stage. A beautiful girl was singing, her wrists and neck covered in chaste lace. Her pure voice sounded like something from a past that was now lost and forever out of reach.

It seemed that everything was over,
That we had long since lost the war,
Yet our hearts beat as strong as ever—
We have a goal worth fighting for.

A storm of applause swept through the auditorium. People sprang to their feet in a standing ovation. The singer smiled, blushing, unsure how to react to this sudden outburst of rapture.

"Bravo!" cried Khitruk, pulling Klim's sleeve. "What about that, eh? What do you say to that?"

"It's beautiful," Klim said.

It took some time for the audience to calm down, and the concert-goers only began to disperse when the lights were dimmed. But as they made their way down the marble staircase in the semi-darkness, a male voice began to sing, "It seemed that everything was over," and soon, the whole crowd joined in. The chorus of voices rang out deep and rich beneath the painted ceiling.

"We're not finished yet," said Khitruk, deeply moved. "See? The Bolsheviks can deprive us of many things, but they can't take away our spirit."

Back at Khitruk's apartment, Klim entered his room flooded with a dusky twilight and sat down on his sofa. He could still hear that song in his head as pure as a sparkling stream.

He took out his notebook, and by the light of the Petrograd white night, he wrote across the page:

Tomorrow morning, I'll burn my boats. I do have something worth fighting for, and I'm not about to give it up. No matter what.

If you are enjoying *Russian Treasures*, please
leave a review on Amazon and Goodreads.
Your feedback is very important for the author.

THANKS!

9. THE BAGMEN'S ROUTE

1

As soon as the ice on the Volga River melted, a network of trade routes opened up along its sandy banks. Two streams of bagmen converged at the great river's villages, bringing grain, salt, and dried fish from the south and the last of the manufactured goods stolen from the industrial warehouses in the north.

Fomin's men had documents for all occasions. Some passed themselves off as employees of the Commissariat for Agriculture while others pretended to be procuring animal fodder. They hid their cargo in the false bottoms of boats and covered it with the hay intended for cavalry horses or nailed it up in coffins. Some stuffed mattresses with flour, and others swaddled sacks of grain and passed them off as babies. It took less than half a year to turn this disparate, wary cohort of bagmen into a well-organized secret army with commanders, guards, spies, and quartermasters. Dozens of drinking dens appeared, offering places where bagmen could rest, eat, and hide from the Cheka.

Nina was now the manager of a consumer cooperative. The city officials eyed her with suspicion but had nevertheless granted her permission to open a shop in the former grocery—again in return for a bribe. From the outside, everything looked quite aboveboard: a group of people from the local neighborhood put up some money to send buyers out to the grain-producing regions. Nina provided these buyers with an official paper sealed with the stamps of the cooperative and the Provisions Committee to keep them safe from the attention of the local Bolsheviks. On their return, she sold the food they brought back from these trips but only to members of the cooperative.

"The most important thing is to get the formalities right," Fomin told Nina. "If the Bolsheviks ask for records of the proceedings at general meetings, you have to provide them with all the paperwork. Let them have your charter, your accounts, even the cleaner's rota if they ask for it. Nobody's going to read them in any case. You just have to make sure they have them. It's a ritual of submission, and we have to play along with it for a while."

Nevertheless, one day the police burst into Nina's shop, and she almost turned gray, convinced that they had come to arrest her. However, they only turned out to be more bribe-seeking criminals in uniform.

Nina had to employ all of her feminine charms to persuade them not to ruin her. She also gave them her own "tribute": a bottle of home-distilled vodka, a pound of tobacco, and a round loaf of pure rye bread.

"Please make sure your bosses never send anyone else but you to inspect my shop," she said. "If they raid it, there'll be nothing left for you either."

After that day, there was a policeman on permanent duty next to her shop. He would not only chase away the local hooligans but also the indignant housewives who resented the fact that Nina's prices were higher than those in the state stores (where, in any case, there was nothing for sale except piles of out of date government newspapers).

Nina spent her days in the store checking membership and ration cards, counting change, and weighing grain on her rusty scales.

Meanwhile, Elena stood on the back porch handing piles of sacks to quiet, unexceptional men who were their most valuable customers.

However, deep inside, Nina felt like a machine trying to run with a broken drive belt. The smaller cogs and wheels might appear to be turning, but the main drive was at a standstill.

Klim had disappeared from her life.

Naturally, Fomin learned that she had found herself another man, but he was too wise and experienced to make a scene. He never reproached Nina and referred to Klim as her "friend." He even expressed his "sincere condolences."

"Anything might have happened to Mr. Rogov," Fomin told Nina. "A train crash, assault and robbery, or a raid by the Cheka. But we must hope for the best."

What does he really mean by that? Nina wondered. What is "the best" for him? Fomin now positioned himself in her life not so much as her former lover but as a kindly uncle, and that perplexed Nina.

Fomin was the only man she considered much smarter and stronger than herself, and she knew he could be dangerous. There were many occasions when he had done away with inconvenient soldiers manning roadblocks who had got in his way.

Every now and then, he would spend the night in Nina's former husband's study, and each time, she was terrified. What if the Cheka were to come after him? What if he started making advances toward her? What if Klim were to come back and find him in her house? But the truth was, Nina couldn't stop Fomin from visiting her.

Her brother and Elena adored him. Thanks to Fomin, Zhora had got a job as a medical assistant at the Martynov Hospital, and that had saved him from conscription. As for Elena, he helped her to get the papers to visit her parents in prison. Even the old countess was inclined to pardon him for his past sins. Her elderly friends had started falling sick from malnutrition, and one after the other had died. There was no one to bury them, and Fomin would send his men to take the deceased to the cemetery and dig graves for them.

Nina knew that when Klim came back (if he ever came back), he would think that she had just switched from one admirer to another. He would probably doubt that she was worthy of the sacrifices he had made for her, and that was possibly what Fomin was hoping for.

But with each day, her own hopes for Klim's safe return faded. When Nina thought about it, she felt as if her entire world was disintegrating. *Stop thinking about that!* she ordered herself. *Come up with something to distract yourself.*

How Nina begrudged giving away those worn, faded banknotes to Fomin! It was easy enough to give money away to charity when you can see the results then and there, but Nina's donations disappeared without a trace. Sometimes she would keep herself awake at night with thoughts of raiding her own cash till, getting herself some false papers, and setting out to Petrograd in search of Klim.

2

As soon as the Volga flooded the grounds of the Nizhny Novgorod Fair, Fomin and Zhora sailed out there looking for abandoned goods. The most valuable of these were sewing materials. In the countryside, the local peasants would give as much as five pounds of flour for a good needle and even more for a pair of scissors.

A lot of the goods had not even been removed out of the fair for safekeeping. It was less risky and cheaper to take them to the upper floors of the warehouses and hide them there until the next season. At one time, the merchants had hired watchmen to keep thieves away, but now—since all the owners were either in prison or on the run—the fair was completely defenseless.

At first, Nina had objected. "That's just breaking and entering!"

"No," Fomin had said. "We're just being 'self-sufficient,' which is precisely what the Bolsheviks are urging us to be."

Looting and petty thievery had become rampant in Russia. People were cutting off the seals of shop doors and drilling holes into the bottoms and sides of boxcars. Sales assistants would add water to the flour to increase its weight. There were constant fires in the warehouses started by employees to hide their tracks after stealing the very supplies they were meant to be protecting. But the worst looters of all were the Bolshevik "food brigades," armed groups of workers who came to villages to requisition grain and other "surplus supplies." They declared anything and everything they could their hands on to be "surplus," from the bread baking in the peasants' ovens to seeds set aside for next year's harvest.

Nina was shocked at how quickly people's attitudes and behavior changed. Now, even the old countess wasn't above petty thievery. She had picked up and brought home a plank that had fallen off the back of a Red Army truck and even boasted about her crime.

That day, Fomin and Zhora had brought back two sacks filled with boxes of needles.

"We were sailing down Teatralnaya Street," Zhora told Nina excitedly, "and then we saw another boat. They wanted to rob us, but Mr. Fomin took a pistol from his bag and splintered one of their oars to matchwood."

Nina gasped. "Did they shoot at you?"

Fomin waved his hand dismissively. "If they did shoot at us, they didn't make any impression on us or the boat."

Elena knocked on the door. "Nina, the old countess would like to see you."

3

When Nina entered the room, the old countess was busy writing at her desk.

"Good evening," Nina said. "Elena said that you wanted to speak to me?"

Sofia Karlovna nodded. "Yesterday, I noticed from my window that Mr. Fomin was walking down the street between you and Elena. Could you tell him that a gentleman should always keep to the roadside when he is escorting ladies?"

"I will," Nina said with a sigh. "Is that all?"

The old countess looked at her through her lorgnette, her eyes flashing scornfully. "I suppose you think good manners are only relevant in peacetime? If so, you are very much mistaken."

She took a stained envelope from the drawer and gave it to Nina. "I was at the post office this morning, and they gave me this letter for you from Mr. Rogov. I do apologize. I forgot all about it."

Nina felt as though every sight and sound around her had suddenly receded into the distance, and she stood transfixed to the spot, unable to breathe or move. It took some time before she came to her senses, and when she did, she found herself in an armchair, not sure how she had gotten there.

She stared at the envelope in her hand with the torn mail stamps along its sides.

"Are you all right?" she heard her mother-in-law's voice. "I noticed that the letter had been opened, but the clerk at the post office told me that that's how they receive them these days."

Nina nodded and pulled out a sheet of lined paper. It was a letter from a woman she didn't know asking for a pair of canvas shoes and a set of drawing instruments to be sent to her.

Nina looked at the envelope. The address was in Klim's handwriting.

"It would appear that the letter has gone astray," said Sofia Karlovna, taking it from Nina's shaking hand. "Princess Anna Evgenievna told me that the Cheka censors are opening and inspecting all correspondences before they get to their recipients. The censors have probably made a mistake and put Mr. Rogov's letter in the wrong envelope."

"His letter has gone astray," Nina repeated in despair.

"You're lucky to get at least something from Mr. Rogov," said Sofia Karlovna. "I've heard that the Cheka destroy all letters that look like they've been written by anyone who is half-educated, assuming that they must be counter-revolutionaries. At least you know that Mr. Rogov has reached Petrograd safely. According to the stamp, this letter was sent a month and a half ago."

Nina snatched the envelope out of the old countess's hand. "What's the return address?"

But it was impossible to read. Someone had placed a sticky cup of tea on the corner of the envelope and torn off the top layer of paper. Nina could make out nothing but the word "Petrograd" and the apartment number.

"Please don't mention this to Mr. Fomin," Nina whispered.

The old countess gave her a reproachful look. "Why do you think I summoned you here instead of bringing you the letter in the dining room?"

"Thank you!" Nina found herself breaking down in tears. "I'm so afraid that if Klim comes back, Mr. Fomin will—"

Suddenly, the old countess did something unthinkable: she patted Nina on the shoulder.

"To be honest with you, I didn't expect Mr. Rogov to stay in Russia," Sofia Karlovna said. "Since he hasn't betrayed you, he deserves to be treated with the same respect as he has evidently shown us. As for Mr. Fomin, don't worry too much about him. Right now, there is nothing you can do about your situation, but later, who knows how things will turn out? As you grow older, you start to notice that most of the alarms in our lives turn out to be false ones."

10. THE DEFECTOR

1

Dr. Sablin was perfectly aware that his wife had taken a lover. The squat, red-faced soldier called Osip who now worked at the regional Military Commissariat and had appointed Lubochka head of its canteen. If in the past, she had channeled her energy into putting the lives of her friends in order, now she did the same for that vats of sour cream and other provisions that had been confiscated by the Cheka and handed over to the Commissariat. Lubochka could keep track of hundreds of names in her head and knew exactly who needed what, and that made her very useful.

Everybody in the hospital knew about Dr. Sablin's misfortune.

"I simply don't understand it!" Ilya Nikolaevich, the chief doctor at the hospital, had exclaimed when he next saw Sablin. "You need to put your foot down. I know that morals are in decline and that we live in troubled times—but you know as well as I do how it will end: one day this fine fellow will stick a knife in her ribs. Do you remember that young cabaret girl who was brought in to us recently? Well, it'll be the same story with your Lubochka."

"If Lubochka ends up on my operation table, I'll shove the knife into her ribs myself," Sablin had said in a husky voice.

Ilya Nikolaevich had gaped at him for a moment. "If I ever hear you talk like that again, you'll be out of a job."

Sablin didn't care. He felt as if his life was pouring out of him, as though he were hemorrhaging to death and there was no way to staunch the flow.

When Sablin had suggested to Lubochka that they divorce, she had merely nodded but hadn't brought the subject up again since.

The problem was that she had no place to go. Initially, Lubochka had hoped that she and Osip could move into her father's house, but it had been requisitioned as a "shelter for proletarian widows." Osip lived in his office in the building of the former seminary and didn't want to ask his bosses for anything. He believed that a private apartment was too much of a luxury, and a true Bolshevik should share the same hardships the people suffered.

Sablin and Lubochka now slept in different bedrooms and barely exchanged a word beyond icy greetings as they passed each other in the house. Sablin left money on the chest of drawers in his wife's room, and Lubochka made sure that there was food in the house for dinner.

Sablin had no idea and didn't care to know where Lubochka spent her days. When he pictured his wife in the arms of another man, he—whom his wife thought "incapable of real emotion"—wanted nothing more than to plunge a scalpel into his heart.

2

Osip Drugov had been born in the village of Chukino in the Balakhna rural district. His mother's hands had been so calloused from work that they would catch in his hair when she stroked his head. His father was a drinker and a fighter, but when he was sober, he tried to do his best for his family.

Once, he went to the market and brought Osip a brand new pair of leather boots. "You should only wear them in church," he said to his son. "You'll never get another pair. Our kind were born to wear bast shoes."

However, Osip dreamed of wearing leather boots every day and also a large peaked cap and a brass chain for his waistcoat. He begged his parents to let him go to Sormovo, Nizhny Novgorod's industrial district. Osip had imagined life in a factory would be some sort of proletarian workers' paradise—full of strong, jovial young men who had left their villages to make their fortunes in the city. They learned all sorts of things, they went away to distant lands, and they even traveled to work on a tram—a sort of huge metal carriage that moved without horses.

But in reality, Osip found himself in hell, not paradise. The workshops of the Sormovo factory were illuminated by the crimson flames of the constantly burning furnaces and the streams of red-hot metal flowing down the gutters, and it was made even more unbearable by the roar of the machinery. Here, even the healthiest of men became crippled by work in the span of a few years.

Osip didn't understand why things were as they were. Why was it that some had money to burn, and others had to sweat and slave in scorching factory workshops? The priest told him that it had ever been thus and that it was sinful to ask such questions.

Osip started to drink and often ended up at the police station. There he came into contact with Bolsheviks who gave him his purpose in life back and cured his sick soul. He felt like a wounded soldier who had been rescued from the field of battle. The Bolsheviks were clever; they understood the great science of Marxism that explained who was to blame for the misery of factory workers like Osip and what those workers needed to do to improve their lives.

The Bolshevik revolution was the biggest event in Osip's life, and his greatest achievement was Lubochka. He found it hard to believe that a doctor's wife could have fallen in love with him, an uneducated man.

He did his best to mask his confusion by making impassioned political speeches to her.

"We are forging a new way of life," Osip told Lubochka. "We will build new communal houses. All of us will work in teams. Every one of us shall have the same sort of accommodation, furniture, and clothes. No one will have luxuries, so there will be no envy or greed. Won't that be wonderful?"

She smiled enigmatically. "I'm afraid we probably won't live long enough to see that become a reality."

"We will!" Osip exclaimed but then fell silent, abashed.

Above all, he was afraid that Lubochka would become disappointed—in him, in the revolution, and in the Bolshevik Party. And there were plenty of reasons to be disappointed.

During the first months of the revolution, Osip had been fond of repeating Lenin's statement that it would be simple for the state to be run by the people themselves. But nothing was going according to plan. Criminals and madmen had joined the Cheka while the workers who had been put in charge of factories had allowed them to idle into talking shops.

An epidemic of food riots engulfed the city. Osip traveled from factory to factory trying to drum up support and issuing empty threats. Nothing he did had any effect.

"Down with Lenin and horse meat!" the crowd started to shout as soon as he mounted the rostrum. "Give us the Tsar and our salted bacon back!"

Osip knew that a counter-revolution could only be controlled with force. On the instruction of his Commissariat, he combed military warehouses, gathered up broken weaponry, and organized repair shops. No one—not even Lubochka—knew how hard this work was for Osip.

3

The food situation in Russia was deteriorating every day. It seemed that the well-to-do peasants—the *kulaks*—were setting out to starve the revolutionary government. They hid their grain and refused to give it up to the hungry cities. As soon as the food brigades went into the countryside, the peasants would start rioting.

Osip studied the reports about the rebellions. The scenario was always the same: the men from the food brigades didn't care who was rich and who was poor. They went from home to home taking any food they could find and stockpiling it at random. The grain and meat spoiled, and anything that actually made it to the city was embezzled by the local officials.

Some of the peasants had brought sawn-off rifles back from the front, and they greeted the food brigades with hails of bullets. To keep them under control, the Bolsheviks periodically bombarded villages with artillery fire.

During the next meeting of the Regional Executive Committee, Osip met the issue head-on. "We need to change the makeup of our food brigades. If we only accept working-class people and not bourgeois types masquerading as workers, then all this abuse of power will stop. The commanders should be trustworthy party members devoted to our communist ideals."

He received an unexpected reply.

"You are just the sort of person we need, Comrade Drugov. You should head a food brigade and set an example for everyone."

4

Osip pored over the map.

Where should we go? he thought. *To my home village? But there are no more than a couple of kulak households there, and my men will eat the village's supplies in a matter of days.*

Osip's finger hovered over the rural district of Bolsheyelnitskaya. A friend of his had once told him that the people there were quite prosperous.

Osip summoned a couple dozen volunteers for his food brigade, workers from the Etna factory.

When they reached their destination, Osip asked a terrified signalman where they might find the local kulaks.

"Go to Utechino," he said. "They're a bad lot there—greedy, the lot of them."

It was dark when they arrived in Utechino. Osip told his men to scatter throughout the village and explain to the locals that they were Red Army soldiers who had become separated from their regiment. He, his assistant Fedunya, and another lad, red-haired Andreika, went up to the last house on the street. Osip struck a match and looked over the sturdy gates. It seemed that the signalman had been telling the truth: Utechino was indeed a prosperous village.

A guard dog on a chain barked behind the gates in a frenzy. Osip shifted from one foot to the other, reluctant to knock at the gate. The villagers were unpredictable and could well be violent. Many a food brigade volunteer had been killed or gone missing in the countryside.

The men drew lots. It fell to Osip to lead the way. He pulled his pistol out of his holster and thumped loudly on the gate with his fist.

"Who's there?" called a suspicious male voice.

"Red Army soldiers," Osip said. "Only three of us. Can we spend the night in your house? We have supplies—there's no need to feed us."

That was a lie too. They had eaten their ration—a pound of bread and a small kettle of soup—earlier that morning.

The master of the house unbolted the gates. Osip struck another match. *Pah,* he thought. *Just an old man with an oven fork.*

"Who might you be then: Bolsheviks or Communists?" the old man asked. Evidently, he wasn't the sharpest tool in the box when it came to state ideology.

"Neither," Osip said with relief. "We're just common folks."

The old man welcomed them inside his dark house. While they were settling themselves down for the night on the floor, he asked them about the city, the war, and the prices, but he didn't offer them any food, although it was clear that they had had nothing to eat.

Parasite! Osip thought indignantly. *We'll deal with you in the morning.*

"Your rifles don't go off by themselves, do they?" asked a young woman lying on the big brick oven. "We had another lot here before you, and one of the soldier's rifles went off in the middle of the night."

Their hosts didn't have the slightest interest in politics. Only their little boy—seven to ten years old judging by his voice—asked if it was true that the Tsar had been sent into exile.

When the family was sound asleep, Fedunya moved closer to Osip.

"I had to run outside earlier, and I heard the sound of a cow—more than one, I think. These people are rich, I tell you."

Osip pushed him away. "Hush! Don't give us away."

5

In the morning, the old man went to the fields—so he had a horse—and the woman gave Osip and his men milk and stale bread. Osip gazed around the house. It wasn't as large as he had thought. However, the backyard was covered with an awning, and there were apple trees in the orchard.

Osip was at a loss as to how to begin the requisition process.

He started a conversation about the hungry workers in the cities. The woman listened to him in silence, spinning wool, her spindle humming quietly on the floor. Her little son, a handsome, fair-haired boy, was mending a fishing net and casting sidelong glances at Fedunya's rifle. He had already tried to touch it once, but his mother had shooed him away.

"My husband is missing at the front," the woman said. "I think the Germans have taken him prisoner. Our neighbors' son was missing too. Then they got a letter from him, and he came back home on Palm Sunday. But he's no worker now that he's lost his left arm."

It was time to get down to business. Osip rose from his seat, and Andreika and Fedunya followed him. But the next moment, they heard women's screams outside. Apparently, Osip's men had begun throwing their weight around without waiting for his order.

As they all ran outside, Andreika without a thought shot down a man trying to raise the alarm by banging on a piece of metal rail hanging from a tree.

"Just do what you've been instructed to do," Osip ordered his assistants.

When Fedunya tried to drag a goat out of the yard, the woman who had sheltered them stabbed him in the side with a pitchfork. Osip pulled out his pistol and fired.

"Mama!" shouted the fair-haired boy.

Osip's men pulled out sacks of grain from the granaries, grabbed chickens, and seized jars of preserved goods from cellars.

The villagers howled in terror, "Have mercy on us, master!"

Osip didn't know how it all happened. He had come here with a clear aim in mind to commandeer surplus food, uphold the honor of the proletariat, and be stern but fair. But everything had gone completely wrong.

"There's no law that allows you to take the grain I planted and harvested with my own hands," yelled a black-bearded man, trying to push his way through to Osip.

Osip's men held him back by the elbows to stop him clawing at the commissar's throat. Osip gave him a hard blow in the jaw.

They found several sacks of grain stashed away at the man's house. Then Osip found a bigger store of grain in a pit in the garden. It was covered with turf, but the grass over it had turned yellow, indicating the hiding place.

A hunched old woman in a black shawl watched as members of the brigade dragged struggling geese along by their necks.

"Stinking thieves!" she cried, pointing at Osip with a gnarled finger.

"Shut up, or I'll burn your house down, you old witch!" he yelled in reply.

They didn't leave a single house untouched. It seemed to them that Utechino must be full of hiding places, yet the amount of food they managed to collect was pitiful.

They needed to justify their behavior to themselves. They weren't shooting and beating the villagers for nothing but for a great cause—to feed the hungry. The only way they could feed the people of Sormovo was by pillaging Utechino and the nearby villages. But they found little or nothing there. The locals had been warned and had escaped to the forest along with their stocks and supplies.

Osip had become a Bolshevik to deliver the working class from slavery, yet now the peasants were calling him a "master" and a "thief."

It was clear that these people had no idea how serious the situation was. If they refused to feed the starving cities, there would be nobody to stand up for them. The landlords and factory owners would come back, and the Tsar's regime would be restored with all its injustice. The poor would remain as miserable as they had always been.

Yet now that the revolution had delivered the peasants from their former oppressors, they felt they had no obligations to the new government. Mired in primitive ignorance, they gave no thought to the cities. As soon as they lost the right to trade their grain there, they began to use the grain to distill raw vodka. Osip was under orders from Moscow to execute anyone who made illicit spirits on the spot, but the men of Utechino had pooled their money together to buy their hooch still and consequently were all as guilty as each other. What was Osip supposed to do? Shoot every man in the village?

Seeing red, Osip ordered a meeting.

"If I find out that you're speculating in grain or making vodka instead of giving your surpluses to the state, I'll blow up your mill. Got it?"

"What?" the villagers were shocked. "But how will we mill our flour?"

Osip told them to bury their dead without ceremony and to get the carts ready to take the food to the railroad station.

6

All the way to the station the one-eyed cart-driver tried to curry favor with Osip, feigning sympathy.

"The folks around here are a feckless lot," he sighed. "They get orders from the city and use them to make cigarette papers."

Osip strode in silence beside the cart. He was deliberately letting Fedunya's rifle strap rub the bare skin of his neck at his open collar. He hoped it would rub his skin raw. He felt an overwhelming urge to mortify himself.

"Hey, boss, are you from Penza city?" the cart-driver asked.

"No. I'm from Nizhny Novgorod," Osip said.

"My son told me that over in Penza, there's a train full of Chacks, former prisoners of war."

"You mean Czechs, not Chacks," Osip muttered. "The Austrians mobilized them to fight against Russia, but they said they didn't want to fight their fellow Slavs. So, they gave themselves up."

The cart-driver was delighted that this stern Bolshevik had deigned to join him in conversation.

"I saw them on the way back from the front," the cart-driver said. "Our generals issued them with rifles and rations so that they would fight on our side against the Germans."

Osip had heard about these Czechs before. The Provisional Government had divided the Czech and Slovak prisoners of war into three divisions and had intended to send them to the Western Front via the Pacific to North America and then to Europe. But due to the usual Russian red tape, the matter had dragged on, and the Czechoslovak trains were stuck at various railroad stations all the way from the Volga River to the Sea of Japan. After the Bolshevik coup, no one knew what to do with this armed legion of forty thousand men. One thing was obvious—they posed a serious threat.

"So, what else did this son of yours happen to let slip?" Osip asked the cart-driver.

"The new government wanted to disarm the Czechs, but instead, they mutinied. They were afraid that under the peace treaty, the Bolsheviks would hand them over to the Germans. Then the Germans would shoot them on the spot as traitors."

7

When Osip arrived in Nizhny Novgorod, he found that the cart-driver's story was true, and the Military Commissariat needed to hastily muster troops to suppress the rebellion.

Osip's homecoming caused quite a stir. The local newspaper published a long article about his heroic deeds, and he was awarded a cigarette case with an engraved inscription on the lid.

However, all he could think about was the woman he had shot, the old hag who had cursed him, and the previously docile peasants who now hated him and all the Bolsheviks with a passion.

8

Three days later, Lubochka found Osip in the cloakroom of the former seminary surrounded by stacks of broken desks. He was sitting on the floor with his head in his hands and a bottle of vodka beside him.

"Come on," Lubochka said. "Let's get you back on your feet."

Osip looked at her with his bloodshot eyes. "I killed a woman."

"Let's go. You need to sleep. Don't blame yourself—it's war."

"We weren't up against soldiers," Osip persisted. "We shot unarmed people."

Lubochka fell silent and took a step back.

"Listen to me, Osip Drugov, and listen carefully. No more vodka, do you understand? I'm not going to waste my life on a drunkard. You have to stand up and be a man."

Osip wiped his face with his sleeve. "Sorry...I'll pull myself together. I promise."

She took him downstairs, called for a cab driver, and told him to take them to her father's house.

"The authorities have listed it as a cultural heritage site," she said. "The revolutionary widows who were quartered there made such a mess of it that the Culture Commission threw them out and appointed me curator. From now on, it's going to be our home."

11. THE CHINESE MERCENARIES

1

Klim had no choice but to renounce his Argentine citizenship and apply for a Soviet passport.

By now, anyone wanting to leave Russia had to pay bribes running into thousands of rubles. Becoming a Soviet citizen, on the other hand, cost next to nothing and usually went smoothly except for the tiring delays and queues.

The door to the Bureau for the Registration of Foreign Citizens opened once every thirty minutes or so. Former prisoners of war sat on the floor in front of the door with their legs stretched out. Next to them stood dozens of Chinese men dressed in ragged oriental robes belted with hemp cords.

"Where are you from?" Klim asked the men in Shanghainese.

The Chinese gawped at him in disbelief. They had never seen a white person who spoke their language before.

A shock-headed, thick-lipped young man bowed to Klim. "My name is Ho," he said. "My mother is from the province of Jiangsu, and I know some Shanghainese. My friends don't speak it though. They are from the northern provinces."

Somehow, the two of them managed to make themselves understood. Ho told Klim that two years earlier, he and his fellow countrymen had come as laborers to work on the construction of the Murmansk Railroad. To compensate for the shortage of labor during wartime, Russian merchants who had settled in China had recruited teams of Chinese workers from the villages and sent them to construction sites across Russia, mostly the railroads. After the Bolshevik coup, the government had stopped paying the Chinese, and they had made the long journey to Petrograd in the hope that the state would pay for their passage back to China.

The door of the Bureau for the Registration opened again, and a scrawny man stuck his head around it. He was narrow-shouldered and dark and looked like a young gypsy. Shifting from one foot to another, he scrutinized the silent queue for a moment and then spoke, "Oppressed workers of China, follow me please!"

Nobody moved, so the young man went up to one of the Chinese and tried to take his hand. The man recoiled in fear.

"He wants you to go with him," Klim explained in Shanghainese.

"Do you understand their language?" exclaimed the scrawny young man, staring at Klim. "Listen, I could do with someone like you."

"But I have my own business here in the Bureau for the Registration," Klim protested.

The young man paid no attention. "Don't worry. I can get you to the front of the queue once you've helped me. Do you need bread? I can arrange for you to get a loaf. And some tallow and tea." He thrust out a skinny hand. "I'm Lyosha Pukhov. I've been charged with creating a detachment of proletarians from the yellow races."

2

Pukhov ushered the awed cluster of Chinese men into a huge hall with crystal chandeliers.

"Ask them to take a seat," he told Klim. "We'll have a political meeting first, and then we'll move onto practical arrangements."

Pukhov took a piece of paper out of his pocket. "Dear Chinese comrades!" he began to read. "Those of you who support the liberation of the oppressed and the protection of the power of the workers and peasants come and join us in the ranks of the Red Armyd. Come and join its Chinese battalion."

Klim had no idea how to say words like "comrade," "oppressed," and in particular "battalion" in Shanghainese, so he just provided a basic translation: Pukhov would give the Chinese food and money if they followed his orders. Ho listened to Klim and then interpreted Pukhov's speech into the northern dialect.

"Our revolution is working miracles," Pukhov called out. "We all are brothers. The same red blood runs under yours and our skin. The same stout hearts beat in all our chests, at one with those of the world's proletariat. Please step up one at a time and fill in a form for us with your details."

"I'd be surprised if they can write," said Klim.

Pukhov scratched his head. "Well—they can dictate their details to you, and you can just write everything down in Russian. By the way, I have sunflower oil too. I'll give you some of that as well."

It was late evening by the time Klim had finished filling out the forms.

After the Chinese had left, Pukhov spent some time reading the biographies of his soldiers-to-be.

"What a life!" he exclaimed angrily. "What cynical exploitation! They were being paid a measly ruble and a half a day, half of what a Russian worker got. They had no recourse to the law and no chance of having any complaints heard. The slightest dissension and they would be sacked on the spot."

Klim nodded, glancing uneasily through the window at the darkening sky. The twenty-four-hour period had expired, he still hadn't been to the Bureau for the Registration of Foreign Citizens and could now be arrested on the spot.

"According to the statistics, we have about four million foreign nationals in Russia," Pukhov continued nonchalantly. "Half of them are prisoners of war, and the rest are immigrants and seasonal workers from all around the world. They're working-class people, and they've already organized themselves into their own little communities. I tell you, these people make the best proletarian fighters. Have you heard about the Finnish Detachment of the Red Guards? And the Latvian Riflemen are a great help to the Cheka too."

"So I hear," Klim said, smiling bitterly.

"Now, we have to organize the Chinese," Pukhov said. "There are about five thousand of them in Petrograd. They live in ramshackle, overcrowded huts in unimaginable filth. Almost none of them have a permanent job. The police have received a number of reports about them being involved in robbery and rape. There are only nine Chinese women per five hundred men living in one barrack. These men are young, and they have—well, you know—perfectly natural instincts. But if a man has no money to take a girl to the pictures, let alone start a family, something is eventually going to give."

"Yes, obviously rape is the inevitable consequence," Klim said through gritted teeth. "You'll have to excuse me, but I have to go."

"Oh, I almost forgot," Pukhov said. "I owe you your wages."

He took Klim into a small office piled high with boxes labeled "Red Cross."

"These are the rations for our Chinese recruits," Pukhov said. "So, tell me, why were you in the queue at the Bureau for Registration? Do you need documents?"

Klim described his situation.

"What nonsense!" Pukhov cried. "The Cheka has no right to cancel your visa. It's not their business but ours—the People's Commissariat of Foreign Affairs. I'll take you to Comrade Zalkind. He'll fix things."

"What if he doesn't agree to help me?" Klim asked.

"He will. If need be, I'll send a messenger to Gorokhovaya Street. You have to stay in Petrograd. Otherwise, how will I be able to speak to my Chinese recruits tomorrow?"

His words set Klim's heart pounding.

"Could you help get my fiancée permission to come to Petrograd?" he asked. "The authorities in Nizhny Novgorod have forbidden her to leave the city."

"Well—you know," Pukhov grimaced, "the local executive committees do pretty well what they please. At the moment, we don't have any control over them."

"I could go to Nizhny Novgorod myself and bring her back."

Pukhov shook his head. "I need you here. We'll be training the Chinese for a couple of months, and then we'll send them to Moscow as reinforcements for the Cheka. After that, I can organize your trip to Novgorod or wherever it is. But you have to make a good showing."

Pukhov was offering Klim a position as an interpreter for a Cheka hit squad.

"I accept," Klim nodded slowly. "But may I ask you a favor? I need to send a telegram to Nizhny Novgorod, and I want it to be handed directly to the addressee. And I need a response."

"That's easy. We'll send the telegram immediately. We have a telegraph operator on duty around the clock."

Pukhov advised Klim not to give up his Argentine passport. "They've just begun a general mobilization of the population. As soon as you become a Russian citizen, they'll have you in the army like a shot. It will be much harder for me to get you out of there. No, I have a better idea—we'll just extend your visa."

3

Khitruk had done nothing but anxiously mope around his apartment since losing his paper. His editorial staff had gradually gone their separate ways to the countryside, Ukraine, or Finland. The days of fearless journalistic scoops had been consigned to history.

Khitruk correctly surmised that Klim had made a deal with the Bolsheviks to let him stay in Russia without changing his citizenship. He didn't ask Klim to play chess anymore and looked at him suspiciously. The two men could no longer find anything to talk about, but this was not the most important thing on Klim's mind at the moment. He had finally had word from Nina. It turned out that she had never received any of his letters, but she assured him she was alive and well.

Klim telegraphed that he would come to Nizhny Novgorod in early September. Pukhov had promised to provide him with the necessary documents, from train tickets to a travel pass from the Cheka. Klim had no idea what to do next, but that mattered little either.

Every morning, he went out to meet Pukhov at the commissar's luxurious lodgings in the Astoria Hotel. A shiny-black, chauffeur-driven car would arrive at the entrance, and they would speed along the grassy, deserted streets to the barracks of the Grenadier Regiment where the Chinese recruits were billeted.

Klim kept himself aloof from Pukhov and his assistants, former Imperial Army officers who had offered their services to the Bolsheviks in exchange for rations. These men quickly began to look down on Klim after it became clear that only about twenty out of the three hundred Chinese recruits understood Klim's Shanghainese. Klim talked, and then Ho had to interpret to the rest of the men. To make matters worse, neither Klim nor Ho knew any military terms, so almost everything had to be explained using gestures.

"There are no other interpreters!" Pukhov shouted in a rage. "We've been everywhere from the university to the Academy of Sciences. Even when we do find someone who knows Chinese, they refuse to cooperate."

He looked gloomily at his warriors kitted out in a motley array of oriental robes, striped sailor's vests, and tattered trousers. "The ill-fated soldiers of the revolution," he sighed.

Gradually, the Chinese learned how to understand "fall in" and "forward, march" and "hurrah" in Russian. But they failed to recognize their commanders because all white people looked alike to them. The guards often even prevented Lyosha Pukhov from entering the barracks. "Halt!" they yelled in broken Russian, and only after they realized that it was Commissar *Le Sha*, as they called him, did they let him through. The sound of Pukhov's first name made them snigger. Klim guessed that *sha* meant something like "stupid" in their language.

The instructors worked their recruits into the ground from dawn to dusk, making them run, aim, and fire.

Klim got back home at around nine in the evening, tired and hoarse from shouting pointless commands.

Durga usually waited for him on the stairs, and he would greet her gloomily.

"Don't you want to write another book?" she asked. "I have a marvelous idea. What about *Pest Control for the Home and Workplace*?"

Klim shook his head. "These days, the censors wouldn't allow it. They'd suspect some political subtext or other."

As he made his way upstairs, Durga's voice floated up from the darkness below, "What about *Official Claims and Complaints for All Occasions*?"

As soon as Klim got into the apartment, he gave his groceries to the cook and retreated to the guest room. He had pinned a calendar out of a newspaper onto the wall, and every day, he crossed out another day—not the current day but the day ahead. That way he could fool himself into thinking that he had a little less time to wait.

4

Finally, the day came for Klim to say goodbye to Khitruk.

"War has broken out," he said. "The Czechs have rebelled on the Volga, and my Chinese are being sent to defend Kazan. We'll go on the troop ship *Nakhimovets* through the Mariinsk Canal System."

"Well, good luck to you," said Khitruk, giving him a mocking look.

Klim made a curious sight in his new guise as a Russo-Argentine Chinese interpreter for the Bolsheviks. His haute couture gray overcoat sewn by the best tailor in Florida Street in downtown Buenos

Aires hung incongruously over his brand-new Red Army uniform.

"I'm going to find Nina," said Klim. "Nizhny Novgorod is on the way to Kazan."

Khitruk averted his eyes. "Well, may God help you." He patted at his pockets in search of a cigarette lighter, muttering away and pretending not to notice Klim's outstretched hand.

"Thank you for everything," said Klim, picking up his kit bag from the floor.

Durga met him on the stairs.

"I really don't know what I should wish you," she said angrily. "Go now before I say something stupid and jinx you. I don't want you to catch a bullet in your first battle."

5

The rivers were shallow in summer and full of hidden shoals and sandbanks, and the troopships made slow, tortuous progress. There were twenty-eight ascending locks and four descending ones on the Sheksna River alone. The rickety wooden holds were so small that the sailors had to load all the coal and ammunition onto barges. Even the water for the boilers had to be stored on them. The troopships were towed to the town of Rybinsk by tugboats at an agonizingly slow speed of two and a half knots.

Klim grew weary and impatient. He paced the burning hot deck, shading his eyes to look at the ancient monasteries on the riverbanks with their towers and arrow-slit windows. The air was filled with the smell of cut grass and river mud.

Pukhov kept pestering the Chinese soldiers as they lay listlessly in the heat.

"How do you say 'hello' in your language?"

The Chinese would say something to him and cackle gleefully. Pukhov repeated what they said and burst into shrill laughter too, not realizing that he had just called himself a donkey and that they were having a laugh at his expense.

After dinner, Klim took refuge behind a lifeboat in the stern. He wanted to spend some time alone away from the Chinese, who were constantly asking him to interpret something. But Pukhov always managed to find him and sat down beside him with his thin hands pressed between his knees.

"The Whites have a fleet of their own now," he said. "I never thought I'd ever be taking part in a river battle. I remember reading about warships, cannons, and cutlasses as a child, but now, I'm going to experience it all for myself."

Klim remained tight-lipped. The civil war was none of his business. He had decided long ago that as soon as they got to Nizhny Novgorod, he would go ashore and escape.

The mowers on the riverbank began to cook their lunch. The waves lapped quietly against the side of the ship. Klim tried to work out how long it would take the *Nakhimovets* to get to Nizhny Novgorod, given all the stops, locks, loading, and unloading.

"Klim?" came Pukhov's voice.

"Hmm?"

"Do you ever get scared at the thought that they might kill us? Personally, I simply can't imagine how the world could possibly exist without me in it."

12. MOBILIZATION

1

Nina was overjoyed when she received Klim's telegram, but out of fear of Fomin, she kept it a secret from everyone and celebrated the good news on her own.

In the evenings, she would dance around her bedroom barefoot, rushing up to the mirror every now and then to inspect her reflection. Was she still pretty? Had she changed very much since Klim had left? Like a child, she jumped onto the bed, fell onto the pillows, and hugged them tightly to her.

Recently, she, her brother, and Elena had become as thick as thieves. They liked to sit together on the small sofa in the library and read aloud to each other in turns. They went to the cinema where they watched the audience rather than the screen and giggled together at the most dramatic moments. They pottered around in the garden they had planted on the slope behind the house, proud of their homegrown cucumbers and radishes.

Nina bit the bullet and allowed Zhora to hold parties at the house for his fellow poets. They came to Crest Hill in the evenings to read their poetry, sing to the guitar, and share news in excited whispers. After the Czechs' rebellion, fighting had flared up all over the country. There were countless peasant uprisings, the Cossacks and Whites had launched attacks on the Red Army in the south, and the Czechs and Slovaks were fighting the Bolsheviks in the Volga region and along the Trans-Siberian Railway.

Nina touched Klim's key. She didn't care about anything in this country anymore and least of all her mill and store. She just wanted Klim back.

The really good thing was that Nina wouldn't have to come up with any schemes to keep Klim and Fomin apart. Everything had turned out perfectly. The conspirators in Nizhny Novgorod were planning to stage a coup in late August. Fomin was one of the ringleaders, and he would be too busy to give Nina much thought.

2

Sablin had been genuinely amazed when Zhora had announced that he wanted to become a medic, but the boy had studied hard in the dissecting room and pretended to mind neither the heavy smell of the formaldehyde nor the dissected corpses lying on the tables. He had watched Sablin perform operations several times and managed not only to take everything on board but also chat to the nurses about the price of butter and millet.

He'll do, thought Sablin, smiling to himself. *He's a born medic.*

One day, Zhora approached Sablin. "I'd like to have a word with you, Doctor, if I may?" And this had marked the beginning of a clandestine alliance between the two men.

Sablin took the most direct part in the preparations for the uprising. He had trained up medical teams and organized secret locations where the wounded would be treated.

When Sablin came in to work at the hospital, he went straight to find Zhora.

"What's the latest news?" he asked.

"The White Army and the Czechs have occupied Simbirsk city," Zhora answered in an excited whisper, "and they are on their way up the Volga."

The Bolsheviks, fearing that their fragile grasp of power might be slipping, were resorting to ever more brutal measures. Sablin gaped dumbstruck as Zhora told him the news from Yekaterinburg that the Bolsheviks had just shot the entire Russian royal family, including the young grand duchesses and the thirteen-year-old Tsarevich.

Soon, the news had spread throughout the hospital, but few people expressed much pity or compassion. Most of the staff and patients confined themselves to obscure phrases such as, "Well, the Tsar has come to a bad end." Others openly reveled in his death, saying that it had served him right.

The city was in a state of feverish activity. Huge posters were plastered all over the fences calling on river transport workers to join the Red Volga Flotilla. In the Kunavino district and around the fair, sailors' hats bearing the names of ships no one on the Volga had ever heard of became a common sight. The Bolsheviks had destroyed the Russian Black Sea Fleet near the port of Novorossiysk so that their battleships would not fall into German hands. Now, their crews were traveling overland to Nizhny Novgorod to set off down the Volga on merchant boats that had been fitted out as gunships in the Sormovo factories.

On the morning of July 27, 1918, two Red Army soldiers came to visit Dr. Sablin.

"Get ready to leave, Doctor," they said. "We have orders to take you as a member of the Red Volga Flotilla staff."

At the headquarters, Sablin was told that he had been appointed head of a field hospital and that the next day, he was to leave for the front on a new gunboat called the *Lady* that had been converted out of a tugboat. Sablin tried to argue that he didn't want to enlist and wasn't even fit to fight on account of his bad leg, but the Flotilla commissar—a strapping, clear-eyed giant of a man—replied that this was no time for arguing and that Sablin would be shot if he didn't report first thing the next morning.

3

Another party for the young poets was in full swing at Nina's house. Zhora was reading a comic epitaph he had composed for Lubochka:

We never learned her dying wish,
So buried her with all her treasures,
The little things that gave her pleasure:
A pair of fine embroidered shoes,
The scented soap she liked to use,

Her cigarettes, red wine, and brandy,
Hair combs, hairpins, and sugar candy,
The caviar she ate so often.
Alas, one thing won't fit her coffin:
That Drugov chap, her Bolshie friend,
Who won't be with her at the end.
How sad, despite the joy he gave,
He can't be with her in the grave.

The poets stayed up until late at night, playing cards using their own autographed poems as the stakes. Every one of them was convinced that one day their manuscripts would be worth their weight in gold.

The candles were lit, ragged shadows flickered on the walls, and the crystal drops of the chandelier swayed gently in the draught.

Suddenly, there was a knock at the front door. Everyone froze and stared at one another. Nina hurriedly blew out the candles.

There was another bang at the door.

"Go!" Zhora told his friends. "I'll go and see who it is."

One by one, the poets leaped through the window and ran down the slope across Nina's vegetable garden. Nina and Elena wrapped the remnants of their food in the tablecloth, shoved it under the sofa, and pulled the cover down to the floor. Within seconds, there wasn't the slightest sign that the drawing room had just been filled with guests.

Any kind of gathering in a bourgeois house was seen as tantamount to a political meeting, and it was the host's responsibility to prove that their guests had been doing nothing but chatting, singing harmless songs, and reciting romantic poems.

There were steps in the hallway and then the squeak of the door handle. Nina and Elena held hands as though they were about to face the imminent impact of a storm. Then Zhora and Dr. Sablin entered the moonlit room.

"What happened?" whispered Nina.

Elena lit a candle, and the flame illuminated Sablin's bloodless face.

"I've been drafted into the Red Army," he said. "Did you know that the Bolsheviks have found the *Lady*?"

"Our *Lady*?" gasped Zhora. It was the best riverboat owned by Elena's father.

"Yes," Sablin nodded.

"Where are they sending you?" Nina asked anxiously.

"To the city of Kazan. They're setting up a field hospital there, and their commissar said he would shoot me if I refused."

4

"I won't let them take my *Lady*," Elena whispered to Zhora.

The *Lady* had only been built three years earlier and was fitted with a diesel engine instead of a steam one, which made her one of the fastest boats on the Volga.

While Nina questioned Sablin about the details, Zhora and Elena quietly slipped out of the house. They went through the bushes down to the Oka

Waterfront to the house of Postromkin, a pilot who had once worked for Elena's father.

The dark street was empty. Zhora and Elena darted through the gate and knocked at the window.

"Who's there?" asked an alarmed male voice.

"Postromkin, it's me!" Elena whispered. "Let us in."

The pilot's family lived in a small two-bedroom apartment.

"Come into the kitchen," Postromkin said, giving Zhora the oil lamp. "My family is sleeping, so try not to make too much noise."

They sat down at a table that had been scored with deep knife cuts.

"What's happened?" asked Postromkin. He was wearing nothing but a pair of drawers and a small copper cross that gleamed in the thick hair on his chest. Confronted with his fat, half-naked body, Elena was so embarrassed that she didn't know where to look.

Zhora told him what he had just found out from Dr. Sablin.

"I know," Postromkin said gloomily. "The Bolsheviks have mobilized everyone—from the captains and chief engineers to the dock hands. I've been called up too."

Elena gasped. "So, will you go?"

"They said they'd shoot my wife if I didn't."

"We must burn the *Lady*," Zhora said firmly. "Where is she?"

"Not far from here. Right next to the cabstand."

"Is there anyone on guard?"

"What do you think? Of course, there is."

Zhora fell silent, thinking.

"We need a rowing boat and some paraffin," he said finally. "We'll approach the *Lady* from the water. That way it will be easier to pass unnoticed."

Postromkin stared at him thunderstruck. "Are you completely crazy?"

Elena took Zhora's hand and squeezed it. "Postromkin, we'll do everything ourselves. Please just give us a little help!"

He left the kitchen and returned several minutes later, dressed to go out. "Stay here. I'll be back soon."

5

He was away for more than an hour.

"Do you think we can trust him?" asked Zhora.

Elena raised an eyebrow. "When he and my father were young, they used to be barge haulers pulling boats upstream. When people work as hard as that in a team, they become like brothers. It's impossible to survive otherwise."

Zhora put his arms around Elena, kissed her soft hair, and whispered in her ear:

Now, light the fuse, my friend, have faith,
Tonight we settle all our scores.
One day, perhaps our names will grace
The pages of police reports.

Elena laughed but stopped suddenly, seeing an old woman barefoot in her nightgown in the doorway.

"You're nothing but children!" she lamented. "My husband has run off to the Cheka. He's going to turn you in. You need to get out of here now!"

13. THE RED VOLGA FLOTILLA

1

The captain announced that the *Nakhimovetz* would be anchored in Nizhny Novgorod for no more than a couple of hours, and Pukhov forbade the Chinese to go ashore.

"I know you, you devils. If I let you go, you'll wander off, and we won't be able to find you."

He didn't want his interpreter to leave the ship either, but Klim, enraged, grasped him by the lapels. "I need to go into the city!"

Pukhov tried to escape Klim's grip. "Stop that! I can't let you go. What if you don't get back?"

"If you don't, then—you mark my words—you'll have an interpreter who'll be worse than an enemy for you."

"Are you threatening a commissar?"

"You promised to help me!"

In the end, Pukhov agreed to let Klim go for an hour but sent two Chinese soldiers to escort him.

"Watch him closely," Pukhov said to Ho, who had already picked up some Russian. "And don't even think about coming back without him, or you'll be brought before a tribunal."

Nizhny Novgorod had been transformed into one enormous army camp. No longer were there any soldiers to be seen idling in the streets. From time to time, military units, field kitchens, and rattling carts loaded with ammunition came driving by.

Klim could barely bring himself to wait for a cable car to take him uphill and was on the point of setting off on foot when a car finally arrived.

"Where are we going?" Ho asked, studying the green ravines and the houses with elaborately carved wooden window frames.

"To see my wife," said Klim, who didn't know how to say "fiancée" in Shanghainese.

The Chinese exchanged glances and smiled.

There wasn't a soul to be seen on Crest Hill. The streets were overgrown with dandelions, and not a shadow moved behind the blank windows.

Klim caught sight of a dusty truck parked outside Nina's porch. Written on its side was the word "Cheka."

Klim felt his blood run cold. He ran up the steps and threw open the front door. After the bright sun outside, it took some time for his eyes to grow accustomed to the dim light of the hallway.

The house was quiet.

"Is there no one here?" asked Ho.

Suddenly, there was a heavy crash, a wild cry, and two men came into the hall dragging Nina behind them.

"Where is that little son of a bitch?" one of them yelled.

The next minute, he had knocked Nina to the ground and kicked her with his heavy boot. Blinded with rage, Klim rushed at the Cheka officer and dealt him a blow to his startled face. The officer fell, knocking over a coat stand. His partner pulled out a revolver, but Ho went for his arm. A shot rang out, and the mirror on the wall shattered.

"Help!" shouted the Cheka officer.

The sound of running feet could be heard from the back rooms.

Klim grasped Nina's hand. "Run!"

They ran down the steep slope through the thicket of bird cherries with burdocks and branches breaking under their feet. Shots rang out behind their backs.

2

Klim pushed his way through to the gangplank where stevedores were running back and forth with enormous sacks on their backs. Pukhov was waiting for him, looking at his watch.

"Good God! What happened to you?" he cried.

Klim's sleeve was torn, his trousers were stained with mud, and there was blood on his shoulder. Pukhov caught sight of Nina being held up by the Chinese guards.

"Who on earth is this?" he asked.

"Please," said Klim, panting for breath, "save her!"

Pukhov stepped to one side and let them board the ship.

Klim took Nina to the cabin he shared with Pukhov and put her into bed. Her face was ashen, and her lips were caked with dried blood.

"You came for me after all," she said almost inaudibly.

Klim sat down on the bed. "Everything's going to be all right," he whispered. "We'll be leaving soon."

He felt dumbfounded. *They've beaten her up.*

Nina didn't look at Klim. She was panting as though she couldn't get enough air and kept one hand pressed to her stomach all the time. Klim wanted to take her hand in his, but she didn't let him. Her muscles were clenched tight, hard as stone.

"Would you kindly explain to me what's going on?" Klim heard Pukhov's voice.

He looked behind him. The commissar was standing in the doorway with a crowd of inquisitive Chinese peering from behind his back.

"Please go away!" Klim pleaded. He forced Pukhov back into the corridor. "Thank you for helping Nina. I'm indebted to you." Klim rubbed his hands over his face, trying to collect his scattered thoughts. His fingers were covered in Nina's blood. "If I'd got there a minute later, that would have been that."

"Was it the Cheka who attacked her?" asked Pukhov, frowning.

"Yes. I saw their truck by her house."

"You've put me in the firing line now, you know. What if that woman is a counter-revolutionary?"

"What the hell does it matter?" Klim grasped Pukhov by his shoulders. "Here we are standing in front of you alive—and the Cheka wants to kill us. Remember, you just told me that you couldn't imagine the world existing without you. We feel the same!"

Pukhov pried himself free from Klim's grip. "Now, listen to me," he whispered. "You never said a word about the Cheka. You've brought her as a kitchen girl to help the cook peel potatoes. As soon as we set sail, she needs to get to work."

"Thank you, but—"

"And I need you to interpret for me now. I'm about to read a report to the Chinese on recent events at home and abroad."

3

The warship sailed along between wooded shores.

It seemed to Klim that Pukhov was deliberately prolonging his pointless and tedious report. He was reading aloud a summary he had written the night before, the bored interpreters were ready to climb the wall, and the Chinese soldiers were nodding off.

Klim's gratitude began to give way to hatred. How could Pukhov be so hard-hearted? He knew that Klim hadn't seen Nina for six months, and now, he had sent her half-dead to the kitchen to work for the benefit of the revolution.

"Counter-revolutionary forces have occupied the Volga Region," announced Pukhov, shouting in an effort to be heard above the sound of the engine. "Central Asia and Siberia are cut off from us, and Ukraine has been occupied by the Germans. Our most important task now is to defend the major railroads and river routes—Kazan in particular. Whoever has Kazan controls the route to Moscow and the Urals."

A seagull hovered above the deck as though hanging on an invisible string, and brown smoke crept across the sky.

"So, I urge you, my Chinese brothers," said Pukhov, "to look sharp and be on your mettle. We are in for some furious battles."

At long last, Pukhov closed his notebook. "That's all I want to say for now."

Klim didn't wait for Pukhov to ask if anybody had any questions and ran to the galley.

"Where's Nina?" he asked the cook, a fat man as heavily tattooed as a convict.

The cook wiped the sweat from his face. "What the hell were you thinking of sending me a kitchen assistant like that? She keeps fainting. I'm not a nanny—I haven't the time to look after her."

Klim rushed back on deck and asked the deckhands if anyone had seen Nina.

"The curly-haired one?" one of the sailors winked at him. "She's right there by the gangway."

Nina was sitting against the wall with her knees pressed to her chin. Her features were drawn and her pupils wide.

Klim sat down next to her. "How are you?" He didn't need a doctor to tell that she was in a terrible way.

"The Cheka people came for Zhora and Elena," she said.

"And what did they do to you?" interrupted Klim.

Suddenly, Nina lost her balance, slumped sideways, and hit her head against the wall.

"Nina!" yelled Klim, grabbing her around the shoulders and pressing her to his chest.

4

Back in the cabin, she regained consciousness. Once again, she pulled her knees up to her chest.

"Show me," demanded Klim.

"No—don't—"

Without another word, he lifted her skirt, pulled down her drawers a little way—and froze. There was a huge black and crimson bruise on her belly in the spot where the Cheka man had kicked her with his boot.

Klim had been in fistfights with Italian immigrants in La Boca, one of the roughest districts in Buenos Aires, and he knew what that bruise meant. A strong, direct blow in the stomach could result in the rupture of internal organs, unbearable pain, and eventually death.

There was neither a doctor nor even a first aid kit on board. A Chinese soldier who had recently come down with food poisoning had been treated with nothing but condolences. The limit of Klim's own medical knowledge was that gargling helps a sore throat and scratches should be treated with iodine.

There wasn't a thing he could do.

Klim went to Pukhov and told him everything. The commissar swore, annoyed that he now had some stranger's problem on his hands.

"As soon as we arrive in Kazan, you can send your girlfriend to the hospital," he grunted. "And don't stare at me like that! Would you like me to anchor the ship in the middle of nowhere? You won't get any medicines there, do you understand? And no doctors either—not since the government declared a general mobilization of health-care workers."

Klim went back to the cabin and sat down beside Nina. "Can you wait a little?" he asked in a wavering voice. "Tomorrow, I'll find a doctor for you."

She closed her eyes. "Tell me about something...the way you used to. About China."

Klim took a deep breath. "China is a very mysterious country. A country where the women wear trousers and the men wear skirts—"

He had imagined so many times how he would eventually be reunited with Nina, and he had kept himself alive with these fantasies. She would be happy to see him, and everything would be fine again even if they had to live on a razor's edge in constant fear. But everything had turned out so badly!

His mind simply refused to accept the fact that in all likelihood, this was the end. The woman he had loved so much was gone, murdered by a scoundrel from the Cheka.

14. THE SIEGE OF KAZAN

1

That night, Nina felt better and managed to sleep. Klim held her hand, trying to imagine that his own vital energy was being passed to her in some mysterious way. He looked into the humid darkness behind the porthole, listening to the drone of the engine and praying, "Faster—faster—"

They reached Kazan at dawn. The *Nakhimovets* anchored in the middle of the river, and Pukhov went ashore by boat to receive further orders from the high command.

Klim went on deck. Between the city and the river bank was a dreary-looking plain crisscrossed by the light ruts of roads. On the pier, crowds of people were running to and fro with lanterns and flashlights. Dogs barked, and a rumble like heavy thunder could be heard in the distance.

"That's our artillery," one of the sailors said, approaching Klim. "Haven't you heard it before?"

The sailor had been to Kazan many times, and now, he told Klim how to find the Shamov Hospital, which, he said, was the best in the city.

A fiery flash lit up the sullen clouds, and several powerful explosions came from the direction of the city: first one, then a second, and a third. A cloud of black smoke rose over the distant roofs.

Pukhov came back to the ship.

"What's going on over there?" Klim asked.

"The Red Army have shelled railroad cars." Pukhov swallowed nervously. "The Czechs are already on the outskirts of Kazan, and we don't have enough soldiers to resist them. Get the Chinese together quickly. We're leaving now."

"Where to?"

"We're going to the center of Kazan, and you're coming with us."

"But listen, I—"

Pukhov glared furiously at Klim. "One more word about your girlfriend, and I'll shoot you."

2

Nina raised her head as Klim ran into the cabin.

"Listen to me," he whispered hurriedly. "Here's the money, and here's the address of the hospital. Pukhov has ordered the Chinese to go ashore, damn him—and he wants me to interpret for him. As soon as we leave, give the sailors some money and have them take you to the pier. There are always cabs there waiting for customers. Just say you need to get to the Shamov Hospital."

"But what about you?" Nina said, looking at him fearfully.

Klim put his arms around her and kissed her. "I'll come and find you later. Don't worry about me. You have to get to the hospital—spend all the money you have if necessary, but get yourself a doctor. Do you think you can manage?"

Nina nodded.

"Rogov, damn you! Where are you?" came a voice from the corridor.

Klim stood up without letting go of Nina's hand. "I love you, do you understand? I need you. Please do as I say."

"Rogov!" The cabin's door banged open, and Pukhov appeared on the threshold with a revolver in his hand. "Are you crazy?" he shouted. "The Czechs are on their way!"

"Don't yell at me," snapped Klim.

They went on deck where the Chinese were already lined up in formation.

"Dear comrades!" Pukhov shouted. "You are entrusted with an extremely important task. We have been ordered to evacuate valuable property from the city. We need to take this mission very seriously. If we succeed, anyone showing outstanding service will be rewarded. Long live the world revolution! Now, to the boats!"

3

The beautiful, ancient city of Kazan was almost empty with only the occasional small cavalry unit or truck sweeping through the straight streets every now and again. There was the smell of burning in the air.

Pukhov and the local commissar—a man whose eyebrows met in the middle—were urging the Chinese forward. "Come on! Come on!"

Sweat flew down the men's dusty foreheads. They passed a flask of water between them and drank as they ran.

"Where are we going now?" Klim asked the commissar.

"To the state bank."

The gloomy sky was split by a deafening howl, and a second later, an explosion struck close at hand.

"The Whites!" yelped Pukhov.

The heavy-browed commissar rushed to Klim. "Tell the Chinese that that was our troops shelling the approach roads to the river bank to give us a chance to take state property out of the city."

They turned onto Prolomnaya Street. Several carts were standing outside a large columned building. All around sailors and soldiers were running back and forth. One of them dropped a tightly packed bag. Small coins scattered all over the pavement, but nobody bothered to pick them up.

"Comrade Tarasov has brought the Chinese," somebody shouted. "Let them take on the loading."

The dim lobby of the bank was piled with wooden boxes. Klim noticed writing on their sides in charcoal: "State Bank" or "Winter Palace" or "Anichkov Palace." Khitruk had told him that during the German offensive, the Bolsheviks had seized imperial treasures from the capital and moved them somewhere inland. Maybe they had sent them to Kazan?

Tarasov ordered the Chinese to take one box at a time and load it carefully onto a tramcar that had just come in. Klim heard him explaining to Pukhov, "Until we have electricity, it's easier to transport everything by tram. The rails go right up to the pier."

Pukhov nodded grimly. He pulled a sheet of paper from his map-case, wrote something with his indelible pencil, and slipped the note behind the wooden slat on the bank front door.

We are now leaving the city of Kazan, but on our return, we will drive out the Whites. Anyone found to have helped them will be hanged.

So, the Reds are retreating, thought Klim.

Pukhov grasped a box and tried to lift it, the veins in his temples standing out with the effort.

"What are you staring at?" he shouted at Klim. "Help me!"

The box was extremely heavy. Together, they dragged it to the tramcar.

"Get inside and help take things on from that end," Pukhov ordered.

Klim stepped up the footboard.

"Hurry! Hurry!" the tram driver groaned.

The aisle and seats of the tramcar were already filled with boxes. Tarasov gave Klim a heavy bundle wrapped in sackcloth.

"Be careful—it's a statue," he said. "The crate broke, and we don't have a hammer and nails to fix it. Just take it like this."

Klim made his way into the center of the tramcar where there was free space.

A loud crash came overhead so powerful and unexpected that Klim missed his footing and fell, showered with pieces of broken window glass. The tramcar jerked and bounced down the street.

Klim was lying flat on top of the boxes. In the rearview mirror of the cabin, he could see the wild eyes of the tram driver. The tramcar turned onto another street where houses were ablaze at its far end.

Once again, Klim heard the howl of an approaching shell. The blow derailed the tramcar, and it fell onto its side, smashing through a shop window.

4

Klim's head was ringing, and the skin on his forehead was tight with dried blood. He could barely make out anything in the darkness. The tramcar had entered the building like a dagger going into a sheath, and all that could be seen now in the narrow gaps between the boxes was the dim glow of fire from the street.

Klim tried to get up, but the edge of a box wedged between the seats was digging into his chest.

"Help!" he called. "Somebody, help!" But no one answered.

Klim had no idea how long it took for him to work himself free and climb out of the tramcar. It seemed to be evening already. He was weak with exhaustion, his hands were torn and full of splinters, and he was terribly thirsty.

He looked into the cabin at the driver. The poor wretch was dead—one of the boxes had smashed his skull.

Klim forced his way between the wall of the shop and the roof of the tramcar and peered out. The building on the other side of the street was burned out, its beams collapsing. Flakes of ash drifted in the air.

Klim tried to remember the directions the sailor had given him for the Shamov Hospital. *It'll be pandemonium there now,* he thought. To find a cab was out of the question; moreover, Klim didn't have two coins to rub together since he had given all of his money to Nina.

Then he remembered that the boxes he had loaded were full with the treasures of the Tsar.

Klim went back to the tramcar and made desperate attempts to open several boxes to no avail. They were well-made, none of them had broken in the crash, and Klim couldn't do anything with his shaking bare hands. What a joke to have a whole tramcar full of valuables at your disposal but neither the time nor strength to get at the treasure.

As he was climbing out again, Klim caught sight of the bundle Commissar Tarasov had given him. He undid the twine and unwrapped a beautifully sculpted bust of a satyr with small blunt horns above a wide forehead. A label glued to the base read, "The Winter Palace, a gift to Alexander III from French industrialists. Sterling silver."

Klim tore off the label and wrapped up the satyr in the sackcloth again. The sculpture was heavy, but at least he could carry it.

5

Shells were still falling now and again on Kazan. Klim watched as one of them demolished the corner of a house, another knocked down a chimney, yet another brought down an old birch tree, which fell with a crash and blocked the road. Shrapnel rained down on iron roofs, and from somewhere came the rattle of machine guns.

When Klim reached the redbrick building of the hospital, his heart was empty of all emotions save one: the sense of a huge, overwhelming disaster swallowing up everything and everyone he saw around him—soldiers, sailors, Tatar women and children, bearded men, and mullahs in their long robes.

He noticed a wagon with a red cross on its side standing at the hospital gate. An elderly nun wearing a stained cassock and round-rimmed spectacles was berating her white horse. "Don't just stand there, you stupid animal! People are waiting, and we're letting them down."

Klim walked past them and into the courtyard, which was full of injured, groaning people—soldiers and civilians. Nurses in bloodstained aprons were rushing to and fro with basins and trays of surgical instruments. The wounded were lying on the ground, and other people were stepping over them as though they were logs.

Needless to say, nobody had any news of Nina.

"How the hell should I know where your wife is?" a medical orderly yelled when Klim ask him. "You can see for yourself what's going on here."

Klim spent a long time walking from one ward to another looking at the faces of all the patients. Finally, he went back into the courtyard where the nun was still trying to go through the gate.

"You're not a mare; you're a lazy dog!" she shouted. "And don't you look at me like that! I know there's nothing wrong with you. I saw you gobbling oats from that other horse's sack."

The horse kept pulling hard at the wagon, which refused to budge.

"Your rear axle is caught in the gate," Klim told her.

The nun went around to take a look. "Oh, dear, so it is!"

Klim helped her to make the horse move back so that she could release the axle. Then the wagon rolled onto the road.

"Which way are you going, soldier?" the nun asked. "I'm going to catch up with the train of carts taking patients to Sviyazhsk."

"Are any of the patients civilians?"

"The head of the hospital had ordered us to take all those in need of urgent help. Sviyazhsk is full of monasteries. There's plenty of space for the wounded. Come with me, soldier. I'm afraid someone might try to steal my mare, Matrona. She's a good horse, and I wouldn't want to lose her. I have to deliver dressings to the hospital. Sit up here beside me on the box. I'm Sister Photinia. And what's your name?"

6

The rain had all but washed away the road, and a slow train of refugees was dragging itself along through the mud in carts, wagons, and wheelbarrows. Everybody moved blindly forward, unthinking, like small fish in a shoal.

In Abbot Village on the outskirts of Kazan, Klim saw a dead man hanging from the tree by his leg, his entire body bruised black and blue. The sailors stopped as they went past, removed their caps, and crossed themselves. For a long time afterward, Klim couldn't bring himself to look up. He couldn't bear the thought of seeing yet more death.

Sister Photinia sniffed and wrinkled her snub, sunburned nose. "Soon, we'll be in Sviyazhsk—it's a special place, a very holy place."

Drowsily, Klim listened to the murmur of her voice, the distant rumble of artillery, and the swish of hundreds of wet bast shoes in the mud. A sharp piece of the satyr sculpture was poking him in the ribs despite the sackcloth wrapping. From time to time, he noticed a shadow flitting along in the bushes at the side of the road and felt his stomach cave in as he thought, *It's an ambush!* A second later, he realized it was only a bird.

His muscles were trembling, and he could feel his pulse beating somewhere beneath his knee. The faces of refugees loomed up and dissolved in the gathering darkness, and all the time, the rounded white rump of the horse shone dimly before his eyes.

It began to rain.

"Drop anchor!" shouted one of the sailors.

They were entering a village. Paying no attention to the indignant shouts of the villagers, people poured into the houses and flopped down wherever they could find a spare corner, falling asleep where they lay.

Klim and Sister Photinia shared a bathhouse with a dozen Red Army soldiers. The air smelled of soap. The window was broken, letting in a cold, damp draft along with the noise of the rain. Occasionally, tiny raindrops hit the windowsill and splashed Klim's face.

"Mama called our pig Contra," came a boyish voice from outside. "And yesterday, the Red soldiers arrested it and shot it behind the barn."

"You should have called your pig Lenin," another boy said. "Then no one would have dared to touch it."

"Quiet, you fool!" said the third boy. "Who do you have billeted in your house? Soldiers?"

"No. Patients from the Kazan hospital. The men who arrested our pig were from the Red Army headquarters."

Klim sprang to his feet and ran outside. It was pitch dark, and he couldn't see the boys' faces.

"Hey, lads," he called, "which of you has patients from Kazan staying in his house?"

The boys didn't answer.

"I'm looking for my wife. She must be here."

"What does she look like?" one of the boys asked in a cautious voice. "We've only got one woman—with curly hair. Mama says she is dying."

Klim started forward and bumped straight into a wooden pillar supporting a canopy.

The boys laughed. "Look where you're going!"

"Please, lads," Klim said, "take me to see this woman."

7

Nina could barely remember how she had gotten to the hospital. Somebody must have helped her. She was dizzy, and her head swarmed with a mixture of real impressions and delirious visions.

A terrible pain in her abdomen, a white ceiling above her, a bright lamp. A doctor in a surgical mask bending over her. "It's peritonitis. My dear lady, you must be operated on immediately."

Then exploding shells and panic. Somebody running by had said, "If we leave this one behind, she'll die. Let's try to take her to Sviyazhsk."

Then a bumpy journey along the road in a shaking wagon and a dreadful pain that had made Nina want to throw herself out and dash her head against the cobblestones. After that, a strange, numb weakness.

She had watched the spruce branches arching over the road like the vaults of a temple, wreathed with sparkling raindrops. Stream rose from the drying rain, and rays of sun slanted through the treetops.

The Cheka arrested Zhora and Elena. Nina was certain of it.

The voice of a doctor again, "In no circumstances should she be given anything to eat or drink."

Now, Nina saw Klim silhouetted against the dark blue sky outside the window. He pressed his unshaven cheek to her hand. "Don't leave me," he whispered.

Then he began to speak in Spanish so quietly she could barely hear him, repeating the same words again and again like a prayer.

15. SVIYAZHSK

1

Sablin took a hip flask of diluted medical spirit out of his pocket and took a sip. His eyes widened. *That's some strong stuff!* He had been drunk every day now for more days than he could count.

Lubochka had seen him off to war in the time-honored fashion: she had shed a few tears, hung an amulet around his neck, and made the sign of the cross over him. "Take care!"

Sablin had no intention of taking care. He was determined not to offer any help to the Bolsheviks. Let them shoot him—he wasn't afraid to die. The medical spirit was effective not only against infection but also, thank God, against his instinct for self-preservation.

The Bolsheviks had not taken Sablin to Kazan; instead, they had put him ashore on the peninsula of Sviyazhsk, home to a number of ancient monasteries and their suburbs. The monks had all been driven out, and the buildings were now being put to use as hospitals and soldiers' barracks.

"Choose any unoccupied house," the commandant told Sablin. "You'll have to set everything up from scratch. They'll be bringing in the wounded soon, so get ready. You'll need to go to the railroad station for supplies and find some assistants as well."

Sablin wandered aimlessly around the empty streets for a while, occasionally shading his eyes to look up at the golden crosses of the churches and the St. Nicholas bell tower with its ancient clock. The watchman—an old man in bast shoes—showed him the convent, prison, and school building. The whole place had been completely devastated and was utterly filthy.

Rounding the mayor's house, Sablin went up onto the cliff and looked out over the river. Dozens of boats were heading toward Sviyazhsk.

"God almighty—" Sablin muttered.

He reached for his flask again, took a sip, and wiped his mouth on his sleeve.

One by one, the tugs, ferries, and rowboats reached land, and soon, the area around the pier was flooded with servicemen and refugees who began streaming up the wooden stairway. The air was full of shouts, the clatter of weapons, and the whinnying of horses.

A little nun wearing spectacles darted around the crowd asking, "Is there a doctor here? Where can I find a doctor?"

"This man's a doctor," the watchman said, pointing at Sablin.

The nun came running up to Sablin, grasped him by the shoulders, and then recoiled in shock. "But the man's blind drunk!"

The soldiers had begun bringing up the stretchers with the wounded. Mechanically, Sablin counted the bodies wrapped in blood-soaked bandages. *Ten, twenty, thirty—*

"Are you a doctor?" a breathless nurse asked him. "Where can we take people?"

Sablin looked at her vaguely. "Go to the school building. It's not far from here. Hey, old man," he called to the watchman. "Show them the way."

I've no medicine, no staff, and no equipment, Sablin thought.

All around, people were shouting, "Morphine! Water! Where's the doctor?"

The nun approached a young man holding a dead woman in his arms. "I'll just get my Matrona from the ferry, and we can get going," the nun told him and ran downstairs.

The man laid the woman on the grass near the fence, took off his long overcoat, and spread it over her.

"Klim, is that you?" Sablin asked in amazement, staggering toward him. "What are you doing here? And who's this?"

He bent down over the woman, studied her sallow, drawn face, and gasped as he recognized Nina Odintzova.

"The doctor in Kazan said she has peritonitis," Klim said, his voice shaking. "He promised to operate on her, but then he ran away."

Sablin slapped at his cheeks, trying to shake himself out of his drunken stupor. He took Nina by the wrist. She barely had a pulse.

Peritonitis, damn it! Sablin thought. *What am I supposed to do about that with nothing but a penknife?*

"If you have a horse," he said, turning to Klim, "you must take Nina to the railroad station. Apparently, there's a hospital there, and they might have what you need for an operation. Otherwise—God help us, man, you can see for yourself."

Klim grasped Sablin's hand. "We do have a horse. Doctor, come with me! You're a surgeon—you—" He fell silent, his shoulders drooped, and his eyes were desperate.

Sablin surveyed the wounded.

Call yourself a doctor? he thought. *You're nothing but a rotten swine. You haven't lifted a finger for days; you were drunk all yesterday and the day before that. By this evening, there will be more than a dozen dead, and it'll all be your fault.*

The medics kept bringing more and more stretchers, and boats scurried to and fro across the slate gray river. The crossing was only just beginning.

The nurse ran up to Sablin again. "Doctor, there are no mattresses in the school. Who's in charge here? Is there anyone responsible?"

Sablin pulled himself together. "You'll have to be in charge for now," he told the nurse. "I'm going to the station to get everything we need for the hospital."

2

All the way to the station, Sablin exasperated Klim with his nonstop chatter. "Let's pray they have an operating room there. Good God! What am I supposed to do without a surgical nurse and assistants? My hands are shaking from the drink."

Sister Photinia urged the horse with her whip, and the wagon moved swiftly on, bouncing over the potholes. Klim held Nina's head on his lap. Her temples were cold, and her forehead beaded with sweat. He kept his fingers under her ear where he could feel her pulse, but every now and then, it seemed to him that everything was over.

What if Nina dies? Klim kept asking himself. *What am I going to do?*

Should he find the wretch who had killed Nina and pay him back in kind?

Dear God, what do you want from me? he prayed silently. *What sacrifice can I offer? Please don't take my Nina away! And if you still need me to do something in return, let me know what. You know me. I'm a man of my word.*

The remnants of the Red Army were now crossing the Volga and gathering near the bridge on the west bank of the river. Every single depot, warehouse, and workshop was packed with soldiers who had no idea what to do or where to go.

The hospital at the station was so full of patients that some of the wounded had even been left lying in the woodshed.

"Go and see Trotsky!" the paramedic yelled at Klim. "If you've got a complaint, make it to him."

He told Klim that Leon Trotsky, the newly appointed People's Commissar for Military and Naval Affairs, had arrived at the Eastern Front after the fall of Simbirsk. Despite all of the propaganda efforts, Russian soldiers were far from eager to fight another war, and Trotsky had assumed the function of Head of Persuasion for the Red Army.

The chances of being granted an audience with the People's Commissar for Military and Naval Affairs seemed about as likely to Klim as securing an appointment with the devil himself. It was even more ridiculous to hope for any help from Trotsky. Nevertheless, Klim left Nina with Sister Photinia and Sablin and forced his way through the nervous crowd surrounding Trotsky's special propaganda train decorated with red banners and the slogans, "Long Live the World Revolution" and "Victory or Death."

Soldiers pressed toward the sleeping car, and the line of Latvian riflemen was barely able to hold back the sheer mass of human flesh that weighed against them.

"What the hell is going on?" the soldiers swore angrily. "We've had no rations for two days."

A disheveled young officer ran along the line arguing with the soldiers and trying to persuade them to leave, but nobody paid him any attention.

"To hell with the lot of you!" they cried. "We've had enough. Let Trotsky come out and talk to us himself."

Suddenly, the sleeping car door clanked open, and a short, wiry man with a pointed beard stepped down onto the footboard. Without a word, he glared at the anxious faces through his rimless pince-nez. The cries of the crowd subsided.

Trotsky unbuttoned his leather overcoat, flashing the scarlet lining, and rolled up his sleeves as though preparing to take on an arduous yet familiar task.

What a buffoon! Klim thought, eyeing the commissar.

"We could have held onto Kazan," Trotsky began in slow, fearsome tones. "The city was abandoned in a state of panic. And what, may I ask, was the cause of this panic? The bourgeoisie had sabotaged the country's economy and its network of communications, supplies, and transport. You felt cut off from the rest of the world. You thought help would never come. And you began to think our cause was lost. Am I right? But never forget, the Russian proletariat is on your side. The Red peasants won't let you starve. Tomorrow, you shall have bacon, boots, matches, and tobacco."

Comrade Trotsky was a great propaganda specialist. He didn't blame the retreating soldiers for the catastrophe unfolding around them. Instead, he explained his version of events to them and promised them that tomorrow, all would be well.

The faces in the crowd brightened as they stood listening, spellbound.

"The workers of the world are closely following everything that is happening here on this section of the front," Trotsky thundered. "We have a radio mast that can receive signals from the Eiffel Tower in France, the Nauen transmission site in Germany, and, of course, Moscow. We send back the most important news for immediate publication in the world press. What will the workers of Liverpool think of you? What shall we report to the dockers of Marseilles? Are we going to have to tell them that Russian workers are cowards ready to betray them at the first sign of failure? Or will you show them that the world has yet to see more steadfast warriors for the happiness of the international proletariat?"

Suddenly, Trotsky jumped off the footboard, headed toward Klim, and grasped him by the shoulders.

"Brother!" he exclaimed. "You and I need freedom. The Bolsheviks have given us freedom, and we must not allow the landlords and capitalists to turn us back into slaves. Tell me, who are you?"

"I'm a journalist from Argentina," Klim began. "My wife is very ill—"

Trotsky looked at him with keen interest. "So, you've come here to report on revolutionary events? Can I see your press accreditation?"

Klim put his trembling hand in his overcoat pocket and took out a colorful document in Spanish. Trotsky examined the elaborate handwriting and the large red seal.

"I need your help, sir," Klim said. "You have a hospital car in your train—and doctors—"

Trotsky gave the paper back to him, embraced him, and raised his voice to speak to the crowd. "You see? The people of Argentina are with us. They are keen to hear the outcome of our struggle, and they have sent their correspondent to us. Of course, we shall show them solidarity. We shall help our Argentinean comrade in every possible way."

Trotsky ordered his aides to take Klim and his sick wife to the hospital car and mounted the footboard again.

"We pledge our allegiance to the Republic of the Soviets. We are prepared to defend the revolution with our lives. Forward to Kazan! Hurrah!"

"Hurrah!" came the exhilarated roar of the crowd.

It seemed to Klim that he could hear his pulse beating in his temples. Not a single person on the railroad platform had the faintest notion that the paper he had shown to Trotsky was a certificate confirming that Klim's overcoat had been made at the studio of Mr. Tréjean on Florida Street in Buenos Aires.

3

Trotsky's attendants laid Nina on the table under the circular ceiling lamps, and Klim brushed a moist strand of hair from her forehead.

"Do you realize who's going to be operating?" Sablin asked, coming up to him. "Gabriel Mikhailovich! Even a luminary like him has been mobilized."

Klim turned his head and saw a haughty-looking old man in a white coat.

"Anyone who is not authorized to be here must leave immediately," the old man snapped.

The nurse pulled at Klim's sleeve. "We'll call you in later."

He went back onto the platform and was distracted by a huge crater in the middle of it.

"The Whites dropped a bomb on the station, hoping to destroy Trotsky's train," explained Sister Photinia, coming up to join Klim. "But they missed."

He nodded without looking at her. She placed something heavy down next to him. It was the satyr statue. The twine had come undone, and the long silver nose and beard protruded from the sackcloth.

"You forgot this," Sister Photinia said. "It was so heavy that I could barely carry it."

"Thank you," Klim said.

"Well—" She hesitated. "Dr. Sablin has arranged for some medical supplies from the hospital to be sent to the wounded back at the monastery. Matrona and I will deliver them."

"I see."

Sister Photinia patted him on the shoulder. "Get in touch with us if anything—well, you know—"

4

Klim was making an ant run along a blade of grass. Once it got to the top, he turned the blade upside down and made it start over again.

What are they doing with Nina now? Klim thought. *Have they cut her open?*

It was hard to imagine that such a thing could happen to a live human being. It was unbearable to admit that Nina's fate was in the hands of people who were largely indifferent about whether she lived or died.

Klim heard the sound of footsteps on the platform but didn't turn his head. Were they coming to tell him it was all over?

No, it was only some sentries and medical orderlies.

All Klim could do now was put his trust in God. The surgeon operating was called Gabriel, like the angelic messenger, and that was probably a good sign.

As a teenager, Klim had served as an altar boy in the church. The high-school boys liked to make an impression, taking the collection bowl around the left-hand side of the church where the female parishioners stood. The service boys were allowed to join the priests behind the altar screen to gain a "better understanding of the church service," but it was there that Klim had parted company with the Orthodox faith once and for all. One day, he had caught the priest taking snuff on the quiet. On another occasion, he had seen the deacon polishing off the last of the sacramental wine. After that, Klim and his friends took to sneaking the occasional nip from the bottles of altar wine themselves.

Klim wore a cross around his neck like an amulet and generally spoke to God in a familiar tone. He grumbled at him when something was wrong and went to church when he needed something. It didn't matter to him whether the church was an Orthodox or a Catholic one.

Now, Klim felt as though everything he was going through was a punishment for his lack of faith back then. He was experiencing that fiery torment that his divinity teacher at school had promised awaited all lapsed believers.

5

Again, Klim heard rapid footsteps behind his back and felt himself tense in anticipation.

"So, what have we here?" Trotsky asked, pointing at the satyr peeping out of the sackcloth.

"It's nothing—" Klim said. "A souvenir. I bought it at the market."

Trotsky squatted down and gazed at the sculpture. He and the satyr looked rather alike: both had a broad forehead and a similar style beard, only one had no pince-nez, and the other lacked horns.

"Well, well, Comrade Argentinean," Trotsky mused. "Perhaps you could let us have your souvenir?

I think we might be able to use it for propaganda purposes."

Klim nodded. "Sure."

"And one more thing," Trotsky added. "The doctor told me that your wife needs to stay in the hospital car for some time. I don't want you to be left without anything to do, so we'll provide you with some socially useful work. Seeing as you're a journalist, you can write us leaflets about the dangers of religious indoctrination. Comrade Skudra will explain to you what you need to do. He's a great expert on propaganda. Come with me, and I'll introduce you to one another."

Klim rose to his feet, overcome by the unexpected and joyful news. Nina had survived the operation.

He had asked God for a sign as to how to repay him if Nina's life were spared, and now, Klim had his answer: he was now to write sermons denouncing God's divinity for these devils in the Red Army. He felt sure that the Almighty was enjoying the irony immensely.

16. LUCIFER

1

EL CUADERNO NEGRO

Klim Rogov's little black notebook

Nina is quite weak and can barely lift her head. Her hair has been cut short, and now, she looks like a sick little pixie with her distant eyes, thin neck, and willowy arms. But she already wants me to come and sit with her. She looks forward to my visits and makes a fuss if Skudra keeps me away for too long. This makes me happy. If my darling is annoyed about something, then that means she still has an interest in this world and has no plans to go drifting off to the next.

She's worried sick about her family. Zhora and Elena were plotting something, it seems, and were caught in the act. As for the old countess, we've no idea what's become of her.

Nina has decided to go back to Nizhny Novgorod as soon as she's well enough. She asked me if I would go with her as if I have a choice. I have more important questions on my mind, however. What if Trotsky goes off somewhere with his propaganda train and takes Nina along with him? What if the Whites try to bomb the train again?

I don't want to move Nina from the hospital car—she's getting the sort of food and medical attention here that the wounded and sick elsewhere can only dream of.

She has no right to this special treatment, and the only reason she's still getting it is because Trotsky hasn't yet had time to reconsider the decision he took in a fit of melodramatic generosity. Now that I've sold my soul to the devil, all that remains is for me to carry out my part of the bargain as best I can in the hope that he'll forget about us.

Our angel, Dr. Gabriel, has said that as long as there are no complications and Nina gets plenty of rest, she ought to recover. Sablin asked to have a look at the patient and went into raptures over her perfect stitches.

"I'm green with envy," he said as he came out of the hospital car. "What I wouldn't give to be able to suture a wound like that!"

I only hope that the Red Army will stay put for the time being, and Nina will have time to get better.

The military camp in Sviyazhsk is swelling and growing before our very eyes. Every day, new trains bring reinforcements, but the Reds have taken no military action apart from shelling some of the White steamships since most of the recruits don't know how to handle their rifles and still need to be trained.

Apparently, the Whites are not strong enough to move up the river Volga. Skudra told me there are plenty of White agitators making speeches in Kazan, but very few soldiers prepared to defend the city. The only troops the Whites can count on are the Czechs, but they're not ready to die to save Russia. All they want is to get out of here as soon as possible.

I spend my days with the propaganda boys in the former telegraph station. We design posters, put together an army newspaper, and assemble newsstands. We also cut printing paper into strips and trade it for raw vodka. The local peasants glue these strips of paper over their windows to prevent the glass breaking from the bomb and shell blasts.

My job is to write the texts for propaganda leaflets debunking religion under the supervision of Skudra, a former pharmacist's assistant from Riga.

For example, what is the secret of the sacred, luminous inscriptions that sometimes appear on the walls of churches? The truth of the matter is that there's no miracle involved at all—just simple chemistry. All you need to do is take some softened beeswax, add white phosphorus, and then use this mixture to draw mysterious symbols that will glow in the dark.

Similarly, if you dissolve white phosphorus in carbon disulfide and dip the wicks of candles in the solution, the solvent will evaporate, and the phosphorus will ignite spontaneously in the open air. That's how you produce the miracle of Holy Fire.

The people who have gathered in Sviyazhsk are like hordes of army ants. Here the survival of every individual depends on the success of the colony as a whole. Anyone who breaks away from their group will find themselves dead in no time. These "strays" quickly meet their deaths either at the hands of the Reds, the Whites, or the "neutral peasants" whose motto is "A plague on both your houses." Nina and I have found refuge and protection with the Red Army, so we call it "our army." I am sure the majority of my "comrades in arms" feel much the same way as we do.

Individual desires or ambitions count for nothing now; the collective is our only hope. God help anyone admitting that they want personal comfort or to be safe, well-fed, rested, and satisfied! As a result, we're all leading a double life. We're all pretending to be devoted ants—proud carriers of straw and dead caterpillars. But deep down inside, we're still humans, and the more human you feel, the more difficult it is to pretend that instead of a heart, you have a dorsal vessel in your chest.

It's a perfect recipe for daily misery. The worst sort of slavery you can imagine. You are bound not by shackles but the realization that if you refuse to be an ant, you will lose the support of the colony, and then you might as well be dead. You have to live your life not as you want to but as the collective dictates. The irony is that you are part of it and, therefore, your own slave.

What should we do then? Toughen up the outer shells of our bodies? Sharpen our mandibles? Arm ourselves with poison? We'll definitely need it at some point. And we'll have to master the art of mimicry—to pass ourselves off as ants. According to zoologists, small spiders and grasshoppers use this form of self-defense very effectively.

2

All day long, Nina stared through the gap in the white curtains at the stinging nettles growing by the fence, the sentry walking to and fro, or the mangy stray dog that had made its home on the station platform.

"Dogs aren't allowed here!" the nurse cried. "Get it away from here!"

She didn't know that Nina had been secretly pinching off pieces of bread and throwing them out of the window. When you can't get up and are bored to death, there are still the pleasures of petty disobedience to be had.

Behind the thin screen that divided the hospital car were two sailors with broken legs who were acting up too. They constantly told ribald jokes and talked about their girlfriends in the most colorful language and shocking detail. For some reason, Nina found this unbearably funny.

Maybe it was just her nerves. The doctor had told Nina not to laugh for fear of bursting her stitches, but now, the slightest tomfoolery would reduce her to feeble, debilitating laughter. She asked the sailors to stop, but they continued to tell each other their outrageous stories, claiming a good laugh is the best cure for any ill.

Klim would come after lunch. The nurses were glad to see him because he always brought them something—a bouquet of daisies picked at the fence, a few cigarettes, or some other small gift. Nina felt proud to see the nurses fussing around Klim but annoyed at them for taking up her precious time with him. Skudra never let him get away for more than half an hour.

When Klim came to visit Nina, he would sit beside her, and the two of them would talk in whispers about how wretched and terrified of losing each other they had been during their separation.

Nina never admitted that Fomin had visited her, but she did hint that she and Zhora had taken part in preparing the uprising.

"Why?" Klim gasped. "Why did you risk so much for the sake of someone else's interests?"

"They are not someone else's," Nina protested. "There is something in this world worth fighting and dying for."

"What exactly is it that you are planning to die for? Some 'Just Cause' nobody will remember in ten years?"

Nina didn't know what to say when she realized how upsetting it had all been for Klim. He had sacrificed everything he had had to save her, and it appeared to him that she hadn't been taking her own life seriously.

"Zhora and I couldn't just sit on our hands," she said, looking down. "If you do nothing, you begin to feel that you don't exist."

The next day, Klim brought Nina the ring from the safety pin of a hand grenade, which consisted of two rings joined together.

"I've found something that symbolizes us in a funny way," Klim said. "Individually, we're nothing but zeros, but together, we become a symbol of infinity and perfection." He straightened the ring into a figure of eight. "We must never part from each other again."

Nina asked Klim to put the symbol of infinity onto the chain that held the "key from his heart" as well as a small anchor that had been made for her by one of the sailors. The sailor had said it was a symbol of hope, a sign that one day Nina would return to her home harbor.

I wish I could go home and find my brother, she thought.

Klim kissed Nina goodbye and ruffled her cropped curls—he found her boyish hairstyle amusing. "See you tomorrow."

He paused at the screen, pretending he had something to say but had forgotten what it was. In fact, he was just trying to prolong the final precious moments of his visit.

"Well, bye-bye for now."

Nina heard his footsteps, the creak of the door as it closed, and then a knock at the window. Then there were more farewells, waves, smiles, and faces traced in the dusty glass of the car window.

Nina stared after him as he made his way down the empty platform.

"You're truly lucky to have made such a rare catch," said one of the nurses.

3

The Red Army troops were lined up on Kafedralnaya Square. As a foreign journalist, Klim had a prime view of the parade from the roof of a staff automobile.

It was a curious sight to see an army of atheists parading against the backdrop of ancient churches. The clouds were riding high in the sky, the golden domes shone brightly, and a little further along next to the cliff's edge stood a veiled monument to a revolutionary hero.

"The Volga River must and will belong to the Soviets!" shouted Trotsky from the stage in the middle of the square. "There are far many more of us than the Whites. Our forces in Sviyazhsk number nearly fifteen thousand men."

I don't suppose anyone knows that for sure, thought Klim.

The Red Army was difficult to quantify, taking into account mass desertion and the lack of uniforms and documents. Some regiments had no more than two or three dozen men, and they only lent half an ear to their commanders.

Klim had talked to the mobilized Red Army soldiers and the captured Whites, who were peasants recruited by force from the local villages. No one wanted to fight.

"What the hell are we doing here?" they complained. "They promised us peace!"

At the first opportunity, both Reds and Whites were ready to surrender just to have a chance to avoid any fighting.

"Hey there!" someone called.

Klim turned his head, and his heart grew cold as he recognized Pukhov standing on the footboard of a staff automobile.

"I saw you from miles away perched up here above the crowd," Pukhov said. "Where have you been all this time?"

He pulled himself up and sat next to Klim.

Klim was feverishly racking his brain, trying to come up with a story that would satisfy his former boss. Pukhov knew that Klim wasn't here representing an Argentine newspaper, and if he found out that Countess Odintzova was being cared for in Trotsky's hospital car, he would have a fit. Why should a class enemy have special treatment while wounded Red Army soldiers were rotting to death in the overcrowded field hospitals?

Klim told Pukhov about what had happened to the tramcar that had taken him away from the bank in Kazan.

"It was derailed, and I suffered shellshock."

Pukhov looked suspiciously at Klim. "Oh, really? So, what are you doing now?"

"I've joined the propaganda team."

"I need you back. We can't do without an interpreter. I managed to get my Chinese soldiers away from Kazan and bring them here. Unfortunately, we weren't able to get the valuables out of the bank, and the Whites have got their hands on all of it. By the time we got here, all we had were thirty pots and twelve spoons between two hundred men. And the supply officer still yelled at us, telling us we had no right to have even that. Come with me when the rally's over. I need to take the Chinese to the bathhouse. I'm afraid they'll get lice and come down with typhus."

"Raise your hands," demanded Trotsky, "if you want the land go back to the landlords."

The crowd stood silent and motionless, only a stray goat scratched its burr-covered flank against the corner of the stage.

"Which of you is prepared to slave away in a factory from dawn to dusk? Which of you wants a coddled few to live in mansions while others huddle ten to a room?"

The faces of the crowd became stern, their jaws rigid.

A village idiot by the name of Maxim tried to elbow his way toward the stage. "That's my goat—give it back, for the love of God!"

The Latvian guards grasped Maxim by the arm and his goat by the horns and dragged them both away.

Trotsky took off his cap and wiped his perspiring forehead. "Does anyone have any questions?"

"When will you allow God to exist?" came the distant voice of Maxim.

Trotsky grinned, descended from the stage, and walked up to the covered statue.

"Here is your god!" he proclaimed, ripping away the canvas.

The crowd winced. The statue he had revealed was the bust of a satyr on a marble column.

"For centuries, priests have told people stories about Lucifer," cried Trotsky, pointing at the French industrialists' gift to Alexander III. "Religious bigots have always said that he is the source of all evil. But why was he the figure that they were all so terrified of? The reason is simple—he was the first revolutionary. Lucifer refused to obey a decrepit God and rebelled against his despotism. So now, let this monument to his proud spirit stand in the very place where priests and misguided fools have groveled on their knees for centuries. This legendary figure never bowed down to a tyrant despite the threat of expulsion from paradise and damnation forever and ever."

The orchestra struck up "The Internationale," the Bolshevik anthem.

Klim cast a sidelong look at Pukhov staring dumbstruck at the satyr.

"How did that end up here?" Pukov asked. "That's one of the sculptures from the bank, don't you remember? It fell out of its box, and Tarasov gave it to you."

Suddenly, there was a roar of engines, and two planes emerged from the clouds.

"The Whites!" shrieked a voice from the crowd.

The ranks of parading soldiers fell into complete disorder, and Klim and Pukhov dived down from the roof of the automobile and crawled underneath it.

"They're going to bomb us!" wailed Pukhov, covering his head with his hands.

But instead of bombs, the planes showered Sviyazhsk with leaflets and disappeared with rifle shots ringing out after them.

Klim reached to take one of the leaflets, but Pukhov snatched it away. "Don't you dare to touch it!"

He began hastily to gather up the leaflets, crumpling and shoving them into his jacket.

"Don't panic! Fall in!" yelled the commissars, no less terrified than everybody else.

Klim crawled out from under the automobile and ran off behind the churchyard toward the road leading to the railroad station.

Pukhov is bound to ask Trotsky where he got the satyr, thought Klim. *And then they'll figure out between them that I am a deserter, a looter, and an imposter.*

The conclusion that they would come to would be inevitable: the swift dispatch of two executioner's bullets—one for Klim and one for Nina.

4

It was growing dark over the station. A choir of Red Army soldiers sang a song, and a small locomotive was being shunted along the sidetrack. Nina and the sailors were playing a game of Battleship, and she was giving them a thorough thrashing.

"Stop!" the nurse shrieked suddenly. "You can't come in here now! Where do you think you are?"

There was the sound of footsteps and the crash of the wheeled table. The room divider was flung aside. Klim rushed up to Nina and bent over her.

"I have to take you away from here," he whispered. "Put your arm around my neck."

"What's happened?"

Klim didn't answer but picked Nina up along with her blanket.

The nursed tried to stop him. "I'll tell the doctor!"

"You can tell the pope for all I care."

The sailors stared at the two of them, their eyes wild with incomprehension.

Klim carried Nina out of the car and onto the cart waiting for them next to the platform.

"We're going to go to Sablin," he said, panting as he laid Nina in the hay and covered her with her blanket. "You can't stay here. If anything should happen, you must tell everyone you don't know me. You're just a refugee from Kazan."

Nina grasped his hand. "What is it? What's happened?"

"I'll tell you everything later. This is a bad road, I'm afraid. I hope you won't be jolted too much along the way."

Klim kissed her forehead and sat down on the box next to the driver.

"Here, take these," he said, handing the driver a handful of cartridges. "But mind," he added in a menacing voice, "keep your mouth shut about who you've taken and where, or I'll wring your neck."

Nina had never heard him talk like this before.

5

When the cart reached the hospital that had been set up in the ancient Cathedral of the Assumption, it was already dark. The room was full of wounded people lying side by side on the straw. Here and there, haggard faces loomed in pools of candlelight.

Sablin, disheveled and unshaven, showed Klim where to put Nina.

"Don't worry. I'll look after her," the doctor said.

After the sterile hospital car, Nina was now laid on a bed of rotten straw along with a hundred lice-ridden men in stinking bandages.

Sablin squatted down beside her and brought a candle up to her face. "How are you?"

"Fine," Nina said in a weak voice. But she was more dead than alive after her journey along the bumpy road.

Klim adjusted her blanket. His head was in a whirl. What was he going to do now? Maybe he could waylay and kill Pukhov to stop him from spilling the beans? Had he done the right thing by moving Nina here? *Yes, you've found the ideal solution,* Klim thought. *She'll come down with typhus in no time now.*

The nurse called Sablin away to see another patient, and he went off, leaving Klim sitting beside Nina and holding her hand.

"Who is that?" she whispered pointing at a fresco depicting a holy knight with the head of a dog.

Stunned, Klim stared at it for a while. He thought the knight looked like Anubis, an Egyptian god from the realm of the dead. How had it ended up here in an Orthodox church?

Suddenly, a shell howled, and the cathedral walls shuddered from an explosion close by. All of the candles went out, and the room was plunged into darkness.

"What was that?" voices wailed in the gloom. "They're firing at us!"

"Quiet!" Sablin shouted. "Don't panic!"

Klim bent down to Nina. "I'll be back soon. I have to find out what's going on."

He picked his way between the bodies on the floor and went outside.

Everyone had run for shelter, and the street was empty. From somewhere over by the railroad line, the roar of artillery fire could be heard, which jarred shockingly with the serenity of the clear starry sky and the golden domes that gleamed in the moonlight.

"Klim, is that you?" someone called.

He flinched. "Sister Photinia?"

"I'm glad I've found you." She grasped Klim by the wrist and began to pull him after her. "You have to get rid of that devil of yours. You're the one that brought his statue here, so it's your responsibility. I'd try to remove it myself, but it's too heavy."

Klim looked around. "The Reds will notice it's gone."

"I don't care. Take it away from here!"

They hurried off to Kafedralnaya Square.

Hiding the satyr is not such a bad idea actually, Klim thought. *That way Pukhov won't be able to prove that it's the same sculpture that I took from the bank.*

But when they got to the edge of the cliff, they found the monument to Lucifer gone and the marble pillar lying on the ground broken into three parts. Klim's heart skipped a beat. Could Pukhov have taken the bust already? A moment later, he realized that the monument had been destroyed by a shell blast and that the satyr had probably fallen over the cliff.

"I hope I don't end up breaking my neck," Klim muttered as he clambered down the slope, his feet sliding on the wet grass.

"Can you see it?" Sister Photinia called from above.

The satyr had become lodged in bushes a little farther downhill. The nun went down by the steps and offered Klim a gunny sack. "Put it in here. Let's drown it in the river and rid Sviyazhsk of this evil pagan spirit once and for all."

Klim gave a wry smile. Throwing away thirty pounds of solid silver wasn't the brightest idea he had come across.

"Well, actually, sister, this sculpture belongs to the science museum," he said off the top of his head. "There was a man in Smolensk Province with horns, and we made a portrait bust of him for scientific purposes. But Trotsky took it and decided to call it Lucifer."

Sister Photinia crossed herself. "Gracious heavens, what a dreadful thing! I don't suppose that poor fellow could take his hat off in church without people laughing at him."

"Let's bury the sculpture in the sand," Klim said. "When Trotsky leaves, we'll dig it up and give it back to the museum."

They made a shallow pit in the sand on the beach.

"It's like burying a body," Sister Photinia whispered. "Anyone passing by will think we've killed someone and are getting rid of the evidence."

Klim smoothed the sand so that there would be no sign of any disturbance and put down a large piece of driftwood to mark the spot where the satyr was buried.

He and Sister Photinia went back up the steps. Over to the west, the sky was ablaze, and artillery fire and rifle shots rang out incessantly. Evidently, there was a fierce battle taking place over by the station.

"I think the Whites have captured the bridge," Sister Photinia said.

Klim nodded. The unfortunate meeting with Pukhov had turned out to be an unexpected stroke of luck. If it hadn't been for his former boss, he and Nina could well have been at the station when the Whites had attacked.

Skudra and Pukhov will be looking for me, Klim thought. *And if the Reds win this battle, I'll be accused of desertion.*

The best thing would be to make a run for it, hide in the woods, and wait for the Whites to arrive. But how will Nina survive in that overcrowded army hospital without him to help her? Of course, there was Dr. Sablin, but he had so many other things to do that there was no counting on him.

Klim said goodbye to Sister Photinia and went back to the cathedral. On the porch, he met Sablin, who had stepped out for a smoke.

"Where have you been?" the doctor said angrily. "Nina is frantic with worry."

The nurses had already relit the candles. Klim made his way back to Nina and sat down beside her.

"There's a big fight going on by the station now, isn't there?" she asked. "Is that why you took me away?"

"I didn't know that the Whites were about to attack," Klim said, exhausted. "That was just a coincidence."

Each new salvo reverberated under the dome of the cathedral, causing the huge chandeliers to swing from the ceiling, their ancient chains creaking ominously.

"They look like the scales in the ancient Egyptian frescos," Klim said. "The god Anubis used them to weigh the hearts of the dead and separate the righteous from the sinners. If the dead person's heart was lighter than a feather, the symbol of truth and justice, then the soul would go to the realm of the dead in peace, but if the heart was heavy with sin, then it would be devoured by a monster."

17. THE MEANING OF LIFE

1

Klim was arrested at dawn. The Red soldiers entered the cathedral, kicked him awake, and ordered him to go with them. Nina wanted to run after them, but when she tried to get up, she fainted from the pain.

She came around to find Sister Photinia patting her cheeks. "There, there, my dear. Are you all right?"

Painfully, Nina attempted to sit up. Sunlight was pouring through the cathedral windows, lighting up the stone arches overhead, the enormous, solemn figures of the saints on the frescoes, and the mass of suffering humanity on the floor below.

Nina's head was spinning. "Where's Klim?" she asked.

Sister Photinia took off her glasses and wiped them with the hem of her cassock. Her face seemed blank and eyeless to Nina.

"The Whites have been on the march for two days," the nun said without looking at Nina. "They got tired, and their attack got bogged down. Now, the station and the area around it has been devastated. Half the propaganda train was burned—a shell hit a fuel tank right next to it. So, you were very lucky, my dear, that you got away."

Weak as she was, Nina felt a cold chill of presentiment. The nun's face swam before her eyes.

"The Reds survived in the end," Sister Photinia said. "Although, goodness only knows how they did it. I think they find it hard to believe themselves. After all, the Second Petrograd Regiment—including all the Chinese soldiers—deserted the battlefield. They boarded a steamer reserved for Trotsky, but they didn't get away in time. They're all going to be court-martialed."

"Those scum deserve everything that's coming to them," said a soldier next to Nina who had lost an arm. "Good for Comrade Trotsky. He knows what he's doing."

There was a ripple of agreement among the wounded soldiers.

"Some of us are out there getting torn to pieces while others are hiding behind women's skirts."

"They should be given the choice: face a firing squad or go into battle and put their faith in God. Who knows? Some of them might even come out alive."

Nina stared at the damaged, angry men around her. *It isn't enough that they have their own troubles,* she thought. *They want to compound others' misery too.*

For them, Klim was a traitor and a deserter. He had chosen to fight for Nina, not the Red Army, and, therefore, deserved to be executed.

Suddenly, they heard the rumble of carts and the neighing of horses outside. Sablin burst into the cathedral as pale as a ghost, limping hurriedly to the operating area screened off by some makeshift blankets hanging from a rope.

"Nurse!" he cried, putting on his overalls. "There are more wounded outside. We need to sort out where to put them."

"But where—?"

"I don't know, and I don't care!"

"Dr. Sablin," Nina called. "What's going on?"

A volley of rifle shots came from the street, and Sablin winced. The grumbling voices of the wounded died down, and the only sound that could be heard was a pigeon fluttering high up in the dome.

"Why are you all staring at?" Sablin shouted. "They're executing deserters. Right here on Kafedralnaya Square."

Nina bit down on her fist, and Sister Photinia gasped. Another volley of shots rang out. Sablin limped off without looking back.

Another volley came and then another. Sister Photinia stroked Nina's hand. "You must pray, my dear."

Nina looked at her wild-eyed. "To whom should I pray? No one is listening to us."

"The Lord sees everything and helps all those who suffer," Sister Photinia said in a firm voice. "Do you see that saint with a dog's head? That is St. Christopher. A very handsome young man he was. He didn't want the girls to tempt him, so he asked God to make him as ugly as a dog. Miraculously, God granted his wish."

Nina pulled her knees to her chest. Klim had been arrested as a deserter for not taking part in yesterday's battle, and that meant…oh, no…God, please, no!

Sister Photinia rose, shaking off the pieces of straw that clung to her skirt. "I'll go and find out what's happened."

2

Nina stayed sitting up and awake until evening, unable to move a muscle. Her body felt frozen, and her scattered thoughts ran through her head like dry sand.

Here in Sviyazhsk, it felt as though they had all fallen through a hole in time and gone back to the Dark Ages, a time when it was considered an act of glorious righteousness to ask the Lord not for love and joy but for the face of a dog to prove one's faith. If you didn't believe in what you were supposed to and if you weren't ready to kill or maim for that belief, then you deserved to die.

Sister Photinia had still not returned, but a wounded soldier who was able to walk brought news.

"Trotsky lined up all the deserters," he said, "and ordered every tenth man to be shot as a warning to the others. The commissar announced that this method had been very effective in improving discipline in the Roman army."

As night fell, Nina was still sitting and gazing into the flame of the oil lamp on the duty doctor's desk. She felt as though the souls of the executed soldiers were roaming the cathedral among the rows of sleeping men. They hadn't yet grown used to death. They might try to take a cup of water or say something to one of those still left alive. But their weightless fingers passed straight through these earthly things, and their voices couldn't be heard.

She felt a tap on her shoulder and turned to see Sister Photinia.

"Your young man is alive!" the nun whispered excitedly. "He's at the station with the Chinese. He gave me this note for you."

Her hands shaking, Nina took the piece of paper but could make out nothing in the darkness.

"He asked me to tell you, 'Wait for me, and I'll come as soon as I can,'" the nun said and put a small white feather into Nina's hand. "He also asked me to pass on this gift for you, but I don't really understand what it means."

"What's happening at the station?" Nina asked, tears of joy pouring down her cheeks.

"Trotsky has gone to Moscow. He ordered the train master to hitch up the remaining cars to a new engine, and off he went. Apparently, there's been an attack on Lenin. He was seriously wounded by a terrorist."

3

EL CUADERNO NEGRO

Klim Rogov's little black notebook

The Chinese saved me from the firing squad. They threw themselves at Trotsky's feet and, with my help, informed him that they had only deserted because they hadn't understood the orders they had been given, and if the last remaining Chinese interpreter is killed, their detachment will be totally unable to fight.

Trotsky took mercy on us, but he gave the order for Pukhov to be shot for failing to organize effective communication between the military command and his soldiers. The poor fellow didn't even try to defend himself. He just stood there in front of a firing squad, barefoot with his shirt hanging out of his trousers, weeping silently. The revolution has betrayed him—its most loyal disciple, the man who loved it more than any other.

The Chinese were determined to take me with them. Ho, the new commander of the battalion, assigned two Chinese men to guard me, but Skudra had no intention of giving me up because he wanted me to write propaganda leaflets about the attempt on Lenin's life. So, he also sent his soldiers for me, and while the command was deliberating what to do with me, the guards and I had a fine old time playing cards. As a result, I won myself a very nice pair of German binoculars.

On September 2, 1918, the matter was settled when Trotsky came back from Moscow bringing two Chinese interpreters, so I've stayed with Skudra.

Thinking back, my work at *La Prensa* newspaper seems like a distant dream. I remember Buenos Aires and our building with its gilded dome topped with the statue of Athena who represented the freedom of speech. The feisty editorial staff, the atmosphere of fervent competition—where are they all now?

I—like everybody else in Sviyazhsk—am in the business of building communism. There's only one problem: we are trying to make a beautiful palace using plans for a city crematorium. Alas, it doesn't even occur to my colleagues for a fraction of a second that there is something seriously wrong with their blueprints. The piles have been driven into the ground, the cranes are already lifting pipes over the building site, and it's too late to start the project from scratch—the Bolsheviks have invested too much time, money, and effort into it. They'll realize their mistake later when the red ribbon has been cut and the orchestra has struck up its triumphant fanfare. Only then will the Bolsheviks see that instead of a paradise for the living, they have built a palace for the dead in which they too are doomed to be cremated alive like poor old Pukhov.

I don't dare state this obvious truth or try to prove my colleagues wrong in any way. The devil has given me the fright of my life, and I'm not going to forget our deal again. He is keeping his end of our bargain, so I must keep mine.

4

The most terrible events often become myths, and every myth needs a hero. The hero's job is to perform miracles and suffer for the people. Rising from the dead is always a handy trick to have up your sleeve as well.

Lenin's miraculous recovery from his recent attempted assassination has transformed him into a hero of epic proportions, and I've now become an expert at creating the myths that will fix him on this pedestal for time immemorial. I write that Lenin works tirelessly for the revolution day and night despite the hole in his lung. A man of his caliber and intellect is born only once every thousand years. Workers all over the world adore him, and delegates from villages flock around the Kremlin to pay homage to their great leader. His name will resound through the centuries, his achievements are immutable and immortal, and so on and so forth.

My Sunday school education and the time I spent serving in church as an altar boy has turned out to be of some use after all. I have developed a flair for writing panegyric material of an almost religious fervor. The thing that truly amazes me is that my over-the-top, ironic toadying is taken at face value and applauded as a resounding success. The more colorful and vulgar my turn of phrase, the more satisfied Skudra is with my work.

I never imagined that anything I ever wrote would be distributed to a hundred thousand readers, yet that's precisely what is happening now. Yesterday, Skudra sent a courier off to Moscow with a manuscript of mine entitled *The Great Leader of the Rural Poor*. For my pains, I received the princely fee of two hundred rubles and a looted toiletry bag replete with a bar of soap, a box of tooth powder, a new toothbrush, and a Gillette razor.

ELVIRA BARYAKINA

The railroad station—or rather, what's left of it—is overrun with children selling trading cards with pictures of Lenin on them. Some soldiers buy them for good luck in battle, others for good luck in their career, but most take them back home and pin them on the walls above their beds.

All of this makes Nina and me laugh. Not very wholesome laughter, it's true, but there's no other kind to be had at the moment.

Nina is still in the Cathedral of the Assumption. She's getting better and has already been out to join me on walks to the bluff overlooking the river. In spite of everything, she wants to go back to Nizhny Novgorod and find Zhora. I've tried to talk her out of it but to no avail. She just gets upset and takes offense when I do.

"If you had a brother," she said, "would you leave him behind?"

I realize that we have to find Zhora, but I've been reading newspapers from Nizhny Novgorod. The situation there does not sound promising.

The revenge of the proletariat for the attack on Lenin will make the entire bourgeoisie shudder in horror.
—*Izvestia* (The News)

From now on, the clarion call of the working class will be a call for hatred and revenge.
—*Pravda* (Truth)

We shall kill our enemies in their hundreds. Let thousands be killed; let them drown in their own blood. We shall avenge Lenin's sufferings by shedding rivers of bourgeois blood.

—Krasnaya Gazeta (The Red Gazette)

What is this? Some sort of mass hysteria? A witch-hunt? Nina and I are bourgeois by definition. We're exactly the type they're out to kill. We need to stay away from the cities, particularly Nizhny Novgorod, where someone might recognize us, but nothing will stop my stubborn Nina.

All that remains for me to do is to take each day as it comes and try to be happy as I can for as long as I can. The Whites have stopped attacking Sviyazhsk, which is a blessing. Trotsky has brought back plenty of medicine and food, and my beloved is safe for the time being. What else could I hope for?

Yesterday, I was on my way back to the station when I saw dark clouds on the horizon and heard the sparrows making a frantic commotion in the bushes. A storm was coming. I hurried along hungry, penniless, and helpless, head over heels in love with my woman. I was already dreaming of the next time I would be able to sit with her on our windy bluff, admiring her beauty and secretly thanking God for all his blessings.

I got soaked to the skin on my way back to the station. Half-blinded by the rain and out of breath, I found shelter under a canopy and stood there wiping my face with my hands and shaking the raindrops out of my hair. And blow me down with a feather if I didn't feel just fine! I felt on top of the world.

Two little girls were standing there with baskets full of mushrooms. They looked at me, and I imagine they were trying to guess what this bedraggled soldier was feeling so happy about.

Nothing special, little ones. I'm just reveling in the true meaning of life.

5

Sviyazhsk was swept by an epidemic of a particularly virulent form of influenza. Dr. Sablin was one of the first to fall ill and was sent back to Nizhny Novgorod. The disease spread so rapidly that soon the number of influenza patients far exceeded the number of wounded.

Klim almost died from the disease, but it did, however, save him from the fate that befell his colleagues during the storming of Kazan. On the way, the ship carrying the propaganda boys hit a mine and sank with no survivors.

The Bolsheviks had transported naval guns down from the Baltic Sea and shelled the Whites who were helpless to retaliate. All they had were light field guns with half the range of the Red's artillery. The Czechs and Slovaks boarded their trains and left Kazan, and the city was immediately taken by the Baltic and Black Sea sailors who were greeted with rejoicing in the outskirts and silence in the deserted streets of the city center. Thousands of civilian refugees had left with the Whites as they retreated. The Red Volga Flotilla and the troops moved east up the Kama River, and the camp at Sviyazhsk gradually dispersed.

Klim wondered why the Red Army, which resembled nothing so much as a horde of bandits, was succeeding in overpowering the Whites. Did the

Whites really have no resources at their disposal to defend the Volga region?

It seemed that this was indeed the case if only because he and others had chosen to work for the Bolsheviks or to remain neutral. Some had made an informed choice while others had simply followed the crowd. The fall of Kazan was a natural consequence of this.

6

Sister Photinia managed to get Nina and Klim on board the hospital ship *Death to the Bourgeoisie*, which was bound for Nizhny Novgorod.

"Oh, you poor things," she sighed, looking at them sadly.

When the steamer was about to leave, she smuggled the village fool Maxim on board. He had agreed to carry a heavy bundle onto the ship in exchange for a piece of hard tack.

"Take your devil away with you," Sister Photinia whispered into Klim's ear. "I don't know if it really is an exhibit from a museum as you say, but it's brought nothing but misfortune to Sviyazhsk. It's a good thing we didn't throw it into the river—it would probably have killed all the fish as well."

The hospital ship sailed out of the harbor to a chorus of sirens from the other steamers. Nina and Klim found a place to sit down at the side of the boat, which was lined with sandbags. To the right of them was a machine-gun nest, and to the left were boxes of ammunition. Hidden behind their backs was the satyr carefully wrapped in cloth.

Klim was still suffering from a terrible migraine after his bout of influenza. The only thing that soothed it was to lay his head on Nina's lap and have her smooth his brow and stroke his head while he gazed up at the curls on her cheek, which reminded him of the curlicue flourishes of traditional Russian Khokhloma folk designs.

We are making a very bad decision going back to Nizhny Novgorod, thought Klim. But they didn't have any other option. They couldn't leave Zhora behind.

18. THE PROLETARIAN POETS

1

Zhora knew that whatever they did, he and Elena must not go home. Postromkin would have passed their names to the Cheka as "enemies of the people," and now, it would only be a matter of minutes before they would run them to earth.

They hid behind the sheds at the power station until morning, and it was only then that Zhora realized that the Bolsheviks might arrest Nina and the old countess instead of them.

How could he have been so stupid? Like some intrepid freedom fighter, he had planned to set fire to the *Lady*, but all he had done was put his own family in danger.

Now, the Cheka will shut down the cooperative, Zhora thought, terrified. *Mr. Fomin will arrive at Crest Hill and walk into an ambush.*

Elena was thinking the same thing. "We have to warn Nina," she said firmly.

They crept up to the house from the river side and almost ran straight into a patrol sweeping the thickets on the slope.

"Run!" Zhora whispered to Elena.

They wandered the city all day. They had nowhere to go. All of their friends were involved in the anti-Bolshevik conspiracy, and Zhora and Elena didn't want to compromise them. One deft pull on the thread, and the Cheka could unravel the entire plot.

As they were walking past the Bubnov Hotel, Elena had an idea. "Why don't we spend the night here?" she asked. "We can say we're young proletarian poets from Moscow who have been attacked and had all their belongings stolen."

The ancient former doorman who had now become the manager of the recently nationalized hotel told them to go to the Housing Department of the Regional Executive Committee. "You need a permit from them. Then we can talk."

"But it's already too late, and everything is closed," Zhora said. "If you won't let us in, we'll just spend the night right here on the porch."

"I'll call the Cheka!" the old man retorted.

After much swearing and grumbling, he said he would let the proletarian poets in if they brought him a bottle of vodka. "Go to Nikolaevna. She sells tobacco at the corner. She always has booze for sale."

Nikolaevna—an unkempt, toothless old woman—took Zhora into a dark doorway and handed him a large vial.

"Just the right strength," she said. "Can you smell the alcohol? I'm not out to swindle you unlike some I could mention. There're plenty of people these days who palm their customers off with water or worse."

2

After he had taken Zhora's bribe, the old man took a lantern and led Zhora and Elena up the dirty stairs to the second floor.

"As though I had nothing better to do than traipse around after the likes of you," he grumbled. "Nowadays, guests don't pay for their rooms anymore. They just bring me permits from the Housing Department. They don't even tip me for service either. And folk don't want to work for nothing, so the staff has all left. I'm the only one left here."

The old man opened the door and put down the lantern. "Here you are."

Elena looked in and gasped. Inside the dimly lit room, dozens of soldiers lay snoring side by side on rows of tightly packed trestle beds.

"But there's no room for us in here," Zhora protested.

"Aristocrats, are you?" the old man grinned. "Tell me, what's wrong with sharing a room with the delegates of the Red Army Congress? They're leaving tomorrow anyway. You can sleep right here," he said pointing to a cramped couch with a curved back.

Somehow, Elena squeezed herself onto it while Zhora settled himself below her on a dirty rug on the floor.

He couldn't stop thinking about Nina. Had she been arrested? Had she had a chance to escape?

Zhora didn't sleep a wink. He spent all night composing epitaphs in his head.

The first one was for the hotel manager:

Here lies a whistle
and a cap,
and a very
     kind
          old chap.

Another was for Zhora himself:

This young man never did fit in.
He wasn't one to hide or squeal.
A Cheka job was not for him.
He'd never give up his ideals.

A bullet to his head one night
Set his idyllic spirit free.
He flew up to the angels bright
To treat them to his poetry.

Where should he and Elena go in the morning? To Osinki without documents? Or should they try to find a place for themselves in Nizhny Novgorod? But how would they manage to get ahold of food? Zhora had only twenty rubles left.

Oh, what an idiot he was! He had tried to save the *Lady* and ended up destroying them all.

3

Zhora woke Elena at dawn, and they went downstairs. During the night, Zhora had decided that he would try to persuade the old man to take them on as staff in return for permission to live in some cubbyhole, but the hotel manager was nowhere to be seen.

They waited in the dim lobby, fingering the keys of a broken pianola in the corner.

"Oh, for goodness sake, where has the old fellow gotten to?" Zhora puffed impatiently, jumping up to sit sideways on the counter. "Elena...the old man..." he whispered, his eyes wide with horror.

Zhora jumped down onto the other side of the counter. The manager was lying on the floor under the leaf of the writing desk, which was why they hadn't noticed him at first. Next to him lay an empty vial.

Elena looked behind the counter. "My goodness, what happened? Has he taken poison?"

"To think that I wrote an epitaph for him yesterday," Zhora said in a trembling voice.

He could see what had happened at a single glance. The manager's face was bluish, there were signs of bruising on his skin, and a sickly sweet odor could be smelled coming from his mouth.

Zhora had seen plenty of victims of methanol poisoning in the morgue of the Martynov Hospital. It was virtually indistinguishable from alcohol in appearance and smell, and cunning traders often peddled it to unsuspecting customers. Some drunks died immediately, some slowly in agony, and anyone who survived would be sure to go blind.

Thunderous footsteps echoed on the staircase. Zhora gave a start, but it was too late to run. The next minute, the lobby was swarming with Red Army delegates.

"We're leaving," one of them said and threw his key to Zhora. "I'll be damned if I ever stay in your hotel again. It's crawling with lice."

"As if any of the other hotels are any better," his friends laughed.

"I don't give a damn. I want to check out."

While Zhora stood staring dumbly at the soldiers, Elena opened the drawer, took out the inkwell, and began to write in the registry book.

"Your signature, please," she said, handing the book to the delegates. "If you can't write your name, then put a cross just here."

She smiled brightly, as though she had no idea there was a dead man lying under the desk.

Finally, the delegates left.

"Zhora, we have to hide the old man," Elena whispered, pointing to the back room.

They found the key on the counter, opened the door, and laid the old man's body on the sagging couch.

"This must be where he lived," Elena said, glancing at the spirit lamp on the table and the sheepskin coat hanging up behind a cloth curtain.

"We have to go," said Zhora.

"Where?"

"I don't know—anywhere. Just as far away from here as possible before they catch us."

Elena shook her head. "If we become vagrants, we'll be picked up by the Cheka in no time. Let's stay here. If anyone asks who we are, we can tell them we're employed to service the rooms."

"What about the body?"

"We'll just leave it somewhere. Do you think the police will care who the old man is and where he came from? There are lots of old people dying on the streets these days."

Zhora covered his face with his hands. He couldn't believe that any of this was actually happening.

4

They found a wheelbarrow in the shed. Zhora took the old man to the Peter and Paul Cemetery, and while nobody was looking, he dumped the body beside the fence.

The days passed, but nobody noticed the manager was missing. Zhora and Elena did his work, and it never occurred to any of the hotel guests that they were impostors. However, they had no money, so they began to sell off the old man's belongings, from the sofa to the sheepskin coat.

Zhora was horrified by his descent to this brutal, cold-blooded pragmatism, but what could he do? Should he run into the street shouting that they had killed a man and were now selling off his possessions?

They were so hungry and desperate that they felt as though their bodies had been partially abandoned by their spirits. They had forfeited their right to live and had severed all ties to their families and friends. At night, Elena wept because she couldn't even go to prison to take food to her parents.

But for the time being, nobody bothered them. Only the lice made their lives unbearable.

After speaking to some women at the market, Zhora prepared a foul-smelling ointment to rub on his skin, and Elena began to wear a magic charm on her wrist. They tried everything they could from naphthalene to camphor oil and spent all of the money they got from selling the old man's skirting boards in the battle with the lice. Both science and witchcraft proved powerless.

Zhora wrote a poem and submitted it to the local newspaper.

It seems the devil has connived
To have the lice eat us all alive.
We'd dearly like to pay them back,
But lice don't make a pleasant snack.

The editor bought Zhora's poem but rewrote the first line as "It seems the Whites have now connived."

Zhora and Elena split the money and went to the public bathhouse.

5

The dark, steamy room smelled of soap and soaked birch switches. Naked, swearing men fought for a place beside the hot tap. Zhora gazed horrified at their swollen feet and scrofulous backs raked with scratch marks.

Then he saw Fomin's bearded face looming out of the steam.

"Just look who it is!" Fomin roared. "I thought you'd left the city long ago."

Zhora was beside himself with joy. Fomin told him that Nina had managed to escape. The neighbors had heard that the Cheka men had been furious about it, but nobody knew what had happened to the old countess.

"The Bolsheviks have nationalized our mill," Fomin said as he soaked and wrung out a back-scrubber made from a piece of bast fiber. "I can't go to Osinki now," he added in a quiet voice. "I don't know how my workers are coping."

"Where are you living then?" asked Zhora.

"At Mitya's."

At that moment, the door swung open. A crowd of uniformed soldiers was standing on the threshold.

"There he is!" shouted one of the men, pointing at Fomin.

The soldiers took them outside in their underclothes without allowing them to get dressed. People queuing at the ticket box stared at them nervously.

Elena ran out of the bathhouse with her face flushed and her wet hair hanging down her back. She dashed over to the Cheka truck. "Wait!" she cried.

"Take this one as well," a Cheka officer with a hooked nose ordered.

The soldiers pushed Elena and Zhora into the back of the truck, open to the heat of the blazing sun.

"What have you done?" Zhora shouted at Elena. "Why did you have to give yourself away?"

She buried her face in his shoulder. "If you're going, I'm going with you."

6

Zhora had shown his naivety again. When he had put his arms around Elena, he had shown the Cheka officers exactly where to find the chink in his armor. When he refused to identify himself or to testify against Fomin, who was accused of illegal trade and counter-revolutionary activities, the guards brought the weeping Elena into the interrogation room.

"So, this is your fiancée, is it?" the investigator sneered. "Then, Mr. No-Name, let us start from the beginning. What's your name, and what exactly is your relationship with Fomin?"

The investigator stepped up to Elena and hit her hard in the face. Zhora rushed at him, but the guards held him back, pinning him by the arms.

"Have you had enough?" the investigator asked in a quiet voice. "Or do you want to see some more?"

He aimed another blow at Elena.

"Don't!" yelped Zhora. "I'll tell you whatever you want! Don't touch her—please!"

Afterward, he couldn't remember what he had said. They kept banging his head against the wall and the windowsill until he saw stars and felt as though he were about to black out.

"Shoot him," the investigator said, and the guards dragged Zhora into the courtyard, leaving Elena in the room.

7

There were about twenty prisoners in the backyard. Zhora stood frozen, staring blankly at them. His throat was swollen from crying, his twisted joints ached, and his knees shook.

He barely recognized Fomin sitting against the wall with his face and beard a bloody mess.

"Come here, kid," he called.

Zhora approached, sat down, and rested his head against the cold stones of the wall.

What are they doing to Elena?

"We weren't very good conspirators, it seems," Fomin said. He spoke with a thick lisp as he had had his teeth knocked out during interrogation. "I suppose we did what we could."

In a state of near delirium, Zhora heard one guard say to another that for several days, the Cheka had been carrying out mass arrests in the city. Somebody had noticed that the commander of the garrison had been sending almost all his soldiers to distant villages as a preventative measure to control rebels, and almost none had been left in Nizhny Novgorod. It had looked suspicious, and it turned out that the commander had actually been a White underground leader. He had named several accomplices under torture, and three days before the rebellion had been due to happen, it had been foiled.

The sun hung motionless over the tops of the apple trees in what had once been the merchant's garden.

Is this it? Zhora thought in a daze. *Are they really going to kill us?* He covered his face with his hands and wept.

"There, there…" Fomin whispered and stroked his hair. But Zhora sobbed hopelessly, the sound of Elena's desperate scream still reverberating in his head.

The guards kept bringing new prisoners into the yard, all of them mauled and torn, near hysterical, and utterly broken. But Elena wasn't among them.

Whispers went through the crowd of prisoners like the wind in the dry grass.

"The Allies have promised to stand up for us. The Red Cross won't allow such an outrage—"

"I heard of a case where they sentenced a colonel to death but forgot to shoot him—"

At sunset, the guards brought Zhora and several other prisoners to the edge of the Pochaina Ravine. Instead, of a verdict, a Cheka man read them an article from a newspaper:

The criminal attempt on the life of our ideological leader, Comrade Lenin, has compelled us to renounce sentimentality and implement the dictatorship of the proletariat with a firm hand. There will be no more words. We will respond to every murder or attempted murder of a Bolshevik by shooting hostages from among the bourgeoisie. The blood of our comrades—dead and wounded—demands vengeance.

The last thing Zhora saw before he was shot was two guards dragging along the body of a girl with long, blond hair. They took her to the mass grave that had been prepared for the rest of the prisoners and threw her in.

19. THE NIZHNY NOVGOROD FAIR

1

Even from a distance, Klim could see that Nizhny Novgorod was in a bad way. Its buildings looked as though they had sunk into the ground, and there wasn't a soul to be seen anywhere. Even the river bank was deserted.

One of the deck hands told Klim that the Bolsheviks had tried to organize a "socialist trading center" there in the hope that the peasants would exchange their crops for industrial products. But the peasants had refused to bring food into the city for fear of being robbed by the policemen or bandits who were virtually indistinguishable from each other. In any case, there were no industrial goods for exchange since all of the factories were at a standstill.

The fair's pavilions had been turned into barracks for troops arriving in Nizhny Novgorod for mobilization. There had been a general breakdown in discipline with soldiers going absent without leave, drinking, and picking up prostitutes, and a number of fires had broken out. Soon after this, the Regional Executive Committee had moved the soldiers out of harm's way and quartered them in the city.

Then the locals had moved in and stripped the fair down to its bones. Many of the houses in the surrounding villages now boasted metal roofs made from shop signs emblazoned with surreal expressions such as "Crystalware" and "Poultry and Wildfowl."

The *Death to the Bourgeoisie* docked at the pier. A group of young Soviet officers in clean new military tunics and smart boots greeted them at the gangway.

"All passengers must present their identification cards," they shouted. "As of the twenty-second of August, anyone entering or leaving Nizhny Novgorod must have a pass."

Nobody paid any attention to them.

"Go on then," said the captain angrily. "I've got five hundred wounded and sick people on board. Why don't you arrest them all? But you'll have to carry all those who can't walk by themselves."

As Nina and Klim walked onto Safronovskaya Square, a woman wearing a muslin mask to protect against disease ran up to them.

"Do you have any flour?" she asked.

Klim shook his head.

"I'll give you twenty-two rubles for a pound," said the woman, looking at the heavy bundle in his hands.

Nina gasped. "How much?"

"Fine—" the woman corrected herself hurriedly. "Thirty then."

The Bolsheviks had decked the square with red flags to celebrate the capture of Kazan. The cab drivers had vanished. Street children were now selling matches not by the box but singly.

While the nurses were loading their patients onto carts, Nina and Klim walked onto Rozhdestvenskaya Street and boarded a half-empty tram.

The city was a mass of blue and gold with the leaves of the trees glistering against the clear, brilliant sky, but there were very few passers-by. Everyone they met was wearing a mask.

"We should do the same," Nina whispered. "Then nobody will know who we are." She took out her handkerchief and began to tear it into pieces.

Klim nodded. *Once people's faces are covered,* he thought, *they are no longer people. They become ghosts.*

All of the houses in Ilinskaya Street had been hung with new signs: "Headquarters of the Commander of the Red Volga Flotilla," "Maritime Investigative Commission," "Red Army Supply Office," and so on. The Rogovs' house had now become the "Board of the Nizhny Novgorod Naval Dockyard." The marble bears were gone, and the blunt muzzle of a machine gun protruded from the open window on the second floor.

Klim felt as though he had been witness to a rape. He told Nina to wait for him by the newspaper stand.

"You look after the satyr. I'll try and find out what's going on."

The front porch was boarded up, and Klim had to enter through the back door. Immediately, he was hit by the smell peculiar to all government offices: a mixture of ink, molten sealing wax, and wet felt boots.

The corridor was empty. In the kitchen, Klim found five hunched figures sitting over desks, wearing masks.

"Do you know where I can find Dr. Sablin?" Klim asked. "He was at the front, but he got sick and was sent home."

"Are you here on official business?" one of the figures asked. "No? Then go away and don't bother us."

Perhaps Sablin is dead, Klim thought. *If so, where can we go? How can we find Zhora and the others?*

As he went back outside, he saw Nina sitting on the ground with her face buried in her hands, sobbing.

He ran up to her. "What is it?"

She pointed to a newspaper stuck up on a display stand. The headline on the front page read, "Rightful Vengeance for the Attempt on Lenin's Life," followed by a list of murdered hostages. On the list, printed alongside the names of the former city governor, merchants, officials, Tsarist army officers, and priests, were the names of Elena, her parents, Zhora, and Fomin.

Klim stared at Nina, who sat crushed with grief. Then he turned to read the newspaper again.

Anyone contributing to the counter-revolution, including those who harbor counter-revolutionaries, will be summarily executed.

"We have to go," Klim urged Nina. "We can't stay here."

She nodded and tried to gather the strength to get to her feet, but her body wouldn't obey her. Eventually, Klim helped her up and clasped her tightly to him.

"I have no one left but you," Nina sobbed.

We should never have come back to Nizhny Novgorod, Klim thought, holding the satyr tightly. *We have no friends or allies here.*

There were plenty of Nina's old acquaintances who would have liked nothing better than to see her arrested. As for the others—who could Klim trust? He was unlikely to find anyone willing to risk their lives for a relative of a counter-revolutionary.

They had to find a place for the night before it got dark. If they were on the street after the nine o'clock curfew, they could end up being arrested or shot, depending on the revolutionary convictions of the patrol that stopped them.

Before the revolution, homeowners had advertised rooms for rent in the windows of their houses, but now, that private ownership was forbidden, all such notices had disappeared. It was futile to try and ask around—people shied away from strangers, fearful that they might be carrying disease or even that they might be Cheka spies.

"We'll have to go to the fair," Klim said to Nina. "I hope we'll find something there."

2

The Nizhny Novgorod Fair used to be the heart of the city with its streets, shopping malls, churches, theaters, and underground galleries. Now, it lay in ruins with all of its windows broken and its roofs dismantled. Ashes and brittle, dry leaves blew around the deserted streets.

Klim felt as though his childhood fantasy had come true.

"What would happen," he had asked his mother as a child, "if everybody disappeared and there was no one left except you and me?"

A stray dog passed with its head drooping, not even stopping to look up at them. A startled mob of crows flew up from the dry basin of the fountain in front of the Fair House.

Klim took Nina to the Figner Theater. As a child, he used to come here to watch almost every show. Every single pane of glass in the building had been broken, and the wide stairs were covered with debris.

Klim opened the door to the auditorium. Columns of light came in through holes in the ceiling, full of circling specks of dust. The chairs had gone, and a huge broken chandelier lay in a heap on the floor. All that remained of the theater's former opulence was a crimson curtain hanging so high above the stage that the looters had been unable to reach it.

"Let's take up residence in the royal box," Klim said. "We might be homeless, but we can at least try to live in style."

Nina nodded silently.

After they had shared the last of the bread they had brought from the boat, Klim went backstage, fiddled with the levers and cables, and managed to lower the dusty bullet-ridden curtain.

"My friends and I used to hang out with the stagehands when we were little boys," said Klim. "We'd bring them beer and dried salted fish, and they'd let us watch the show for free."

He made a bed out of the curtain, laid Nina in it, and lay down beside her.

"You go to sleep. We'll think of something tomorrow."

She closed her eyes. "When I was a little girl, I read *Dracula* by Bram Stoker, and I told Zhora the story. He made up a special prayer. 'Dear Lord, have mercy on my parents, on Nina, on me, and on all Christians. Let me be a better person and deliver us from the bloodsuckers.' I told him that the bloodsuckers didn't exist and would never come to Russia, so he stopped saying the prayer. And now the bloodsuckers have killed him and drained the life out of the rest of us."

Klim felt hopeless. How could he comfort her? What could he do to try to heal this new wound?

Thankfully, Nina fell asleep quickly. She was exhausted and did not even have the strength for tears.

The silence was so intense that Klim felt he had gone deaf. The fair was normally a noisy place with loud, bustling crowds, orchestras, and shopkeepers praising their wares—lambskins, apricots, and rice, which they called "Saracen grain."

Klim sank into fitful, sun-filled dreams, waking up with a start to total darkness and a sepulchral silence.

Life in the city had become impossible, yet Klim and Nina couldn't leave without documents. And soon winter would set in. They might be able to hide from the Cheka, but there would be no way of evading the cold.

3

The following day, Klim and Nina went to the train station to find out if there were any railroad tickets for sale, although they had no idea where they might go. Where did the land of the Soviets begin and end? What was going on in the rest of the world? All the international headlines on the newsstands were about strikes and anti-government demonstrations. "World revolution is coming!" they claimed.

As Klim had feared, it proved impossible to buy a rail ticket without a permit from the Cheka.

He spoke to the bagmen and found that it was still possible to get into one of the boxcars without a ticket if you were quick and cunning. But typhoid spread by lice was rife inside the heated boxcars. The bugs would crawl from one person to another, and all of the train's passengers might end up getting infected. The only safe way to travel was in the cars reserved for the Bolshevik officials.

Had Klim been alone, he would have tried jumping on a train, but he didn't want to put Nina at risk. If there was a crush to get on, her stitches might burst open, and there would be no one to provide her with medical care.

They decided to cut up the satyr and sell the pieces of silver one by one to make it last. Klim spent all of the money he had earned from his propaganda work on a hacksaw, cut off the satyr's beard, and sold it to a jeweler trading in precious metals (evidently under the patronage either of the police or the Cheka).

They had to sort out a place to live and find a source of income urgently, but it was almost impossible to find a room to rent. Nina had no documents and, therefore, couldn't get an official registration permit—and without this, she was liable to be arrested on the spot.

4

Nina was amazed at Klim's ability to adapt to any circumstance. He found a rusty flatiron, took off the handle, and made it into a tiny hotplate that they could use to cook food by heating it from beneath by burning old theater posters and wood chips.

Klim had the vital ability to laugh at misfortune rather than complain about it. What did it matter if they had no spoons or forks? Real gauchos ate with their knives.

"If you eat with a fork," Klim told Nina with a wink, "then you'll need a plate. Before you know it, you'll be wanting tables and chairs, and your problems will never end. You can't carry all that with you when you're out on the pampas. A gaucho should be as free as the wind."

They made a tent out of the theater curtain—luckily, there were needles, thread, and scissors in Klim's toiletry bag. One day, he found a potted palm tree in a bucket that somebody had thrown out, and he brought it back to the theater. Once they had cleaned up the bucket, they had something to carry water in, and they kept the palm tree for decoration.

Klim sat beneath it and told Nina stories about his adventures in faraway countries.

She liked to admire the fine shape of his hairline, which pleasingly circumscribed his high forehead. She liked the way his stubble grew too, forming handsome curves at his cheeks with a narrow strip under his lower lip.

"Kiss me," Nina said.

Klim recoiled in feigned horror. "Don't you know, ma'am, that kissing is a source of infection? I read that on a notice at the Babushkin Hospital."

He kissed her anyway, and quickly becoming dizzy with passion, he held her tightly to him.

"Easy…easy…it's too early now," he whispered.

Reluctantly she obeyed, delighted that although she was thin and only wearing a faded, second-hand dress, Klim still found her desirable.

"Thank you," she whispered—*spasibo*.

He laughed. "According to the new regulations, you should now say 'merci' instead of 'spasibo' because in old Russian, *spasibo* means 'God save you,' and it would appear there is no longer a God—at least not in this country."

Klim didn't allow Nina to leave the theater. The danger that she might run into a patrol was too great. Every now and then, military units marched along the bank of the Oka River a stone's throw away from the theater. Besides, it was likely that criminals and street children were hiding in the ruins of the fair. Klim shuddered to think what they might do if they saw a woman out walking alone.

"I'll see to everything," Klim promised Nina. "Your job is to get better as soon as possible."

But it was hard for Nina to spend all day by herself. Every morning, Klim covered his face with an improvised flu mask and went to look for food while Nina wandered around the theater or made up and performed her own plays on the stage. By turns, she pretended to be an unfortunate heroine and played the roles of her suitors and oppressors. Sometimes she imagined herself dancing the tango with Klim. Sometimes she shed bitter tears thinking of her family.

If someone had told her a year ago that soon she would be a homeless pauper living in a ruin, she would never have believed them. How long was this all going to last?

One day, Klim told Nina that he would have to be out all that night. "Trust me, sweetheart. It's something I have to do. Please don't ask me why."

She panicked and flared up in anger. "Have you gone out of your mind, leaving me alone all night?" she shouted. "What if—"

He winced as though her words had physically wounded him.

"I'm sorry, but I have to go now. Be careful and take care of yourself."

Nina had a terrible night. First, she sobbed, imagining that Klim would never come back and she would be left all alone. Then she remembered what she had said to him in her fit of anger. *He'll never forgive me,* she thought. In a moment of weakness, she screamed and wailed like a desperate child, her cries echoing all around the theater. She stopped as suddenly as she had started, shocked at the sound of her own voice in the silence.

As he had promised, Klim came back in the morning, tired and smelling of tobacco smoke. He crawled into the tent and took Nina in his arms. The sun was shining through the old theater curtain and bathed everything inside with a reddish light.

Nina stroked Klim's hair. "Where have you been? Why don't you want to tell me? Are you mixed up in something bad?"

"I've brought us some bread," he said without opening his eyes.

"So, you won't tell me?"

Klim took a deep breath. "I've been gambling. I know how you feel about it, but we've got to treat it as if it's a new job. I'm sorry, but I can't think of any other way of surviving."

5

Nina viewed gambling with horror as a kind of incurable disease. Her father had been an addictive gambler and quite capable of blowing the family's entire savings in a single night, forcing Nina's mother to borrow money to feed the children.

"I hope you know what you're doing," Nina said to Klim. Her heart sank at the thought that he might gamble away the money from the satyr at the card table.

Now, Klim slept during the day. Nina took his binoculars and went upstairs. From the top floor, she could look out over the grounds of the fair, the Oka River, and the opposite bank. In the distance, the military trucks would drive by, their sides daubed with propaganda slogans:

We welcome the donation of mattresses to the hospitals.
Tailors! Lend your services to make uniforms for the Red Army!

One day, Nina saw a banner demanding that the town's citizens surrender their binoculars.

You won't be getting these, thought Nina. She needed her binoculars to watch what was going on at her house on Crest Hill on the other side of the river.

Klim had tried to find out what had happened to Sofia Karlovna but without success. He had found out, however, that the Bolsheviks had converted Nina's mansion into a telephone exchange and telegraph station. They had cut down the trees in the orchard and put up radio masts all around the house. Everything Nina had once had was now lost—her books, her paintings, and even a reminder of the beauty that had once surrounded her.

By mid-October, the satyr had lost half its head, but the money from the silver together with Klim's occasional winnings was barely enough to buy food that was now being sold at outrageous prices. The nights became colder, but they had no stove and couldn't make a fire in their tent. Their only tool was a hacksaw, so they couldn't build a better shelter for themselves.

Nina crept around stealthily, talked in whispers, and imagined Cheka operatives lurking in every shadow. One night, she had a dream: it had snowed, and the Cheka had tracked Klim down by following his footprints. She woke up in a cold sweat.

I can't live like this anymore, Nina thought. *We have to do something. We have to change things.*

But now she shrank instinctively from the thought of resistance. Memories of that hard blow to her stomach and of her brother being shot were fresh in her mind. Her instinct for self-preservation told her not to stick her neck out, to lay low, and to let no one know of her existence.

In any case, except for Klim, I have no one to live for anymore, thought Nina. *Not even myself.*

20. LUCK OF THE DRAW

1

The underground gambling den, where card players and crooks of every stripe would meet to try their luck or ply their trade, was at the Lukin Tavern next to Kunavino Market. Klim entered the semi-dark room full of drunk people roaring with laughter and found himself a place at the bar.

The waiters hauled up buckets of raw vodka from the basement, and the punters drank it with soaked dried peas and bread sprinkled with salt. Underage prostitutes with hungry eyes did their best to lure crippled bagmen. War invalids always had money because they were allowed to carry more baggage than others.

A pawnbroker sitting next to Klim complained to the chief of police that the cold weather was coming, but the authorities weren't allowing citizens to stock up on firewood. In return, the chief of police complained about the sailors of the Red Volga

Flotilla, who had moved into their winter quarters in Nizhny Novgorod and were raising hell.

"Don't issue them with warm overcoats," the pawnbroker advised. "Then they'll stay quiet until spring."

The police chief nodded. A moment later, he showed his new friend a handful of ladies' rings under the table. "How much will you give me for these?"

Klim recognized the jeweler who had bought pieces of silver from him. The man put on his dark glasses and gestured to Klim, inviting him to take a seat at his table.

"Ladies and gentlemen, let us start the game," he pronounced.

He was playing alongside a blue-eyed woman with a yellowing ermine flung over her bony shoulders. Klim was paired up with a red-faced army man whom everybody addressed by his patronymic, Petrovich. The man held a briefcase in his lap, a sign of state authority. Apparently, he was some kind of a local bigwig.

Klim quickly realized that the jeweler and his blue-eyed girlfriend were cardsharps. They might play into his and Petrovich's hand for a while, but in the long run, they always won. Klim's red-faced partner cursed under his breath and chain-smoked.

The great Don Fernando, the chief gambler of the Shanghai underworld, had taught Klim that with a few exceptions, all cardsharps use three basic strategies:

Card tricks, when a cheat pulls a card from out of his sleeve.

Signaling, when a partner or a specially placed spy passes information to the cheat about his opponents' cards using secret signs.

Marked cards, when cheats would make tiny marks on the cards with a piece of graphite hidden under a fingernail or with a needle.

But no matter how hard Klim tried, he was unable to figure out how the sharpers were managing to swindle him and Petrovich.

The jeweler had begun to shuffle the deck once again when suddenly, the electricity went out.

"I need light!" he shouted. "Quick! Bring me some candles!"

His girlfriend lit a match, and Klim noticed that the jeweler covered the deck with his hand.

Finally, a servant brought in a large candelabra. Klim squinted at the matchbox with its clumsy printed cover. It was crude work, probably made in a basement in the Millionka district.

"Could I have a few matches?" asked Klim.

Just as he had thought, the matches were tipped with phosphorus—a method that had been out of use in Europe and America for at least twenty years.

Well, gentlemen, thought Klim. *You're about to see a magic trick.*

He went to the lavatory, sprinkled the lining of his pocket with water, and put the matches in it. Then he returned to the card table.

Soon, the faces of both the jeweler and his girlfriend had turned sour.

"Let's tally up," grumbled the jeweler, taking his dark glasses off.

Klim took his winnings and went outside. The street was full of drunkards loitering and singing dirty songs, ignoring the curfew.

"Wait!" Petrovich called, running to catching up with Klim. "How did you do it?" His face looked strained in the moonlight.

"Our opponents were playing with marked cards," Klim said quietly.

"Surely not!"

"They were using phosphorus. It's how people make the mysterious symbols that appear on the walls of churches at nighttime. Phosphorous glows in the dark, so as long as the light was on, only someone wearing dark glasses could see the signs. That's why our cardsharp panicked when the power went off."

Klim explained to Petrovich that once he had gotten wise to the ruse, he had put the wet matches in his pocket and dipped into it repeatedly to touch the matches and leave smears of phosphorous all over the deck. Soon, the jeweler could no longer see his marks and had to give up.

"Why didn't you expose the rotten scoundrels?" Petrovich asked.

"At the moment, I'm more interested in money than justice."

"And how did you manage to win anyway? Were you cheating too?"

Klim shook his head. "If you want to cheat, you have to be well-prepared. I didn't have time today."

"I say, will you teach me how to play cards?"

"If you pay me, I will."

2

The next evening, Klim was told not to try to be smart. If he moved in on other people's targets, he would get his neck wrung. Now, he had no choice but to play with occasional penniless visitors and from time to time with Petrovich. Klim's new partner would stake his own money, keeping the winnings to himself, but giving Klim food in return for his instructions in gambling.

Petrovich treated Klim with wary curiosity.

"I see those casino people for what they are," he said, looking at the other card players. "I come here to beat these bastards down, at least at cards, but I can't figure you out. Are you a former bourgeois? You don't look like one." He eyed Klim's frayed outfit doubtfully. "The devil only knows who you are. But one thing's for sure—you're a cheat and a son of a bitch."

Petrovich was a fanatic of the first water who believed absolutely in the infallibility of the Bolshevik Party. He was completely disinterested in money. When he had been younger, he had never had a penny to his name, and now, everything came his way without any effort from him because of his position. He toiled away morning and night, taking everything on himself, jumpy and crotchety, yelling at his subordinates, forgetting to eat, and chain-smoking lethally strong, hand-rolled cigarettes. He was a man equally capable of signing a death sentence and giving away all of his possessions to the poor.

Petrovich never spoke of worldly matters. He always steered the conversation around to his favorite subject: preaching Bolshevik ideology even when he was sitting at the card table.

"The revolution was a historical necessity," he said. "The vast majority of the population lived in poverty with neither the right nor the ability to alleviate their fate. There, take that! King of clubs. The Tsarist police arrested the mechanic from our factory shop. Why? His only fault was that he gave shelter to revolutionaries who had escaped from exile in Siberia. He was locked up for his kindness."

"Nothing much has changed since then," the pawnbroker grinned. "Except that now the Cheka arrests those who give shelter to Whites."

"And rightly so," Petrovich barked. "Those who oppose the people deserve to be punished. What's this—are you bidding misère now?"

Playing cards was Petrovich's only weakness—and an understandable one. When everything inside a man is going at full blast, he needs to let off steam once in a while. Petrovich had asked many times if he could be sent to fight at the front, but his superiors didn't allow him to go because there was no one who could replace him in his present civilian post.

Klim noted rather sadly the new signs of the times. The revolution had replaced one aristocracy with another, but the essence of Russian despotism remained unchanged. In the past, people could be threatened with the words, "Are you against the Tsar?" Now, they heard, "Are you against the people?" In reality, both phrases meant more or less the same: "Woe betide you if you encroach on the privileges of the ruling class."

Things were much the same as they had been for centuries. The population still had no civil rights and retained a medieval sense of servility, believing that the people should serve the rulers and not the other way around, no matter what the propaganda posters proclaimed about the dominance of the working class.

One night, the Cheka raided the tavern. They took the card players out onto the street and began to load them onto a truck, but Petrovich stopped them taking Klim with them.

"This man is with me," he told the Cheka officers.

When they left, Petrovich got into his car. "It's a shame they've shut down the tavern," he said. "But it's for the best. These crooks aren't our people."

Klim said nothing. His last source of income was now gone.

"I'm leaving for Moscow," Petrovich said. "I'll be away for a month or so. Maybe we'll meet again when I get back."

3

Klim crawled out of the tent and shivered. God, how cold it was outside! Overnight, the theater had turned into an ice palace with its walls covered with frost.

Nina followed him out. "One of these days, we won't wake up."

There was a sound of chopping and splintering wood outside. They ran into the corridor and looked out the window. A group of Red Army soldiers cut down the wooden pillars holding up the awning of a shop on the other side of the road. Another brigade armed with saws and axes came from the riverbank.

"Get to work!" the brigade leader shouted through his megaphone. "The more wood you chop, the warmer your barracks will be in the winter. Smash the fair!"

The soldiers spread out around the square. Some began to tear the panels off boarded up windows, and others hacked at doors and broke down doorframes.

"We must go," Klim whispered to Nina.

The only thing they managed to take with them were the remnants of the satyr. As they left by the back door of the theater, they found themselves facing a crowd of young people wearing red ribbons on their chests. Luckily, nobody paid much attention to Nina and Klim.

"Celebrate Revolution Day with shock work!" the leaders urged them on.

Wood chips flew in the air, and clouds of dust blotted out the weak November sun. Someone started singing the famous ditty *"Dubinushka"*—"The Cudgel"—and dozens of voices picked up the song.

A tramcar decorated with red flags stopped opposite the Fair House, and another group of workers swarmed onto the street—some with wheelbarrows and some with fire hooks.

"Down with the fair!" they yelled. "Destroy the cesspit of capitalism!"

"We'll take it to pieces and burn it in our stoves!"

Klim and Nina got into the empty tramcar.

"Once, Comrade Trotsky let me have a look through his book on the history of the Roman Empire," Klim said, trying to act tongue-in-cheek. "The book told the story of the Stoic philosopher Epictetus. According to him, everything can be divided into two categories: things we can control and things we can't control. A person should do his duty no matter what and not bother himself with things he has no power to change anyway. This is the only way to be truly free, whether in poverty or in wealth. What do you think? Perhaps we should have a go at being Stoics."

Nina nodded slowly, looking straight ahead. She was shivering with cold.

They huddled close together, sharing the only overcoat they had between them. Klim clenched his teeth, seething with helpless rage at himself, his unhappy fate, and the city of his childhood now mutilated and rotten to the core.

Perhaps they should try to find Lubochka? Surely she wouldn't give them away to the Cheka. But then, who knew? Anyway, he had no idea where she lived now.

If Petrovich hadn't left Nizhny Novgorod, Klim would have gone to him for help. Now, even that path wasn't open to him.

He looked sideways at Nina. Her lips were blue, and her worn dress was too thin to protect her from the bitter cold. *If I don't find us shelter tonight,* Klim thought, *she'll come down with pneumonia or worse.*

The tramcar rattled over the pontoon bridge. The gray river water had a gelid look, and mist swirled over the waves, a sure sign that the river would freeze over early.

Fresh flags had been put up on Rozhdestvenskaya Street, and there were huge portraits of Bolshevik leaders in the shop windows. The ancient Ivan Tower was decorated with fir branches and a huge banner: "Glory to the Great Anniversary of the Revolution!" It was hard to believe that a whole year had passed.

The tramcar went uphill to the kremlin and stopped. The driver told the passengers that a demonstration was about to begin, and the police had blocked off Blagoveschenskaya Square and Pokrovskaya Street.

"I wonder for whose benefit this demonstration is being staged?" Nina muttered. "For the benefit of the demonstrators themselves?"

"I think it's for our benefit," Klim said. "To scare us."

"Then let's go and watch the performance. It would be sad for the actors to put on a show without an audience."

Klim frowned. "What if somebody recognizes you in the crowd?"

"I don't care," Nina said, looking into his eyes. "I can't hide anymore."

4

At twelve o'clock, a chorus of all the whistles, sirens, and signals of Nizhny Novgorod split the air. Marching bands struck up the "Internationale," planes showered the city with propaganda leaflets, and a procession of delegates from the Regional Party Committee, the Executive Committee, the city Soviet, and other organizations started to make its way along Pokrovskaya Street.

To Klim, this Bolshevik parade looked very like a religious procession only with rifles instead of crosses and banners instead of icons.

"Those who oppose the grain monopoly are the enemies of the proletariat," they chanted. "Kill the parasites! Distribute food according to class!"

Then came several carts that had been converted into floats. Klim noticed one with a papier-mâché spider under the sign that read "Capital." Another carried a huge dustbin in which sat a group of gloomy actors in greasepaint decked out as a priest, a member of the Tsarist police, and the Tsar himself—this costume clearly from the opera *Boris Godunov.* In the third cart were several effigies of White officers tied to a pillory under a sign that read, "Death to the White Scoundrels."

The crowd gazed at all of this splendor in silence like the citizens of a conquered country watching a parade staged by the conquerors. They could be sure that plenty of Cheka agents were nosing around among them just in case anyone was watching the Bolshevik demonstration without a properly joyful look on their faces.

The event ended with the ceremonial burning of the effigies of the White officers and the spider named Capital.

5

For some time now, Lubochka had been standing in the crowd observing Nina and Klim from a distance. *Good Lord,* she thought, *how thin they are!*

Not long ago, a cat had started to visit the canteen where Lubochka worked. The cat was so skinny that its ribs could be seen through his gray marbled fur. It was wild and nervous, and it had never tried to ingratiate itself with Lubochka or beg for food. It had just sat on the doorstep for hours looking at the meat on the chopping board.

The cook had chased the cat away, but it had been too weak to jump the fence and had fallen. The cook had picked it up by the scruff of its neck so that the cat had hung from her hand pitifully, its ears flattened, and its long body stretched out.

"We should kill this damn creature," the cook had said, grabbing a piece of a brick. "One of these days, it'll steal our meat."

But Lubochka had snatched the cat away. She had taken it back to her house and fed it. Still, it refused to acknowledge her and hissed and raised its paw to her if she tried to pet it.

To Lubochka, her cousin Klim now looked like that feral cat. And Nina, clearly half-starved, was all but unrecognizable.

Should I go up to speak to them? Lubochka thought. But what if they shrank away from her? She too had changed but in quite a different way.

Lubochka now lived in her father's house with all of her beloved men around her: Sablin, Osip, and Anton Emilievich.

Lubochka's father had come back to Nizhny Novgorod early in the August of 1918. He had gone quite gray, and what was left of his hair stood out in clumps. His left ear had been torn and failed to heal properly. He had never reached Finland but had been arrested on the border and imprisoned, his money taken away. Whenever his daughter tried to quiz him about what had happened, he either tried to laugh it off with feeble jokes or fell into a sudden rage and demanded that she leave him alone.

In early September, Lubochka had run into the head doctor of the Martynov Hospital.

"Sablin is dying," he had said disdainfully. "Haven't you even gone to see him?"

She had found her former husband in a terrible state, lying on the floor in the hospital corridor. She had presented her father and Osip with a fait accompli: she would bring Sablin into the house and nurse him until he was fully recovered.

"I'm not going to go back to him," she had told Osip, who was seething with jealousy. "Sablin will get better, and then he'll go. What opinion can you have of me, thinking that I could give up on someone so close to me?"

"But Sablin's not close to you," Osip protested.

"I would never give up on any of my family members, including you. Under no circumstances."

Osip looked at her sullenly, unable to find the words to convince her.

Sablin had indeed recovered and returned to work at the Martynov Hospital after being pronounced unfit for military service. But he had had nowhere to go since the house on Ilinskaya Street had been requisitioned, so, he had stayed on in Anton Emilievich's former library.

In her heart of hearts, Lubochka didn't want Sablin to move out. Every now and again, Osip went on a business trip, and sometimes he was away from home for weeks. Then Lubochka whiled away the time with her ex-husband.

She still admired him for his education and impressive intellect. She could talk to him on topics that Osip knew nothing about, such as history, science, and culture. This was something she missed terribly in her present marriage.

Lubochka realized that she needed both of them at once: Comrade Drugov and Dr. Sablin.

"You, my daughter, are playing with fire," Anton Emilievich had said, shaking his head.

During the first year of Soviet rule, Lubochka had believed in miracles and hadn't refused herself anything. She had realized that everything was possible if you have something to exchange and know how to trade it.

By November 1918, a web of invisible but strong threads had grown up throughout the city, linking all of those who received privileges of one sort or another. It covered all industries and sectors from the newly established University of Nizhny Novgorod to cobbler's workshops and dental surgeries, and the center of this elaborate network was the Regional Provisions Committee. Those who knew on which side their bread was buttered had lost interest in the dangerous trade of the bagmen and joined the ranks of bureaucrats, trying to get work that allowed them access to consumer goods, communications, or valuable information, all of which were worth a lot more than money.

Lubochka had access to food supplies and high-ranking military officials in the Red Army, and she set up her business in such a way that her family members had been spared mandatory public work and civil defense work. Thanks to her efforts, Sablin had received the position of head of the surgical department, and her father had become executive editor of a newspaper, the *Nizhny Novgorod Commune*.

Lubochka's new partners and friends were all people who had adapted to the new regime, something which, in itself, required quick wits and intelligence. And now she found herself staring at her former idol, Klim Rogov. He had stayed on in Russia with his precious girlfriend, sunk right to the bottom, and Nina—of whom she had been so jealous—had ended up with a gaunt, unshaven beggar with haunted eyes.

Congratulations, Lubochka thought. *Now, you have one overcoat between the two of you. Quite romantic, I suppose.*

Klim turned his head just as though he had felt Lubochka's gaze on them.

She set off purposefully toward them. "Come with me."

Now was no time to bear a grudge. Klim and Nina needed to be saved.

21. THE ART OF LIVING

1

On the day of the anniversary of the revolution, Sablin was given a day off and found himself alone in the house for the first time in a long while. His former father-in-law had gone to a gala concert, his surrogate for marital duties had been summoned to Moscow again, and Lubochka had gone out to watch the Bolshevik parade.

Sablin had become accustomed to doing everything at a frenetic pace, and now, he felt himself at a loose end. Deciding to go for a stroll, he put on his overcoat, took his cane, and went outside. He walked for twenty minutes without meeting a single living soul.

It's like a city after the plague, thought Sablin.

To him, there was a remarkable similarity between the Bolshevik revolution and the pandemics of Black Death in the Middle Ages. The plague of ideas—like the plague bacterium—were passed on by contact with infected individuals, and both were incurable unless steps were taken quickly. The Black Death had destroyed around a half of the population of Western

Europe, leaving its cities and village empty, its moral standards in decline, and riots breaking out all over the countryside. The same was happening in Russia now. In both cases, nobody had known the cause of the disease, and people blamed demons or foreigners for their misfortune. In Nizhny Novgorod at the moment, there was much speculation about which members of the Bolshevik government were Jewish and which were from the Baltic provinces.

People had tried all sorts of remedies against the plague, from drinking raw vodka on an empty stomach to going to mass, but all of them had proved useless. In any case, prayer meetings—like political demonstrations—only helped the disease spread faster.

Bolshevism is a malignant virus, thought Sablin. When somebody becomes infected, one thing leads to another: hallucinations, fever, and a burning desire to cut the painful swelling—the "bubo"—out of the body even if it only makes things worse.

Sablin knew that he too was infected. He could feel nothing but hatred toward those who had brought Russia to its knees and were now finishing it off for good—Trotsky signing death sentences for his fellow countrymen without batting an eyelid, Osip Drugov, who had stolen Sablin's wife, and Lubochka herself.

Once Zhora Kupin had written a poem about Comrade Drugov:

This fellow never had enough.
He needed other people's stuff.
He stole somebody else's wife,
Hoping to get a brand new life.

Good at division and subtraction—
But ruling held the most attraction.
His school, the College of Hard Knocks,
Has dealt his brain too many shocks.
The doctors tried, it must be said,
But couldn't mend this young man's head.

Zhora and others like him were always the first to die in the troubled times. He was too principled; he stood out too much to survive. Would it ever be possible to forgive his murderers? The Cheka had wiped out an entire generation of youngsters who could have been the flowers of the nation. Passionate, talented boys with a burning desire to make the world a better place, these were the young men who had volunteered for the White Army and performed heroic feats for a cause they had believed in. Who was there now to replace them? Of course, there were enthusiastic, dedicated young men among the urban working class and rural poor. But while the Whites had culture and knowledge behind them, these young Reds had to start at the very beginning from a position of medieval ignorance.

How will we survive the plague? Sablin wondered, walking down the street. Some people will develop immunity—they'll remain untouched by the disease or not be badly affected. Those who survive will have to rebuild everything after the epidemic, which could drag on for years.

Three people were coming around the corner: a man and two women. Sablin peered at them and, to his great surprise, saw that it was Lubochka with Klim and Nina.

Sablin limped toward them. "Good God, you're alive! How are you? What are you doing here?"

Lubochka looked around anxiously. "Let's go home. Nina and Klim have nowhere to go, and I think they should stay with us. I'll arrange everything."

2

Lubochka clearly couldn't resist showing her guests how much she had achieved. It was a great pleasure for her to act the hostess, boasting of the fine food at her table.

"*Pelmeny* should be made as they are in the Perm Province," Lubochka said to Klim and Nina as she ladled out the meat dumplings. "About the size of a walnut and wrapped in dough as thin as linen. The stuffing should have finely minced onion and cream mixed with the ground pork and beef, and they should be cooked in a veal broth and served with red vinegar, ground pepper, and parsley."

It was the first time in months that Nina and Klim had enjoyed a good meal in peace, warmth, and comfort. Nina sat on the sofa with her hands under her knees. She was ashamed that the skin around her nails was black with deeply ingrained dirt.

Nina felt overwhelmed by the opulence that Lubochka lived in, but the overriding feelings that she was currently experiencing were shock and indignation. How could her old friend possibly serve the Bolsheviks? How could she have possibly abandoned all her ideals for these pelmeni? However, Nina felt she had no right to condemn Lubochka as she herself was eating her meal courtesy of her former friend's hospitality. Nina's self-righteous anger would have appeared to everyone, including herself, as bitter and petty envy.

"Come on. I'll show you your room," Lubochka said and took Nina and Klim to a small, wood-paneled room above the porch. It had once been used by Anton Emilievich as a storage room.

"Are you sure your father won't mind us staying here?" Klim asked when Lubochka told him about everything that had happened to Anton Emilievich.

"What are you talking about? You're his nephew."

"And what will your new husband say?"

"Nothing."

"So, you have all of them under your thumb?"

Lubochka rolled her eyes. "Oh, you—you're incorrigible!"

While Klim was taking a bath, Lubochka brought Nina a set of bed linen.

"Will you be sleeping together? Unmarried?" Lubochka asked, pretending to be scandalized. "But I really don't care. Osip and I didn't have a church marriage either."

"So—what's going on between you and Sablin then?" Nina blurted out, unable to help herself. "He must see everything…and I'm sure it's breaking his heart."

"I love him too," Lubochka shrugged. "I love them both in different ways."

"How is that possible?"

"I've come to realize that one man can't provide you with everything you want. Take Klim as an example. He is a nice guy, but he's let all his opportunities pass him by."

"It's not his fault there's been a revolution," Nina objected.

Lubochka laughed. "That's not what I meant. Klim is vain, and all he needs to be happy is for someone to pay him a compliment. He hasn't the slightest interest in money and power, and he's always been that way. He'll never be rich again. He doesn't know how to make money and doesn't want to learn."

Don't argue, Nina told herself. *Let her believe she's in the right.*

"I'm sure you won't have to go begging," Lubochka said as she plumped up the pillow, "but I don't imagine you'll do very well for yourselves either. One day, you'll remember Mr. Fomin and your dreams of a beautiful life. If he was alive and you were with him, you'd be living like a queen, no matter who was in power."

"If the Bolsheviks hadn't confiscated my mill, I'd have provided for myself pretty well," Nina said.

"I don't think so." Lubochka laughed. "There are flowers that can't grow without support. You know you would never achieve anything without Fomin."

Nina was at a complete loss as to what to say.

"You know what's your problem is?" Lubochka asked in a confidential tone. "It never occurred to you that Klim is the one who's responsible for your present penury. If you had found yourself a more capable man, you wouldn't have been starving and hiding from the Cheka, and you could always keep a man like my cousin by your side just for the sake of pleasure. After all, he does bring you pleasure, doesn't he?"

Klim returned from the bathroom clean-shaven and wearing a new shirt and trousers provided by Lubochka.

"That's much better!" Lubochka said. "You look like yourself again."

He smiled. "All I needed was some hot water and a bar of soap, and suddenly, everything is right with the world."

Lubochka gave Nina a folded towel and one of her dresses. "Your turn."

3

The mirror in the bathroom was misty with condensation. Nina wiped her hand across it and stared at her reflection.

A couple of well-directed blows were all it had taken to get right under Nina's defenses. Lubochka had immediately sensed that Nina did not approve of her and couldn't help enjoying her little revenge.

"Here you are, little countess, so noble and scrupulous...but who has been more successful in life? You or me? Who has come begging to whom with their arms outstretched? So, be quiet, and I'll preach a couple of home truths to you and say whatever mean things about your man that I like."

And there was nothing Nina could do about it.

All those months she had been tormented with anxiety about what the future would hold. Would her life ever go back to normal? If the Reds won the war, the only way for her to have a half-way decent life would be to serve the same people who had killed her brother.

Even if the Whites prevailed, Klim would never get back his inheritance, and there would be next to nothing left of the mill at Osinki or the rest of the property confiscated by the Bolsheviks. Without a visa, Nina wouldn't be able to go to Argentina. So, what should she do? What should she hope for?

Nina had expected her former friend to show them some sympathy and even admire their courage and fortitude, but for Lubochka, they were just a couple of fools who only had themselves to blame for all the unnecessary misery they had experienced.

Lubochka was ready to play any game according to any rule as long as there was a guaranteed prize for her at the end of it while Nina still insisted on playing the old game that she had always used to win. It was little surprise that she had been so unceremoniously kicked out from the table.

It's not Klim who's responsible for our trouble but me, Nina thought.

Her reflection misted over again, and now, all she could see of herself was a shapeless smudge.

4

When Anton Emilievich arrived home, he was amazed to find the new visitors.

"Good Lord! Klim, is that you? Where have you been?"

Klim told him what had happened.

"So, Nina has no documents?" mused Anton Emilievich. "I think we can do something about that. She should go to the Regional Executive Committee and tell them her papers were stolen on a tram. It's important she gives a different name—then she won't have to answer any awkward questions. When they ask her about her place of birth, she should say she was born in Kiev. The local registry archive was destroyed by fire last year, so she'll be issued with a temporary ID card that she can use for two years."

Klim was stunned. "Is it that simple?"

"What did you think? That all the people working in the Bolsheviks' offices have great minds? Most of them are just ordinary women. All they care about is keeping their jobs and pleasing their bosses. When they get instructions from other women just like themselves, they don't question them; they simply follow them to the letter."

5

Nina and Klim lay side by side in a clean bed in the warm room. It was impossible to sleep; everything seemed so unreal. They were worried about what would happen when Lubochka's new husband came back. What would he say about his new tenants? And what would they do for money now? Whatever happened, they wouldn't be able to rely on Lubochka for long.

Klim leaned on his elbow and looked at Nina for a long time. "Will you marry me?"

She smiled bitterly. "Don't you think I've already dragged you down far enough?"

"My love for you is boundless and bottomless, and I want to dive down to its most profound depths."

"If it weren't for me, your life would have been completely different."

"That might be. But in the current circumstances, you're my only hope. There's no other woman who would marry me anyway."

Nina laughed. "All right then, but I'm keeping my maiden name, Kupina."

"Why?"

"I want you to have a better chance of surviving if I'm arrested."

6

They were married in the Church of St. George on the high bank overlooking the Volga River. It was the most beautiful church in the city with its white walls coated with lace-like stucco and its two golden domes gleaming against the cloudy gray sky.

"Glory to Thee, our God!" the choir sang.

Lubochka gazed at the newlyweds standing in front of the lectern. The bride was dressed in Lubochka's old dress—*not white, of course, not white.* Against the background of the rows of candles that lit up the church, Nina's head looked like a dark silhouette cut from paper.

"You're nobody," Lubochka whispered to herself. "An empty space."

A young black-bearded priest looked up at Klim.

"Have you, Kliment, come here to enter into marriage with this woman, Nina, without coercion, freely and wholeheartedly?"

"I have," Klim said, and as he said so, it seemed to Lubochka that he quickly glanced at her.

Finally, he had given in and acknowledged her preeminence. Indeed, Klim treated her with a deference so pronounced that sometimes Lubochka felt he was mocking her. But then again, how could he mock her when he was entirely dependent on her charity?

Lubochka felt particularly sorry for Nina. In no more than a year, she had changed beyond recognition not only in appearance but also in character. Once an elegant, business-like young woman, she was now little more than a skinny scarecrow. Nina seemed to see signs of ill will everywhere around her, and that was why Lubochka had been unable to resist the urge to tease her.

It would be nice, for example, to seduce her husband. Nina was no match for pretty, pampered, and perfumed Lubochka. Surely, Klim would never risk refusing the irresistible lady of the house and being thrown out into the freezing cold.

Lubochka smiled at her sinful thoughts and sighed. No, she wouldn't cheat on Osip, at least for now. But then who knew what the future might bring?

7

After the church ceremony, Lubochka took the newlyweds to the registry office in the basement of a former merchant's house. The Soviet Republic only recognized civil marriages.

"Father and I have decided to make you a wedding gift," Lubochka told Klim when the formalities were over. "He's going to give you a job in his newspaper. You'll get ration cards and a union membership card and the right to use the canteen at the Journalists' House."

"What will I have to do?" he asked.

"Write me a sample article."

"Something along the line of a *Passionate Appeal to the Workers*?"

"Exactly. But don't try to be clever. Nowadays, journalism isn't about bringing readership and profits. All that matters is to get the approval of the Regional Executive Committee."

After much thought and numerous edits and revisions, Klim brought Lubochka his work. "I think I've done a reasonable job. It's full of nonsense and 'comrades,' 'long lives,' and exclamation marks."

Lubochka read the article and patted Klim on the shoulder.

"Very good. You have a special gift for nonsense."

22. THE SOVIET JOURNALIST

1

EL CUADERNO NEGRO

Klim Rogov's little black notebook

I am now a Soviet worker and enjoy a third category allowance of ration cards, which entitles me to ten pounds of rotten potatoes a month. The authorities have promised a delivery next week on the barge *Friedrich Engels*, but if the Oka River freezes over, the *Friedrich* will take my potatoes somewhere else.

The print-run of the *Nizhny Novgorod Commune* varies between two and six thousand copies, depending upon the availability of paper. You could hardly call our work "journalism." Almost all news worth reporting is a state secret. In the meantime, we occupy ourselves with publishing Soviet decrees and appeals and insulting the bourgeoisie.

I'm the one responsible for the workers' letters. All of the tolerably educated Bolsheviks are busy with party work, and the local correspondents tend to have a rather shaky grasp of Russian prose.

I have to edit their letters, and if we don't have enough material, I just write them myself. Recently, we had a competition for the best short story. As we didn't get any entries, I dashed off ten stories and then chose the winner and received the prize—a subscription to the *Nizhny Novgorod Commune*.

There have been coups in Germany and Austria-Hungary, and the Allies have won the war. Uncle Anton was almost in tears when he learned about that. For months, he had been hoping that the Germans would come deep into Russia and overthrow the Bolsheviks.

"If only the Allies would attack us!" he said hopefully. "On the other hand, if they'd wanted to attack, they would have done so long ago. It's beyond a joke! They're sending tiny landing parties in at the ports and pretending to be at war with the Bolsheviks. Still, who knows what will happen? The Whites are moving in from the east under Admiral Kolchak, and General Krasnov is coming up from the south with his army."

I widened my eyes, pretending to be skeptical. "Surely not!"

Uncle Anton showed me the map and pointed to the villages and towns now occupied by the Whites.

He told me details of the news from the frontline—not the contradictory nonsense that the public gets from the newspapers but the latest reports straight from the headquarters. Only kremlin officials and chief editors can read these reports, and they have to sign for them.

From time to time, Uncle Anton shares some other choice pieces of news with me. Accurate information is vital to me, Nina, and Dr. Sablin as we have decided to escape from the land of the Soviets.

At first, I thought we should invite Uncle Anton to join our conspiracy, but the more I see of him at work, the more relieved I am that I've told him nothing.

He turns a blind eye to the fact that his daughter has two husbands, and he is reluctant to argue with Osip or Sablin because both of them are very useful to him.

"It's not my business to give other people advice," he says.

At the same time, if some girl sends in a letter to the newspaper, pleading, "Dear Comrade Schuster, please tell me how to live—I'm at the end of my tether." Uncle Anton will write a five-page letter full of recommendations and exhortations. And what's more, he'll send the poor girl a copy of one of his books.

It turns out that Uncle Anton writes novels about courtly love and reverence before some mysterious, beautiful lady. Often when we are alone in his office, he walks over to the window and, tugging his beard, asks if I would object if he recites certain passages from his novel to me, which he knows by heart.

Marusya, the secretary, enters the room.

"What are you doing in here, you fool?" the knight in shining armor screams. "Can't you see we're busy? You're fired! Don't bother coming in to work tomorrow."

Marusya begins to cry, and Anton Emilievich grudgingly relents. "All right then. Forget what I said just now. I tell you, Klim, these girls couldn't tell a work of art if it came up and introduced itself to them. All they care about is getting home early at the end of the day."

I don't remember him being like this. Could the Bolsheviks have sent us back an imposter in place of the old Uncle Anton? Or does he only bother to behave like a gentleman when he's around people who can be of use to him and make no effort with anyone else? My stock is so low just now that he doesn't have to worry about making a scene in my presence. As for Marusya, she's quite beneath his notice.

In our household, a secret religious conflict is smoldering below the surface. The abyss between the sects is so deep and wide that reconciliation is quite impossible. We have the great reformer, Comrade Osip, who is absent for the time being. Lubochka and her father belong to the Order of Opportunists who—while they might not believe in anything—diligently serve the powers that be as long as they get some benefit from doing so. Nina, Sablin, and I are dissenters. We stand firmly for the old faith. If we're not allowed to serve our ideals, we'll set sail and travel to the end of the world to get as far away from the infidels as possible. We don't intend, God forbid, to openly challenge the official religion. We even pretend that we are ready to renounce our mistaken beliefs. But at night, when the opportunists go to bed, we call secret meetings to exercise the right to assembly and freedom of speech.

Lubochka is desperate to lure us into her sect. She tempts us with food rations in the present and salvation in the future. As a sweetener, she has offered Nina a job as a dishwasher in her canteen. It's a prestigious job because it entails proximity to both food and the warmth of the kitchen.

At first, my proud wife just laughed. Then she cried. Finally, she agreed. We're going to need money if we want to get out of Nizhny Novgorod.

My longing for Argentina has become an obsession. On my way to the editorial office, I lose myself so deeply in my memories that it seems I can feel the fresh breeze from the Rio de la Plata and hear people talking in Spanish with a strong Italian accent, the incomparable language of Buenos Aires.

When our office girls wonder what to do with tough horse meat, I remember the recipe of the gauchos. They soften tough meat by putting it under the saddle and then riding the horse at a gallop. Sometimes I catch a glimpse of somebody gesticulating like an Argentinean, and of course, it always turns out I'm mistaken. It's just a mirage, but it says a lot about my state of mind. My old life has become a symbol of peace for me while the present is a symbol of war.

I'm sure Nina has already had enough of me telling her stories about the *asado*. This is a special Argentinean ritual, a whole day spent preparing food on a barbecue and then a feast. People eat at nine or even ten in the evening and then stay up late drinking homemade wine, talking, and dancing. I miss those Argentinean nights most of all.

I try to keep Nina's hopes up. I promise her that I'll get an Argentine visa for her, whatever the cost. But sometimes I feel her faith in that fading away, and that scares me more than anything. She needs big goals, not a vegetable existence. It's insulting for her that someone else is in charge of her time and energy even if that person is Lubochka. And that's why I love my Nina—for her inability to go with the flow and for her burning desire to become a successful person and do something significant. She has a strong will, a kind heart, and a good head on her shoulders. She's the kind that could never live in slavery even if that slavery comes complete with prestige and every comfort.

If only she saw a future for us as I do! I know that one day, we'll wander through the center of Buenos Aires gazing up at the elegant facades of the buildings with their stucco ornaments. We'll look at the closed shutters and try to guess who lives behind them. When we get tired, we'll go to Café Tortoni with its stained glass ceilings and distinguished gray-haired waiters like English aristocrats. We'll eat delectable *medialunas* croissants and cakes and—

That's enough for today. I don't want to get too carried away.

2

Nina never left the house without her flu mask, but she was no longer afraid that anyone would recognize her. Her life was like that of a forest animal. She knew there were wolves around, she knew they attacked and devoured prey every day, but what could she do about it?

Every morning, she went to the Military Commissariat. The city was covered with snow. Trees and bushes that had survived the fuel collection sparkled with frost in the sunlight, and the houses looked like gnomes wearing huge white caps and necklaces of icicles. It was so cold that there was a halo around the pale winter sun.

Women standing around outside the locked door of the grocery shop were cursing the Soviet government in whispers. "Why do all the Bolsheviks jump the queue? They should clear out."

A saleswoman wrapped in an eiderdown was slowly moving the weights on the scales.

Why can't they have two women serving instead of one? Nina thought. *And why is this woman allowed to force people to stand in line in the cold? She should be punished like a thief for stealing the most valuable thing of all—time.*

Still, maybe it was a good idea to kill time in the land of the Soviets because then perhaps everything would be over as soon as possible.

Nina had no real cause to complain. She worked in the best "public catering point" in the city. The canteen boasted gilded chairs stolen from a theater and dining tables confiscated from merchants' houses. And while the spoons might have been made of wood and the tablecloths of newspaper, the tableware bore the monograms of princely families.

While the standard fare in other catering establishments was salted herring, in Lubochka's canteen, the cook's handwritten menu boasted "pilaf with beef" or "lingonberry dessert with shugar." But even this menu had been drawn up for the ordinary customers and didn't tell the full story. Lubochka also had dried fruit, rice, and flour from Tashkent, canned fish from the Baltic states, and even caviar and sturgeon from the Lower Volga region. She had plenty of food, but not for everyone.

There were always street children crowded around the entrance to the canteen. As soon as a visitor walked up to the door, they rushed forward shouting, "Mister! Ma'am! A spoonful, please!"

Trying not to look at their dirty faces, Nina stamped the snow from her felt boots—a gift from Lubochka—and went to the kitchen. She had to bring in firewood, light the oven, and heat a whole tank of water before the first guests appeared.

The canteen opened at twelve, and the kitchen filled with the sound of clattering dishes and running feet. Sometimes Lubochka came to the kitchen to announce that they needed "first-class service." That meant that somebody important had arrived.

"How are you?" Lubochka asked Nina.

Nina, breathless with exertion, wiped her wet hands on her apron and tucked a stray lock of her hair under her kerchief. "I'm fine."

Lubochka cast an eye over the piles of clean dishes. "Good for you. But do me a favor, don't stack the cups like that. They could break."

"I won't."

Nina and Klim had no right to hate Lubochka, but they hated her nonetheless. As they saw it, it was only thanks to her and her kind that the Bolsheviks were able to remain in power.

Countless Lubochkas had filled the state offices and institutions, feathering their nests in the process. Now, they were ready to fight tooth and nail to keep their jobs, which meant defending the Soviet state.

Of course, there was resistance but mainly in the form of petty sabotage and widespread theft. It gave Nina great satisfaction to steal millet from the canteen pantry and feed it to her hen, Speckle. This hen was the object of pride and constant concern because it laid golden eggs—golden because every one of them fetched eighty rubles at the market.

Nina was terrified at the thought that Lubochka's cat might catch Speckle. She would often jump up in the night to check whether the hen was all right.

Klim had named the cat Kaiser because of its bellicose whiskers and recent misfortune. Like the former German emperor, it had lost its territory and was now forced to live at the mercy of strangers.

"If that cat of yours eats Speckle, I'll give it short shrift," Nina threatened.

"Oh, come on!" Klim laughed. "A hen is nothing compared to a cat. Cats are princes of the animal kingdom. After all, they're cousins to the king of beasts. Personally, I feel a sense of kinship with Kaiser. Perhaps you could call it class solidarity."

Kaiser had grown fond of Klim too. The cat slept on his lap and let him scratch it behind the ears.

3

In order to escape from the land of the Soviets, Sablin, Klim, and Nina had to get to the frontline, and to do that, they needed the following documents:

1) passports
2) certificates of exemption from military service for the men
3) letters of assignment from work
4) passes from the Regional Executive Committee
5) permits to buy railroad tickets
6) railroad tickets
7) permits from the Cheka

Soviet bureaucrats who issued travel papers made a fortune in bribes. Sometimes they would be caught and executed. But then new officials would step into their shoes, and everything would go on as before. All that happened was that the bribes increased.

Money was scarce. Sablin, Klim, and Nina were all earning next to nothing. The shapeless lump of silver that was all that remained of the satyr couldn't cover more than a tenth of their travel costs, and Sablin had nothing to his name but an amber cigarette case missing one corner. Things looked particularly bleak regarding the third item on the list—the letters from their workplaces—since neither the local newspaper nor the hospital ever sent staff to the frontline. As for Nina, her profession involved no travel whatsoever.

4

Sometimes Sablin's acquaintances would bring news of a successful escape from the land of the Soviets. Excited, he would permit himself cautious questions: "Where is the frontline, and how did they get across it?" But no one could tell if these rumors were even true because no one ever came back from the other side of the frontline.

It was so hard for Sablin to tell himself that he would be leaving Lubochka forever in the spring. He kept questioning his decision, wondering if perhaps he ought to stay, clinging to what remained of his former domestic happiness.

"I'm sorry," he told Klim, "but I really don't think I can leave the hospital. People here are so hungry that they're eating God knows what, poisoning themselves. And we don't have even emetics, so—"

"Let your patients read our newspaper," Klim said. "Listen, you have to get out of here. Otherwise, you'll lose your mind."

"You must start afresh," Nina told Sablin. "You won't find new love as long as you're still carrying a torch for Lubochka. I know what I'm talking about."

Sablin frowned. He didn't like to discuss such things, particularly not with a woman.

He kept thinking of how Lubochka had nursed him back to health when she had found him dying. In the past, she had complained that Sablin didn't love her enough. He had been at a loss when he had heard this unfair accusation. For Sablin, love meant family, and family meant respect, cooperation, friendship, and loyalty. Lubochka had had all of these things. What more did she want?

He could find only one explanation, the vilest and unbearable: she had been disappointed in him as a lover. He had asked her if this was true, terrified at what she might say, but Lubochka had only thrown her hands up, "Lord, how vulgar you are! It wasn't about that."

But what was it then?

Sablin tried to figure out how Klim had made Nina fall in love with him. Obviously, it wasn't about his money—she hadn't cared much for him when he had been rich. Perhaps his secret was his charisma. Sablin had never had this quality.

There was no point in cursing his fate. Some people have a talent for dancing, and some don't. Some lucky souls are easygoing while others are born pedantic and boring. Sablin accepted his shortcomings in the same way that he had accepted his limp.

He spent evenings playing against Klim and staking his amber cigarette case as a bet. If they played cards, Klim usually won, but if they played chess, Sablin would beat him every time.

"What a stupid game this is!" Klim said angrily after Sablin had beaten him yet again. "In my opinion, there should be a special chess piece that both players are fighting over—a dragon, for instance. What's the point in just knocking out all your opponents' pieces? I need something to fight for."

That was Sablin's problem in real life: he had nothing to fight for.

Klim and Nina's room was next to Sablin's, and hearing the muffled sounds of their passion at night, he would feel sickened and angered. He wanted to bang on the thin wall with his fist and yell, "You're not alone here, damn you!"

In the morning, Nina came out of her room still sleepy with a blissful, distracted expression, and Sablin could barely restrain himself from asking, "So, what do you plan to do if you get pregnant?"

Then Lubochka appeared in the corridor as solicitous as a gardener tending her plants. "Sablin, have you taken your medicine? Don't forget, please. And put your gloves on when you go outside, or your hands will get cold."

Imagine that we did manage to escape, thought Sablin. After traveling for weeks on a lice-ridden train in constant danger of being robbed or killed, imagine that they got as far as the frontline and survived the shelling and the raids. When everything was over, would he regret his decision? Would he go out of his mind with longing for Lubochka, for Nizhny Novgorod, for his job? There, on the other side of the frontline, Sablin couldn't just walk into a hospital and say, "Take me on as a surgeon."

What would happen to him there? How could he find a place for himself? And what use would he be to anyone there anyway as lame, shy, and unsociable as he was?

23. THE OLD COUNTESS'S DIAMONDS

1

There was no point getting up before nine o'clock. It was still dark, and there was no electricity in the mornings.

With his hard-earned pay from his work on the *Nizhny Novgorod Commune*, Klim could afford half his breakfast: carrot tea and a piece of bread cut from a frozen loaf he had bought two weeks earlier for a hundred rubles. The other half—a slice of lemon, butter, and cheese—came courtesy of his generous cousin.

Lubochka smiled at his hesitation. "Are you ashamed to be taking gifts from me? Look at it this way—perhaps God is fond of you and using an intermediary to make sure you have lemon for your tea."

"God must have a dubious sense of humor," Klim said. "If He really wanted to send me provisions, He should have sent Admiral Kolchak with his White

Army. After all, to judge by the Red propaganda posters, the admiral has seized all the food in Russia, including champagne and sausages."

"At the moment, your Admiral Kolchak is stuck somewhere near the Ural Mountains," Lubochka said as she poured herself a cup of tea. "He wouldn't be able to get to Nizhny Novgorod in time for dinner, let alone breakfast."

Klim left the house at eleven.

Perhaps it was true that everyone else in the world was descended from monkeys, he thought, *or from Adam and Eve, but the Soviets must have had hamsters for ancestors.* They were all constantly on the lookout for food and squirreling it away—if not into cheek pouches, then into bags and knapsacks.

Klim himself was no exception. There was a very good vegetarian canteen on the way to his newspaper office, and he usually dropped in when he could. The prices there might have been outrageous, but it was the only establishment in Nizhny Novgorod where you could eat without a union card or a special pass.

Unfortunately, the canteen was closed because it had been burglarized the previous night.

Klim decided to go to the Journalists' House.

But he was out of luck. When he got there, he found an enormous queue of desperately hungry people, most of whom looked as though they could never have even read a newspaper article, let alone written one.

"Our oven isn't working," announced the cook, appearing on the porch. "It'll be at least an hour before it's fixed."

There was nothing for it but to go into work.

It was awfully cold in the editorial office. Klim's colleagues were already busy warming up homemade ink with their breath.

"Klim, you're late," said Zotov, a young man with a somewhat vague job description who always kept a watchful eye on his coworkers and informed his superiors about everything that went on. Anton Emilievich—who had a good nose for useful people—held him in high regard.

Zotov pulled a red pencil from his pocket and walked over to a large cardboard sign on the wall. On one side of the sign was the slogan, "Praise to honest workers." Below was a list of all those who came into work before Zotov and left after he did. The other side proclaimed, "Shame on idlers and loafers." Naturally, Klim Rogov's was the first name on this list.

Zotov put yet another big black cross next to Klim's name and announced that all of the editorial staff had to sign up for a volunteer workday.

"Where are you sending us this time?" Klim asked. "To a sweets factory?"

The office girls laughed. "You wish! We're being sent to unload freight cars."

"Then I'm afraid I'm busy."

Zotov wasn't sure he could force Comrade Rogov to sign up to compulsory "voluntary" work because not only was Klim technically a foreigner but also apparently personally acquainted with Trotsky.

With a determined look, Zotov set off to see Anton Emilievich's office. He spent some time inside airing his grievances. As a result, Anton Emilievich gave his nephew a very public reprimand so that nobody should accuse him of nepotism.

"Klim, we have a team here. You behave as though you're not part of that team."

To hell with them, Klim thought and went off to the accounts department. He was more interested in when they would get the promised delivery of cabbage from the Journalists' Union.

The woman in the accounts department told him that the cabbage would be coming in tomorrow. However, it wouldn't be given to the journalists but to the guards outside the newspaper office. A machine gun detachment had been assigned to protect the *Nizhny Novgorod Commune* in case the Whites should take it into their heads to seize the newspaper.

Klim wasn't at all in the mood for work. All he wanted was to go home and sit by the warm stove. Nevertheless, he went over to his place by the windowsill next to a frozen rubber plant, sat down on his broken-backed chair, and unfastened the top button of his overcoat. Today, he had to write a letter from a worker in a steel factory wishing Comrade Lenin a speedy recovery.

The resulting letter was as full of emotion as a passionate love poem. If Lenin had only known how many fervent lines Klim had dedicated to him, he might have shown his gratitude by issuing Comrade Rogov the pair of shoes he needed so badly. But how would the great and glorious Soviet leader ever find out about the heroic labors of a humble journalist?

There was a flutter among the female members of staff as the military instructor, a handsome man in a fur hat, came into the office. The newspaper workers sat themselves down in a circle to listen to him. Klim noticed that the proofreaders were wearing lipstick.

Where do you even get ahold of lipstick these days? he wondered.

The instructor read out "Order #4 of the Military Affairs Committee":

Forthwith, all Soviet office employees are to learn revolutionary songs. The singing of ideologically empty songs from the prerevolutionary period is prohibited.

No one came forward to say they knew any revolutionary songs.

"Then we shall write down the lyrics," ordered the instructor.

But this was impossible since the ink was still frozen.

"Then we'll learn the songs by heart," he declared.

By the time they had gotten to the second verse, the military instructor was also shivering with cold. "That's all for today. Any questions?"

The proofreaders raised their hands.

"If the authorities don't allocate us firewood to heat the editorial office," Zotov interrupted, "I shall resign and go to the frontline."

Zotov was just bluffing, of course. *But it would be good,* thought Klim, *if the bluff paid off and something was done about the heating.*

As night fell, the editorial staff went home. On his way back, Klim visited the Journalists' House again. People were still queuing in front of the closed doors.

"When are they going to open the canteen?" Klim asked.

"We don't know."

"Why are you waiting then?"

"Just in case."

A grubby-faced street boy came up to Klim and winked at him. Klim needed no further explanation. He was to follow the boy to a side street where a citizen keen to keep a low profile would be waiting to do business with him.

It was a good thing these days to look young and healthy and, therefore, well-off. The street boys who worked for the bagmen would pick you out of the crowd and take you to where you could buy coveted supplies: buckwheat, bread crumbs, or even birch logs for the fire. Those who looked shabbier had to rely on the canteens because all of the markets had been shut down. At the same time, anyone who looked wealthy ran a greater risk of being knocked over the head in a dark alley. So, Klim followed the boy with no idea of what was waiting for him around the corner.

2

"Sofia Karlovna! Can it really be you?"

The old countess put her finger to her lips. She gave the boy a tip and waited until he had dashed off before shaking Klim by the hand.

"There was a Cheka man standing in the queue," she said. "He was the one who searched our house. I was afraid he might recognize me if I went any closer. Tell me, how are you?"

Though the old countess had aged considerably, she still cut an impressive figure in her worn moleskin overcoat, velvet hat, and white headscarf. She was pulling her bags along using a child's sled.

"Nina and I have been looking for you everywhere," said Klim.

The old countess' face lit up. "So, Nina is still alive? I lit a candle in her memory after I read in the newspaper that poor Zhora and Elena had been shot. I thought the Cheka had killed Nina too."

Klim told her everything that had happened.

"So, you helped her escape arrest?" the old countess gasped. "You must come and visit us. I live with Anna Evgenievna now. Do you know her? She's a wonderful lady. There aren't so many of her kind left these days."

3

Sofia Karlovna and Anna Evgenievna lived in what had once been the cook's room with a window half-buried in the ground. The mansion had been turned into a barracks, and now, there were three-tier bunk beds in the princess' former apartments.

One corner of the old ladies' room was hung with icons, and another with portraits of sons killed in the war.

Anna Evgenievna looked ill, her neck puffy and her body swollen with dropsy.

"Pleased to meet you," she said, bowing to Klim.

The old countess lit the gas lamp.

"Fortunately, the temperature here never drops below fifteen," she said. "Our neighbor's oven is right next to our wall. He's a senior quartermaster of the Red Army. As you can imagine, he's not very happy that we get his heat for free, but he can't help it."

The old ladies earned their living mending and patching the Red Army soldiers' clothes.

The pair barely ever went out, so their only source of food and news were their new "tenants."

Surprisingly, the ladies had retained the elegant standards of former days and kept their room spotless. The floor looked swept, the door handles polished, and their room was fresh with the scent of pine essence.

Once Klim had laughed at Sofia Karlovna and her old-fashioned ways. Now, he saw that her exacting standards allowed her and her friend to maintain their sense of dignity.

Klim brought a log from the yard and helped saw it up so that the old ladies could heat water and do their laundry.

"Thank you so much!" Sofia Karlovna said. "It's very difficult for us to manage a saw."

She went to see Klim off to the gate. The city was lit up starkly black and white under a full moon, and the snow crunched beneath their feet.

"I'm glad I ran into you," the old countess said quietly. "Anna Evgenievna is dying, you know. These days, I look at the people as I walk around, and I have a feeling that all of us are heading toward death. I went to the cemetery yesterday and saw so many familiar names on the grave crosses! The cream of Nizhny Novgorod society is gradually making its way to the Peter and Paul Cemetery, leaving nothing behind—no descendants and no property. We're not simply dying. We're disappearing without a trace. How old are you, may I ask?"

"Twenty-nine," Klim answered.

"And I'm sixty-five. I've lost everything—my husband, my son, and my house. I shall never have any grandchildren. I am quite destitute, and my life is passing me by. But I want to live! Tell me, what are you going to do next?"

"We're going to leave the country this spring," Klim said. "Nina, Dr. Sablin, and I."

"Where to?"

"We don't know yet."

"You need to go to Novorossiysk," Sofia Karlovna whispered excitedly. "I've heard from the senior quartermaster that the Allies' ships are in the harbor there. If you take me with you, we can go to France from there."

Klim was embarrassed. "We don't have any money for the journey," he explained. "And to be honest, I haven't the slightest idea where we are going to get any."

Sofia Karlovna took a small velvet bag out of her pocket and put it into Klim's hand. "These diamond earrings were my mother's wedding gift. I think you can get a lot of money for them."

"But how can I—"

It was unbelievable: the old countess had never been fond of Klim, and now, she was entrusting him with the last of her possessions.

"Just take them," she said. "I don't need any oaths or promises from you. I still don't approve of how you live your life, but you haven't deserted Nina, and I can tell that you belong to the nobler class of person."

4

The day was a fortunate one indeed—the electricity was still on after seven that evening.

"There's no call for rejoicing," Marisha said gloomily. "All it means is that the Cheka wants to search somebody's house."

But Klim, Nina, and Sablin weren't listening to her. They were too excited by the news of the old countess.

"I wonder how she managed to hide these earrings?" Nina asked, turning over the glittering diamonds. "And she told me she had nothing left."

Lubochka called them to dinner.

At home, Uncle Anton didn't lecture anyone about "team spirit" as he did at the office. He even allowed himself to criticize the government.

"Do you think that forced labor and food requisitions were invented by the Bolsheviks?" he asked as he poured sour cream sauce over his potatoes. "Nothing of the kind. That's exactly how the grand dukes of Moscow used to tax their subjects in the Middle Ages. It was the territory rather than the individual that was responsible for paying tax, and the local authorities had to work out who would do the work and what to pay. Back then, the only way to avoid paying taxes was by serving the grand duke. Now, being a member of the Bolshevik Party works the same way."

"Papa, please eat up," Lubochka said. "Your food will get cold."

Klim was irritated by their chatter. He couldn't wait to go to his room and think about how to sell the diamond earrings. Where could he find a buyer, and how much could he get for them? And how could he keep himself safe from the Cheka agents who were out to trap people selling gold and precious stones on the black market?

Suddenly, they heard the sound of footsteps in the street and a loud knock at the front door. Klim froze at the sound. It must be a search!

His first thought was how to hide the earrings. He stood up, but Lubochka stopped him. "Sit down, please. Marisha, go see who it is."

Klim passed one of the earrings under the table to Nina. If the Cheka found one of them, perhaps they could save the other? Nina put the earring into her stocking.

Klim's nerves were strained to breaking point. Marisha rattled the door bolts, and then he heard a deep male voice and the creak of footsteps on the floorboards.

"What's going on in here? Some sort of party?" asked a red-faced man, appearing at the door of the dining room.

It was Petrovich, the military man who had been Klim's partner at the card table.

"Osip!" Lubochka cried and threw her arms around the newcomer's neck.

5

After dinner, Osip and Lubochka went to their room and talked for a long time. Nina tiptoed to their door several times and returned to the dining room pale and anxious. "I can't hear a thing."

Marisha had cleared away the dishes, and Anton Emilievich had gone to his room, but Nina, Klim, and Sablin were still sitting at the table.

Klim remembered the Russian folk tale about a little house that stood in the middle of a field. A mouse, a frog, and several other animals lived in the house, but one day, a bear stopped by, and all of the inhabitants of the little house froze in horror at the intruder. Would the bear destroy everything, or let them live happily ever after? The story ended with the bear trying to get into the little house and pulling it down.

Klim tossed the salt cellar from hand to hand. Who would have thought that Osip and Petrovich were the same person? And how on earth could Lubochka have fallen in love with such a character?

The doctor looked as though he had been slapped in the face. Klim imagined himself in Sablin's shoes, and the very idea of being betrayed by his wife—the dearest person of all—made him feel sick. Up until now, whenever he had seen marriages and affairs come to an end, he had always thought that it was simply a part of life. But now—looking at his friend crushed with sorrow—his blood ran cold.

Finally, Lubochka stepped into the dining room. "Klim, come here, please."

Just as she spoke, the electricity went out.

6

Osip's tired face glimmered in the light of a single church candle. Lubochka stood behind him looking at Klim and smiling.

"I didn't expect to see you here," Osip said. "Lubochka tells me you're her cousin."

"I am," Klim said warily.

"She also mentioned that you're a journalist, and you're good with people."

"That's about right."

"And she tells me you're well-traveled. Which countries have you been to?"

"Persia, China, and Argentina. And I did a tour of Europe when I was a child."

"I hear your wife escaped arrest," Osip said, his blue eyes piercing Klim. "Is that true?"

Klim flinched and shot a glance at Lubochka. Why had she told Osip about that?

Osip ran his hand through his close-cropped gray hair. "Lubochka told me the Cheka wanted to arrest your wife because of her brother," he said. "The devil knows what to do with the pair of you. If your wife is innocent and we put her in jail, she'll be a burden on the state. But if we allow her to remain at liberty, she won't forgive us killing her brother. And she'll try to sabotage us—"

Lubochka put her hands on Osip's shoulders. "If you arrest people just to be on the safe side, the whole city will be in jail in no time," she said softly. Then she turned to Klim. "Look, we have a proposition for you. There are two thousand sailors in the city, and they have nothing to do all winter. The Regional Executive Committee is going to open a special university for the sailors, but we need very special professors who can deal with—well, you know—general populace."

"What do you want me to teach them?" Klim asked, surprised.

"We want you to keep them busy," Lubochka said. "You can tell them about faraway countries and teach them to wash their hands before eating."

"It's very important work," Osip said. "Comrade Lenin has told us it's essential to raise the cultural level of our troops. If you agree, you'll be given the highest category of food ration. After you've completed a trial period, of course."

Klim hesitated. "So, you don't mind if Nina and I stay here for a while?"

"What is it to me?" Osip shrugged. "This house isn't mine anyway. It belongs to the city's Executive Committee."

"Just as I told you," Lubochka said, winking at Klim.

7

Back in the dining room, Klim closed the door and told Nina and Sablin what had passed between himself and Osip.

"I have an idea," he said under his breath. "I'll suggest that Osip organize a train with a propaganda car, and as soon as the waterways become navigable in spring and the sailors go back to their ships, I'll ask him to send the train to the frontline to help spur on the Red Army soldiers to heroic deeds. We will sign up to be propagandists. That way we'll have a car to ourselves, and the scoundrels in the Cheka won't dare touch us."

Nina looked at Klim with shining eyes. "Do you think Osip will agree to help you?"

"I don't see why not. He seems to think I have the gift of setting soldiers on the right path."

Sablin smiled wryly. "Poor Lubochka—imagine if she knew what we were up to."

"So what?" Nina said in a dispassionate tone. "She treats us like a peasant woman treats her chickens. She feeds us with one hand and pulls out our feathers with the other. And all just to feather her own bed."

Sablin sighed. "Yes, I know."

24. THE SAILORS' UNIVERSITY

1

The Sailors' University was set up in a former girls' school on Ilinskaya Street. Anton Emilievich had also volunteered to give lectures there. Enthusiastic, disheveled, and perspiring from effort, he took turns reading his own stories and extracts from the Bolshevik political agenda to "our brothers the sailors," who sat yawning and scratching their shaven heads.

This wasn't the sort of audience to which Anton Emilievich was accustomed. The sailors had no use for his ironic comments or intriguing historical parallels. Propaganda had convinced them that they were the pride and strength of the revolution, and that everybody—including the generally despised lecturers—was obliged to bow down to them.

They interrupted Anton Emilievich or stood up during a lecture and announced, "I need to take a crap." Sometimes Anton Emilievich felt like giving up altogether. These men had no respect for culture and education. They slept with their shoes on, blew their noses into their fingers, and the moment any problem arose there was an outcry: "Why are there no potatoes in our soup? You tell the kitchen staff from us that if they're stealing our food, we'll beat the living daylights out of them."

What on earth could Anton Emilievich hope to do in this situation?

"Comrades," he said in a shaky voice, "I'd like to tell you a story about a noble knight."

The sea of brutish faces before him looked blank and indifferent. Some were chewing tobacco, and others were picking their noses.

Suddenly, there was a burst of laughter from the next classroom.

"What is it now?" Anton Emilievich exclaimed angrily. "It's impossible to work in these conditions."

He was annoyed to see that nobody was paying any attention to him. They were all listening to the sounds coming from Klim's classroom on the other side of the wall.

At recess, the sailors met up together for a smoke. Anton Emilievich pushed his way through the crowd of laughing, cursing sailors.

"We were acting out the trial of a prostitute, Miss Roll-me-ova, who was accused of seducing a soldier. Our boatswain was gotten up as a woman in a shawl and kept pawing away at Vaska. Cracked us up, he did. And tomorrow, Comrade Rogov has told us we're going to have a Funeral of the Superstitions. The lads have already knocked up a coffin."

Klim clearly pulled out all the stops trying to keep the sailors entertained.

"No wonder they're so fond of you," Anton Emilievich told him. "It's as they say—birds of a feather flock together."

But to Anton Emilievich's surprise and indignation, Klim's popularity extended beyond the sailors. It was rumored that when he gave public lectures, the assembly hall was filled with hundreds of people, mostly young ladies and students.

Anton Emilievich went along, curious to see what his nephew had to say, although the subject seemed unremarkable—"The Nature of Power and Control Over the Masses."

The assembly hall was packed, indeed. The audience shivered from cold. The feeble light of the electric lamps shone through the mist of breath that had gathered over the heads of the people.

"Several days ago, I was leafing through an old copy of the periodical *Annals of the Fatherland*," Klim said as he went up on stage. "And I came across a phrase written in 1811 by Count de Maistre, ambassador to the Russian court from the King of Piedmont-Sardinia: 'Every nation has the government it deserves.' Would you agree with that?"

The listeners began to exchange glances. Some people became indignant, some shrugged, and some nodded, "We don't deserve anything better."

Klim sat down in the chair in the middle of the stage.

"As I see it, the ambassador was wrong," he said. "There is a method that can be used by any government to hang onto power, which has nothing to do with the individual qualities of their citizens or the things they deserve. My father was a prosecutor, and when I was a child, he regularly took me to jail to see life as it really was, warts and all. Do you want to know what I discovered there? A jail is ruled not by the authorities or the wardens. It's a system conceived and governed by the prisoners themselves, and the prison guards' job is solely to keep it running."

Klim was a natural-born actor. He dramatically described what had happened to the noblest souls who had been deprived of their freedom of speech, freedom of movement, and their freedom to survive and live honestly. They were forced to bow and scrape to the most powerful inmates to save themselves from a beating or to get an extra ladleful of soup. And the privileged criminals and their patrons from the prison administration made sure that this predetermined order of poverty, violence, and hierarchy never changed.

"If you want to live, become a part of the system," Klim said in a quiet, menacing voice. "If you want to succeed, protect the system and remember that universal freedom is an abstract idea while the freedom to hand out food and thrash your subordinates is very real."

Klim broadened his shoulders, and the character he was playing, the scoundrel who had risen through the ranks, disappeared before his audience's eyes.

They were stunned. Everyone knew that what Klim had been talking about wasn't the prison of his childhood but the events that were unfolding here in the country right now.

"This system feeds on human flesh," Klim said, "it reproduces itself, and heals its wounds very quickly. If you remove one petty tyrant, somebody else will take his place in no time."

"What if a system like that were to be put in place throughout a whole country?" someone asked.

There was an uproar in the audience.

"We should organize strikes."

"The international community should treat a country like that as a pariah state."

Klim shook his head. "The worse the economic conditions get, the stronger the system becomes because people become even more dependent on their rulers."

"So, what should we do?" cried a girl in the front row.

"Those who are trapped inside the system have only two choices," Klim said, "either serve their time in prison, hoping that one day it will turn into a resort, or…escape."

The audience left the assembly hall in shocked silence. Klim had forced each and every one of them to confront their future face to face.

"It takes a lot of courage to say such things openly," a man with a goatee said to Anton Emilievich. "But still, to me, it smacks of desperation or mad posturing."

"He's just a fool," Anton Emilievich snapped. He was aware that his nephew's lack of caution might end up costing him dearly.

2

Coming home, Anton Emilievich called for Klim and told him in no uncertain terms that—while he was welcome to go around asking for trouble—he should leave the house immediately if that was what he planned to do.

Then Anton Emilievich talked to Nina. "Do you want to be widowed a second time? Isn't it enough that your brother has been shot?"

He was gratified to hear Nina scolding her husband. And then it was Osip's turn to give Klim the tongue lashing he deserved. Anton Emilievich's description of Klim's lecture was laid on a bit thick, and Osip had yelled at Klim so terribly that Marisha gave a start and dropped the soup tureen.

Lubochka managed to calm Osip down.

"So, what did he say?" Anton Emilievich asked when she came to his room.

"Osip says that if anything like that happens again, he'll shoot Klim himself as a traitor to the revolution."

Anton Emilievich cracked his knuckles. He deeply regretted that in a fit of altruism his daughter had invited Klim and Nina to stay with them.

"How are we going to get rid of Klim?" Anton Emilievich asked Lubochka. "How long is he going to live here? He's a foreign citizen, so he could easily leave the city with no questions asked. But he refuses to go because of his precious Nina. I don't see what the fuss is about. It's not as though there weren't any dishwashers in Argentina. Still, if he does go back, he'll get his head bashed in soon enough."

Lubochka frowned. "What are you talking about?"

Anton Emilievich showed her an extract from the Bulletin of the Russian News Agency:

On January 7, 1919, a riot took place in Buenos Aires, ending in clashes with the police. Many blamed the communists, and in the days that followed, the crowd carried out a pogrom against the houses and shops of immigrants from Russia. More than seven hundred people died during the massacre, and more than four thousand were wounded.

Lubochka snatched the paper from her father's hands and headed for the door. "I need to show this to Klim."

"Don't!" Anton Emilievich cried. "If you do, he'll stay here forever."

Lubochka looked at him, her eyes narrowed. "That's fine by me."

3

EL CUADERNO NEGRO

Klim Rogov's little black notebook

In the past, I found it hard not to reproach Nina for not coming with me when it was still possible to leave Russia. I thought that if we'd gone then, we could have saved not only ourselves but also Zhora. But evidently, Nina's instinct of self-preservation is keener than mine. If we'd been in Buenos Aires, we'd probably be dead by now. After all, everyone there knows I'm Russian.

Seven hundred killed. It's impossible to grasp that the good old *porteños* are capable of such a crime.

I feel helpless. Nina and Sofia Karlovna think they'll find a safe haven in France. Like hell they will. It'll just be more of the same. We're condemned everywhere to be outsiders—an unknown quantity and, therefore, guilty of all the troubles of the universe.

The world has gone mad, and we have nowhere to run. Except perhaps to the end of the earth, Patagonia, where you can go for months without seeing a single soul. All you see are the blue snow-capped mountains, crystal-clear lakes, and the grass rippling in the wind. We could set up an estancia and farm sheep—that would be the life, all right. But I'll never get my wife to agree to it. Sofia Karlovna has already seduced her with her Parisian scheme. Nina isn't daunted at the idea of France—she knows some French, and she's been there before. As for me, to be honest, I no longer care.

After my public lecture, everyone in the house attacked me, accusing me of stupidity, selfishness, and short-sightedness. Nina reminded me how harshly I had condemned her for her participation in the underground resistance movement.

"But what you are doing," she said, "is utterly suicidal. Do you have some kind of a death wish?"

In fact, I suppose I have a "life wish"—a craving for a normal life, and it's very difficult to suppress it. If I have something to say, and I see other people ready to listen, it's the most natural thing in the world for me to get it off my chest.

For the same reason I want to put my heart into my teaching.

"What are you trying to prove to your sailors?" Nina asked me. "They're hopeless savages, and you can't improve them."

But I'm not interested in trying to improve anyone. I just show my students that there are many ways to live their lives. We're all different, and we all have a right to exist so long as we don't cause troubles for our neighbors.

People at war become deaf and dumb. To keep one's mouth shut and stop even trying to explain yourself is to maintain a state of war. If all I see when I look at my sailors are violent degenerates, then I'm at war with them. But we can all get along together! They're simply different from us, and we need to accept them as they are. Then everything will fall into place.

I'm not saying that everyone has to love one other. Say what you like, but I can't stand Lubochka. I'm not fond of Uncle Anton either. Still, I'm talking about basic principles: if you don't like a person, avoid them by all means, but don't try to destroy them or remake them in your own image and likeness.

There's no point in me scribbling these angry notes. Nina believes it's another sign of my careless nature—to keep a diary that might cost me my life. Well—I did promise her that I would be careful. And in any case, it's too late to lament our fate.

4

Nina came into the room and loosened the knot of her headscarf. "Have you been burning papers?" she asked.

Klim was sitting by the stove stirring at the coals with a poker. An empty leather binding lay on the floor beside him.

"What happened?" Nina said, alarmed.

"Nothing." Klim sighed. "I just decided to get rid of a witness."

Nina sat down next to him. She picked up the leather cord that Klim used to bind his notebook.

"Once Zhora wrote a poem," she said.

The strings of life are tied in a knot?
It doesn't mean they break or rot.
Sometimes you win, sometimes you don't,
But you must survive, no matter what.

Nina decorated the cord with several ornate knots and then tied it around Klim's wrist.

25. PREPARING TO RUN

1

The spring and the early summer of 1919 were fraught with expectation and filled with frantic activity. Klim managed to obtain official permission for a railroad car for his propaganda efforts. The car had once been used as a mobile chapel and was now lying disused in a siding. But although the cogs of the bureaucratic machine continued to turn and meetings were held to decide on programs and budgets, no locomotive could be found to pull the propaganda car. All serviceable engines were working at maximum capacity, transporting troops, ammunition, and food.

Admiral Kolchak was advancing from the east, General Yudenich was coming in to attack the Bolsheviks from the north, and General Denikin was moving up from the south. The newspapers were reporting that "the ring of the frontline is closing in."

Clearly, things were looking bad for the Soviets to judge by the panic and frenzy in government offices. The city was in an agony of suspense, and senses were heightened. No one knew in which direction the Whites were moving, how strong they were, and which of the "damned imperialists" was giving them support.

Nina tried to remain skeptical. A year earlier, it had also looked as though the defeat of the Reds was inevitable. There was nothing for it but to wait and listen, to keep their ears and eyes open.

Klim drew up the staffing plan for the members of his propaganda team himself. He now had a number of official documents covered in stamps and signatures, according to which Dr. Sablin was charged with explaining the health benefits of personal hygiene to Red Army soldiers, Sofia Karlovna was to handle supplies and requisites, Nina Kupina was to work as an administrative assistant, and Klim himself was to provide ideological leadership.

"We'll need to hope Osip doesn't check the staff list," he said. "Otherwise, he'll realize in no time that we're planning to bail out."

They bided their time and waited for their chance, saving what they could for scraping together an "escape fund." They sold Sofia Karlovna's earrings, but by spring of 1919, the Russian ruble had lost all of its value. The People's Bank might as well have been printing candy wrappers—nothing to be ashamed of perhaps for those who espoused the Bolshevik view that the communist state would eventually have no need of money. In the meantime, banknote printing became the most efficient and fastest growing industry in Russia. The only thing that kept a check on rising inflation was the availability of paper.

"Soon, we'll see announcements in the street," Klim said, "for sale: an elegant snuffbox for your monthly food ration and a large wheelbarrow for your monthly wages."

But the situation had serious implications for their "escape fund," which had to be kept in foreign currency if they wanted it kept safe. Meanwhile, the deutsche mark, the French franc, and the British pound were all losing value due to postwar inflation. And in any case, the banknotes rustled if you hid them in your clothes, as Nina soon found out.

"If the Cheka searches us, they'll definitely find the money," she said after a few experiments. "Perhaps we should try dollars."

But while it might still have been possible to find European currency at the flea market or in the alleys beside the railroad station, American dollars weren't to be had at any price, and there were provocateurs and counterfeiters on all sides. Once Sablin brought home a forged banknote signed by the "Komissar of Finanse."

In the end, they decided it would be best to convert their savings into alcohol. Klim and Sablin made a wooden field kit with slots for tubes, and Nina labeled each tube with a label saying, "Caution! Typhoid bacteria!" On the side of the box, she wrote, "Medical equipment of vital importance."

The question of clothes was a worry. Should they buy them or not? On the one hand, it would be good to take as many clothes as possible because garments could be swapped for food. On the other hand, anyone traveling with luggage was asking to be robbed by local commissars eager to requisition "bourgeois property." At the very least, they needed military uniforms for Klim and Sablin so that they could pass themselves off as frontline soldiers. It was rumored that the barrier troopers were afraid of them.

The most difficult problem of all was how to disguise the old countess. Sofia Karlovna was horrified at the thought of pretending to be a simple old peasant woman. Moreover, since the death of Anna Evgenievna, the old countess' mind was beginning to wander, and on occasion, her tongue ran away with her.

"Good gracious, their butler has a mustache!" she exclaimed upon seeing a policeman in the waiting room at the Executive Committee offices. "When did you ever see a butler with a mustache? He should wear side whiskers."

Nina felt very uneasy at the thought of traveling with her mother-in-law. What if she was to let slip something like that in the presence of Bolsheviks and give them all away?

Sofia Karlovna lectured Nina time and again.

"At the market today you called out for Mr. Rogov by name. A well-brought up young lady never raises her voice. If she wants to be noticed in a crowd, she must take off her hat, put it on her parasol, and raise it above her head."

"But, Sofia Karlovna, I have neither a parasol nor a hat."

"That won't do. And don't look at me like that. I understand that your family believed that a woman's place was in her kitchen and thus didn't set great store by your upbringing. But how are you supposed to raise a child if you know nothing yourself?"

Sometimes Nina wished that Klim had never met the old countess in the street. But, however difficult life was with Sofia Karlovna, they couldn't have done without her diamonds. And besides, the old countess had influential relatives in Paris who could help them find visas and accommodation once they got to France.

2

Lubochka was pregnant, and she had decided that Nina could be of help to her running errands now and looking after the baby in the future.

"It will be hard to cope with the baby and the canteen at the same time," she told Nina. "You will help me, won't you?"

Nina went with her to market. On the first day, they bought swaddling clothes and on the next, a goat.

"I'm afraid my nerves will affect my milk," Lubochka fretted, "and I won't be able to feed the baby myself. We need to get a goat just in case. Do you know how to milk them? I've heard it's not that difficult. I'm sure you'll learn."

Lubochka quite legitimately asked for favors in return for her kindness, and Nina couldn't refuse her. She tried to put Lubochka's mind at rest, did everything she was asked, and assured her that her figure would soon get back to normal after childbirth.

"I'm so ugly these days," Lubochka sobbed. "Osip doesn't pay me the slightest attention anymore."

Indeed, Osip came home, and every night after dinner, he suddenly got up from the table and went to Klim's room.

"Are you there?" he asked, knocking on the door. "May I come in?"

They played cards and always ended up in heated arguments.

"You think that society is divided into classes that have to compete with each other," Klim said to Osip. "But I still can't figure out for the life of me which class I belong to. I was born into the nobility, but I've lived my life like a tramp. Whose side am I supposed to be on?"

"You're a declassed element," Osip told him, "and you have to decide which side you should move to. Look, some live by their own work while others exploit them, and we need to put a stop to it."

"I don't mind being exploited," Klim said, shrugging his shoulders. "If a publisher pays me well and stays out of my private life, why should I fight him? If I fight him and win—God forbid—there won't be anyone to pay my wages."

"Then the products of your labor will be yours, and you can do with them as you like."

"But what if that doesn't suit me? For me, it's much more convenient to write an article and sell it to an exploiter."

"Pah!" Osip spat in disgust. "Why do you always bring everything back to yourself?"

"All right then, let's talk about you. What class are you?"

"I'm a worker, of course. What else?"

"I don't think so. You haven't worked in a factory since 1914. You're a bureaucrat just like my father."

Osip laughed. He was amused by the comparison with the Public Prosecutor.

Klim feigned innocence. "What are you laughing at? Who rides the workers? Who produces nothing but paperwork?"

"But I don't assume the products of someone else's labor."

"Really? Then where do your party rations come from? Some might say you're an exploiter yourself."

"I've never heard such rubbish in my life!" Osip exclaimed, blood rushing to his face.

"That's exactly what my father used to say."

Nina pleaded with Klim to stop arguing with Osip. "What if he gets angry and does something to harm you?"

But Klim thought that the arguments with Osip were helping them find common ground.

"Osip doesn't trust anyone, you see. He thinks everyone is out to exploit him, but he feels safe with me because he knows exactly what to expect. He's lonely, and all he's trying to do is make friends."

"But you're completely different from one another."

"So what? We're honest, and we respect each other."

"You respect Osip?" Nina asked in surprise.

"Absolutely."

3

The pregnancy took its toll on Lubochka. First, she suffered from sickness and then from back pain. She was terribly anxious that she might not be able to carry on working at the canteen after having her baby. If she lost her job and access to provisions, how could she hope to feed a child? She no longer put her faith in Osip. Recently, he seemed to have lost interest in everything except his precious Military Commissariat, his card games, and his political discussions. He wasn't happy at all about her pregnancy and treated her as though she had a serious illness.

She tried to alarm him by telling him that Sablin had become particularly attentive toward her, but Osip didn't believe a pregnant woman could be of any interest to any man in his right mind.

"Have you looked at yourself in the mirror lately?"

It was true. Lubochka had all but lost what looks she had. Her thighs, chest, and neck had puffed up, and her fingers were now so fat that her rings no longer fit her.

"Will I stay like this?" Lubochka pestered Sablin. "Why don't you say anything? You're a doctor. You should know."

"It's not really my field," Sablin said, averting his gaze.

Anton Emilievich also felt nervous about her situation.

"If you ask me, you made a bad choice," he told Lubochka one day. "You couldn't have found yourself a worse husband."

She lost her temper. "If it weren't for Osip, we wouldn't be living in this house, and there would be no canteen."

"Look at you now weeping and wailing," Anton Emilievich said. "And where is he? Playing cards with Klim, that's where. You were the one who brought your cousin here, so it serves you right."

4

Lubochka had gathered various strands of love under one roof. For Sablin, she felt the sort of pitying love that one feels for a child; she loved Osip for his ability to provide for her, but her passion was reserved for Klim and Klim alone.

Lubochka watched him sitting in the armchair and writing something down in the notebook she had given him. He scratched his thick eyebrow and chuckled to himself. He had probably thought of a joke but didn't want to share it with anyone yet.

She cherished every memory of him ever touching her. The one when he had brought her a shawl and wrapped it around her shoulders to keep her warm or when he had gently placed his hand on her belly after she had told him the baby was kicking.

Lubochka did her best to persuade herself that she wasn't feeling jealous, but one day, as she was walking down the corridor, she heard Klim's voice.

"If you cut my hair crooked," he said, "that hard-boiled crew will laugh me out of the classroom."

The door to the bathroom was slightly ajar. Lubochka tiptoed to it and saw Klim sitting on a low stool. His shoulders were covered with a white sheet, and he was trying to sit still while Nina trimmed his hair.

"How much longer?" he asked.

"Hold on a minute."

She blew the cut hair from his neck and took the sheet off his shoulders. Lubochka had never seen her cousin half-naked like this before. She drank in the sight of his broad, swarthy back and his reflection in a mirror—his chest covered with dark hair and the narrow strip of hair running down into the waistband of his trousers.

"I think it's turned out well," Nina said. "Do you want me to cut a little more from the left side?"

"No, I don't."

Suddenly, Klim pulled Nina close to him.

"Stop—" she gasped. "What if someone—"

He lifted his wife and put her on a low cabinet by the wall. Klim parted Nina's knees and pressed himself to her, and Lubochka felt as though her heart was about to burst. Nina put her arms around him and sank onto his shoulder. Suddenly, her gaze met Lubochka's.

"Don't forget to clean up after yourselves," Lubochka said and staggered to the kitchen, scarlet with emotion and with tears starting in her eyes.

26. THE SAFE

1

Osip met Klim after the lecture.

"I've arranged everything. Get your team ready—you leave at nine this evening."

"Where am I going?" Klim asked.

"The Whites have broken the front near Kursk. Morale is low, and soldiers are deserting, so, the army's political administration is summoning all of the propaganda reserves. The propaganda car stays here, I'm afraid. You'll travel in a separate compartment, and you can find yourself a transport when you get there. Here's your warrant." Osip handed Klim a piece of paper. "I called the Cheka office—the secretary will wait for you until six. Bring your team's employment cards, and she'll give you all permission to leave. They're expecting you in Kursk."

Klim turned pale. "What about you?"

"I'm also going to the front, but not with you. My train leaves in two hours." Osip squeezed Klim's hand. "Stay faithful to the revolution! When you talk to the soldiers, remind them that the Red Army has to be invincible. If the Whites defeat us, they'll restore the Tsarist government, bring back the landlords, and punish the workers for rebellion. They should remember that they have created the world's first state of workers and peasants."

2

Osip called in at the canteen to speak to Lubochka.

She went into the corridor holding a coffee grinder in her hands. "We got a hold of real coffee," she said. "Smell!"

Osip dutifully inhaled the scent of the coffee but breathed out too hard so that the dark brown powder went all over Lubochka's dress. "Sorry," he said, embarrassed.

She shook the coffee grounds from her skirt. "Don't worry. I've gotten ten pounds of the stuff. Do you want a cup of coffee?"

Osip shook his head. "Thank you, no. I've come to ask a favor. Do you think you could visit my parents and bring them something—maybe bread or money?"

Lubochka looked at him, frowning. "What are you going to do?"

"I'm going to the front."

"When?"

"Now. This moment."

3

Lubochka dashed home with her heart thumping and tears running down her cheeks, still holding the coffee grinder in her hands. She wished that she could just drop down dead in the street. One minute she was cursing Osip, and the next, she was remembering how tightly he had held her when he had said goodbye.

She had begun to scream so loudly that the entire kitchen staff had run into the corridor to see what was going on.

Osip had looked at Lubochka with a pained expression. "You have to understand. Now isn't the time to think only of saving your own skin."

"I'm only thinking about our baby! Don't you understand it could be left an orphan?"

She had told him that he didn't love her anymore and would rather risk a bullet to the head than go on living with her. "Go to hell," she had said. "Just see if I care."

Osip had grabbed her by the arms.

"Don't think badly of me, Lubochka," he had said. "Drop me a line if you have a chance—I'll look forward to getting a letter from you."

4

On the porch of her house, Lubochka met Sablin. He looked unlike himself in his new soldier's overcoat with a knapsack on his back.

"Where are you going?" Lubochka asked.

It was clear that Sablin wasn't expecting to see her there. "I'm going to the front," he said, tipping his cap.

She took a step backward and hit her back hard on the railing of the porch. "What do you mean? Have you all gone mad? You can't go! What about your leg—"

She stopped as she heard the gate squeak. Nina and Klim ran into the yard.

"Dr. Sablin, we are ready," Nina cried.

"Tell me what's going on!" Lubochka demanded.

Klim looked at Nina. "Go with the doc. I'll catch up with you two later."

He took Lubochka gently by her shoulders. "We need to talk. Let's go inside."

They entered the house and went into Lubochka's room glowing with the evening sun. She put the grinder on the table strewn with half-made swaddling clothes.

"Do you still have Nina's employment card?" Klim asked.

"Yes," Lubochka said.

"Is it at the canteen office?"

"No, it's here." She pointed at the safe that had once kept Klim's father's legacy. "The burglars often rob canteens, so I had to bring the papers here. Just in case."

"Can I have it, please?"

Lubochka looked at him in surprise. "Is Nina going to leave her job?"

"Yes. We want to get out of Nizhny Novgorod," Klim said. "Without her employment card, we can't get permission from the Cheka."

Finally, Lubochka realized that they were planning to escape from the land of the Soviets. She crossed her arms over her chest and glared at Klim. How dare he ask her for anything? She had given him shelter and helped him find work, and now, he was going to leave her alone and pregnant just when she had been abandoned by her husband.

"I hope this is some sort of joke," she said and, beside herself, hurled the grinder at Klim. It missed and hit the wall, and coffee grounds scattered onto the carpet.

"Lubochka, don't be ridiculous—" began Klim, but she interrupted him.

"Or what? Are you going to kill me to get into the safe? Come on, then, why don't you? I know that physically you are more than a match for me, but you're not getting the code from me no matter what."

Klim sighed, walked to the safe, and pushed it over onto the carpet. Then he pressed at the bottom of the safe, which gave way. Putting his hand inside, Klim drew out a pile of papers.

"Father got this safe," he said, "as a souvenir from the insurance company after he'd gotten two burglars sent to jail. They had opened the safe so neatly that no one could guess what had happened to the two hundred thousand rubles locked inside. The door was intact, and the lock closed. It was only later that the investigator realized they had cut out the bottom with a special tool from America."

Tears streamed down Lubochka's cheeks. "Why are you leaving me behind? You still don't understand that I love you, do you?"

"Lubochka…" Klim said in a reproachful tone. "Possessing doesn't mean loving."

"Do you think Nina loves you? She wrecked your life. She took away everything you had. And I pulled you out of the mire, and after that, you—"

Klim put Nina's employment card in his pocket. "I know you've done your best, and I'm very grateful. But Nina and I are unhappy here." He paused, not knowing what to add. "Thanks for everything," he said at last.

"Damn you!" Lubochka yelled after him as he left.

She stood in the middle of the room next to the overturned safe surrounded by scattered papers. The house was as quiet as an abandoned mine.

Gradually, it dawned on Lubochka that she had no one left. It had all happened so quickly! Clearly, Klim had planned his escape. While she had struggled to guarantee him benefits that ordinary people couldn't have dreamed of, he had been plotting against her all of the time.

But what about Sablin? How could he have abandoned her?

With a decisive step, Lubochka went into the hall and reached for the telephone on the wall.

"May I help you?" asked the operator.

"Nine-forty, please," said Lubochka.

Suddenly, the connection was broken off.

"Don't." Her father came into the hall holding an unplugged telephone wire. "Don't call the Cheka."

"So, you're on their side too, are you?" asked Lubochka, taking a step back from him.

Anton Emilievich shook his grizzled head. "Let them go," he said. "They'll have their necks wrung somewhere along the way. But if we call the Cheka, there will be an investigation, and the first thing they'll do is come here. Is that really what you want?"

He stepped toward his daughter and took her in his arms. She sobbed on his shoulder like a child.

5

On their way to the special service train standing on the sidetrack, the "Red propagandists" were constantly stopped by patrols who demanded their documents. Nina held Klim's hand and kept looking behind her to check that the old countess and Dr. Sablin were able to keep up.

It was horrible—creeping away like this with their tails between their legs and feeling so vulnerable at every moment. All they could do was keep praying silently, "Lord, have mercy on us!"

What if something went wrong? What if there was no locomotive? What if there was some sort of mistake in their documents?

A Cheka man at the footsteps of the railroad car examined their documents for a few agonizing minutes, scraping at the paper with his fingernail while his lips moved. It took some time for Nina to realize that he was holding the permits upside down. The man was illiterate.

Deliriously happy, they got into their compartment and locked the door. Could it be that they had made it? But, no—it was still too early to rejoice.

Klim put the field kit on the top shelf.

"Sofia Karlovna," he said, "I forgot to ask—should a gentleman carry a lady's knapsack?"

He was still able to joke.

"What are you talking about?" the old countess sniffed. "A gentleman shouldn't carry anything for a lady except perhaps one or two books or a beautifully wrapped box of chocolates."

"We're fine then," sighed Klim with relief, helping Nina to take off her knapsack. "Still, I feel sorry for Kaiser. Lubochka is sure to deny him his rations as punishment for our sins, and I'm sure she'll eat Speckle."

"Oh, do be quiet!" Sablin pleaded.

At nine o'clock, the train was still standing motionless in the same place. They spent another two hours in silence, devastated and jittery with anxiety. They heard soldiers running on the roof of the train and someone shouting at the conductor on the other side of the wall.

Finally, the engine whistled, the train jerked, and the grim buildings of railroad depots began to slide past the window.

"Rissoles—a hundred rubles each," the attendant said, sticking his head around the door of the compartment. "White flatbread—forty rubles. Hot water—two rubles."

6

Before the revolution, it had been possible to board a train in the evening and arrive in Moscow the following day.

The day after they had boarded the special service train, it had only gotten as far as Doskino two stations away from Nizhny Novgorod. Even the commander of an infantry regiment in the neighboring compartment—a very stern character—was unable to figure out the mysterious ways in which the railroad administration worked. He tried everything, including threats to shoot the staff, but neither swearing nor pointing a gun at the engine driver's head had any effect.

"What am I supposed to do if I've been ordered to let the troop trains go ahead?" snapped the engine driver.

There was no other choice but to watch the boxcars full of recruits roll by. The sides of the cars were painted with slogans: "All forces join the fight against General Denikin!" Soldiers sat in the open doorways with row upon row of heads behind them.

"Cannon fodder," Sablin whispered under his breath.

The "propagandists" arrived in Moscow the following week only to learn that the Whites under General Denikin had taken Poltava, Kremenchug, and Ekaterinoslav and launched an offensive against Kiev and Odessa.

It took them three weeks to receive passes from the Central Office of Military Communications. Unfortunately, by that time, the papers issued by Osip had expired. The Bolshevik officials were scared witless and claimed to have no idea what was going on at the front. The situation was changing every day, and communications with Kursk were sporadic.

Finally, all permissions were granted.

7

The "propagandists" boarded another special service train. This time, the neighboring compartment was occupied by a group of Red Army officers newly graduated from military school. Sablin gazed at the peasant boys. They were neatly dressed, polite, and modest, and their heads were filled with Bolshevik propaganda, nationalism, and flag-waving. They were clearly proud of the fact that the important folk in Moscow had such high expectations of them.

With no watches or calendars, the passengers could only guess at how much time was passing. They ate what the cook sent from the dining car and washed using the services of women who came to the station platforms with soap, towels, and buckets of water.

During the first days of their journey, Sablin was still having trouble taking in the enormity of what he had done. Every second took him closer to the frontline, and the only thing he knew for certain was that there was no way back.

He had not imagined how unbearable it would be to live in one compartment with Klim and Nina. She cut up an apple, stood on her bed, and passed the pieces one by one to Klim as he lay on the upper berth. Then instead of sitting down, she remained standing there whispering in Klim's ear and laughing softly, making Sablin feel awkward, unwanted, and in the way.

The old countess sat playing patience, and Sablin thought longingly of Lubochka and the look she had given him when he had waved her goodbye. Really, when all was said and done, they had repaid her kindness very poorly.

I should have stayed in Nizhny Novgorod with her, Sablin thought for the hundredth time. *I don't care if she's having another man's baby. I love her.*

But still, he had been right to leave his hometown. The past was dead and buried, and now, he had to learn how to live again just as he had learned to walk again after being wounded in the leg. And while he had no idea how things would turn out, he felt in his bones that soon he would be able to talk, think, and work without idiotic government controls and degrading permits. It wouldn't be long now.

In the night, when the "propagandists" were sitting in the neighboring compartment talking to the young officers, they heard the distant rumble of cannons.

"It sounds as though we're close to the frontline," Klim said, his eyes shining with anxiety.

One of the young men raised his hand as though he were about to smooth his hair and quickly crossed himself. The other officers did the same.

27. THE RED PROPAGANDISTS

1

The "propagandists" were up half of the night whispering and trying to work out how to get across the frontline.

Sablin knew that it was useless to discuss it at this point—they needed to get to Kursk first of all and see how the land lay—but he still found himself arguing with Klim. "We mustn't take on any guides. They might lure us into a trap and kill us, or they'll give us away to the Reds."

"First of all, we need a map," Nina insisted. "If we had a good map, we could figure it out."

Sablin could hardly contain himself. "If they search us and find a map, they'll know exactly what we're up to."

Sofia Karlovna couldn't offer any advice but sat fretting silently and swallowing the sedative drops she had brought with her.

At last, quite worn out, they climbed into their berths. Sablin listened to the drumming of the wheels on the track. A single thought went around and around in his head: *Will we get through?* He folded his arms behind his head and caught the smell of sweat from the underarms of his dirty tunic, the smell of a live body. Still alive.

The window curtains fluttered, and an enamel cup on the table tinkled softly.

Suddenly, there was a knock at the door. "Get up! Show your documents!"

Sablin sat up suddenly and hit his head on the luggage rack. The old countess lit a candle in a tin.

"What's going on?" asked Klim.

"I don't know—" Sofia Karlovna said. "I suppose they're looking for deserters again."

People were stirring in the next-door compartment. The guard was walking down the corridor crying, "Look lively there, comrades!"

Sablin climbed down and sat next to Sofia Karlovna. She had covered herself with her overcoat—she always shivered during searches.

Klim opened the door and peered out. "It seems there's a whole congress of soldiers' deputies here," he said. "Dr. Sablin, give me the documents."

Sablin shoved the tattered papers into Klim's hand.

"Here are our propagandists, sir," the guard said respectfully to someone standing in the corridor with a crowd of Red Army soldiers and other passengers behind his back.

"Goodnight, comrades. Sorry to disturb you."

Klim yawned into his fist. "That's fine."

The guard looked over his shoulder again, the soldiers stepped aside, and Osip Drugov entered the compartment.

In a flash, he understood everything. Sablin sat speechless with his heart thumping in his ears. *That's it. We're done for,* he thought in horror. But Osip wasn't looking at him.

"So, you took Nina with you, did you?" he asked, glaring at Klim. "Weren't you afraid she'd be killed?"

Klim bit his lip and said nothing. Osip snatched the documents from his hand, took a flashlight from his pocket, and carefully scanned the papers. Then he tore them all to pieces—permits, identity cards, and even Klim's Argentine passport.

His face contorted by a nervous grimace, Osip directed the flashlight into Klim's eyes. "When they told me you were in the fourth car, I immediately made up my mind to come. I was hoping to see a friend. I hoped we'd go to the front together." Osip turned to the soldiers. "These traitors are making their way to the Whites—as a family, so to speak. So, Dr. Sablin, you're going to join General Denikin too, are you? You decided to leave Lubochka behind?"

Sablin tugged at the collar of his tunic as though it were choking him.

"Search the place," Osip ordered the soldiers. "Check their clothing. They might have jewels hidden anywhere—in pencils, candles, or bread. They might have coins in the soles of their shoes or covered with cloth and sewn on instead of buttons. As for you," he turned to Klim, "you come with me."

Nina rushed to Osip and clung to his arm. "No! Please—don't!"

Osip pushed her away so hard that she fell against the table.

"Good God, are you out of your mind?" Sofia Karlovna shrieked.

The soldiers dragged Klim out of the compartment.

"Wait!" cried Sablin. Elbowing his way through the soldiers, he rushed into the corridor and then along to the rattling gangway at the end of the car.

"Open the door," Osip told the terrified guard, "unless you want to clean up the blood from the floor."

The door clanked open. A gust of cold air filled the gangway, and the sound of the wheels grew louder. The early morning sky glowed pale behind the surging mass of the dark forest.

The soldiers put Klim against the door. Osip gave his flashlight to the guard—"Point this at him!"—and pulled his revolver out of its holster.

"Osip, don't you dare!" Sablin shouted, grabbing him by the arm.

A gunshot rang out, and Klim fell from the car. A woman's desperate shriek echoed inside the compartment.

Osip fastened his holster slowly and carefully. Then without warning, he slammed his fist hard into the doctor's head. Sablin fell facedown on the spittle-covered floor.

"Comrade Drugov, they have a box full of spirits," a soldier shouted from the compartment.

Trembling all over, the guard gazed pleadingly at Osip. "Believe me, I didn't know they were deserters."

"You should have been more careful," Osip said through his teeth and strode away.

2

The Red Army soldiers took Sablin, Nina, and Sofia Karlovna off the train at an unnamed station and brought them to a military checkpoint in a requisitioned grain elevator. Grain lay scattered all over the ground. People trampled it into the mud, and cavalry horses strained their necks to reach it with their lips.

From time to time, artillery fire boomed in the distance.

The prisoners were all put into a large hall, men and women together. There were two guards at the door: one was in a soldier's uniform with a revolver in his hand, and the other was wearing torn trousers and a sailor's cap with a handwritten inscription: "Red Terror." His only weapon was an ax.

"Is the *Red Terror* the name of your ship?" Sablin asked.

"It's the name of our campaign," the guard answered grimly.

Sofia Karlovna was fussing around Nina. "Do you want me to see if I can get you some water?"

Nina didn't even look at the old countess. Her face was bloodless, and her pupils were so dilated that her eyes looked black.

Sablin too was having trouble grasping what had just happened. How had Osip ended up in their railroad car? Why had he killed Klim and then disappeared without showing the slightest interest in the rest of the "traitors"?

Sablin's throat tightened with sorrow for his friend. Klim had come bursting into their world and turned it upside down, stealing Nina's heart, poor girl.

And they'll kill you in a couple of hours too. The sudden thought brought Sablin up short. *Oh, Lubochka—you chose to love a murderer.*

There were about thirty prisoners in the room. Some were telling others the stories of their arrests.

One seventy-year-old man, formerly a village chief, had been arrested for pinning on his medal when he had heard that the Whites were on their way.

Two other prisoners said that they had come to the railroad station to try to exchange a barrel of pickled mushrooms for agricultural tools. They were arrested and charged with profiteering.

Sablin stood at the window watching as an endless train of carts passed by. The Bolsheviks were hastily evacuating the town. He already knew that their situation was hopeless. The *Red Terror* sailor had told them that prisoners wouldn't be taken back behind the lines but executed.

The sailor was nervous. He kept leaving the room to find out when the military checkpoint was to be evacuated. A second guard stayed with the prisoners in his absence.

Sablin felt his whole body burning as though seized by a fever. At first, just one thought kept going around and around in his head: *Are they really going to kill us?* Then he felt a rising sense of indignation and outrage. *We have to do something. We have to fight!*

He gazed at the remaining guard. The man was about forty-five, his face tanned and weather-beaten with bags under his eyes and a prominent mole on his nostril. He was sitting in the doorway and—for lack of anything to do—spitting at his feet trying to make the string of saliva reach to the ground.

Should I talk to him? Sablin thought. *Try to frighten him? Tell him that the other Red Army soldiers have left him behind?*

Now, the street outside was empty, and only the occasional messenger galloped by from time to time.

Sablin approached the remaining guard, trying his best to appear confident.

"Wait a minute," he said with a fake smile plastered on his face, "I think I know you. Where are you from?"

The soldier glared sullenly at him. "From Vladimir Region."

"What village?"

"Kostrovo."

"I knew it!" Sablin exclaimed. "I was there on holiday. I lived at the old woman's house. What was her name? She was all hunched and bent."

The soldier raised his eyebrows. "Do you mean old Nura?"

"That's it! Have you been there recently? How is she?"

"She's fine. Her hut is two streets away from where I live."

Sablin gave the guard a friendly slap on the shoulder. "That means you and I are almost family, aren't we? Fancy meeting you here!"

The soldier's name was Damian. He told Sablin in great detail all about his village, old Nura, and his family. Sablin found to his surprise that he was an inspired liar, telling the soldier that during the Great War, he had fought on the same part of the front as Damian and been wounded in the leg. They reminisced about battles, spoke critically of their commanders, and complained about the poor quality of their army greatcoats, which would come apart at the seams if they caught on anything.

I hope that damn sailor won't be back anytime soon, thought Sablin, peering out the window.

"Hey, Damian, do you know where your friend with the ax went?" Sablin asked.

The guard grinned. "He's gone off to ask for a machine gun to finish you all off."

"Are you going to shoot me?" Sablin asked, looking the guard in the eye.

Damian turned away. "Oh, come on!"

"So, you're going to let your friend do it for you?"

Damian quickly looked out. There was no one in the street.

"Go on," he hissed, "get out of here. Now. Don't worry about me—they won't touch me. They haven't registered the people who were arrested this morning. I'll say I never saw you."

"What about this lot?" Sablin asked, pointing at the silent prisoners. "After all, they might report that you let me go. What if you let all of us go home? Why bring more misery on everyone? Come to that, it's probably time you ran away yourself. The Whites are coming, and if they catch you here, they'll shoot you."

3

The square in front of the church was crowded with people. A Bolshevik agitator on a cart was calling on the women and children to resist provocation. "The colossal propaganda machine of imperialism is trying to corrupt the minds of our people," he ranted.

It's no good coming here, thought Sablin, stepping back to the alley where he had left Sofia Karlovna and Nina.

They had been circling around the town for more than an hour trying to find a place to hide until the arrival of the Whites. Sablin's knees were shaking from excitement or exhaustion. He still couldn't believe they had been set free. He glanced anxiously at the two women. The old countess was half-dead with fear while Nina looked as though she didn't care anymore where she was going or what was going to happen to her.

There was the sound of hooves, and a mounted patrol turned into the alley. Sablin held his breath: the Whites!

They rode along quite openly in their black and red caps and epaulets. They stopped, dismounted, and walked to the church square, leading their horses by the bridles.

The Bolshevik agitator was so carried away with his own eloquence that he failed to notice anything. "We'll crush the White bandits with the full might of our proletarian wrath—"

At that moment, his gaze fell on a White officer standing and swishing at his boots with a horsewhip.

"Go on, comrade, don't be shy," the officer prompted. "We're all ears."

The crowd burst into laughter.

A bell on the church tower pealed once and then twice. Large and small bells rang out in a merry chorus just as if it were Easter.

4

Sablin walked down the street limping even more heavily than usual. He felt joy bubbling up inside him from his heart to his throat, a joy so intense that it exceeded even his grief at the loss of his friend and the fear of death he had just experienced. The Whites were in town!

Everything around him had become meaningful again. The colors had become brighter, the air fresher. Never before had Sablin felt such a feeling of inspiration, such gratitude before fate. He wanted to kneel down in the middle of the road and weep for joy.

The dashing soldiers of the Kornilov Regiment, sunburned and dust-covered, filled the streets of the town. Children hung around them, boys gaping at the skull motif on the men's caps and badges.

"Look, look! See the skull and crossbones?" they whispered in awe. "That means, 'We'll destroy you all, sons of bitches.'"

"No, boys," Sofia Karlovna said, her voice trembling with emotion. "That symbol is known as 'Adam's Head.' It stands for the resurrection of the dead after the sacrifice of the body for one's country and one's people."

The orchestra in the church square struck up a tune—not any tune but none other than "God Save the Tsar."

Sablin turned to Nina and Sofia Karlovna. "I'm sorry, my dears, but I've made up my mind. I'm going to join the White Army. You'll have to find your way to Novorossiysk by yourselves."

"Oh," gasped the old countess. She stared at him for a while and then shook his hand. "It's a sacred cause, doctor. God bless you."

Nina said nothing. She stood at the old countess' side looking at the ground with a curl of hair come loose from her comb and hanging over her cheek. She was fingering mindlessly at the flap of her jacket.

Sablin felt alarmed. "Nina—dear—"

She looked at him vacantly. "Klim didn't make it by one day."

5

As soon as the railroads were working again, Sablin found places for Nina and Sofia Karlovna on a train to Novorossiysk. The acting commander was so happy with Sablin's work in caring for the wounded that he had issued a special pass for the "doctor's family," and the women were given places in a second-class officers' car.

Sablin—now wearing a cap with the emblem of the skull and crossbones—came to see them off.

"Do take care of yourself," the old countess said as she made the sign of the cross over him. "We shall try to get to Paris via Novorossiysk. Promise you'll write to us. Send us a letter to the Central Post Office, general delivery."

Sablin nodded gloomily. "If I'm still alive." He stood on the platform, waving them goodbye.

"He'll be killed for certain," Nina said with conviction as the train started moving.

"Why do you say that?" the old countess asked.

"Because it's obvious. It's always the good people who die. Always."

"Well, we're still alive."

"And we'll be killed too unless we learn how to—" Nina passed her hands over her face. "I don't know—to rob and murder. We're penniless, and I don't see how we're going to get to France with no money."

Sofia moved closer to Nina. "I have something hidden in here," she whispered, tapping her cheek. "It's in my tooth—or rather what's left of it. It's a half-carat diamond. It will keep us going for a while. Forgive me for these anatomical details, but I had no other hiding place."

The train slowed down and stopped to let an oncoming train pass. Nina was silent.

"A shrewd housewife never puts all her eggs in one basket," Sofia Karlovna added.

The old countess was eager for Nina to appreciate her prudence and foresight, but her daughter-in-law was staring out the window. Sofia Karlovna followed her gaze and saw the body of a hanged man dangling from a signal post.

It was Osip Drugov.

6

Sofia Karlovna couldn't remember at what point she had stopped seeing Nina simply as *that woman* and begun to look on her as a daughter. At first, the old countess had been unable to forgive Nina for marrying Vladimir. Later, Sofia Karlovna had been furious with Nina for having an affair with Fomin, and then she had smarted at her marrying Klim Rogov. The very idea that Nina had found comfort in the arms of a stranger was insulting, but Sofia Karlovna had been forced to hide her feelings because her daughter-in-law and Klim were the only people she had left in the world.

After Klim's death, she had become reconciled to Nina. *As for etiquette,* thought the old countess, *let he who is without sin throw the first stone.*

Now, Sofia Karlovna kept an eye on her daughter-in-law's state of mind and tried to make sure that Nina ate.

After the death of her first husband, Nina had been hysterical, which had been understandable. Now, she was calm and didn't even cry, although Sofia Karlovna could tell that something was very wrong. In an attempt to reassure Nina, the old countess babbled away about the life they would have together in France.

"We'll spend winters in Paris," she said, "and go to Burgundy in summer. I have some money in Crédit Lyonnais, and I'm thinking about buying a vineyard not far from Dijon. When I was your age, what I really wanted to do was to make wine. So, why not?"

Sofia Karlovna could almost see the dusty purple bunches of grapes and taste the juice of the first berry.

"Your grief will pass," she told Nina. "Not immediately, of course, but eventually, everything will fall into place. I loved my husband very much too. He was killed by a terrorist—in those days, students kept assassinating government officials one after the other."

"I'll never forget Klim," Nina replied and fell silent, realizing that not so long ago she had said the same thing about Vladimir.

Sofia Karlovna sighed.

"Only the first love stays with you forever, and the older you get, the more it means to you. When I was fourteen years old, my family lived in St. Petersburg right next to the residence of the Japanese consul. His son—we called him Jap—was always spying on us through the hole in the fence as we played in the backyard. One day, he sent me a letter: 'My dear cherry blossom, Sofia-san—' He finished with the line, 'As my body does its work, my soul is always with you.'

"I was stupid and showed the letter to my friends. They teased him, 'Hey, lover boy, do you want us to call for Sofia-san while your body is doing its work?' Soon, his family went away, and I never saw him again. Fifty years have passed, but I still remember him. And you will remember my son in that way too."

"Yes, I will," Nina said faintly.

7

Sofia Karlovna kept asking Nina, "Why are you so silent?"

Because there was nothing to talk about anymore. Nina had turned to stone: a swift reaction had swept through her body so that everything—her skin, muscles, and even her thoughts—had curdled and solidified.

What can I do with myself now? Nina wondered. She spent her days mired in contemptuous hatred of those who were still alive while Klim was dead. These other people breathed his air and ate his bread, and they had stolen the time that Nina had intended to spend with him alone. It was a daily desecration and sacrilege.

At night, she lay on her bed curled into a ball and repeated to the rhythm of the wheels, "Come back, come back—" She tried, again and again, to realize that never again would she look into Klim's laughing dark brown eyes.

The second-class car was dark, filled with a foul haze and the sound of snoring.

Do you want me to learn to live without you? But there's so much I still want to say to you. I want to sleep in your arms, watch you drink your tea in the morning, smooth down your hair, help you find your keys that have fallen under the table in the hall, bend to reach for them at the same time as you, and forget everything to kiss you on the lips. I want to wait for you to come home in the evening, look forward to it, be angry with you for always being late—always late—

28. THE WHITE ARMY

1

Fomin had paid the Cheka men off by giving them a huge bribe—all the money collected for the uprising. He felt terribly sorry for Zhora and Elena, but there was nothing he could do for them. He had had no choice but to drop everything and run away as fast as he could.

By November 1918, he had ended up in the headquarters of General Denikin. The White Army grew from nothing, thanks to the enthusiasm of volunteers willing to fight to save their country. But there weren't enough of them to defeat Bolshevism, and they had nothing with which to inspire the masses.

Nobody was able to explain in popular terms what the Whites were fighting for. The words "monarchy," "freedom," "constituent assembly," or "rule of law" meant nothing to the illiterate peasants. They understood only that the Whites would bring back landlords and make the peasants pay for the land they had gotten ahold of illegally. In such a situation, it was useless to expect them to offer help with food or to join up for the army.

The Bolsheviks had a much better position in terms of geography. They had gained control of almost all of the country's industrial enterprises and railroads. The population in the territory occupied by the Red Army was far greater and more ethnically homogeneous while the Whites had to deal with the border regions, each of which was seeking separatism. As long as the White generals stood up stubbornly for "one indivisible Russia," they alienated their potential allies from local elites.

But the main difficulty was the eternal problem of money—damn money!

Lack of funds led to a lack of supplies. White officers and officials were paid a pittance and so were prone to bribery and looting. One thing led to another, and by the summer of 1919, General Denikin and his army couldn't even find support far behind the frontlines in White-occupied territory.

Fomin did everything he could to convince the White generals that they needed a well-thought-out and easily understood political program that would clearly benefit the common people. But for them, the simplicity of slogans meant appealing to the most primitive popular beliefs. While the Bolsheviks blamed everything on the bourgeois, the Whites decided to blame everything on the Jews. The only idea that united the broad anti-Bolshevik coalition from monarchists to anarchists was blind, ruthless anti-Semitism. They believed that since there were so many Jews among the Bolshevik high officials and Red Army commanders, the revolution and the civil war in Russia were a part of the conspiracy of Jews seeking world domination. These sentiments resulted in anti-Semitic attacks of an unprecedented scale and brutality.

Fomin invested all of his energy in trying to establish quality propaganda in the White Army. He argued that they should stress the idea of patriotism, not nationalism or revenge. The Whites had to seek compromises, promote democracy, and campaign for help from abroad since only the Allies would give loans to fund the White Army.

But the generals didn't support Fomin's program. "Let the Europeans do things their way," they said. "In Russia, people aren't ready for democracy."

It was useless to appeal to common sense; they didn't want to listen.

Fomin went to Novorossiysk where he found work as a local representative for the Interdepartmental Commission for the Recording of State Property taken from the Bolsheviks. His new position meant that he had money to run his newspapers. Fomin decided that he would independently campaign for what he thought was right.

2

Novorossiysk was a small southern town surrounded by bluish mountains and a dirty sea. All the town offered in the way of local sights were the silhouettes of Allied steamers standing dark against the horizon and the masts of sunken battleships—the remnants of Russia's Black Sea Navy, which could be glimpsed among the waves not far from the pier.

Fomin rode into town along Serebryakovskaya Street in his battered motor. The street was full of nervous, bustling people. Ragged soldiers loitered beside government buildings. A cart passed slowly in a cloud of white cement dust with bluish arms and legs protruding from under its tarpaulin cover.

"Typhoid victims," the chauffeur told Fomin. "Essentially, we're in the middle of a funeral procession, but nobody has bothered to take off their hats."

A large poster hung over the entrance to the cinema: "Horrors perpetrated by the Bolsheviks from 1917 to 1919 in Moscow—in four parts." Fomin knew that all of these "horrors" had been filmed by the White propaganda bureau.

In the window of the grocery store was a map of military operations. The little paper flags that marked the frontline had not changed positions for three weeks.

A crippled man stood on the sidewalk with a tin in his hand. "Citizens, please make your donation for a monument to the heroes who have died from Bolshevik atrocities."

Fomin looked at the continuous flow of people in faded bowlers, soldiers' caps, and ladies' hats apparently made of baize taken from card tables.

Refugees, damn it, he thought.

Until September, Fomin had still believed victory was possible, but when the head of the supply bureau had told him that there were no winter boots for foot soldiers, he had realized that the game was up.

The White Army couldn't have managed without supplies from the Allies. Fomin talked many times with Lieutenant Colonel De Wolff, the representative of the British military mission. "Why don't you send more troops?" Fomin asked him. "The Bolsheviks wouldn't stand another month against the regular British army."

"War is an expensive enterprise," De Wolff said, shaking his head. "What will the British people get out of it besides tens of thousands of graves and a hole in the national budget? Russia has nothing to pay us with. Your industry is in ruins, and mining operations aren't profitable without investments and long-term loans, which are huge risks. Bad climate and poor logistics will eat up any potential profits. You have to understand that the British are tired of war, and when all's said and done, they couldn't care less about the fate of the White Army. It's a bitter pill to swallow perhaps, but it's the truth."

Fomin nodded. "I see."

"Denikin's government has already received large loans from us," De Wolff continued. "The Whites promised us they'd be in Moscow by October, but it hasn't happened. And Admiral Kolchak has been routed in Siberia. Our bankers are nervous. If you lose the war, they lose money. As for me, what I want to know is given that the United Kingdom and Russia are allies and we're committed to a common good, should my country take part in killing Russian citizens? Do we really have the right to break into someone's house if we think that something reprehensible is going on inside? I'm not so sure."

Fomin understood him perfectly from the point of view of diplomacy, finance, and philosophy. If an enterprise is failing, the sooner you pull out the less money and authority you stand to lose. But close up, things looked very different. In Russia there and then, thousands of people were succumbing to typhoid due to a shortage of medicine. White officers had not been paid for six months and left the frontline in desperation so that they could feed their hungry children.

There and then, Fomin published lies in his newspaper, claiming, "The Allies will help us," and that was all he could do for the White cause.

Fomin's friends kept asking him these days where he was planning to go when he emigrated. Should he go to Switzerland to the wife he didn't love and hadn't seen for five years? But how would he get there?

No European country was keen to accept sick, penniless, and traumatized Russian refugees. So far, they were being taken to Crimea, the Greek island of Lemnos, Serbia, Constantinople, and the Princes Islands off the Turkish coast. The first evacuees were sick and wounded soldiers, then their families, and then the civilian personnel of military institutions. The remaining women and children were taken onboard for a fee.

At one time, Fomin had considered himself a big fish, a man to whom all doors were open, but he now realized that he was just another one of the countless "bourgeois" vainly besieging foreign missions and the Committee for Evacuation.

The White government officials were the last to be evacuated.

3

The best place in town to get the latest news was the Makhno Café, frequented by members of the so-called Black Horde, a formidable fellowship of profiteers. The café wasn't so much an eating place as a gentlemen's club and exchange market. You could buy all manner of things from soldiers' undergarments to steel factory shares. So great was the influence of the Makhno that newspapers published currency rates under the heading "Café."

It was an odd place, large and dirty with potted palms in every corner and a stove in the center. The waiters wore their hair neatly parted and kept their shirtfronts white and their nails clean. The waitresses wore fine jewelry. As the waitstaff flitted to and fro, customers would shout out for champagne and sunflower seeds.

Fomin went to his table, on which the word "Reserved" had been scrawled in chalk.

"Capri Salad with tomatoes and black olives," Vadik the waiter informed Fomin. He was an old hand at the art of pleasing. "Fillet of plaice with grapes. Skewer-grilled shrimp with lemon."

Fomin wasn't listening. A young woman sitting at an empty table by the window had caught his eye. She looked strangely like Nina Odintzova.

Of course, it wasn't her. This woman had her hair cut short and was wearing a dress that looked like a school uniform.

The woman was sitting sideways to Fomin with her legs crossed. Her folded overcoat, felt hat, and a small bag were on a chair next to her.

It was Nina, Fomin realized. She looked older, and her face had become thinner and her chin sharper.

"Duck in sweet and sour sauce," Vadik murmured.

Fomin waved him away and walked over to Nina. "What a coincidence!"

She looked at him, started. "Oh…is it you?" She seemed pleased to see him.

Fomin held her hand in his coarse paw. "Good God, Nina—I never thought— How long is it since we last saw each another?"

"A little more than a year." She smiled, and Fomin's heart melted. "I thought you were dead. Your name was on a list of people who had been executed."

"I'm fine," he said. "How are you managing?"

Nina looked down, pulled her hand away, and hid it under the table.

She's been through the mill by the looks of things, thought Fomin.

"Is Zhora dead?" he asked.

Nina nodded. "Everybody is dead: Elena, her parents—Sofia Karlovna and I are the only ones left."

Fomin crossed himself. "May they rest in peace."

He found out that Nina and the old countess had just arrived from Rostov, and that they had nowhere to go. Sofia Karlovna had gone to the French mission to negotiate their departure. Meanwhile, Nina was waiting for her in Makhno Café.

"Did you say that your mother-in-law is well-connected in Paris?" Fomin asked.

It would be nice to get to France with the help of the old countess, avoiding quarantine camps and the humiliating process of registering as a refugee.

"Where are you going to stay while you're in town?" he asked next.

Nina shrugged. "I don't know. We've heard the hotels are full."

"Why don't you come stay with me?"

"How much are you asking for a room?"

Fomin laughed. "Nina, what's wrong with you? Keep your money for yourself. The prices here are outrageous. An apple at Privoz Market costs fifty rubles."

Nina was shocked. "Why so expensive? We came here by train and saw plenty of gardens around the town."

"Nobody goes there for fear of the Greens."

"Who are the Greens?"

"Partisans. Or rather, gangs of deserters evading the draft. They're fighting everybody—the Whites and the Reds—and sometimes they come into the town from the mountains and kill the guards. So, you'd better get your papers ready if you want to go outside. Otherwise, you're at risk of being taken off to counterintelligence on suspicion of being a supporter of the partisans. If you have money, you can pay your way out, but if not, the guards will flog you—and that's the best that will happen."

Nina grew pale. "But we don't have any documents yet. Sofia Karlovna is hoping to get them from the French."

"I strongly recommend you come to stay with me then. You'll be safe in my house—I have reliable bodyguards."

Nina looked him coldly up and down, and Fomin suddenly realized that she didn't want him to get too close.

"What happened to that Argentine?" he asked bluntly. "Did he come back from Petrograd?"

"Yes. And then I married him."

"Really? And where is he now?"

"He was killed two months ago."

Sofia Karlovna returned excited and told them that she had met Colonel Guyomard and Colonel Corbeil, and both of them were very nice and friendly. They had promised the old countess to do everything possible to help her and her daughter-in-law get to France.

Fomin listened without taking his eyes off Nina.

She was somebody else's fortune now, he thought, out of his reach because of his age, his post in the White administration, and his military duties. She would go abroad, and he would die here in Novorossiysk from a Red Army bullet or perhaps from a broken heart.

It seemed he was doomed to have his feelings unrequited—both by his motherland and by the woman he loved.

29. THE BRITISH LIEUTENANT

1

The sun beat down on Klim's eyelids, unbearably bright. He felt as dry and scorched as a dead leaf, his body no more than an outline and a handful of dried-out veins.

He was aware of a terrible weakness and a tugging pain in his chest every time he took a breath. And what was that buzzing sound? Was it the sound of cicadas, or was it inside his head?

Suddenly, there was a roar like thunder, and a hot wind fanned his cheeks.

Klim opened his eyes and saw an armored train racing along the embankment in a cloud of dust, black smoke, and sparks. The rattling cars flashed by, and then all was quiet again, although the earth kept trembling as though beaten.

Klim tried to sit up but felt such excruciating pain that he fell back. Catching his breath, he tried again, this time more carefully. His tunic was covered with half-clotted blood. It was terrifying even to take a look at the gaping wound in his chest. *Has Osip wounded me fatally? Will I recover, or am I done for?* It took some time for Klim to realize that his lung had been spared, and the bullet to his chest had only damaged the flesh.

He had a vague, delirious recollection of the events of the previous night. He remembered jumping out through the open car door, his body angled to the side perhaps a split second before Osip had fired the gun. After that, Klim had hit the ground, and, it seemed, he had concussed himself. That was why he felt so sick.

Nina? Klim choked and clutched his forehead. Oh, God! He had left her behind; she was still on the train.

2

Klim bandaged his wound clumsily with a strip torn from his tunic and dragged himself along the railroad tracks barefoot and leaning on a stick that he had found lying on the ground. There wasn't a soul around, just hunchbacked slopes, dry grass, and trees. He had no food and no water to drink or to bathe his wound. Without medicine, it wouldn't be long before his wound became infected.

Several times, Klim stumbled and fell and lay there motionless feeling nothing but his own pulse. If only someone would come! Whites or Reds, he didn't care. *Just give me some water, and you can finish me off.*

A sense of inexorable horror was bearing down on Klim: *What has happened to my wife? Those beasts might rape or mutilate her. Osip, please don't touch her...please...please!*

Klim prayed silently and pointlessly as he stumbled along. He knew he had seen Nina for the last time, and no one would be able to tell him where to look for her.

At first, Klim felt he was losing his hearing—he could no longer hear the birds or the snap of twigs under his feet. Then came visions: gray huts floating above the horizon and a large bed on the path with its bedposts adorned with round metal knobs that gleamed in the sunset. Two boys dressed in rags were sitting on top of it.

Klim wanted to talk to them, but they disappeared in the thick shimmering air. He staggered to the bed—what a convenient mirage!—and lay down on it.

That's it, he thought. *I'll just lie here. I'm not going anywhere.*

3

Klim was woken by two thin menacing boys—one with a kitchen knife and other with a scythe and dressed in an adult's shirt with a hood that made him look like a miniature Grim Reaper.

"Get off!" they yelled. "This is our bed."

Two girls approached, timid and wary. They circled Klim at a safe distance for some time, unsure what to do. In the end, they brought him water.

"Are there any adults in the village?" Klim asked, catching his breath as he spoke.

"No," said the younger of the two girls, whose head was shaven. "The Reds mobilized all the men and took all food away, so the women have gone too. There's nothing to eat. We live in the mansion over there on top of the hill."

"Shut up, Leech!" ordered the older girl.

Klim agreed to get off the bed in exchange for a potato.

As soon as he got down, the boys lifted the bed up by its legs.

"Where are you taking it?" asked Klim.

"To the mansion," one of the boys said. "There's a wounded pilot there. A foreigner. It's for him. We hope he'll take us up in his plane when he gets better."

Klim spent the night in an empty hut and the next morning trudged up the hill to the mansion.

Clearly, the house had been used as a military base. It had been looted and badly damaged. The ceiling in the hall was peppered with gunshot, the parquet floor was broken, all of the larger pieces of furniture had been cut up, and torn books and photographs littered the floor. Only the antique tapestries remained intact. No one had bothered with them because the cloth they were made of was so worn that it was no use for making clothes.

Klim didn't hear the girl they called Leech approach him.

"Come on," she said. "I'll take you to the pilot. He's in the main bedroom with the pink wallpaper and stained-glass windows."

Klim's head was spinning from hunger and fatigue.

"How do you find food?" he asked the girl.

Leech shrugged her bony shoulders. "We look for cigarette butts along the railroad. Passengers throw them out the windows, and we pick them up, take out what's left of the tobacco, and exchange it for potatoes."

"And is that it?"

The girl stood on one leg to scratch her calf with her foot. "We go into the big village and beg too. Sometimes we get a slap, but sometimes we get bread."

4

Lieutenant Eddie Moss had been assigned to deliver a package to British military observers with the Kornilov Shock Regiment. On his way back, his plane had been shot down by machine-gun fire from a Red armored train. The pilot had been shot dead, and Eddie had survived only because the plane fell into trees. He had fallen out of the cockpit and so escaped being burned alive. Only his legs and his right arm had been covered with deep burns.

The gang of homeless children had found Eddie and dragged him into the ransacked mansion. The oldest of them was no more than twelve years old, yet they had fed Eddie and helped change his bandages. He didn't speak Russian and had to explain himself using gestures and drawings. But he had little talent for arts and had to use his left hand, so, often the children couldn't understand what he wanted.

Eddie was desperate to get back to his own side. He struggled for more than an hour drawing in his notebook, trying to ask the children in pictures if they had seen another plane of the same kind as his. He was sure that his fellow soldiers must be out searching for him.

But the children had not understood and thought Eddie was telling them he was uncomfortable on the floor, asking them to find him a bed. So, they had brought one for him—albeit without a mattress—happy to be helping a wounded aviator.

They had mistaken him for a pilot and were fascinated by the fact that Eddie had so recently been up in the sky. The boys kept bringing him charred pieces of the wreckage of the plane that they had found in the forest. They would run around the ruined house with their arms outstretched, pretending to be fighter planes.

Eddie was in despair. *I'm missing in action,* he thought. *Nobody knows where I am, and I can't get out of here by myself.* His legs and right arm were in such agony that there were times when he would have welcomed a bullet to the head. But one day, a miracle happened—a man came into Eddie's room and, speaking with a strong Russian accent, asked him in English, "How did you get here?"

5

On November 11, 1918, London had learned about victory in the Great War. That afternoon, cables came into news agencies announcing that Germany had surrendered. The city was celebrating with a joyful chorus of factory sirens, ships' whistles, and car horns. Parishioners gathered in churches to give prayers of thanks, all of the pubs were full, and people danced in the streets, drunk and happy.

Eddie Moss was in a cab riding along Pall Mall. He was ready to weep at the thought that he was young and still alive, there was the bright moon in the sky, and the blackout blinds had been taken off the windows. Not so long ago, German zeppelins had bombed London and killed more than seven hundred people.

Eddie stopped his cab at the Royal Automobile Club. On the marble steps, gentlemen with their overcoats unbuttoned were bawling out "The Mademoiselle from Armentières."

Eddie entered the bar.

"Over here!" his friends greeted him with shouts. "Give him an extra drink for being late."

There was a crash of broken glass outside and the sound of a police whistle, and everyone ran out to see what was going on.

Lieutenant Bolt sat down next to Eddie and put an arm around his shoulders. "What are you going to do after the war?" he asked.

"Well—" Eddie hesitated. "I don't know. My brother has a firm in Yorkshire that produces fertilizer."

"What? Cow shit?" Bolt laughed. "I can just imagine you selling that."

"Not shit, chemicals!"

Eddie felt embarrassed, but he had nothing better to do now that he had been demobilized.

"We're going to Russia," Bolt said. "We're organizing a military campaign in the south, and we need about three hundred volunteers. Want to join us?"

Eddie tried to bring to mind what he knew about Russia. All he could think of was snow and a picture of the bearded Tsar in epaulets, which he had once seen on the cover of a magazine.

"The rabble has mutinied there," said Bolt, "and now, the noble Russian ladies are waiting for their knights in shining armor to save them. The War

Office wants to help General Denikin restore law and order in the country. Just think—soon we'll be celebrating in Moscow!"

The boys came back into the bar, pleased to have saved from the police patrol a US Marine, who had caused the disturbance outside.

"So, you're all going to Russia, are you?" Eddie asked his friends.

"All except you, seeing as you prefer to work as a shit peddler," Bolt said.

He proposed that they have a gentlemen's agreement: the first one of them to be awarded a medal would get the pick of the Russian duchesses.

"Are you sure they have duchesses in Russia?" Eddie asked.

"I think so. Russia has everything you can imagine. Then the rest of us will get second or third choice of all the duchesses and countesses and what have you. You just wait and see—they'll welcome us with open arms and tears of gratitude. After all, we're saving their bloody motherland."

They drank to their new US Marine friend, to Mother Russia, to Moscow, and to the Tsar and Tsarina, if they were still alive. They laughed and roared out at the top of their voices:

Ho!—for the cognac!
Ho!—for the wine!
Ho!—for the mam'selles,
Everyone's fine.
Ho!—for the hardtack, bully beef, and beans!
To hell with the Kaiser and the goddamn Marines!

6

They had taken a long journey by sea to the dirty port of Novorossiysk and then on by train to Ekaterinodar where the British mission was based. They didn't, of course, meet any duchesses, but still, the White Russians doted on the British. The representative for the United Kingdom, Major General Poole, vowed to do everything possible to get his government to send troops to help Denikin. It was rumored that in return for petitioning the British government, Poole had been given a large share in an oil company exploiting reserves on the north-eastern coast of the Caspian Sea.

"He got one hundred and fifty thousand pounds in shares from the Russians," Bolt told Eddie in confidence, "just for writing a fifty-five-page report."

But the British government was skeptical about Poole's proposal and soon replaced him with Lieutenant General Briggs. Briggs was put in charge of military supplies for the White Army.

Every now and then, Eddie was sent to Novo—as they called Novorossiysk. He delivered packages or watched British tanks, rusty-gray monsters that thrilled everyone who saw them being unloaded at the port. According to the newspapers, these "self-propelled armored vehicles" had arrived at the front in wooden containers labeled "tank" to conceal their actual purpose, and the name had stuck.

The British staged a demonstration battle on the outskirts of Novo. The tanks drove down into a steep ravine one after another, clattering and thundering, and then moving heavily on their tracks crawled up the opposite slope. The spectators watched in awe.

"We need to explain to the Russians that the Mark V tanks come in two types: 'males' and 'females,'" said Captain Pride, chief commander of the armored unit. "Males are armed with six-pounder guns and machine guns, and females have machine guns only."

However, there was no one to translate his words. Some Russian officers knew basic English, but when it came to "transmissions" or "air-intake systems," they were struck dumb. There were no dictionaries, and the allies had to learn from each other by pointing at things and naming them.

There was food in Southern Russia but no industry. The White commissaries made endless lists of what was needed at the front, but there was no one to translate them. The British looked at the dense Cyrillic letters, shrugged, and sent whatever military supplies happened to be left after the Great War.

They sent bayonets that didn't fit the Russian rifles, cartridge belts incompatible with Russian machine guns, and shells the wrong size for Russian cannons. Studebaker field ambulances were too heavy for the Russian roads, and the British horseshoes were too big for Cossack horses—while the White cavalry was given a hundred and sixteen thousand of them. A hundred thousand steel helmets gathered dust in warehouses because the Russian soldiers never used them. Huge shipments of goods flowed in from the Mediterranean military bases without the slightest understanding of for whom or for what they were intended.

The Russians were driven to protesting angrily, shouting and waving their arms.

"They say that the British are mocking them deliberately," the interpreter explained dispassionately. "They think the objective of the United Kingdom is not to get Russia back on its feet but to destroy it."

Needless to say, sentences such as this were easy enough to translate.

While General Denikin blamed the Allies for the chaos at the rear, the Allies blamed thieving supplies officers. Everything that was brought into the military warehouses appeared immediately on sale at local markets—at exorbitant prices, of course.

Six months later, Briggs was called home.

London bided its time. No one could predict whether or not it was worth taking a bet on Denikin. On the one hand, Bolshevism was a threat to world order, and the United Kingdom was itself subject to debilitating strikes. On the other hand, Lenin's government had ravaged his country to such an extent that Russia no longer posed a threat to the interests of the English king. This, of course, was a relief.

Eddie didn't care much about politics. His job was straightforward enough, British currency was highly valued at the Ekaterinodar market, and Novo was full of restaurants and beautiful girls (although he had still to meet any duchesses).

Eddie was pleased when the next man put in charge of the British mission, General Holman, kept sending him off to deliver packages to military observers. After all, that meant he had the chance to fly.

Whereas before he had sent his brother photographs on which he had written, "Here I am with a Mark V tank," now he sent more impressive pictures on which he wrote, "This is me with the

Bomber DH.9" and a detailed description of what it was like to fly in a plane.

He sent postcards home saying, "Greetings from Rostov" and "We're on the advance" and so on. But now it looked to Eddie Moss as though he would end his life in a ruined mansion in the middle of nowhere.

7

Eddie clutched Klim's hand. "Don't leave me! There's no one here besides you who understands English—I'll die without your help."

Klim looked at Eddie's face caked with grime and soot. The young man had a short nose thickly covered with freckles and shining blue eyes with matted eyelashes.

"I'm sorry, but I have to find my wife," said Klim.

He asked Leech how to get to the nearest railroad station. The girl looked doubtfully at his bandage, now stiff with dried blood, and at his bare scratched feet. "You won't get that far," she murmured.

And she was right. Klim got no farther than the porch before he fell down unconscious. The children dragged him back to the room with the pink wallpaper, and there he and Eddie spent more than a month.

Klim floated in and out a feverish delirium. Sometimes the image of Nina swam before him, and he would think, *I'll never see her again,* and feel fear and pain burn him up inside. If it weren't for the black infected wound in his chest and this nausea that made it impossible to stand, he felt he might have been able to find her, to save her. But now it was too late anyway. The worst had probably already happened.

Lubochka had cursed Klim, and it had turned out as she had wished. *We should have stayed in Nizhny Novgorod,* he thought again and again. *So what if we were freeloaders in somebody else's house there? So what if we were serfs of the Bolshevik state?*

Klim's only memento of Nina was the knotted leather cord that she had given him—to remind him that no matter what, he had to survive. But would he?

Eddie was tormented more by this uncertainty than by his burns.

"Where's the frontline?" he kept pestering Klim. "Why can't we hear guns? What are the children saying?"

The children had no idea where the frontline was. There was nobody in charge at all in the surrounding villages—neither Reds nor Whites.

"If the Reds find us, will they kill us immediately?" Eddie asked Klim.

"Most likely."

"What about the Whites? Could you explain to them that I'm in the service of His Majesty?"

"I could."

When Eddie felt better, he told Klim about the British mission in Ekaterinodar.

"There is a whole crowd of us. A hundred officers and a hundred and thirty soldiers, all volunteers. One fellow came because he heard Churchill's appeal about military aid to Russia on the radio, and he joined the British Military Mission because Churchill is his idol. Another fellow thought he heard God's voice in his head telling him to go to Russia. Yet another spent the Great War as a prisoner of the Germans, came out without a single medal, and decided to catch up with all his friends. And our machine-gun instructor openly admits that he escaped from the police. Russia might be a god-forsaken hole, but it's still better than Scotland Yard."

"And what about you—why are you here?" Klim asked.

"I wanted to see the world. If I'd been demobilized, I'd have ended up in Yorkshire. I've seen everything there is to see already."

The two of them talked to each other for days. Klim told his new friend about Argentina, and Eddie told him of the gas attacks at Ypres and how he had narrowly escaped being gassed. On the day that the Germans had fired their toxic shells, he had been sent to the rear to pick up the mail. When he'd returned, his whole company had been blinded, and none could even read the letters.

Eddie had been born the same year as Nina and had seen nothing in life except war. He was surprised that Klim didn't want to join the White Army.

"If you hate the Bolsheviks so much, why don't you fight them?"

"This isn't my war," Klim said.

"If everyone thought like you, the Bolsheviks would win."

"It's all the same now."

8

Klim felt sorry for the children who had saved him and Eddie. What did the future hold in store for gangly Fyodor? Or for Yuri, who never parted with his weapon, the rusty scythe? Or for snotty-nosed Janka or the shaven-headed Leech? They stole from peasants and were often beaten. If they fought among themselves, Fyodor would thrash the other children brutally, particularly the girls.

"They need to learn to respect me," he said.

Sometimes Klim told the children fairytales or showed them card tricks. It turned out that Eddie had a deck of playing cards—albeit indecent ones—in his map-case.

Leech stared at Klim with adoring eyes. "How do you do that? What are you, a magician?"

At night, she fell asleep next to Klim. "I'll stay with you. If I have a bad dream and start screaming, wake me up."

"What do you dream about?"

"Well—different things."

Later, Fyodor told Klim that Leech's entire family had been shot.

"Who killed them?"

"Hell knows."

At first, Klim couldn't understand why the children, who were always hungry, shared all of their meals with two wounded men.

It wasn't because of the card tricks or because they wanted a ride in a plane. It was simply that as children, they needed adults who would take an interest in them. As a little boy, Klim had always thought his father hated him, and it had made his life miserable. But these young criminals were hated by the whole world. To them, it was a miracle to find people who wouldn't chase them away and who expected food from them rather than a dirty trick.

"You need to get well quick," Janka kept saying. "We're going to the city soon to spend winter there. We have a good place in a factory boiler room. It's like heaven there. You can stay with us, and if the police come, you can tell them we're your kids. The main thing is that we don't want to get taken to the orphanage. They don't feed children there, and we'll die of hunger."

It was easy enough to say "get well quick." It was cold now, and Klim and Eddie—both bearded, thin, and shaggy—wrapped themselves up in antique tapestries to keep warm.

Klim scoured the house and park for anything edible, but the only things he could find were berries at the very top of a spindly rowan tree. It was impossible to reach them because they were too high and the branches of the tree were too thin. Even Leech wouldn't have been able to climb up there, and Klim was far too weak to think of breaking the tree down.

They burned what was left of the furniture in the cast-iron stove in the pink room. The varnish and paint smelled terrible, and the burning wood gave off a thick brown smoke, but the fire kept them warm at night. Now, when the children went out to look for food, they went farther afield and came back with less. Fyodor had become broody and irritable and lost his interest in planes.

9

"They'll leave us soon," Eddie said.

Yuri, looking sullen, had just brought in a moldy crust of bread for the two men to share and disappeared again out the door.

Klim thought he knew what was going to happen. The day before, Leech had been crying and refused to explain what the matter was. Clearly, the children had discussed things together and decided to go off to the city because they could no longer provide for the two adults.

Klim reckoned that it must be about fifteen miles to the city. If he could get ahold of some kind of footwear, he could probably reach it, but Eddie was quite unable to walk. His legs were covered with scabs, and the slightest movement caused him pain.

If I stay, we'll starve together, Klim pondered. *But if I leave, Eddie hasn't a chance of surviving.*

One morning, the children went off and didn't come back. Klim had to make a decision. One minute, Eddie told him that all he needed was one or two more days to get back on his feet, but the next minute, he begged Klim to shoot him.

"Shut up, for God's sake!" Klim said, frowning.

He concocted all sorts of fantastical schemes in his mind. He would have to go to the city and persuade somebody to come back and rescue Eddie. But why would anyone take a horse back along the frontline for the sake of an Englishman of no use to anyone?

Klim could hear trains racing past behind the trees a stone's throw from the mansion. *They'll never stop to pick up two wounded men,* he thought. *Even if I got up on the railroad tracks and waved my arms to attract their attention, they'd probably just run me down and keep going.*

In fact, this was what Klim wanted most of all. He had had enough, and in any case, he had nothing left to fight for.

30. THE ARMY INTERPRETER

1

Klim and Eddie's rescuers arrived one day in a tank. It tore off the gate at its hinges and rolled up to the porch, leaving behind it the smell of fumes and black, ribbed tracks in the freshly fallen snow.

A man wearing a British uniform pushed up the hatch and jumped out. "C'mon, lads!" he shouted above the sound of the engine. "There's got to be a stove here!"

He ran up the steps followed by five other men from the tank.

Eddie couldn't believe his luck when he realized that the soldiers were his fellow countrymen for whom he had helped organize the tank demonstration in Novorossiysk.

"How did you get here?" he asked as the soldiers picked him up to carry him to the tank.

Captain Pride explained to Eddie and Klim that the British troop train had been traveling with the White Army. Along the way, the crews brought their tanks down from the open trucks where necessary to put the Reds to flight. The tanks never failed to strike terror into the hearts of the recently mobilized villagers, and they had only once encountered serious resistance when the Reds had fought so fiercely that the British had been astonished. Why were the Russians attacking a combat vehicle armed with no more than rifles? The episode had ended in a bloody massacre. Later, the British had learned from Russian captives that these zealous soldiers were military cadets from the city of Tver. Their commanders had convinced them that the British tanks were fakes made of painted plywood that would shatter at the blow of a bayonet.

The tanks were unable to cover long distances, so they never went far from the railroad. The crews tried not to use them too much because the machines were expensive, and if something happened to them, they couldn't be taken away from the battlefield to be mended.

The tank crews lived in freight cars converted into sleeping compartments, which were terribly cold at night. Captain Pride had decided that they needed a stove. He had seen thick brown smoke rising above the trees and, training his binoculars on it, noticed a European-style roof. He had decided that he should go to the mansion to look for a small stove unlike the enormous brick monsters they had found in Russian villages so far.

Pride had told the driver to stop the engine and set off on a treasure hunt.

"We didn't have any firewood," Eddie explained to his rescuers, "so Klim burned broken furniture in the stove. This man saved my life. He made an Argentinean hunting weapon, a *bolas*, out of stones and rope and used it to hit the hares that came into the garden."

The captain shook Klim firmly by the hand. "How long have you been here?"

"I don't know," said Klim. "We lost track of time long ago."

The soldiers knocked the cast-iron stove out of its place, took it to the railroad by tank, and put it into their car.

"Now, we'll be warm as toast in here," Pride said. "And those machine-gun instructors will be freezing their arses off outside. After all, they wouldn't help us get the stove, would they? Now, we won't let them in our sleeping carriage to warm up."

Then Captain Pride summoned Klim. "Where did you learn English?" he asked.

"I had an English tutor when I was a child. Later, I worked at the British mission in Tehran and then in Shanghai."

"How would you like to interpret for us?"

Pride told Klim that at the previous stop, he had had to court-martial the unit's orderlies and interpreters after he had discovered that they were stealing anything from the train that wasn't nailed down—from officers' boots to the new Ricardo engine—in order to sell it.

"It's a nightmare trying to find interpreters," Pride told Klim. "We've tried to hire Russians, but they're either thieves or their English isn't good enough. Then we had some Jewish immigrants from the East End of London sent out, but that only made things worse. The Russians hated them so much that they refused to talk to them. They even shot one interpreter in front of our eyes. Some of our men know French from learning it at school, and they can make themselves understood when they speak to the

Russian aristocrats, lucky beggars. But I'm not one of them. The only French phrase I've learned since the war started is 'Ça coûte combien?'—'How much?' If I want to find a girl for the night—"

"I don't know much military vocabulary," Klim admitted.

"That doesn't matter," Pride said. "It's the machine-gun instructors who need to talk to Russians about their equipment. All we need is to find washerwomen to do our laundry now that we've lost our orderlies."

Klim agreed to sign a contract and was taken on to the payroll with the unit.

2

Klim translated cable after cable for Captain Pride—reports of General Yudenich's defeat in the north and Admiral Kolchak's retreat from Omsk. In mid-November, the Red Army seized an important railroad station, Kastornoye, and after that, it became clear that the Whites would never make it to Moscow.

They never stayed long anywhere, so they soon received the nickname "tourists." They had stormed a locality, killed the Red garrison, and gathered the citizens in the central square.

"Now, you and Russia are saved," they had proclaimed. Then they had left, taking with them whatever they had managed to get from the "grateful people."

Many times, Klim had witnessed epic scenes of looting. Soldiers had run from boxcar to boxcar smashing locks with their rifle butts and tearing off seals.

"There's underwear in here, lads. Real underpants!"

"And artillery parts."

"Hey, quick, this one's full of saddles!"

The army priest had beaten at the looters with his umbrella. "Take your hands off! That's a sin! Don't you dare!"

But the soldiers had shoved him down in the mud.

The Whites forced the peasants to carry their loot and refused to let them go, taking them farther and farther away from their native villages. The army neither paid civilians for their services nor gave them hay for their horses. Many times, a peasant willingly gave up a good horse for an injured one simply for a chance to get back home. And when he reached his village, he found a new man in charge there, a Red commissar who had been dispatched to take the place of a predecessor who had been hanged.

"Citizens," the commissar exhorted the frightened villagers, "you have been freed from your chains. A new day is dawning."

The White army kept losing soldiers and gaining refugees. Hordes of people trudged alongside, carried their belongings, and drove herds of animals along the roads.

"I just don't get it," Pride said with a shrug. "Why the hell have we stopped our offensive against Moscow?"

For Klim, it was quite clear what was happening. The White Army had simply gone bankrupt. It hadn't enough resources—neither material nor human.

The White Army retreated because it was impossible for them to wage war without reinforcements. The soldiers had been fighting for months until they were numb and almost dead with exhaustion. All they had by way of rations was moldy hardtack; all other food had to be procured from the locals. The volunteers knew that there was nobody to come to relieve them, and gradually, they gave in to a despair close to indifference.

When your lungs are racked by chronic bronchitis, all your comrades have died, and your stomach is aching with hunger, the only thing you feel is a fierce hatred of all those who stayed away from the front and survived at your expense.

3

Most of the time, the British troop train stood idle on railroad sidings. The tanks were no longer being taken down from their trucks because there was no more fuel. There was an air of nervous merriment among the British soldiers very similar to the atmosphere Klim had observed in the gamblers' den. Rather than fighting the Bolsheviks, the tank crews were more interested in waging their own brand of guerrilla warfare against the machine-gun and artillery instructors. The tank crews called the instructors "schoolmistresses" while they themselves proudly bore the name of "canned meat."

"Look out! It's the tinned stew!" the instructors yelled, catching sight of their adversaries.

The tank crew curtseyed facetiously. "Good afternoon, ladies! How are your lessons?"

The instructors were sitting around with nothing to do too. In the first months of the war, they had played an important role as advisors to the Russians, instructing them in the use of British weapons, but now, nobody had any need of them.

The tank crews and instructors competed against each other in every possible way from bottle-shooting competitions to friendly boxing matches. They agreed to a truce only when an express train brought them French magazines, *L'Illustration* and *La Vie Parisienne*. Then a frantic trade started up involving pictures of girls, especially glamorous pin-ups showing off cleavage or bare legs.

But deep down, everyone was tormented by the same question: "What are we doing here? What's it all for?"

The British had plenty of food from condensed milk to canned beef, and soon, Klim felt far better and stronger than he had before. However, all this time, he felt not as if he were living but merely enduring life.

His duty was to translate the news releases, manage the newly hired orderlies, and assist the British in their short-lived love affairs. The instructors were extremely jealous of the tank boys for having Klim to help them, and now and then, Captain Pride would "rent out" their interpreter, overcharging the instructors shamelessly for Klim's services.

"I suppose a crate of whiskey will just about do it, but you can bring me a new samovar as well."

While on his Russian mission, Captain Pride had assembled a magnificent collection of samovars and kept it in the ammunition car under the strict surveillance by the guards.

The instructors laughed at him. "The Bolsheviks will blow up our train sooner or later, and your samovars will be scattered all over. Just imagine, the

Russians will write in their chronicles, 'In the year of 1919, extraordinary weather conditions were observed: it rained samovars.'"

At night, the tank boys gathered by their fireplace. Klim drank with them, laughed at their dirty jokes, and gazed at the map on the wall. The railroad line was like a black funeral ribbon stretching down to the south through Rostov and Ekaterinodar to Novorossiysk.

What if Nina has managed to escape from the Reds and reach Novorossiysk? Klim thought, and every time, he pulled himself up. *Who are you kidding? You'll never find her. Even if Osip by some miracle did spare her life, and even if she wasn't killed or injured on the journey, she'll have left Russia long ago. And God only knows where she is now. Maybe in France, maybe not. But in any case, she thinks I'm dead. She won't be expecting to see me again.*

His mind ran this way and that like a caged animal throwing itself against the bars of its enclosure, unable to see a way out.

"Got the blues again?" Pride asked, looking into Klim's eyes. "I've seen a lot of that at the front. Give us your cup—I'll give you a shot of rum."

4

Klim went to see Eddie in the hospital car.

"How are you, old boy?" he asked.

Eddie put his newspaper aside. "That's it," he said. "We're going home." He began to whistle "It's a Long Way to Tipperary."

"What d'you mean?" Klim asked, surprised.

Eddie handed him the newspaper. At a banquet in London's City Hall, the British Prime Minister Lloyd

George had given a speech in which he had announced that the United Kingdom couldn't afford to continue its costly intervention in the endless Russian civil war. To maintain an effective fighting force, the Britain government needed to send four hundred thousand soldiers to Russia, and this was quite unthinkable. Lloyd George was sure that sooner or later the Bolshevik regime would fall, and he didn't consider General Denikin capable of spearheading the anti-Bolshevik campaign. If the people of Russia had really supported him, the Bolsheviks would never have been able to defeat the White Army.

"What nonsense!" Eddie said with a sad smile. "As though victory in war is down to a popular vote or something. Anyway, from now on, we're only here as observers."

5

The news that Britain would no longer be supplying military aid terrified the Whites. There were calls for Denikin to be replaced by the brilliant cavalry general Wrangel. Political passions were running high in the Caucasus, and the Cossacks were refusing to lend their support to the volunteers unless the White command promised them an independent state. The Whites' retreat began to look more like a stampede.

The locomotive pulling the British train had broken down, and the passengers were forced to celebrate Christmas of 1919 in the middle of the frozen steppe. Outside, the unbroken snow of the plains stretched away like white silk under a velvety-black starry sky as far the eye could see. The tank crew fed their fire with the butts of broken rifles and took turns to crank away at a handheld dynamo flashlight. Christmas dinner was special less for its food than for the elaborate reminiscences of food that it evoked.

"My mother used to cook veal chitterlings," Captain Pride said as he opened a can of the hateful beef stew. "We would stuff ourselves until we hardly could move."

Eddie poured cups of whiskey. "We used to have a Christmas goose dinner."

They talked of stuffing, roast potatoes, bread sauce, and plum duff.

"Gentlemen, please, must you?" someone pleaded from time to time.

But the conversation went on: "Mince pies—ham omelets—"

Eddie raised his cup. "Do you remember how we drank to Christmas in Moscow?"

The door clanged, and a guard walked into the sleeping car to report in Russian.

"They've mended the engine, but they still haven't got any steam," Klim interpreted. "The train manager is asking everyone to help fill the tank with snow."

"We'll be there just as soon as we've had our drink," Captain Pride said. "Merry Christmas, gentlemen, and here's to a happy 1920!"

All night long, all of those who could still stand hauled snow to the engine in buckets, bags, and even capes. A bucket of snow when melted would yield a few cups of water.

6

Finally, they got the train going and managed to go as far as Rostov. The branch lines were flooded with hoards of refugees who tried to storm the railroad cars heading south.

Captain Pride posted men with machine guns on the roofs of the boxcars and ordered them to shoot if anyone tried to get onto the British train.

Then he went into town, taking Klim with him. The mood on the streets was frantic, close to hysteria. Nobody knew where the headquarters were or who was in charge. The telegraph was down because Red partisans had cut the wires.

"How far away are the Bolsheviks?" Klim asked a distraught-looking colonel overseeing the loading of horses into a freight car.

"Wake up!" the colonel barked. "They'll be here any moment now."

"We need to get another locomotive," Captain Pride said, turning pale as he learned the news. "Our own wreck won't last ten miles."

They found a graveyard of abandoned locomotives next to the railroad depot, but there were no working engines to be had either for money or the promise of canned beef. Captain Pride brought in his soldiers and lined all of the railroad employees up against the wall.

"Tell them to find us a damn engine, or we'll shoot the lot of them," the captain told Klim.

"How am I supposed to do that?" howled the depot manager.

The soldiers already had their rifles at the ready.

"Captain Pride! Captain Pride!" called a voice.

They turned to see one of the instructors running toward them.

"We've found an engine. We met the men from the British mission in Rostov. They're evacuating, and they agreed to take us on board. But there are only two cars in their train. Their engine can't pull any more than that."

Captain Pride gave the order to leave everything behind, including all of the tanks, arsenal, and his beloved samovars.

"People are our priority," he said firmly, but nevertheless, he decided to abandon the Russian staff.

"Our officers from Rostov have an interpreter of their own," he told Klim. "If I take you, I'll have to take the rest of the Russians."

Klim told him that he understood perfectly.

Eddie leaned out of the car door and thrust a wad of crumpled banknotes into Klim's hand.

"Here, take this. The lads did a whip-round." His lips were trembling. "I feel like such a pig! I'm sorry it turned out this way."

7

A black and dreadful-looking crowd of White soldiers and refugees was crossing the ice of the frozen Don River.

"Look at the bourgeois army scampering!" commented a homeless boy perched on a boat frozen into the ground.

The "bourgeois" hadn't a penny to their names. Those who had once waltzed in splendid dance halls were no better off than those who had loaded bales in the docks. Nobody knew where they were going, where they could stay the night, or how they would find their next meal.

A huge Kalmyk encampment stretched along the railroad for miles—emaciated horses, huge mud-spattered camels with matted fur, shivering children with blue lips, and stiff old men and women with blank faces.

Nobody knew why the Whites were unable to defend themselves. Why in general did nobody show any faith in their ability to act together? The refugees were all like desperate beggars prepared to kill just for the chance of a frozen carrot, a place in a sleigh, or a night in a warm hut.

Klim submitted to the law of the refugee pack. He tried to keep neutral and inconspicuous—he had no choice if he wanted to get to Novorossiysk, the allied ships, and salvation. However, at the moment, he couldn't for the life of him see any point in being saved.

Fortune had smiled on him again, and now, he was warmly dressed and had money. Nevertheless, at night after the long journey on foot, he—along with many others—began to hallucinate, imagining that he saw thousands of roses in the trampled snow. Many people fell under the same mass illusion and walked as though over a carpet of white and pink flowers, breathing in the delicate, sweet scent.

Klim experienced an even more sublime hallucination of his own. His wife came to him dressed in a blue gown with the shimmering embroidery on the bodice and an ornamental comb in her dark curls. He called out to her, losing himself so completely in his dream that he saw nothing else and bumped into the people around him.

If only he could have administered that vision straight into his veins like a drug in fantastic doses! To the outside world, Klim knew that he must seem like a madman with a twisted sense of humor and a warped view of reality. But inside, he was still living in the world of the tango and the Columbus Theater, the finest in Argentina, ablaze with light from the chandeliers and decorated with flags for opening night.

I don't care if Buenos Aires has gone to the dogs just like everywhere else, Klim thought. *I'm not going back there anyway, and I won't have to witness its disgrace.*

His hallucinations were, in fact, a blessing to him. When people no longer understand what is real and what is not, they are no longer terrified to see the naked bodies of dead children thrown out of train windows or shocked to find velvet furniture and a stuffed tiger in a sleeping car left behind by the White commanders while desperate people trudge through the snow on foot.

The heavy frosts prevented the Red cavalry from catching up with the refugees and hacking them to pieces with their swords, but the same frost spelled doom for the Whites as well. It was rumored that six thousand Cossacks under General Pavlov had frozen to death on the steppe. The Reds emerged from their warm huts one morning to see the entire regiment lying dead and covered with ice.

Klim passed through countless towns, villages, and hamlets on foot, and it was only once he got to Ekaterinodar that he managed to squeeze himself onto a dilapidated train. The more fortunate passengers were snoring triumphantly on their berths while others were sleeping standing up with their heads nodding in time with the wheels.

For a long time, the train made its tortuous way between the mountains, every now and then plunging into a tunnel and crawling slowly on. The sun was rising, and the snow-painted peaks changed from purple to gold.

31. THE JEWISH QUESTION

1

Spring had already come to Novorossiysk. The snow had melted, and the weather was warm and windy.

Klim got off the train at a small dirty station. To judge by the blankets, oil stoves, and swaddling clothes drying on ropes, there had been refugees camped out here for weeks, and people were dying here too. In the waiting room, medical orderlies were picking up the dead and laying them on stretchers. There was an epidemic of typhus in the town.

Klim came onto the crowded square beside the railroad station. A strong gust of wind lifted his cap from his head and dropped it at the feet of a guard sitting on a broken hitching post.

"This is nothing to what we get in winter," he said amiably, "when the Nor'easter starts up."

"Do you know where I can find a room to rent here?" Klim asked.

The guard beamed and put his hand to his mouth. "That's fifty-four!" he called out to a porter nearby.

The porter gave him the thumbs-up.

"We had a bet on how many people would ask for a room to rent," the guard explained to Klim. "I told him there'd be a hundred before lunch."

Klim looked around. Officers, Cossacks, Kalmyks, and aristocratic ladies with children—everyone was hurrying off somewhere, their feet churning up mud.

"There ought to be something available," Klim said.

The guard shrugged. "Go to the market and ask around. Maybe some widow will let you into her bed."

The tin shop signs rattled in the wind, and great clouds were massed in the sky. The sidewalks were so full that people inched forward like passengers on a crowded tram. There were hundreds of beggars—mostly adults and youths—but almost no elderly people or small children to be seen. The streets were lined with rows of covered wagons and broken-down cars used as shelter by soldiers, who were building bonfires and butchering horse carcasses right in front of their makeshift dwellings. The living paid no attention to the corpses lying in the road; they might have been dead dogs for all anyone cared. Some of the dead had gunshot wounds, and some looked as though they had died a "natural" death.

As usual, no one knew where anything was, but after walking for some time around the streets that ran down toward the sea, Klim found the marketplace.

Carts harnessed with long-horned oxen stood close to the stone wall. The smell of damp earth and rotten potatoes mingled with smoke from the braziers.

"Get your barbecued meat here!" the street sellers called. "Kebabs for sale!"

"Pickled watermelon!"

"Dried apricots! Sweeter than a Cossack's kiss."

Buyers could find everything here from cutlasses to oranges, from silver mackerel to watery soup doled out by traders into cups and pots.

Blue-eyed Cossack girls haggled contemptuously with refugee women. They held up the White government banknotes to the sun, grumbled under their breath, and tucked the money into the tops of their men's boots.

The sprawling flea market was full of people buying and selling, gambling and fighting, and everywhere the air was thick with cement dust.

Klim walked up to a cart loaded with newspapers: *Russian Time, Free Speech, Great Russia*, and the like. All of the editorials looked the same: "Let's hear it for our boys and victory!" no matter what.

Klim began to read an appeal to "Our brothers, the peasants":

All the land seized during the revolution must be returned to its rightful owners. But as winter crops have been already planted, one-third of the future harvest will be transferred to the state, another third transferred to the owners, and one-third kept by the peasants in payment for their work.

Are they idiots? Klim thought. *What sort of time is this talk about how crops will be shared out in the future with the White Army on the brink of destruction?*

A little old hunched Jew with an oversized cap pulled down over his big hairy ears was selling copies of *Great Russia.*

"What time is it?" Klim asked him.

The man bowed—just in case. "You can choose any one of five times, sir," he said. "The first is local time, the second is nautical time, the third one is Petrograd time, which is what they use on the railroads. The fourth is marked by the factory sirens, and the fifth is the time in the British mission. So, there's no sense looking at a clock."

The old man's name was Zyama Froiman. He told Klim that the population of Novorossiysk was divided into three categories—the townspeople, the Cossacks, and the guards. The townspeople were refugees in constant search of jobs, accommodation, and food. The Cossacks who lived in the surrounding villages despised the townspeople and deceived them as much as they could. The guards took it in turns to rob both groups.

"Are you a refugee?" Zyama asked Klim. "Just arrived from Nizhny Novgorod? We know your fair very well here. They made Jews pay extra tax there, and then your governor ordered all the Jewish stores to be shut down except the ones belonging to the richest merchants."

The old man dreamed of the day when the Jews could move to Palestine and set up a Jewish state in which there would be no anti-Semitism or pogroms.

"The Whites really hate us, and with the way I look, I can't pass for a Russian. You've no idea what's been going on in Ukraine and here in the south this last winter. There haven't been such brutal pogroms since the sixteenth century. The Whites think that because I'm engaged in trade, I'm a rich man. They tell me, 'You profit from the blood and tears of the Russian people.' If only I knew how to sell blood and tears, it seems I would get along just fine."

"What does General Denikin say about the pogroms?" Klim asked.

Zyama waved his thin hand. "There's no point appealing to the authorities. Even the more kind-hearted officers you will not find standing up for a Jew. They're afraid. They think people will say, 'He's being paid off by the yids.' My son Jacob, a wonderful boy, used to own a newspaper here in Novorossiysk. But the paper was requisitioned, and now, my son is reduced to working in the small ads section—and with his brains! Still, you will not find another man in town who understands advertisements better than my Jacob. The Whites don't dare get rid of him because none of them have the subtlety required for the job, if you'll pardon my opinion."

"I'm a journalist myself," Klim said. "Do you think I can get a job at your Jacob's newspaper?"

Zyama shook his head. "You must understand, sir, what times we live in."

"Couldn't we ask your son?" Klim ventured. "You say he's a wonderful boy. If he's so smart, perhaps he can give me good advice."

2

Zyama's house had been requisitioned by the American Red Cross, and the owners had moved into the basement where Zyama's wife Rivka still managed to maintain a semblance of order and comfort. Their grandchildren, shy adolescents with the same large ears as Zyama, were sitting at a long joiner's bench doing their homework. They were utterly absorbed in their work and paid no attention to their grandfather, Klim, or the complaints of their grandmother.

"You plague!" Rivka lamented. "What have you done, bringing him back here? Don't tell me this is a guest! Not since 1914 have I had guests in my house. I would be happier to see a tax inspector."

"Hush, woman!" Zyama shouted at his wife. "Who is the head of the household here? We shall wait for Jacob to come back from work."

Anxious to keep out of Rivka's sight, Klim went out to the backyard. It was full of trucks, nurses were dashing to and fro, and a long line of people was standing at the porch.

He spoke to one of the US Marines on guard and found that almost all of the foreigners in the city had already moved to the other side of the bay where British mission was stationed on the site of the former cement factories.

"Are they going to give up Novorossiysk?" Klim asked.

The Marine looked up at the mountains, covering his eyes with his hand. "I think we could defend the town if we had the will. It's a natural fortress. But everybody here gave up long ago before the Reds started to advance."

When Klim returned to the basement, Zyama ran up and grasped him by the sleeve. "You speak English! I saw you talking to the American. My Jacob will be so happy! You two can discuss business later today."

"What kind of business?" Klim asked.

"My son will tell you everything. It is a very delicate question. Stay here with us tonight. You can sleep on the joiner's bench."

Klim's accommodation problem was solved. Not only that, but he now seemed to be in Rivka's good books. She made him up a cup of powdered milk.

"Sorry," she said, "but we have no other food besides this powdered milk that we get from the Red Cross. What a blessing that you know how to speak foreign languages! For us, this is like a miracle. There, you dumbheads!" she shouted at her grandchildren. "You must study! Let this educated man be an example to you."

3

It was night, but Jacob had still not come home. The Froimans said their prayers and went to bed.

"They have taken him away to counterintelligence," Rivka sobbed in the darkness. "Don't try to comfort me—I know it's true."

"Don't scare the children!" Zyama said angrily. "Jacob has just stayed late at the office. They can't do without him there."

The general mood of anxiety affected Klim too. The joiner's bench was uncomfortable, and he couldn't get to sleep.

I feel like a corpse laid out for burial, Klim thought.

The Zyama's oldest grandson, fourteen-year-old Syoma, was tossing and turning on the chest that served him as a bed.

"Can't you sleep?" Klim whispered. "Tell me about Novorossiysk. What's going on here?"

Syoma took a deep breath. "When our men were driven out of town—the Reds, I mean…anyway, the White officers took all the sailors who hadn't run away and forced them to dig a pit. Then they shot all of them, about fifteen hundred—they were all flapping around like fish out of water until the Whites filled the pit with dirt. Then the bodies started to stink—you could smell it all over town. So, the women went to the commandant and asked permission to rebury the dead. 'You can do what you like with them,' he said. 'Make a stew out of them if you want.' Later, they found that commandant dead in a lavatory. He was missing his head."

"Hush!" Rivka hissed. "Don't listen to him, sir. He's just a child. He doesn't understand anything."

Klim knew that Syoma understood everything very well. Those who had been victims of the Whites were waiting to be saved by the Bolsheviks. They looked on them as miraculous deliverers just as the citizens of Nizhny Novgorod had looked on the White Army.

They're all hoping for their people to come and punish their oppressors, Klim thought. *But they have no idea what they're wishing for.*

4

"I don't know who he is," Klim heard Rivka's distant voice break into his sleep. "Your father brought him from the market."

Klim sat up.

In candlelight, a short, bald, narrow-shouldered man pulled off his boots. Rivka thrust a mug into his hands. "Jacob, sweetheart, drink some milk."

Zyama sat next to his son, holding him by the shoulder as though he was afraid Jacob would disappear again.

Klim walked over to them. "Good evening."

"Same to you," Jacob grinned wryly, and Klim noticed that his forehead was covered by a large graze.

"They took all his money again," Rivka wailed.

"Listen to me, Jacob Froiman," Zyama whispered excitedly and pointed to Klim. "This young man can speak English. He has been sent to us by God."

The Froimans knew that they couldn't count on being evacuated—they had no money for tickets on civilian ships and couldn't dream of getting a place on a naval ship. They had no idea what to do. Should they throw themselves on the mercy of the Bolsheviks? Their children—who seemed to have picked up socialist ideas from somewhere—thought they should wait for the Reds.

"I don't want to scare them," Jacob said, "but when everything here blows up—which could happen any day—there'll be panic in Novorossiysk, and the only safe place for Jews will be the graveyard. Anyway, I'm not sure the Bolsheviks will overlook my 'bourgeois past' because I've been working on a White newspaper. We have relatives in New York—wealthy people. I'm sure that my cousin will help us get to America. We just need to contact him."

"What do you want me to do?" Klim asked.

"The American Red Cross is up there now in our house." Jacob pointed to the ceiling. "We need to write a petition to their commander and explain our situation. They've been sent here to help, and I'm sure they won't ignore our request. When we reach America, we'll find a way to repay them."

Klim shook his head in disbelief. Even princes in possession of fortunes were finding it impossible to get out of Novorossiysk, let alone impoverished Jews.

But the Froimans were determined.

"You're our only hope," Zyama told Klim. "Please write a petition for us! Perhaps the man in charge of the Red Cross is from New York. He might even know our Solomon."

"There are millions of people living in New York."

"We have to try," Zyama insisted. "We asked a Russian translator to help before, but that young man didn't like Jews. He even insisted that the Red Cross stop giving us powdered milk—although we have four children to feed. The boys have been left without their mother. She was murdered for 'espionage.' Whenever they arrest a 'Bolshevik,' the counterintelligence agents get half of the money in his pockets."

"For some people, it's just a way of earning money," Jacob said in a trembling voice. "They find out who has been paid that day, slip communist leaflets into their pockets, and then shoot them, and no one had ever been punished for it."

Zyama had everything ready—a sheet of white paper and a sharp pencil.

"Please be extremely careful," he said nervously. "No smudges, please. Americans are very particular people. Our petition must look like a real official document."

Klim felt uneasy providing the family with false hope. The Froimans stood around him dictating in a whisper what he should write in their petition: their previous achievements, an account of their New York cousin's wealth, and a note of Solomon's address to which the head of the Red Cross should send a cable.

There is simply no way that the Red Cross is going to bother with healthy people when the town is full of sick and wounded in much direr straits, Klim thought. But there was no point trying to dissuade the Froimans.

Jacob put the precious petition in his pocket. "How can we repay you?" he asked Klim.

"I'll be glad of anything you can offer," Klim said with a sigh. "At the moment, I've nowhere to live and no job."

"This young man wanted to ask if he could get a job at your newspaper," Zyama prompted.

Jacob frowned. "It won't work. We already have a crowd of authors—all of them famous—who've come here from the capital. Everyone wants to publish their writing, everyone's looking for money, but we have only four pages in our newspaper."

Klim had an idea. "You're in charge of ads, aren't you? My wife is missing. She was trying to get to Novorossiysk. Maybe someone knows where she is?"

"I can put an ad under Missing Persons," Jacob said. "And we can print it in the largest type to make it more noticeable. I won't take any money. I'm sure the Red Army will take Novorossiysk before our books are checked. And when the Bolsheviks come, we're doomed anyway."

32. THE NEWSPAPER AD

1

Nina hoped to escape with the help of the French government, and now, all she needed was confirmation that she and Sofia Karlovna would get visas. Their case had been delayed for several months because they didn't have passports, and it had taken a long time for the consulate to send a request to Paris and get a positive response.

Fomin had also applied for a French visa.

"You're so anxious about it," Nina teased him, "it's almost as though you think we'll live happily ever after once we're in exile."

"But perhaps there's still time for one final fling?" Fomin replied.

Nina shook her head. "Admit it—we've already had our fill of life's luxuries, and now, it's time to pay for our pleasures."

One day, she overheard the cook talking to a friend.

"The mistress won't be going anywhere," the cook said. "She'll act coy for a while, but eventually, she'll marry Mr. Fomin. He's old enough to be her father, but what choice does she have? He'll give her children, and in five or ten years, he'll keel over with a stroke."

It's true, thought Nina. This was probably what would happen if they ever escaped from Novorossiysk.

Fomin wasn't putting a foot wrong. He never laid a hand on her and just smiled calmly when she talked of her love for Klim. Nina took a grim pleasure in teasing Fomin, deliberately turning the knife in both his and her own wounds. She was like a condemned criminal provoking her jailers before her execution, refusing to accept any favors, and encouraging them to fresh torments as though the worse things were, the better for her.

Nina and Fomin sat up long after Sofia Karlovna had gone to bed, restless night owls drinking champagne requisitioned from the Abrau Durso vineyard. They laughed at themselves and the White cause, sang Russian folk songs, and talked about politics.

Fomin kept claiming that the British were to blame for the Whites' defeat since they were always on the lookout for a chance to bring Russia to its knees.

"You have too high an opinion of yourself," Nina said. "People everywhere tend to mind their own business. They don't concern themselves with the tragedies of strangers. If there's a conflict of interest, there'll be war. If not, no one will bother themselves about us. Here in Novorossiysk, the British and Russian interests don't clash—in fact, they don't even overlap, so no one wants to help us. It's not the fault of the British that the Whites are losing the war. It's because the local people don't support us."

"The devil only knows whom those locals support," Fomin said angrily. "Who even asks them? Who checks the statistics?"

When dawn came, Nina brewed coffee for them, and Fomin started getting ready for work. At the moment, he was busy trying to decide what part of the huge stock of military supplies in Novorossiysk should be taken to Crimea and which part should be destroyed before the evacuation.

2

Cynicism is the best medicine, thought Nina.

Early every morning, she would step onto her balcony, a cup of coffee in hand, to admire the sunrise and watch the panic below.

Once, she recalled, Klim had told her that one day they would drink coffee together on the balcony of his house in Buenos Aires.

As the low clouds above the mountains blushed pink, a blue searchlight from a British dreadnought scoured the slopes and went out. Then came the resounding boom of a gun—the Allies trying to scare away the Green partisans now roaming the town openly. Three days earlier, they had stormed the jail and released all of the prisoners.

There was a biting wind, but Nina stayed on the balcony watching the endless stream of people moving along Vorontzovskaya Street. Exhausted Cossacks led weary horses, automobiles sounded a chorus of horns, and ladies pushed baby carriages loaded with household items.

Nina wrapped her shawl tightly around her and rested her coffee cup on the railing as she watched a handsome man with a fine mustache walk by on the road beneath. The man was dressed in brand-new civilian clothes and held a burlap sack in each hand. A pair of chicken's legs protruded from the top of one of the sacks, and the tops of army boots from the other. Nina was quite sure the poor wretch would have nothing in his pockets but a fake identity card and nothing in his head but the thought, "Every man for himself."

You shouldn't be in such a hurry, Your Honor in Disguise, Nina thought. *You won't get a place on a ship anyway. The Russian ships have no coal, and those who can still sail are stuck in Constantinople and the Greek ports. The foreign governments know about the typhoid epidemic in Novorossiysk, so they're keeping all the refugees quarantined for weeks on the ships. And you can't count on the steamers the Allies have promised to send either. The British squadron has just been hit by a storm—they cabled about it yesterday.*

Nina went back inside and closed the balcony door. Sofia Karlovna was combing her hair in front of the mirror.

"Colonel Guyomard asked me to come to his office at eight o'clock," the old countess said. "Our visas are ready."

"I'll tell Fomin to get you an escort," Nina said. "Have you seen what's going on outside?"

"Oh, dear, oh, dear—" Sofia Karlovna sighed.

They heard the front door slam as the newsboy brought the morning newspapers. Nina went downstairs to the lobby where the bodyguards stood waiting for the master of the house.

"Where's Mr. Fomin?" she asked.

Shushunov, a huge, grim-looking Cossack with a broken nose, pointed to the dining room. Fomin was standing by the window with one arm in the sleeve of his overcoat, reading the newspaper and holding his glasses up to the page.

"Sofia Karlovna needs an escort," said Nina. "She shouldn't go out by herself."

Seeing her, Fomin winced and hurriedly put the newspaper in his pocket.

"Has something happened?" Nina asked, alarmed at the expression on his face.

"It's nothing."

She told him again that the old countess needed a chaperone to take her to the French Mission, but Fomin wasn't listening.

"Don't leave the house today," he said finally before putting his overcoat on and heading for the door.

"Then I'll ask Shushunov to take Sofia Karlovna to the Mission in your automobile," Nina cried after him, but Fomin didn't even turn his head.

3

Jacob had only been able to publish Klim's advertisement a week after he had made his promise. The authorities kept demanding that the newspaper publish instructions and official orders, and he couldn't find space for the announcement stating that "Nina Vasilievna Kupina's husband is anxious to know of her whereabouts."

All this time, Klim had been living with the Froimans, but he had found Rivka's constant lamentations so unbearable that he preferred to go out to work with Jacob at the editorial office.

Klim was consumed by an absurd, irrational hope. Who knew? Perhaps somebody had seen Nina or at the very least heard something about her. Time and again, he pulled himself up and told himself to prepare for the worst—or rather, for the fact that things would simply go on as usual.

Nevertheless, he didn't let Jacob out of sight. What if he should change his mind about publishing Klim's announcement? What if the authorities sent him off to dig trenches? Or what if some scoundrel picked on him again because of his Jewish appearance?

"You're my guardian angel," Jacob said, smiling.

The Froimans had sent the petition up to the Red Cross, and now, Jacob walked around whistling nursery rhymes. At nighttime, the family had gathered in their basement and discussed what to take with them to America and how they would get settled in when they got to New York.

The newspaper was printed at night and went on sale at seven o'clock local time. Klim knew that it was ridiculous to expect any response in the morning. Even if someone were going to take the trouble to come, it was highly unlikely that they would rush into the editorial office immediately after reading the announcement.

You're just fooling yourself, Klim told himself again and again. *A thousand copies in an overcrowded city like this—it's no more than a drop in the ocean.*

Nevertheless, he told everyone in the newspaper office that if anyone should ask for a Klim Rogov, he would be at Froiman's desk right behind the filing cabinet. Meanwhile, Jacob went off to the art department to oversee the illustration of a commercial for breath-freshening peppermint drops. It was a very popular product with the ladies, who were all hoping to entice an influential official and get evacuated with him to Constantinople.

Klim picked up a pencil and balanced it on the pyramid-shaped inkwell on Jacob's desk. It looked like a little set of scales, and he began to place paper clips and drawing pins on the two ends of the pencil to make it balance. But he couldn't get it to work, and the whole thing kept falling down.

He heard footsteps behind the filing cabinet, looked up, and froze.

"How are you, Mr. Argentinean?" Fomin said without offering his hand to Klim. He slumped down on Jacob's rickety stool, which creaked under his weight.

For a few seconds, the two men stared at one another.

Klim was the first to break the silence. "Do you know where Nina is?"

Fomin didn't answer. His left eyelid trembled, and he bared his large teeth in a scowl.

"How did you manage to lose her, a woman like that?" Fomin said. "You should have looked after her better once you had the good fortune to get her. Where are you staying?"

"At the Froimans'."

"I see. As I understand it, your situation is desperate—you've no money, and dinner in the Czechoslovak canteen costs a hundred and fifty rubles. You can't even afford to get a shave because that costs another hundred. What do you intend to do, taking into account the storm brewing here? No evacuation for you, I suppose."

"What do you want?" Klim asked, frowning.

Jacob thrust his nose from behind the file cabinet but backed off, seeing Fomin.

Fomin beckoned him. "Come in, you Jewish scum. What are you afraid of? I must say, it's very interesting—I asked the cashier about the payment received from this man for an announcement that he put in my newspaper. It seems he didn't pay a thing."

Suddenly, crimson with rage, Fomin jumped to his feet. "I didn't grant you permission to sit in my office, Mr. Argentinean. Get out!"

4

Sofia Karlovna had come back from her errand.

"Nina," she said. "I've got my French passport, and I have a visa for you. But the French have rejected Mr. Fomin's application—they only take families of their fellow-citizens on board. I don't know how to break the news to him."

Nina rushed to the telephone. His secretary told her that Fomin had called from his newspaper office and said that he wouldn't be back until evening. Nina knew that something was wrong. During the last weeks, Fomin had not bothered to visit the editorial office at all, claiming that all of the White newspapers were obsolete now. There were no reliable sources of information, and the only people who still cared about appeals to patriotism and poems were the writers desperate to earn money.

Nina remembered that Fomin had been upset that morning but had refused to tell her what had happened.

"Sofia Karlovna, I'm going up to the editorial office," Nina cried as she ran downstairs. "Shushunov, come with me to Serebryakovskaya Street."

The bodyguard put on his cap. "Very good."

Shushunov considered it beneath him to run errands for a lady and disliked it when Nina made him do so. Huge and brawny in a gray coat with cartridge belts slung across his chest, he reminded Nina of an impassive crocodile that might lie still on a beach one minute but the next minute spring to life and sink its teeth into you.

5

They got into the open automobile, and the driver started the engine.

"Any news?" Nina asked Shushunov to make a conversation.

The bodyguard spat over the side of the automobile. "They say they're not going to evacuate any more men except the sick and wounded."

Nina smiled bitterly. The big bosses liked to make grand gestures that looked good in the newspapers. In practice, this new rule would mean several thousand deaths. It was almost impossible to evacuate hospitals in all of the confusion with no transportation on hand. All that this new decree would do would be to cause delay and another round of corruption and trade in medical certificates.

Furiously honking, their automobile sped down the street.

Sofia Karlovna had said that she and Nina now had permission to board the French dreadnought the *Waldeck-Rousseau*. But how could they leave Fomin behind? After all, he had helped them so much by giving them food, shelter, and everything they needed.

If Fomin doesn't leave this town, he'll die, Nina thought.

There was nowhere to go from Novorossiysk with the Greens inundating the mountains and the Sukhumi Highway about to be cut off at any minute. Once the Bolsheviks came into town after long days on the march and desperate battles, they were bound to commit atrocities, massacring any men who had not managed to escape.

Outside of the editorial office, an excited crowd had gathered. A man at the center of the mob was being viciously beaten to the sound of jeers and catcalls.

Shushunov told the driver to stop the engine and got up on his seat to take a better view.

"It looks like they've caught another Bolshevik," he said.

Nina also stood up to take a look, and the street swam before her eyes.

The angry mob was attacking the dark-haired man in a pack, hammering at him with their fists and kicking him, screaming like apes. The man, wearing a bloodstained British uniform, kept trying to get on his feet only to be forced back down to the ground.

Beside herself, Nina dug in her purse, took the small ladies' pistol she had received as a gift from Fomin, and fired it into the air. The crowd froze.

"Shushunov," Nina moaned, "for God's sake—save that man! I'll give you all I have."

The bodyguard gave her a quizzical look, his cigarette between his teeth. He leaped to the ground and made his way through the hushed rabble with a businesslike air.

"Who's this?"

"A Bolshevik," someone said. "He was distributing leaflets."

Shushunov glanced toward the driver. "Let's take him to the counterintelligence office."

Together, they threw Klim into the back seat.

Shushunov propped his foot on the running board of the automobile. "No rough justice, is that clear?" he barked, addressing the crowd. "If you catch a Bolshevik, bring him in for questioning. We know you'd like to kill him, but what if he has important information? Let him tell us who had sent him and why." Shushunov got into the front seat and ordered to the driver, "Let's go."

33. THE ATTIC

1

All this time, Nina had felt as though she were trapped under the ice, and now, suddenly, she had been pulled into the sun. Her whole body trembling and her breath coming in gasps, she stared dumbstruck at Klim. He was here alive! Beaten black and blue but safe.

He had come to his senses and was gazing at Nina as though he couldn't believe his eyes. He reached out to touch her, but she shook her head in fear. Shushunov and the driver must not find out whom they had just rescued.

Klim smiled knowingly.

"Alive—" Nina breathed with tears in her eyes.

The automobile pulled up to a shabby two-story building on Morskaya Street.

"Did you want to come here, ma'am?" the driver asked as he turned to Nina.

Only then did she realize that he really had taken her and Klim to the counterintelligence office. There was a guard at the door of the building and a long line of people waiting for news of imprisoned relatives. A Russian Imperial flag torn by the wind into three colored strips fluttered on the roof.

Nina tried to take money from her wallet, but her fingers refused to obey her. She thrust the wallet toward Shushunov. "Here, take it. You can share it between the two of you."

Shushunov silently tucked her wallet into his chest pocket.

Nina leaned over to Klim. "Can you walk?" she asked.

He nodded.

"Don't tell anyone about what happened," Nina said to Shushunov. "This man is my friend—I never expected to see him again in such circumstances. Leave us now, please."

Wincing from pain, Klim got out, Nina slammed the door, and the automobile disappeared around the corner.

There was a tang of salt in the air, and they could see the blue-black waves with white crests behind the leafless trees on the embankment.

Nina glanced at Klim. "Let's find a place to sit down."

2

Nina was speechless. She wanted to say something, but all she could do was weep.

As usual, Klim made light of their miseries and even tried to joke. "Who were you aiming at when you fired into the air?" he asked. "Were you angry with the Almighty? I have to say that I was annoyed at Him too. Why is it that every time we see each other after a long separation, He tries to kill one of us?"

"Don't be blasphemous!" Nina snapped. "Not now."

He smiled. There was a huge bruise on his cheekbone and a gash above his eyebrow, but it was still Klim, her beloved husband.

They sat beside the water watching the sunlight glittering on the waves and the clouds parting like theater curtains.

Klim told Nina of his encounter with Fomin. "I suppose he must have been the one who paid those thugs to attack me."

Nina was overcome with hatred and bewilderment. If Fomin cared about her so much, how could he try to take away from her the person she loved most? Then she felt fear. What could she and Klim do now? Where could they go? How could they get out of Novorossiysk? What if the driver or Shushunov were to tell Fomin that Nina had ransomed his enemy using his own money?

"I'll tell you what we'll do," Klim said. "Today, you and Sofia Karlovna will board the French steamer. That way I'll be sure that you're safe."

"I'm not going anywhere without you," Nina said firmly. "We'll get you documents. The French are evacuating relatives and families of their fellow countrymen. You're my husband, so that means they'll give you a visa."

Klim smiled bitterly. "I'm not sure I count as a relative of a Frenchwoman, seeing as I'm the husband of her son's widow. And I don't have any documents—only a translator's identification card that I was given by the British."

"In any case, you can't go back to the Froimans, and you won't find another room at any price. There's no alternative—you'll have to stay in our attic."

Klim stared at her. "What—in Fomin's house?"

Nina nodded. "You'll need to spend a few days in bed while Sofia Karlovna and I apply for your visa."

"And meanwhile you'll be downstairs with Fomin, will you?"

"Don't talk nonsense!"

They argued briefly, but made up at once and began to give each other hasty, muddled promises. Nina wept, holding Klim tightly as she kissed his lips and unshaven cheeks.

"We have to go now," she said, "or we won't have time to arrange everything before Fomin comes back."

3

Nina sent all of the servants on errands and went back to fetch Klim, who was waiting for her around the corner.

As they entered the house, Klim glanced at the dusty curtains and cramped, gloomy rooms cluttered with expensive but shabby furniture. "So, this is where you've been this time," he said. "I've walked past this house a couple of times."

Nina brought him to Sofia Karlovna's room. "Look who I've found!"

The old countess dropped her lorgnette into her lap. "Klim, is it you?"

Nina told her what had happened.

"Are you out of your mind, bringing Klim here?" Sofia Karlovna cried. "What if Mr. Fomin finds out? He came back at lunchtime, and I told him that the French had refused him a visa. He was so angry that I thought he was going to kill someone."

Nina took the revolver out of her purse and gave it to Klim. "Here," she said. "You keep this just in case. Sofia Karlovna, you must go to Colonel Guyomard and tell him we've found Klim, and we're—I mean, I am—not going to go anywhere without him. Klim doesn't have a passport, but you'll have to explain to them that it's nonsense to ask for passports at a time like this."

Nina rushed around the house making sure that Klim had something to eat, heating up water for his bath, and finding clothes he could change into. His whole body was covered with crimson bruises, and her heart sank when she remembered her own experience with peritonitis.

"Are you sure you don't need to see a doctor?" she asked.

"Honey, I'm absolutely fine."

They asked Sofia Karlovna to stay by the window and keep an eye out to see if anyone came to the house, but the old countess kept leaving her post to give Nina an earful about Fomin's treachery.

"I would never have thought that he would attack anybody in such an underhand way."

Klim winked at her. "Quite deplorable. If a gentleman is angry with another gentleman, the proper thing to do is to challenge him to a duel, not pay a bunch of lowlifes to do the job for him. Don't worry. We'll have a duel later."

"Please stop it!" Nina pleaded.

"I don't think Klim should stay in the attic," Sofia Karlovna said, shaking her head in disapproval.

"Where do you suggest we go?" Nina asked. "Do you want us to sleep in the street?"

The attic was dusty and stuffy, and doves cooed behind the dormer window. Nina was worried that Klim wouldn't be comfortable there. She brought him blankets, food, water, and a stack of old issues of the *Niva*, a wholesome family magazine. She stopped in the middle of the room, wondering what else she could do for him.

"At night, I'll heat the stove so it'll be warm from the chimney here," she said. "Stay right above my room, and don't worry about Fomin. He spends all his time at work, so we'll be alone in the daytime. I hope the servants don't find out about you."

"Mr. Fomin is here!" Sofia Karlovna shouted from downstairs.

Nina kissed Klim on the cheek and made the sign of the cross over him.

"Don't fuss too much over me," Klim said with a frown. "Your Fomin can't hurt me."

Nina put a finger to his lips. "Remember when you said, 'I'll arrange everything'? Now, it's my turn."

4

Fomin was quiet and gloomy. Now and again, Nina began to worry that she was overacting—she was being too nervous and ingratiating.

"Are you upset about something?" she asked Fomin at dinner.

He gave her a sullen, bear-like look. "It's nothing. Just a little Jew that played a dirty trick on me. I broke a few of his ribs, and it will be awhile before that son of a bitch is back on his feet."

Nina tried not to show the shock she was feeling. Klim had told her that he was worried Jacob Froiman might come to grief because of him.

"Where were you this afternoon?" Fomin asked suddenly.

Nina flinched. He must have found out about Klim.

Sofia Karlovna, the old fool, looked up at the ceiling, and Nina picked up the meat knife from the table. *If Fomin tries anything, I'll kill him,* she thought.

"I went for a walk," she said, surprised at how hard her voice sounded. "It was nice outside."

"Shushunov told me you didn't take him with you."

Nina stared straight into Fomin's eyes. For a moment, she regretted having given her handgun to Klim.

"It won't do to go out alone, my dear," Fomin said. "You're a young woman, and there are all sorts of riffraff in this town. Next time, take Shushunov with you."

So, it seemed the bodyguard and driver hadn't talked.

Fomin poured himself cognac and knocked it back in one gulp.

"I've had an idea about how to get permission to be evacuated," he said. "But I need your help. We all know that the French are only allowing close relatives of their fellow countrymen on board. So, why don't you marry me? As a pure formality, of course."

"But you're married," Nina said in fear.

"Who's to know that?"

"Mr. Guyomard will immediately find out it's a fake marriage," Sofia Karlovna said. "They've only just given us back your documents, and I already told him all about Nina."

Fomin thought for a moment, drumming his fingers on the tablecloth.

"Then I shall have to become Klim Rogov," he said. "I hate the thought of getting into another man's skin, but I don't have a choice. Recently, I posted an ad in my newspaper about Mr. Rogov looking for his spouse. Let's say he's still alive and has been miraculously reunited with his family. Did you mention to Guyomard that Rogov was an Argentine citizen?" Fomin asked, turning to the old countess.

"Yes, I did."

"Then tell him that you made a mistake, and he just lived in South America for a long time. We can't forge Argentine documents here, but I can get a Russian passport for Klim Rogov tomorrow afternoon along with a certificate of exemption from mobilization. We'll make Rogov the Second a bit older and put my own physical description in his papers. Sofia Karlovna, you'll have to convince Colonel Guyomard to get a visa for this man who is as dear to your heart as your own son. If he asks for money, tell him that I'm prepared to come to an understanding."

Nina and Sofia Karlovna looked at each other.

"I'll do what I can," the old countess said.

Nina was speechless. If everything went according to plan, Fomin was unwittingly about to provide Klim with a passport and a visa. But what would happen to Fomin?

Let him go to hell, Nina thought angrily. *He wanted to kill my husband. I don't owe the man anything.*

5

That night, Fomin had a guest, a Captain Igoshin who served in counterintelligence. The two men shut themselves up in the living room and talked about something for a long time. Exhausted, Nina sat waiting for the captain to leave and Fomin to go to bed.

She had made the stove in her room so hot that she could barely breathe, but she didn't mind as long as Klim was warm. There wasn't a sound from the attic. *Is he all right up there?* she wondered anxiously. At least, thank God, he had done nothing yet to give himself away.

Finally, Igoshin went home, and Fomin knocked on Nina's door. "Would you like a nightcap with me?"

She knew she should be polite and gracious, but she hadn't the strength to dissemble.

"You need to get some rest," she said. "Just look at yourself—you haven't had a good night's sleep for days."

"Speak for yourself, my dear."

"I'm going to bed now."

A naval gun boomed offshore.

Fomin kissed Nina's hand. "Why are you shaking? That's only the British trying to scare off the Greens." His eyes were tired and bloodshot, the pupils dilated.

Nina felt pierced by a sudden, sharp pity for him. He had lost everything, and he was unloved and doomed. But still, she pulled her fingers out of his rough palms.

"Good night."

6

An hour later, she crept carefully up to his bedroom door and looked inside. The light was still burning. An empty bottle of cognac stood on the table, and Fomin snored on the couch still in his clothes and shoes.

Quietly, Nina climbed the ladder to the attic. The stairs creaked treacherously under her feet, and she winced at every step. What if somebody overheard her?

Slowly, Nina opened the hatch. She was greeted by the musty smell of an unlived-in room and a cold breath of air. It was pitch black, and she had nothing to light her way.

"Klim!" she whispered.

"I'm here."

A hot wave of relief swept over her body. Thank God, he was all right.

Groping across the attic, Nina found her way to where Klim was lying and put her head on his shoulder. He covered her with his blanket, pressed her to his chest, and groaned softly.

"Oh, they gave me a thrashing all right," Klim said.

"I don't want anybody else," Nina sobbed quietly. "I just want to love you—and to be with you—"

Klim quietly ran his fingers through her hair. "I still can't believe I've found you. Up here, I can hear everything everyone says downstairs. That counterintelligence agent was lying to Fomin. He told him that his boys had killed me and thrown my body into the sea. He got fifty francs for it—so now I know my true worth. And all the time, I was lying here as though I'd already died and gone to heaven."

"Don't talk about it!" Nina pleaded.

She kissed him in the pitch darkness like a phantom, a spirit she had called up. She tried to be cautious but kept forgetting and surrendering to warm delight.

Somewhere outside came the sound of shooting, and Nina got to her feet. "I have to go, or someone will wake up and find out I'm not in my room."

"Go on then," Klim said, still holding her hand. "Nina—is it true that I've really found you again? Maybe this is just some sort of delirium? If it is delirium, I don't want to wake up."

34. THE GREAT RETREAT

1

Sablin had spent six months in the White Army. He had seen marching columns deployed from horizon to horizon. He had seen brutal cavalry attacks in which avalanches of horsemen would crash into each other at full gallop in an orgy of slaughter.

So much had passed before his eyes: cannons hopelessly stuck in the snow, half-deaf gunners who could talk only in shouts, and Kalmyk troops going into battle accompanied by the crash of tambourines and singing of their shamans. They came back with their enemies' heads on spears.

Don Cossacks in faded tunics and trousers with red stripes, Kuban and Terek Cossacks in astrakhan hats and long, flared chokha coats, and volunteers dressed in the Russian Imperial and British uniforms had only one thing in common: their battered boots, a symbol of the great retreat.

Now, if they came across a dead body lying on the road, the first thing they did was remove the boots, which were far too precious to be allowed to go to waste.

Everyone had long since stopped expecting anything from the commissary. They had only been issued new footwear once in the last two months when they had been sent a consignment of odd army boots, left feet only.

"Don't anger the gods," Kirill Savich, the paramedic, had said to Sablin. "Be thankful for small mercies. Imagine if the Reds shot your right leg off. A left boot would come in handy."

"If only I could be sure they'd shoot off the right leg," Sablin had muttered.

The army fled but slowly. The icy steppe had thawed and was now deep with mud that clogged the wheels so that they could only move the ambulance carts forward by dragging them. Sablin remembered something similar in Manchuria during the Russian-Japanese war of 1904–1905.

The horses collapsed with exhaustion and didn't even try to get back up again. Spattered with mud to his shoulders, Sablin approached a group of medics crowded around a horse, its sides heaving with effort and its ears twitching.

"You need to unharness it," Sablin commanded. "Grab its mane and pull it over onto its side."

Then they freed its bent front legs and pulled at its mane and tail. Finally, the horse was back on its feet, and the medics harnessed it again.

"I just can't bear to watch it," said one of the nurses named Fay, a grotesque-looking girl with a face like an imp. "The poor thing needs rest."

Sablin sniffed. "If we let it rest, it wouldn't move and would be dead before we knew it. A horse needs to be led. Do you remember how my mare Swallow got her hoof stuck in the crack between the planks on that bridge? If I'd left her alone, she would have broken her leg. When a horse panics, it goes crazy."

"It's the same with people," sighed Fay.

Soon, the hospital was left alone, as all of the rest of the army units had overtaken it. Only occasionally a rearguard unit made its way past the ambulance carts. At first, Sablin kept looking behind to see if the Red Army was approaching, but soon, he just forgot about it.

They spent nights camped out on the floor of huts, often abandoned. Sablin always was the last to go to bed. First, he had to make sure that all of the horses were unharnessed and had enough hay. Then two hours later, he got up to check that the horses had been given their water. He couldn't trust anyone else to do it because everyone was dazed by fatigue. They would reply automatically, "Yes, sir," and do nothing. Only Fay helped him, fetching water when necessary or haggling with Cossack women for fodder.

"I need food and hay for the field hospital," she insisted.

"We have nothing," they said.

"Listen, I'll pay you in cash. If you refuse, I'll find what I need and pay you nothing. The Reds will take the hay anyway."

Every now and then, Fay scolded Sablin, "You're always taking care of the horses, but what about taking care of yourself? If one of the horses collapses,

I can find another even if I have to steal it. But where would I find another doctor? Go to sleep now!"

Even in the morning when everyone had already gotten up, she sent the medics away to stop them bothering Sablin. "See to it yourselves," Sablin heard through his sleep. "Let the doctor have a few minutes' rest."

2

After the Whites had surrendered Ekaterinodar, it seemed for a time that they would have a respite. The Bolsheviks were stuck some way behind. The Kuban River had overflowed its banks, and all of the bridges had been blown up by the Whites. It was much easier to walk now. The Kalmyks' herds had passed the hospital unit, and the sheep trampled the mud until it was a solid, springy mass less sticky and easier to walk on than before. The hospital unit was reduced to eight carts: all of the walking wounded had gone on ahead, and half the seriously injured patients had died on the way.

The air was pure and soft, and in the distance, the blue-gray mountains rose up still with patches of snow here and there. Sablin rode along, falling asleep every now and again—or rather, drifting in and out of consciousness. His horse, Swallow, carried him along behind the carts, and he dreamed of Nizhny Novgorod, his house, and his wife. It seemed to him as though none of it had ever actually belonged to him, that he was watching a film of somebody else's life, an unheard-of color film with sound.

"Doctor, look!" called Fay.

The road ahead ran through a crevice in the mountains, and countless convoys and military units were streaming down into it as though into the mouth of a funnel. The sight was majestic and eerie: the White Army disappearing into another world.

They traveled on through rocky mountains, gorges, and tunnels flooded with people, horses, camels, and carts. Partisans could be hiding behind any rock. Sablin struck up a conversation with a lieutenant who had been several times to Novorossiysk. The lieutenant told him that the entire Caucasus region was riddled with Greens like a Cossack hat crawling with lice. They called themselves "The Sochi Raiders," "The Detachment of Thunder and Lightning," the "Team of Avengers," and so on.

"Who'd they want to avenge?" the doctor asked wearily.

"Everyone and everything."

The partisans were impossible to resist: they killed whomever they wanted and snatched whatever they could carry away.

"Sometimes I think, was it really worth fighting?" Kirill Savich, the paramedic, sighed, scanning the endless columns of the retreating people. "If we'd known in advance what would happen, I don't think we'd have formed the White Army and started the war. Russia is done for anyway, and we've done nothing but suffer in vain and get people killed for nothing."

Sablin gave a wry smile. Maybe it hadn't been worth it, but if he had to choose again, he would still have joined the volunteers and made his way from Oryol to the Caucasus Mountains.

Once, Klim Rogov had told Sablin that he didn't want to get involved in the war; he didn't want to waste his time on such a bad business. But war gave you no choice. It sucked in everybody, willing or unwilling.

To fight the Bolsheviks meant to shoot ordinary Russians who had been forcibly conscripted. Not to fight them meant to stand and watch your home being destroyed without even trying to defend it. It was a trap, and once you were in it, there was no good solution. You could either bite your leg off and escape crippled or wait for the hunters to come along, shoot you, stuff you, and mount you in a glass case.

Everyone had to make the choice that suited them best. Sablin had chosen to keep going to the bitter end as long as he was able. That was how Sablin saw himself—a man who never surrendered. As for what it all meant, he had no idea. In general, he often struggled to find meaning in life.

3

Sablin had naively believed that when they got to Novorossiysk, the worst would be over. He had thought the evacuation would be carried out in an orderly manner with the wounded transferred to ships and sent off by the commanders to wherever they saw fit. But as soon as the ambulance carts crossed the mountain pass, his hopes were dashed.

It was a quiet spring evening with the hill slopes lost in a lilac haze, and in the distance, the Black Sea was as calm as a millpond. Below as far as they could see were sprawling camps of army units. Huge pillars of swirling dark gray smoke rose from the foot of the mountains.

"Where are the Allied ships?" Fay asked anxiously.

Kirill Savich handed her his binoculars. "Over there on the horizon. I suppose none of the transports are in the port. Congratulations, ladies and gentlemen—all that remains for us to do now is throw ourselves into the sea."

Sablin ordered them to pitch camp. Then after questioning several people about who was responsible for what, he rode Swallow down the hill to the headquarters of General Kutepov, who was in charge of the evacuation.

The general had his headquarters in a boxcar that stood uncoupled not far from the marina. Beside it were several freight cars in flames.

Sablin had to argue with the guards for some time before they let him squeeze into the hot boxcar filled with cigarette smoke. Cossacks and volunteer army officers shouted at each other, clutching their guns. General Kutepov called them to order, but quarrels kept flaring up again.

"Did you know that General Kirey is evacuating artillery shells and military equipment while people are left stranded?" roared an elderly colonel with a saber scar on his forehead. "The scoundrel announced that anyone who loaded at least two thousand pounds of the stuff onboard would get a place on his steamer."

"Why are they taking equipment and leaving the sick and wounded behind?" Sablin asked a captain from the Drozdov Regiment.

The captain folded his arms on his chest. "Everyone is already thinking about how they'll survive after the war. The sick and wounded can't be sold abroad, but military equipment can."

The meeting lasted four hours. Each division had a steamer assigned to it, and the commanders were to send guards to the ships to keep unauthorized passengers from boarding.

"Gentlemen," Kutepov repeated for the tenth time. "I assure you, you will get your transports. We've already had radio messages from the Allies to that effect."

Try as he might, Sablin couldn't manage to find a place on the ships for his hospital unit. The officers he approached either averted their gaze, told him to go to hell, or advised him to appeal to the Allies.

"The French have said they'll give us forty-five places and no more," the captain of the Drozdov Regiment told Sablin. "The British haven't given us a clear answer yet. They are busy with the second battalion of the Royal Scots Fusiliers, which has just arrived from Constantinople. They're supposed to ensure the evacuation of the foreign missions and, if possible, some of the Whites."

As Sablin left the boxcar, he noticed a faded propaganda poster on its wall. It was Gulliver in a British helmet pulling a fleet of battleships along on strings. "I am an Englishman," read the slogan, "who has given you everything you need for victory."

There was a Bolshevik leaflet on the ground directly under the staff boxcar.

Down with idle landlords, capitalists, and officers with golden epaulets!

All the soldiers of the White Army are now eligible to return home except for monarchists, landlords, kulaks, factory owners,

traders, profiteers, and other parasites, all of whom are expelled from Soviet Russia.

Present this leaflet at any political department of the Red Army.

Stick your bayonet into the ground! Join the Red Army! Join history! Forward toward a new dawn of humanity!

Sablin returned to his camp dazed and numb. For a long time, he sat quietly, staring into the campfire.

"I've just been to the port," Fay said, approaching him. "It's so terrible there that it's indescribable. An Italian ship docked, and everyone rushed to try to get on board. A woman was trampled to death."

Sablin listened with only half an ear. *What am I supposed to do?* he thought. *We have only three or four days of food left and only a couple of thousand rubles in worthless White Army money.*

He looked at the slopes dotted with campfires. There were tens of thousands of people. It was impossible to evacuate them, and they couldn't put up any fight against the Reds. What would happen to them when the Bolsheviks captured the town?

Smoke from the bonfires filled the sky. Sablin could hear rifle shots from the mountain slopes. Had the Reds already reached the passes? Or perhaps that was the Greens attacking and robbing a traveler. It was impossible to tell.

The night drew in quickly, but the camp was still humming and bustling with activity as people settled down for the night. A bird chirruped in the bushes.

Sablin got up—it was time to do the rounds of his patients still lying in carts. The nurses changed their bandages, and their tanned, thin faces were lit up by the gas lights like the faces of icons.

In the last cart lay a twenty-two-year-old patient, Nikita Yeremin. Three days earlier, Sablin had amputated his foot rotten with gangrene.

"How are you doing, young man?" Sablin asked.

Yeremin was lying with his hands behind his head. "I'm fine, doctor," he said. "Look at the moon—how beautiful it is. It looks like a great, big, round cheese full of holes. My mother had a grocery shop in Kiev, and she sold that kind of cheese there."

"Do we have any soap left?" Fay shouted. "We're out of clean bandages too. I'll have to wash dirty ones."

"You should go to the British warehouses and get yourself new bandages there," a male voice said from the darkness.

Sablin turned his head and was startled to see a Cossack right behind him with a dozen medical kits strung over his shoulders.

"Where did you get all this?" Sablin asked.

The Cossack pointed to the city below. "The British are destroying their military warehouses, so they're giving away supplies for free."

Sablin glanced at Fay. "Call Kirill Savich," he said. "We need to go to the British now."

"Doctor, please don't leave us!" Yeremin cried out, grabbing Sablin's sleeve.

"Don't be silly." Sablin pulled away his hand. "I'm not going to leave you behind."

But Yeremin wouldn't listen. "Doctor, promise you won't abandon us! We'll die here without you."

Even when Sablin, Fay, and Kirill Savich had driven far away from the camp, they could still hear him shouting.

35. THE IMPOSTER

1

Colonel Guyomard received his bribe and promised Sofia Karlovna to settle the visa issue, but apart from this, Nina's plan didn't work out as expected. Fomin stopped going into the office. In fact, now he never left her alone at all but constantly demanded her presence.

When Fomin and Nina were sitting on the second floor, Klim could hear almost every word they said. It drove him mad to even think that he must hide from this scoundrel and remain silent while Fomin was tormenting Nina.

She could come up to the attic only late at night when everybody else in the house had finally sunk into a heavy sleep that brought no relief. Klim could only feel the touch of Nina's hands in the darkness and hear her agitated whispers: "Be patient. It won't be long now."

Sometimes a searchlight shone straight in at the dormer window, and then Nina's pale, dark-eyed face appeared to Klim for a second. There was an otherworldly, terrifying beauty about her features.

Nina kissed Klim and made him promise to keep quiet so as not to expose himself to any danger.

"Fomin has ordered the guards not to leave the house," she told him. "There's looting going on all over town. He's afraid we'll have unwelcome visitors."

Klim hated himself for his enforced idleness, but there was nothing he could do. There was only one bullet in Nina's revolver, and with no more ammunition than this, he could never hope to challenge Fomin's bodyguards.

2

During the daytime, the sun came streaming in the dormer windows, and the roof heated up like a furnace. From down below, Klim could hear the roar of engines, the clatter of hooves, and the shouts of the frenzied crowds. It wasn't even possible to stretch his muscles in case he gave himself away with a single careless movement. All he could do was sleep, read, and think.

Klim was surprised at how much Nina had changed in two and a half years. While the war had not broken her entirely, it had warped her character ruthlessly. He admired Nina for her efficiency and resilience but was alarmed to witness her sudden fits of cruelty. Klim heard her arguing with Fomin and wouldn't have wished such harsh words even on his worst enemy. Fomin loved Nina, yet she kept telling him that she didn't even regard him as a man and that the White cause had been lost because of people like him. Once, she told him that he could expect nothing good in exile and had better shoot himself now.

Nina made Fomin suffer for her own feelings of fear and dependence.

While there was no love lost between Klim and Fomin, Klim would have liked to see Nina behaving more kindly. The callous cynicism she displayed was a natural consequence of the deep wounds she had endured.

It will be a long time before she's herself again, thought Klim. *In the meantime, I have to put up with it. Somehow, I have to try to guarantee her a life of peace, comfort, and spiritual warmth. That's the only way to help her get better.*

If the war had made a cynic of Nina, it had made a stoic of Klim. What was it that Epictetus had said?

"When we are invited to a banquet, we take what is set before us; and were one to call upon his host to set fish upon the table or sweet things, he would be deemed absurd. Yet in a word, we ask the gods for what they do not give; and that, although they have given us so many things!"

As Klim saw it, unhappiness was either the result of guilt from the past or fear of the future. It is not the present moment we fear but sufferings that still lie ahead. However, in fact, we will never actually live in that terrible future. All we can only ever live is the present, and we generally manage to deal with it.

The ancient Stoics wouldn't have approved of Klim's passion for Nina. Those wise men of old had frowned on such strong attachments. But then again, they were probably not the best authorities in matters of the heart.

To find out what love is, you have to look at its opposite, and the opposite of love is not hatred but war. When you are loved, you are seen as something sacred, and even when people hate you, you are at least important enough to deserve their hatred. However, war devalues people utterly until they die like ants accidentally crushed underfoot. They become nothing and nobody, and that is something impossible to bear.

During the war, Klim had seen hundreds, maybe thousands of dead people. These priceless human lives had been cut short, and no one cared. That fact was more terrifying for him than death itself. How could you hang onto your moral right to life? How could you prove—at least to yourself—that someone needed you on this old blue sphere? There were only two ways of preserving your integrity in this life, and that was to prove to yourself either your heroism or your love. As military exploits consist mainly of killing others, there is often little choice.

Nina had told Klim that she had kept all his little gifts: the key, the little white feather, and the symbol of eternity he had made out of the safety pin of a hand grenade. Recently, she had added a yellow pebble to her collection: it reminded her of a petrified heart and a candle flame. Nina had decided that it was a symbol of commemoration.

During his time in the attic, Klim also made himself a new treasure—a simple metallic button with the Greek letter Λ that he had inscribed on it. It was his personal symbol of love: each side of the letter holding the other up to keep the whole from collapsing.

3

All morning, there was a continuous cannonade as the Whites detonated shells at the railroad station. The oil tanks were ablaze too, and the air smelled strongly of burning.

Shushunov had taken Sofia Karlovna to see Guyomard at nine o'clock to fetch the visas. But it was already afternoon, and still, they had not returned.

Beneath him, Klim could hear Fomin's heavy tread as he paced his room.

"It looks as though your mother-in-law isn't coming back," Fomin said eventually to Nina. "She's either died, or somebody's killed her. What do you think?"

"How should I know?" Nina snapped.

"I knew I should have gone myself—"

Klim tried to figure out how many bodyguards were still in the house with the driver and Shushunov gone. Had Fomin sent any of the others with them?

He kept wondering what to do when the old countess returned with the papers.

If Klim could only have been sure that the visas would be ready today, he would have left the house the night before to wait for Nina and Sofia Karlovna at a prearranged place. But now what? Should he—in the best tradition of Robin Hood—suddenly rush in on Fomin and rob him?

Klim would have been capable of killing if necessary to defend himself or his loved ones. But this was different; something like grabbing someone else's lifebelt to save himself—even though it was his own passport at stake.

He would find out soon enough, he supposed, when he was forced to make a choice. Besides which, there was a good chance that Klim would be shot himself. Fomin and his Cossacks wouldn't think twice about finishing him off.

"It's one o'clock," announced Fomin presently. "What do you propose we do, Miss Nina? All hell has broken loose in the port. The military is seizing the ships by force and throwing civilians like us overboard."

Nina didn't answer. Klim heard a sudden commotion and running feet and then an order in a stranger's voice, "Go downstairs, ma'am."

Klim froze.

"Counterintelligence has honored us with another visit," said Fomin with forced gaiety. "How can I help you?"

There was the sound of chairs being scraped back.

"Listen, Fomin. I know that you've given up your official duties, but I also know that this January, you got ahold of a stack of promissory notes confiscated from the Kharkov Bank—"

"What are you talking about?" broke in Fomin in a menacing voice.

"You know perfectly well. You never made any record of those notes on the balance sheet. It's as though they'd never existed—isn't that right? I imagine you're hoping you can use them to live comfortably in exile, but they don't belong to you."

"Whose are they then? Yours?"

"I have a proposal for you. If you can relieve me of the necessity of searching your house for the notes, you get a place on the steamer. That way will be in all of our best interests. I don't have a lot of time, and as for you, well—notes or no notes—you'll die without my help."

Klim was unable to catch Fomin's answer. He listened intently for a few long minutes, but now, all was quiet downstairs. Suddenly, there was the roar of a car's motor in the backyard.

"The British mission!" he heard Nina shout suddenly, but her cry was abruptly cut short.

Forgetting all caution, Klim rushed downstairs. The house was empty. He ran outside to see a large black car driving full-speed toward the port.

"Damn it!" Klim kicked at the gates in exasperation, sending an iron echo ringing around the yard.

The British mission is right on the other side of the bay, Klim thought. *By the time I get there on foot, the steamer will have left.*

Another car drove slowly up to the gate.

"What are you doing here?" exclaimed Sofia Karlovna. "Where's Nina?"

"Fomin's abducted her!" Klim cried in despair. "Just a minute ago! They left without waiting for you."

The old countess gasped. Shushunov and the driver exchanged glances.

"We couldn't get back any earlier," Sofia Karlovna said, confused. "We had to wait, but now I have your papers."

Klim pocketed his passport without looking and grasped the handle of the car door. "Please take me to the British mission!" he pleaded with Shushunov.

The Cossack pulled out his tobacco pouch and began to roll himself a cigarette. "How much will you pay?"

Klim hesitated. He had nothing. Those thugs in the pay of counterintelligence had robbed him of all his money.

"I must get to the British," he said.

"Not good enough," Shushunov said as he lit his cigarette.

Sofia Karlovna sighed, shook her head, and took a five-franc note from her purse. "Here, take it," she said. "A gentleman should always have enough money to pay his own passage. If not, he risks finding himself in a very unpleasant situation. Now, get into the car."

36. TRAGEDY IN NOVOROSSIYSK

1

For several days, all of the employees of the British mission had given themselves up to vandalism on an unprecedented scale.

Five hundred gallons of rum had been poured into the sea. All of the artillery breechblocks had been thrown into the water. The tank crews had crushed forty new airplanes straight from the factory and then sent the tanks into the sea with their engines running.

Everyone was trying to stay calm but making a poor job of it. Mountains of rifles, backpacks, saddles, and harnesses had appeared down by the waterfront. The Royal Scots Fusiliers had doused them with kerosene and set them alight. The sea around the pier was full of floating debris with a dead body drifting facedown in the waves here and there.

The British had abandoned all of their warehouses in the city to looters but weren't allowing Russians onto the territory of their mission under any circumstances.

Two days previously, Eddie Moss had received an order to deliver a package to General Kutepov's headquarters. As soon as he had gotten out of the car, he had been surrounded by women carrying small children. They had held up their crying babies and screamed, "*Pozhaluista!* Please!" as though he could do something for them. One of the women had fallen on her knees and grasped Eddie's hand, trying to kiss it. He had pushed her away, feeling like a murderer.

An interpreter at Kutepov's headquarters had told Eddie that the general had issued a new order: now only those servicemen able to continue fighting the Bolsheviks had the right to leave for Crimea. Kutepov had requested that the British command help the Russians with the evacuation.

2

The British were hastily boarding the *SMS Hannover,* a former German battleship that had been transformed into a troop transport. With a great clatter of boots and squeaking of wheels, they made their way up the gangplank, their sweaty faces coated with cement dust. A terrible wailing could be heard over the port as the crowd surged and cried out behind the barbed wire that fenced off the pier. Every now and then, the soldiers on the machine-gun towers fired volleys into the air to hold back the crowd, but even that was useless. The British soldiers had to use their rifle butts to knock down those who climbed the fence.

Eddie tried not to look at the Russians. *It's not our fault that we can't save them,* he thought. *They'll trample us to death if we let them through the fence.*

The Whites felt that the British behavior toward the Russians showed an icy indifference. What Eddie was feeling now wasn't indifference but unspeakable shock and shame.

We're leaving you behind. We promised to help you, and now, we have to leave you to die.

Eddie thought time and time again of Klim Rogov and particularly of the day when they had left him behind in Rostov. But how the hell could he have done anything differently? Should Eddie have stayed with Klim out of solidarity, sick as he was, only to become a burden to him and die somewhere on the frozen steppe?

The Russians are to blame for all this, Eddie kept saying to himself. It made it a little easier to take.

He heard a locomotive whistle from behind the fence.

"Moss, to the gate!" cried Captain Pride.

A small train that had come to fetch the workers from the British mission and take them to the pier came forcing its way through the crowd. There were clouds of steam, a deafening squeal of metal, and dreadful shrieks. Eddie wondered if somebody had fallen under the locomotive.

The Scots Fusiliers closed in on the refugees to stop them forcing their way through the opened gates.

"Get back!" yelled Eddie, waving his gun. "Get back, or I'll shoot!"

The locomotive came slowly in, pulling four cars behind it. Eddie was about to give the order to close the gate when he noticed a man on a horse making his way through the crowd. Judging by his collar insignia and crimson band on his cap, the man was a British officer with the Royal Army Medical Corps.

"What's up?" Eddie shouted.

"I have a hospital here!" the officer cried in a muffled voice. It sounded as though he had caught a cold. "I need help bringing in my patients!"

"Where the hell have you been all this time?" Eddie shouted, aghast. "Why aren't you on the ship yet?"

The officer only waved his hand.

The Fusiliers lined up to make way for eight carts full of wounded soldiers, pale-faced and freshly bandaged.

"Do you belong to our military mission?" Eddie asked them, but no one answered.

The officer dismounted and ordered the medics and nurses to load the wounded onto new stretchers that they had brought with them.

"Faster! Faster! Take them onto the ship!" he shouted in a strange accent.

Russian staff officers were getting out of the railroad cars. According to an agreement with the British command, they had been assigned places on the *Hannover*. A tall man with a shaven head dragged a young woman out by her arm. She tried to pull away from him, shouting something in Russian. The man slapped her across the face, and the woman cried out and pressed her hand to her cheek.

All of the anger that had been boiling up in Eddie came to a head. Running up to the scoundrel, he put a gun to his chin. "Don't you dare!" he shouted.

"You not understand! This my wife," the man protested in broken English.

Eddie grasped the man by the shoulder and pushed him toward the Fusiliers. "Take him out of here!"

Then he approached the weeping woman. "Are you all right, ma'am?" he asked.

She said nothing—it seemed that she didn't speak English. Eddie could see that she was shaking all over.

"Go to the ship, ma'am. We're leaving soon."

Suddenly, the woman caught sight of the R.A.M.C. officer. "Dr. Sablin!" she cried.

The woman rushed to him and started to explain something. Looking at her in confusion, the officer nodded, and Eddie realized that not only the officer but also all of the wounded men with him were Russian. The doctor had changed into British uniform to give himself and his patients a chance to get on the ship.

Should I report them? Eddie thought for a second. His next thought was, *Of course, not. Let the captain find out after we set sail.*

He went up to the doctor. "Keep your people quiet," he said in a whisper. "Try not to talk until we've boarded the ship. I'll help you get settled."

The words of a solemn song kept going around in Eddie's head:

It's the only, only way,
It's the only game to play—

3

The old countess told Klim that she wanted to go straight to the French quay. "Sorry, but I'm too old for all these adventures. I just want to get onto the ship."

For an extra twenty francs, Shushunov had promised to take the old countess to the checkpoint.

"You should come with me," Sofia Karlovna told Klim. "You have documents now, and Fomin will get Nina out."

Klim looked away from the old countess. "The British will take her to Egypt or somewhere, and I'll never find her again."

"You won't find her again anyway," said the old countess with the sigh. "Still, I wish you luck."

They shook hands, and Sofia Karlovna got out of the car. "If by some miracle," she said, "you manage to get out of here, do write to me care of the Paris central post office. Mr. Shushunov, let's go."

Klim had to leave the car behind in the port. It was impossible to get through the endless columns of Don Cossacks. A forest of lances and a sea of horses' heads stretched as far as the eye could see. The ground was littered with cloth, leather, canned food, and rifles.

Klim made his way, ducking under the bellies of the horses.

The cavalry officer ordered the Cossacks to dismount. "Leave your horses behind!"

The Cossacks unfastened their saddles and bridles. Many of them wept silently, tears coursing down their dusty faces. It was unthinkable to leave behind a horse that meant more than a friend. These horses had saved their riders in battle and shared everything that had come their way.

The Cossacks put their arms around their horses' necks and stroked their cheeks. One man put a gun in his horse's ear, but his friends wouldn't let him pull the trigger.

"Do you want me to give up my girl to the Reds?" he yelled as he struggled in the arms of his friends.

The horses whinnied in fear while the men cursed. In a frenzy, the Cossacks began to throw their saddles into the water. "To hell with it all!"

Hundreds and then thousands of feet stomped up the gangplanks as the regiments boarded the steamers, which began to list under the weight.

"Get back! We're setting sail! No more space here!" the captain shouted through his megaphone, but nobody paid any attention.

"We still have three rearguard regiments here!"

An artillery shell wailed and exploded on a nearby slope.

"The Reds are already at Hajduk Station!" someone cried. "They might even have gotten as far as Kirillovka."

"You'll sink the ship!" yelled the captain. "There'll be another transport soon to take you on board."

One by one, the overloaded ships sailed away with clusters of people hanging onto their rigging. Whenever a new vessel sailed toward the quay, the crowd would dash along the side of the water shouting, not knowing where it would berth. Lost children wailed, and women became hysterical.

Klim noticed a Kalmyk with two boys, numb with fear. They were dashing hither and thither among the soldiers, completely lost.

"Where should we go?" the Kalmyk asked Klim. "Where's our boat?"

Several horses jumped into the sea and swam after the steamers as they left the quay.

4

Klim reached the British pier by evening. A huge crowd was standing in front of the closed gate; however, people were now no longer shouting or panicking but staring silently through the rows of barbed wire, watching a warship sail into the distance.

The fog drifting from the mountains mingled with the smoke of the fires on the streets. Some people decided to go to Gelendzhik, and some went back into town. Klim overheard an officer from the Markov Regiment proposing to take by force the next ship that came in. "It's every man for himself now," he said.

"There won't be another ship," a familiar voice said.

Turning, Klim saw Fomin, bareheaded in an overcoat with its buttons torn off, standing a few steps away.

Klim rushed up to him. "Where's Nina?" he asked.

A vague smile appeared on Fomin's face. "If it isn't Mr. Argentinean himself! Nina's gone. Neither you nor I will ever see her again."

5

Sablin ordered Nina to help him carry the wounded onto the ship. When all of the men were aboard, she rushed onto the upper deck.

Sablin tried to hold her back. "Where're you going?"

"Klim's still there," Nina said, panting. "I need to go back to town."

"Are you out of your mind?"

"Dr. Sablin!" cried the nurse running up to him. "The captain found out that a we'd made our way onto his ship unlawfully."

Sablin closed his eyes for a moment.

"I'll go to the captain now," he said. "Fay, I want you to keep an eye on Miss Nina. She's beside herself with grief. She could throw herself overboard."

Fay cast a jealous look in Nina's direction.

"You can go back to Novorossiysk if you want to," she told Nina as soon as Sablin was out of the way.

Nina set off toward the gangplank.

"I can't leave," she tried to explain herself to the British sailors.

They helped her to get to the jetty strewn with abandoned possessions. Thick smoke billowed from the steamer's funnel, and the anchor chain rattled as it was pulled up.

The *Hannover* set out to sea.

For a long time, Nina stood at the railing looking at the fiery glow in the waves of the gulf. The last transport passed, tugging an overcrowded barge behind it.

The crowd behind the barbed wire was thinning out. At first, people left one by one and then in groups. Soon, there was nobody left at the pier.

Darkness set in rapidly as the town struggled in its death throes. From time to time, the pink glare of an explosion flashed behind the dense clouds. The last defenders of Novorossiysk were desperately trying to hold the mountain passes.

Nina picked up an abandoned chocolate bar from the ground and unwrapped it. The smell and taste were like something long-forgotten. She struggled to understand what she had done and why she had refused to be saved.

I don't need that kind of salvation, she thought.

There was nothing in her heart but a sort of dull apathy. Where should she look for Klim? What might have happened to him? She couldn't bear to lose him again.

One of the abandoned horses came up to Nina and laid its head on her shoulder. It was trembling and snorting, and a purple point of fire glowed deep in the pupil of its eye.

Nina picked up her skirt, put her foot in the stirrup, and mounted the horse, feeling the unfamiliar sensation of the breeze on her bare knees.

"Let's go home," she said, touching the reins.

6

The town was in the grip of a pogrom. The streets glowed golden from fires, the low clouds were brown as coffee from the smoke, and the air was filled with flying ash and charred paper.

Nina rode slowly down the middle of the road. Ragged people ran by with bundles of leather jackets, shoes, and belts. People were breaking open crates right there in the street and pouring packets of hardtack, yeast, and starch into their knapsacks. It was beyond belief that all of this food had been kept in warehouses all this time while in Novorossiysk, people had been starving.

The earth trembled with the beat of thousands of hooves. Horses abandoned by the Cossacks had herded together, and bearded Circassians were chasing after them whooping.

Vorontsovskaya Street was empty. It appeared that everyone had taken cover in anticipation of the inevitable trials to come. Nina rode into the backyard, jumped to the ground, and froze in disbelief when she heard laughter inside the house.

She ran onto the porch and pulled open the front door. In the living room by the light of two candles, Klim and Fomin were sitting at the dinner table playing cards.

"I think I'd have made a good Provisions Commissar," Fomin said.

Klim nodded. "I agree." He caught sight of Nina and jumped to his feet, his face transformed. "Why are you still here?"

She rushed to him. "I couldn't go without you!"

Klim's hands were shaking as he took her tightly in his arms and kissed her. "Everything will be fine—you'll see. We'll go East instead. The Bolsheviks won't be able to block the border with China, however hard they try—it's thousands of miles long. We'll find a way to get over it."

Fomin cocked the little revolver in his hand.

"Nina, my dear," he said, "you are distracting us from very important business. After you left, Mr. Argentinean and I decided to have a card duel. We thought it would be entertaining. The winner will die a quick and painless death courtesy of the last precious bullet in this gun. The loser has to wait to be hacked to death by the Red cavalry. I must inform you that your husband beat me."

Nina froze. "Surely, you wouldn't—"

"Mr. Rogov, if you wish, I can let Nina have your prize. Whatever you say."

The reflection of the candle flame flickered on Fomin's forehead, slick with sweat. The corners of his mouth twitched.

"There's no need to look so frightened." He laughed. "After all, you wouldn't be apart for very long. The Reds will be here in a couple of hours, and they'll kill the rest of us. Then we'll meet in heaven and laugh over our memories."

"Hands up!" shouted a clear boyish voice as a group of scrawny teenagers armed with rifles appeared in the doorway.

Startled, Fomin dropped the revolver on the tablecloth and raised his hands. A second later, he realized that the intruders were mere boys trembling at their own effrontery.

"What do you want?" Fomin demanded angrily.

He reached for his revolver, but the older boy pressed his rifle to Fomin's chest while the second boy grasped the gun. "We need to talk about our father—Jacob Froiman."

Fomin grimaced. "I see. Well, young men, have a seat."

The older boy turned to Klim. "You must leave now. We have a score to settle."

Klim grabbed Nina's hand, and they ran outside. The sky above the trees was bathed in an orange glow.

"Who were those boys?" Nina whispered.

"The vanguard of Soviet power," said Klim. "Come on. We need to find a place to hide."

A rifle shot rang out inside the house.

37. EPILOGUE

1

No sooner had Sofia Karlovna boarded the dreadnought *Waldeck-Rousseau* than the nightmare of Novorossiysk fell away, and she found herself in France. She was given a five-course dinner and a cabin with a bath along with a now subdued and obliging Shushunov, who had gotten himself a place on the ship by passing himself off as her butler.

Although the ship was far from shore, clouds of smoke and the glow of fires could still be seen from the direction of the port. Sofia Karlovna wasn't looking in that direction. The sea was calm, the clear sky was the color of lilac, and the moon was rising over the mountains like a worn cameo.

The evacuated cadets from the Alexander Military School lined up on the ship's deck to sing a prayer. The old countess listened to their clear young voices and crossed herself.

Everything was as it should be: the mistress of the ball was bidding farewell to her guests and wishing them a good night. Now, she could rest while the servants swept up the rubbish and cleared the dishes from the tables.

2

A year later in Montmartre, Sofia Karlovna read in a newspaper that—following the tragedy in Novorossiysk—some Whites had fled and others had been taken prisoner. Many more, believing that they would be given amnesty, had taken part in a voluntary registration. All of those who had registered had been arrested. Some had been sent to labor camps while others—drafted into the ranks of the Red Army—had taken part in the bloodbath that was the Polish war.

The Poles had prevented the victorious Red Army from rushing westward, forcing the Bolsheviks to abandon their dream of the World Revolution. At least for a while.

Please support *Russian Treasures* with your reviews on Amazon and Goodreads.

Two or three sentences are enough. Just let other historical fiction fans know what you like about the novel and what kind of readers would enjoy it.

It will help a lot—people make buying decisions on the number of reviews, making every one of them precious.

SUBSCRIBE TO A NEWSLETTER

The only way to know immediately when a new book by Elvira Baryakina comes out is to subscribe to her newsletter at www.baryakina.com/en/

Join and get *The Shaman*, a prequel to the *Russian Treasures* series, for free.

THE SHAMAN

A short story

Klim Rogov, the sole heir to the fortune of a noble family, has disappeared without a trace. Only his fifteen-year-old cousin has any idea what has happened, but she is keeping silent. There is little point trying to explain to adults the nature of the mysterious force that has commanded Klim to leave home, come what may.

If you'd like to talk about life and good books, please join Elvira Baryakina on her Facebook — http://facebook.com/elvira.baryakina

THE RUSSIAN TREASURES SERIES

Russian Treasures. Book One

White Ghosts. Book Two

The Prince of the Soviets. Book Three

Made in the USA
Columbia, SC
10 April 2019